THE WIFE HE NEEDS

BRENDA JACKSON

TEMPTED BY THE BOSS

JULES BENNETT

MILLS & BOON

First Published in Great Britain 2020
by Mills & Boon, an imprint of HarperCollinsPublishers,
1 London Bridge Street, London, SE1 9GF

The Wife He Needs © 2020 Brenda Streater Jackson
Tempted by the Boss © 2020 Harlequin Books S.A.

Special thanks and acknowledgement are given to Jules Bennett for her contribution to the *Texas Cattleman's Club: Rags to Riches* series.

ISBN: 978-0-263-28010-4

1220

Brenda Jackson is a *New York Times* bestselling author of more than one hundred romance titles. Brenda lives in Jacksonville, Florida, and divides her time between family, writing and travelling. Email Brenda at authorbrendajackson@gmail.com or visit her on her website at brendajackson.net

USA TODAY bestselling author **Jules Bennett** has published over sixty books and never tires of writing happy endings. Writing strong heroines and alpha heroes is Jules's favourite way to spend her workdays. Jules hosts weekly contests on her Facebook fan page and loves chatting with readers on Twitter, Facebook and via email through her website. Stay up-to-date by signing up for her newsletter at julesbennett.com

Also by Brenda Jackson

The Westmoreland Legacy

The Rancher Returns
His Secret Son
An Honourable Seduction
His to Claim
Duty or Desire

Forged of Steele

Seduced by a Steele
Claimed by a Steele

Also by Jules Bennett

Twin Secrets
Claimed by the Rancher
Taming the Texan
A Texan for Christmas
An Unexpected Scandal
Scandalous Reunion
Scandalous Engagement

Discover more at millsandboon.co.uk

To the man who will always and forever be the love of my life, Gerald Jackson, Sr.

Hatred stirreth up strifes: but love covereth all sins.
—*Proverbs* 10:12

One

"So, when is the wedding, Garth?"

Garth Outlaw raised his eyes from studying his cards. Was his brother playing mind games to mess with his concentration?

"And just what wedding are you talking about?"

Garth glanced around the table and saw the smirks on the faces of all four of his brothers. Even Jess had made a trip home from the nation's capital for a week long visit.

"Is anyone going to answer?" Garth asked.

Jess grinned as he threw out a card. "I heard it from Dad the moment I walked through the door. He claims you've gotten over Karen Piccard, decided to settle down and do whatever needs to be done for the benefit of the company, which includes getting a wife and making babies to guarantee the Outlaw dynasty. Those were his words, not mine."

"We heard the same thing," Cash said, with Sloan and Maverick nodding in agreement.

Garth didn't say anything. Being the oldest son of Bartram "Bart" Outlaw wasn't easy, especially when his father liked spreading information that wasn't true. However, in this case, it was. At least partly. He was planning to do what needed to be done for the company. But he seriously doubted he would ever get over Karen. She would always have his heart.

"No wedding date has been set because I haven't chosen a bride."

His brother Cash sat up straight in his chair. "Are you really thinking about settling down with a wife and making babies?" he asked, as if the thought of doing such a thing was as unheard of as living in outer space.

Garth threw out some chips. "Why not? I don't see any of you guys rushing to the altar to continue the Outlaw legacy. Not even you, Jess, and you're the politician in the family. You of all people should be thinking about acquiring a wife." A couple of years ago, Jess had gotten elected as a senator from Alaska.

A grin touched Jess's lips. "No, thank you. I'm not ready to fall in love."

Garth shrugged. "Who said anything about falling in love?"

"You're thinking of marrying a woman you don't love?" This question came from Sloan.

"For me there's no other way."

There was no reason to explain what he meant. They knew.

"And you'll do it because Bart says it needs to be done?"

Garth rolled his eyes at his youngest brother, Maverick, who'd been quiet up to now. "No, I'll consider doing it because I think it's about time I settled down. I'm thirty-eight, and dating gets old."

"Speak for yourself," Maverick said, grinning. "I happen to enjoy dating a lot of women."

Garth shook his head. "And Walker got me thinking.

Look how long he was a loner before he got married. If he can do it, then anyone can."

Walker Rafferty was Garth's best friend. A couple of years ago, Walker had met his current wife and now they were parents to twins, a boy and a girl they'd named Walker and Westlyn. Nobody thought Walker would ever remarry after losing his first wife and son in a car accident. Surprisingly, ten years later, Walker had fallen in love again. Garth was happy for Walker, and inspired to settle down, but honestly, he couldn't see himself falling in love. He was convinced Karen was the only woman he was meant to love.

He and Karen had met in the Marines. They'd fallen in love immediately and made plans to marry after their enlistment. They'd dated six months and then one morning during a routine border check in Syria, her military chopper had crashed, killing everyone on board. He'd never even gotten the chance to bring Karen to Fairbanks and introduce the woman he'd loved to his family.

"Walker certainly does seem a lot happier these days, thanks to our cousin," Cash said, intruding into Garth's thoughts.

Garth nodded as he studied his cards. Yes, Walker had become the Outlaws' cousin-in-law after marrying Bailey Westmoreland. Bailey was a cousin they hadn't known existed until it was proven that the Westmorelands and the Outlaws were related. The physical resemblance between the two families could not be disputed, although for some reason their father still would not accept the fact that the Outlaws and Westmorelands were kin. However, like Garth and his siblings had told Bart, it didn't matter whether or not he accepted the kinship, it was the truth.

The Westmoreland extended family spread from Georgia and Texas to Montana, Colorado and California. After growing up with no other relatives, it was fun joining the

Westmorelands whenever they had get-togethers or family events, like the annual Westmoreland Charity Ball in Denver. Garth loved it whenever the Westmorelands and the Outlaws got together.

Hours later, after the poker game ended with Cash winning all their money, everyone retired to bed except for Garth and Jess. Although all six Outlaw offspring owned homes in Fairbanks, every once in a while, to appease the old man, they would stay under his roof at the Outlaw Estates.

Some people found it amazing that the six Outlaw siblings were as close as they were, considering each one of them had a different mother. Unfortunately, some of those women had turned out to be gold diggers. When the divorces became final, Bart's attorneys made sure he was given full custody of his children.

Garth was the oldest. His mother had been Bart's first wife and had come from a wealthy family. She had married Bart against her parents' wishes. And when her family finally got to her, she had asked Bart for a divorce. He told her he would give her one but she couldn't take his child. In the end, she'd left without Garth. She'd remarried a couple years later, to the man her parents had chosen. After marrying her second husband, Juanita pretty much forgot Garth existed. However, his maternal grandparents had left him a pretty hefty trust fund when they'd died twenty or so years ago.

Jessup or Jess, as he preferred to be called, was thirty-six and the second oldest, and had always wanted a career in politics. Jess's mother, Joyce, had been the first gold digger, and Bart had ended his marriage to Joyce before their first anniversary rolled around. Bart had taken her to court for custody of Jess.

Cashen, who was usually called Cash, was thirty-four

and the third-born son. Cash's mother, Ellen, had been a decent woman and Bart's third wife. In a way, she'd been too decent for Bart. She was soft-spoken and had tried bringing out the good in Bart. When she'd realized such a thing wasn't possible, she'd left. Even with Bart's threats, Ellen had called Bart's bluff and tried to take Cash with her. In the end, she'd lost the custody fight after finding out Bart had friends in high places.

Sloan was thirty-two. His mother, Barbie, had been another one who'd picked Bart for his money. Although the marriage had lasted less than six months, that was long enough for Sloan to be conceived. Barbie'd had no problem leaving Sloan behind—for the right amount—when she split. She hadn't been seen or heard from again.

Maverick, at twenty-nine, was the youngest Outlaw son and the most womanizing. Granted, all of them enjoyed their share of the opposite sex from time to time, but Maverick had his share and then some. His mother had been an exploiter, too. Rosalind was the one who'd been caught having an affair right under Bart's nose. However, there hadn't been any question that Maverick was Bart's kid, since he favored the old man more than any of them. Right down to the cleft in his chin.

Last but certainly not least, was Bart's only daughter, definitely his pride and joy, twenty-five-year-old Charm. To this day, Charm's mother, Claudia, was the only woman Bart had ever loved and the one he couldn't handle. And… she'd been the only one Bart hadn't married, but not for lack of trying.

Claudia had refused to accept Bart's marriage proposals. All five of them. The most recent was four years ago, when Charm had turned twenty-one. The Outlaws saw Claudia frequently because, unlike the other mothers, she had an open invitation to visit as often as she liked, but she never visited as often as Bart would have wanted. Claudia didn't tolerate Bart's grouchiness and seemed to bring out the best in Bart…if there was such a thing.

Bart hadn't known Claudia was pregnant when their affair had ended. She'd left for parts unknown. Fifteen years later, Claudia reappeared with Charm in tow, telling Bart she couldn't handle Charm's sassiness anymore and for him to now deal with it.

Unfortunately, Bart dealt with it the wrong way by spoiling Charm even more rotten. It had taken the five older brothers stepping in and applying the firm hand their father had refused to apply. In the end, their spoiled sister had settled down. That didn't mean she didn't try their patience every once in a while, because she did.

"So, what's the real deal with you and this marriage thing, Garth?" Jess asked, intruding into Garth's thoughts. "Unlike what Dad thinks, I find it hard to believe you've gotten over Karen…although it has been close to ten years now."

Garth glanced over at Jess as he took a sip of his wine. Garth was close to all his siblings, but there was a special closeness between him and Jess. Jess had confided his intentions to Garth when he'd decided to run for United States senator. Jess had won the election in a landslide victory. And he knew just what Karen had meant to Garth, because it was all in the letters Garth would write home to Jess.

Garth leaned back in his chair. "It could be twenty years and I still won't get over Karen, Jess. I loved her too much. But I'm not getting any younger, and I want the same happiness I see that Walker and our cousins have. Besides," he said with a chuckle, "I figure if I make the first step, the rest of you will follow suit."

Jess threw his head back and laughed. "Don't expect that

to happen. Some of us aren't ready for home, hearth and the sound of little feet yet." Then Jess added, "Now that you've made up your mind, have you decided on a particular woman? Anyone we know?"

Garth shook his head. "Nope. Taking Charm's advice, I—"

"Wait! Hold up. You took Charm's advice about something?"

Garth chuckled. "Yes. I know it sounds scary, but I liked what she suggested. It's a totally different approach to meeting a woman who is wife material."

"What approach is that?" Jess asked, taking a sip of his beer.

"A private dating service."

Jess nearly choked. "You're serious?"

Garth smiled. "Yes. I thought it was way out there at first, too, until Charm convinced me how productive it would be. She did all the legwork for me and found this high-class dating agency that's located in Beverly Hills, California. Just to be considered as an applicant the men must have a specified financial portfolio, and the women are required to not only be attractive but have a certain level of poise, education, classiness and sophistication."

Shifting in his seat, Garth added. "I further specified I wanted a woman who was trustworthy, had good morals and was one who wants to become a wife and mother one day. Sooner than later. And she must share my interests and hobbies. I provided a list of them."

"Have they found such a paragon of a woman who met all your specifications?"

Garth grinned. "Surprisingly, yes. Trust me, any woman who comes through this particular dating service is well vetted. She'll keep things confidential and private during the entire process."

"Have you met her yet?"

"No, but she has agreed to spend two weeks with me, at a location we both agreed to, so we can get to know each other better. Of course, I'm covering all the expenses, including those to get her there."

"And exactly where is *there*?"

"Santa Cruz, Spain. I'm flying there next week."

"This method sounds so impersonal. More like a business arrangement."

"In a way, it is. I'm hiring the service to match me with someone who's compatible with my needs and desires. I've seen pictures of her and she's beautiful, and her résumé is impressive. If things work out the way I'm hoping they will, after our Spain trip we'll continue to date and then eventually talk marriage."

"A loveless marriage."

"Yes, a loveless marriage. I will honor her, respect her and take care of all her needs, but I won't ever love her," Garth said bluntly. "I'll be honest and forthright with her about that, Jess. I won't have her entering the marriage with false hope or illusions."

"Why use a dating service? I would think you're capable of finding a woman on your own."

"Didn't have time."

"Any reason you're in a rush?" Jess asked.

"No."

Jess studied him intently and Garth wished he wouldn't do that. Jess could always figure out his motives, and Garth hoped like hell that he didn't figure out this one. The less Jess knew, the better.

"Well, you're an ace when it comes to strategic planning, and I wish you the best. I hope the woman is everything you want, Garth, and things work out."

"Thanks, Jess. I hope so, too."

* * *

Regan Fairchild's job as a corporate pilot was one that anyone who enjoyed flying would love. Then why was she thinking of leaving it? The answer to her question was the gorgeous specimen of a man walking toward the plane with his briefcase in one hand and a cell phone in the other. His long black coat whipped against his legs as he headed toward the plane while ignoring the strong gust of Alaskan wind that always accompanied October weather. The shoulders beneath the coat were massive and powerful, which gave him a totally heart-stopping, virile look.

He was handsome, and she was convinced that in another life he'd been an explorer, discovering and invading new territories. He was always busy. He always had a plan. He rarely slowed down, and lately he rarely dated.

Her heart pounded in her chest like it always did whenever she saw him. How long had it been since she'd fallen hopelessly in love with Garth Bartram Outlaw? Had it been ten years ago on her eighteenth birthday, when he'd flown her and two of her besties to Las Vegas as a high school graduation gift? Or had it been at sixteen, when he had helped her father surprise her with a "sweet-sixteen" party at Disney World? Deep down she knew it didn't matter when it had happened. The key thing was that it *had* happened, and she needed to do something about it before Garth became her downfall.

Regan knew that as much as she wished otherwise, realistically, quitting her job was not an option. Her father, Franklin Fairchild, had been the corporate pilot for Outlaw Freight Lines for over forty years. When he retired a few years ago, she had taken over. She loved her job. She also loved the man who was headed toward her with a huge smile on his face. He did that whenever he saw her. She'd

rarely known a time when Garth hadn't given her a smile.
It was a smile that meant everything to her.

She knew Garth's smile was a natural part of his makeup.
He rarely frowned, and when he did, everyone knew there
would be trouble. He was an astute businessman, and the
company had grown in leaps and bounds since he'd taken
over from his father. It wasn't that Bart Outlaw hadn't been
good at his work, but Garth's approach was a lot different
from his father's. Bart ruled with a hard hand and was dis-
trustful by nature. He was hard-nosed and inflexible. On
the other hand, Garth knew the art of compromising, and
he was also brilliant. Everybody liked Garth, and she of
all people knew how easy he was to love.

She also knew about that period of sadness in his life
when he'd returned home from a stint abroad as a marine.
He had come back a broken man, after the woman he loved
had been killed. For a while there had not been any smiles,
and he'd thrown himself into working beside his father to
make the company bigger and bigger.

Then, when Bart retired, or more specifically when the
company's board threatened to oust him, it was Garth who'd
taken over and put in all those long hours, sometimes without a social life, to pull the company through difficult times.
Regan guessed that he'd also been trying to rid himself of
the pain of losing the person he'd loved. More than once,
she had walked in on him unexpectedly, in one of his quiet
moments, to see grief in his eyes.

"Good morning, Regan," he said now, when he came to
a stop in front of her.

She tilted her head back to look up at him. He was tall,
but the first things that caught her attention were Garth's
handsome features. Namely his smooth, coffee-and-cream
complexion, piercing dark brown eyes, a perfectly shaped

nose, a pair of full lips and a sculpted chin. He garnered plenty of feminine attention no matter where he went.

"Same to you, Garth. Ready to fly?" She knew she would be flying him to Santa Cruz, Spain.

"I'm ready whenever you are, and how's Franklin?"

"Dad is fine."

"Good. I need to check up on him soon. Maybe even pay him a visit."

Her father was close to all Bart's offspring but would admit that Garth had always been his favorite. Franklin had been working as Bart's pilot when Garth was born. When Bart had gained full custody of Garth, oftentimes Garth and his nanny had accompanied Bart when he traveled extensively.

"I miss him."

Regan missed her father, too. She hadn't been surprised when her father had left the cold state of Alaska to move to Florida upon retirement. He was enjoying sunshine nearly all year round.

"Everything is in order, Garth, and we'll be taking off soon."

Less than twenty minutes later, she was cruising the skies. They would make a couple of pit stops to refuel before reaching Santa Cruz. She'd never been there but had heard it was beautiful. One thing she did in addition to studying the layout of the private airport of any destination was get familiar with the area. The plan for this trip was for her to drop him off and return to get him in two weeks. She had two rest days before flying back to Alaska and would use them to get in as much sightseeing and shopping as she could. Depending on his business plans, there were times when he asked her to remain with him during the entire trip as his private chauffeur. He hadn't asked for that on this trip.

"Mind if I join you?"

She smiled. "Sure."

It wouldn't be the first time Garth had joined her in the cockpit, claiming he was bored in the seating area. Although calling it a seating area was an understatement when this jet included luxurious sleeping quarters as well as an office.

Out of the corner of her eye she saw how easily he slid into the copilot seat beside her. As usual, he smelled good. She didn't have to glance over at him to know he was gearing up with the headset. Her father had taught a teenage Garth to fly and he'd enhanced those skills while in the Marines. More than once, he'd copiloted with her on long flights.

"Estimated flight time?" he asked her.

"Twelve hours."

"First stop?"

The FAA required her to take a break after piloting for nine hours. "Bolungarvik, Iceland," she replied.

He nodded. "Nice place. I visited there a few years ago while in the Marines. It's a beautiful coastal fishing town with breathtaking scenery. Especially the mountains surrounding the harbor."

"Sounds gorgeous."

"It is."

She eased the jet into a glide while moving around a huge mountain. "You're good at that, Regan," he said.

"Thanks. I was trained by the best."

She considered her father the best pilot there was, and he'd made sure she'd gotten her private pilot license at sixteen. Her mother had died of an aneurysm when Regan was five. She and her father had a close relationship, and she missed him now that he was in Florida. However, she'd understood him wanting to spend his later years in a warmer climate. When he had sold her childhood home, he'd split the proceeds with her. She'd taken the money and purchased a home on the Tanana River.

Because Fairbanks had a military base, most of the men she'd dated had been soldiers. All were nice guys, and although she'd enjoyed their company, she hadn't gotten serious about any of them. At least not as serious as some of them had liked. Earlier in the year, she had broken up with Craig Foster. They'd dated for six months and then he'd developed jealous tendencies she hadn't cared to deal with.

"I love being up here."

She knew what he meant. There was just something about being in the beautiful blue sky, this close to heaven. "Me, too. I guess I don't have to ask if you're prepared for your meetings this trip." She knew that when it came to any business regarding Outlaw Freight Lines, Garth was always prepared.

He chuckled. "Not this trip. It's strictly for pleasure."

"Oh." Suddenly, a pain settled around her heart. That meant his two weeks in Santa Cruz would be with a woman. The thought of that bothered her even when she had no right to let it.

"No one back in Fairbanks will have need for the company jet while I'm in Santa Cruz. They have their own planes anyway," Garth said. "If you like, instead of returning to Fairbanks, you can use the time to visit your father in Florida before returning for me."

He was right; all the Outlaws had their own personal planes and could fly them. Even Charm. Due to Alaska's very limited road system, one of the most common ways of getting around was by aircraft. Locals liked to say that more Alaskans owned personal planes than cars.

"Thanks, but Dad left two days ago for a twenty-day cruise. However, if you don't mind, I'd like to spend a couple of days in Los Angeles to visit Simone." Garth knew Simone was her best friend from college.

"Of course, I don't mind. By the way, chances are we might have a guest flying back with us on the return."

Regan's stomach knotted. "A guest?"

"Yes. I'll let you know when I'm certain so you can file the proper flight information."

"All right, Garth."

The one thing Garth had never done was bring a female friend on board to spend time with him. He always kept his business and personal lives separate. But then, hadn't he said this was not a business trip?

Regan glided around another mountain and tried concentrating on piloting the plane and not on what Garth had told her. Maybe it was time for her to finally accept that the only place she had in Garth's life was this one, as his pilot. She would never be the woman who would one day wiggle her way into his heart to remove that sadness she often saw in his eyes. As much as she wished otherwise, it would never happen, and it was time for her to make her peace with that.

Two

"What do you mean she's not coming?" Garth asked, speaking into his cell phone, while rubbing a frustrated hand down his face. He had arrived in Santa Cruz expecting the woman selected by the dating service to be there already. She wasn't.

"I got a call from the dating service," Charm said. "Evidently there was some kind of mix-up in the dates. They regret their error and are hoping you will consider rescheduling."

Anger rose, heating Garth's face. A mix-up in the dates? He expected better from a company that prided itself on being the best in the business. "Since there's no reason to remain here, I'll let Regan know I'll be on the plane with her when she leaves two days from now."

"Why?"

Garth frowned. "Why what?"

"Why are you coming back home? Don't you think Cash can handle things while you're gone?"

Garth rolled his eyes. "Of course, I do. Had I thought he couldn't, I would not have left him in charge."

"Then let him do it. It will make him feel important to the company."

"He *is* important to the company, Charm. All of you are."

"Then take the time off you so rightly deserve. We've been worried about you. All those long hours you've been working over the past six months. Finalizing that Biggins deal wasn't easy, Garth. You did it and now you need some time off to enjoy yourself." She paused before adding, "I know it's disappointing not meeting your match, but look on the bright side. At least I rented a nice place for you."

Garth glanced around. Charm had made all the arrangements, and she was right. This was a nice place. It was a beautiful château in the mountains, overlooking the sea. It was spacious and the view was breathtaking. "What am I going to do here alone for two weeks?"

"Rest. Relax. Sleep. And who said you had to be alone? I booked several activities for you and your date to enjoy while in Santa Cruz. They were paid for in advance. Just ask Regan to stay and join you."

"Regan?"

"Yes, Regan."

Garth drew in a deep breath. Ever since the night of the Westmorelands' last charity ball on New Year's Eve, when he'd asked Regan to go with him upon the Westmorelands' request, he hadn't been able to think of her in the same way. He blamed this change on the outfit she'd been wearing and the dance they'd shared. When he'd seen her and held her in his arms, desire—which he hadn't thought he was capable of feeling for any woman after Karen—had nearly driven him insane. He'd known Regan all her life and she'd been his pilot for almost five years. But on that night, he'd seen her in a whole new light.

A light he'd been trying to dim since.

"I can't invite Regan to join me at the château for two weeks, Charm."

"Why not?"

He locked his jaw for a minute, refusing to say anything that would give his sister a reason to speculate. She was the last person who needed to know of his attraction to Regan. Nor did he want her to suspect his interest in finding a wife had been driven by his attempt to end his attraction to Regan.

"I think she would prefer leaving Spain, Charm. She even mentioned visiting her girlfriend in LA."

"Trust me, Garth. Any woman would love to spend two weeks in that château. When was the last time Regan took a real vacation that didn't include visiting her father in Florida? She's been your pilot for nearly five years now, and you haven't done anything really nice for her."

He rubbed his hand down his face. "Charm, I've always done nice things for Regan."

"I mean *really* nice. She has decisions to make and…"

When Charm's voice trailed off, Garth raised a brow. "Decisions about what?"

She hesitated and he didn't like that.

"Decisions about what, Charm?" he repeated.

"I wasn't going to say anything because she told me in confidence, but maybe it's something you should know. Especially since he's offering her a lot."

Garth frowned. "What are you talking about? Who is he and what is he offering?"

When she didn't speak, he asked again, "Charm? What are you talking about?"

"You can't tell Regan I told you, but Harold Anders offered her a job as his personal pilot. The salary is good and the benefits are even better."

Garth didn't say anything as the full implications of what

Charm said hit him hard. Harold Anders owned a huge computer software company in Fairbanks, with offices in Los Angeles, Dallas, Atlanta, Portland and several more cities, as well as international offices in London, Rome and Paris. He didn't have one private jet; he had several.

He also knew the man was a forty-one-year-old divorcé with a reputation for womanizing. Anders saw women as conquests and trophies, the younger the better. Garth had heard about the sex scandal involving him and his personal assistant a couple of years ago.

And he wanted Regan to be his pilot.

Anders was the last man Regan should consider working for. Besides, she worked for Garth. A Fairchild had worked for the Outlaws for over forty years. On occasion, when he traveled internationally, she was even his private chauffeur on the ground. For her to be thinking of leaving was ludicrous. He paid her a good salary and gave her generous bonuses. He wasn't complaining about the pay because he certainly felt she deserved every penny. She was valuable to him. Irreplaceable.

"I didn't say she was taking Harold Anders's offer, Garth. She has a month to decide."

"I don't like the thought that she's even considering it."

He knew the ensuing silence meant Charm didn't like it, either, but she wasn't saying anything. Charm thought of Regan like an older sister. Charm had arrived in Alaska at fifteen, full of anger and ready to take a bite out of anyone. At least anyone but Regan. The two had bonded immediately.

"I'm sure Regan won't be taking the job," Charm said. "She loves working for our company. She's said so a number of times, and I also know she enjoys flying you."

Garth wished he could be as certain of that as Charm.

"Why didn't she tell me about the offer?" he asked in an annoyed tone.

"Really, Garth? She's a professional and you're her boss. She probably figured that had she mentioned it, you would have thought she was hitting you up for a raise, to counter Anders's offer."

"I would not have thought that. Besides, I'm more than her boss, Charm. Like all the Outlaws, I consider Regan a friend."

"Well, some friend you are. You'll deny her two weeks to enjoy herself at the château with you. If I were you, I would do whatever it takes to remind her that she's not only your pilot, but also your friend."

He heard what Charm was saying; however, he wasn't sure that was a line he wanted to cross. "I don't think Regan sharing space with me here is a good idea, Charm."

"And why not?"

There was no way he would tell Charm the real reason. "I don't want her to feel uncomfortable."

"Why would she? You're overthinking things. If it was Jess, Cash, Sloan or Maverick, none of them would mind asking Regan to hang out with them for two weeks so she could have fun. I don't understand why you would have a problem with it."

"We don't have that kind of relationship."

"Well, you should. You've known her as long as they have, even longer. And everyone knows what a great bond you share with Franklin. In some ways, you're closer to him than you are to Bart."

When he didn't say anything, Charm added, "You know what I think, Garth?"

A part of him was afraid to ask. "No, what do you think?"

"I think the problem isn't with Regan but with you."

His stomach tightened. Had Charm figured out his attraction to Regan. "It's me in what way?"

"Since taking over the company you've gotten so driven to make the company successful that you've become the ultimate professional, dotting every *i* and crossing every *t*, and you've forgotten how it feels to just chill and hang out with those who remember how fun-loving you were before becoming Mr. CEO. You've become a stuffed shirt."

"A stuffed shirt?"

"Yes, and a stick-in-the-mud, too. I hate to see you become another Bart."

Garth frowned. "That won't ever happen."

"It will if you don't learn how to relax, have fun and enjoy spending time with people you can trust. If you prefer, I can take time off and fly out and spend time with you in Santa Cruz."

That was the last thing he wanted. Charm would drive him batty. "I'll ask Regan about it today."

"Good. Now about your match from the dating service. Do you want me to reschedule your time with her?"

He inhaled deeply. Maybe her not showing up was an omen. If he was honest with himself, he would admit he preferred meeting women the traditional way. "No. Please cancel my relationship with the service."

"Are you sure?"

"Yes, I am."

"All right. I'll notify them to remove you as a client. Enjoy yourself. Love you. Bye." Charm then clicked off the phone.

"You want me to join you at the château?" Regan asked Garth, speaking into her phone and trying to make sense of what he was saying.

"Yes, my original plans have changed and there's no need for everything I had set up to go to waste, so I'm asking you."

Regan could only reach one conclusion. For whatever reason, the woman who was supposed to join him was a no-show, and he was inviting her to be with him instead.

Should Regan be upset that she was being asked by default? First of all, she wasn't really a default. He wouldn't expect her to take the woman's place per se. There was no doubt in her mind that he and the woman would have engaged in an affair. That would not be the case for him and Regan. He was merely being kind by inviting her to enjoy some of the things his date was not there to enjoy. Being in his bed would not be one of them.

Knowing how she felt about Garth, could she share space with him and enjoy his company, just like she would if the invitation had come from Jess, Cash, Sloan or Maverick? Garth was her boss; they weren't. As the firstborn, Garth had been groomed to take Bart's place one day, and lately, he hadn't been as approachable as his siblings.

Since becoming his pilot, she could recognize his moods. Although he always exemplified a kind, caring and thoughtful demeanor toward her, she could tell when he was in a more serious state of mind versus a more relaxed one. She was well aware that his disposition was driven by whatever business deals he had on the table. Lately, she'd seen less of his relaxed mood.

She wanted to see more of it.

"Yes, Garth, I'll join you at the château. Thanks for asking."

"I know you wanted to spend a couple of days in LA with your friend. I'll make sure you still get that time on the back end. While you're visiting her, there's a couple of guys I met while stationed there that I can look up. No problem."

"You don't have to do that."

"I don't mind. It's the least I can do to show my gratitude to you for keeping me from getting bored for two weeks. And I recall you mentioning on the flight here that you intended to do some shopping tomorrow. How about if I join you?"

Regan, who'd been about to take a sip of tea, nearly spilled it out of her cup. "You want to go shopping with me?"

"Sure. Why not? It's not like I'm new to the shopping game. Remember I'm Charm's oldest brother, and if Charm's shopping antics haven't driven me crazy, then I'm sure yours won't, either."

"Oh."

"So when do you want me to pick you up from the hotel?"

"I'll be packed and ready to leave whatever time you decide."

"In that case, I'll be there at ten in the morning, Regan."

At exactly ten the next day, Regan watched Garth stride into the hotel's lobby. Her heart skipped and then began to race when he saw her and gave her that Garth Outlaw smile. The one that made her feel all warm inside.

"Good morning, Regan. Are you ready?"

She wasn't sure if she was. She hadn't gotten much sleep last night, wondering if spending two weeks with him was a good idea. Being his pilot was temptation enough. But there was no way she could back out now without him questioning the reason she was doing so.

"Yes, Garth, I'm ready."

"Need help with your luggage?"

"No, I've got this," she said, taking hold of her luggage handle to walk beside him.

"Walker called before I left to come here. Guess what?" She glanced up at him. "What?"

"The twins were chosen Babies of the Year and will be featured on the cover of some motherhood magazine."

A smile spread across Regan's lips. She'd known Walker Rafferty for as long as she'd known Garth, since the two had been the best of friends from toddlerhood. "That's wonderful."

"I think so, too. Of course, he couldn't wait to tell me since I'm one of the twins' godfathers."

She knew Bailey's oldest brother, Ramsey Westmoreland, was the other godfather. "I haven't seen the twins in a while. I bet they've gotten bigger now," she said.

"They have. I'm happy for Walker. Losing his older son, Connor, was hard on him and he swore he would never have any more children. I'm glad he and Bailey have a beautiful family."

When Garth opened the rental car door for her, he glanced at her and said, "I don't think I've ever heard you say if you plan to settle down, marry and have children, Regan."

She slid onto the seat and snapped her seat belt in place. Pushing her hair back from her face, she said, "Those are my plans one of these days, but I'm in no hurry."

He nodded and then closed the door. Goose bumps formed on her arms as she watched him walk around the front of the car to get in. He had such a sensuous walk. It went well with the rest of him. Today, like her, he was dressed in jeans. The blue polo shirt looked amazing on him and she hoped he thought her blue blouse looked good on her.

"I don't recall sending out the memo," she said.

He glanced over at her as he buckled up. "What memo?"

"The one that told you what colors I was wearing today."

A huge grin spread across his face. "It wouldn't be the first time we've coordinated our outfits without realizing it."

That was true. She'd been his last-minute escort to various functions enough times to know to always pack both semiformal and formal outfits and the necessary accessories.

Before he could start the ignition, she couldn't help but ask, "Why did you want to know about my plans regarding settling down and having children? Dad's been talking to you?"

He shook his head. "No. I asked out of curiosity. Why would you think Franklin has talked to me about that?"

"Because that's all he's been talking about lately. Now that he's retired and has plenty of free time on his hands, he figures he should be spending it with grandchildren he doesn't have yet. He's been dropping hints."

Garth chuckled. "I can see him doing that."

"Dad knows he has to marry me off first. You wouldn't believe how many guys, mainly sons or grandsons of his new collection of friends from Florida, that he's tried fixing me up with whenever I visit him."

"Annoys you much?"

"Yes, like the dickens," she said grinning. Then, because he'd asked her, she felt it should be okay to ask him. "What about you? Now that Walker has gotten married and become a family man, are you thinking of doing the same?"

Regan had expected a quick yes or no. His hesitation gave her pause. "Umm…maybe," he finally said.

Maybe? Now she wondered if his plans to spend two weeks with a woman here in Santa Cruz had been more serious than she thought. All kinds of questions went through her mind. How did the two of them meet? Just how serious were things? If things were serious enough for him to be contemplating settling down, that meant he was finally moving on with his life after losing Karen.

"Where do you want to go first?"

She glanced over at him. "I heard that the best shops and markets are located in the Square."

He smiled as he turned on the car's ignition to pull off. "Then that's where we'll go."

Three

An expression of annoyance flitted across Garth's face. If one more man approached Regan to hit on her, he would step in and say something. It didn't matter one iota that she seemed to be doing a good job of handling them herself; it bothered the hell out of him that she had to handle them at all.

He was sitting on a bench on the other side of the store, which provided a good view of her. Unfortunately, other men, too, saw what he saw—a very beautiful woman. But still, that didn't give any man the right to interrupt her shopping.

The man finally moved away and now she was the only one in Garth's line of focus. He studied her striking features. There was her very smooth-looking mocha complexion, a pair of full lips, high cheekbones and almond-shaped, brown bedroom eyes. Her glossy, dark brown hair curled at the ends and hung around her shoulders. And he couldn't dismiss, any more than those other men could, just how good she looked in her jeans and pullover blouse. Regan Fairchild was definitely one delectable package and he wished he hadn't paid attention to that fact.

When a ping alerted him to a notification from his stock app, Garth stood to pull his phone out of the back pocket of his jeans. He smiled seeing the good news that some of his investments were doing extremely well. After putting his phone back in his pocket, he glanced over to where Regan stood and saw yet another man had approached her.

Garth stiffened when he noticed that unlike the other men, she was pretty damn friendly with this particular guy. She was smiling at whatever he was saying. Why?

Deciding it was time to break up that little party, Garth walked toward her, ignoring the little voice telling him she had a right to talk to whomever she wanted, and it wasn't his place to interfere. He ignored that same voice when it accused him of acting territorial.

From the man's accent, which he heard as he came to a stop beside her, Garth guessed this guy was American. "How's the shopping going, Regan?" Garth asked her.

She smiled up at him. "It's going fine. Garth, I'd like you to meet someone," she said, her smile getting even brighter. "This is Lamont Jefferson. Lamont and I attended college together at UCLA."

She turned to the other man. "Lamont, this is my boss, Garth Outlaw."

Garth didn't flinch at the introduction. He wasn't sure why it had bothered him, when technically he *was* her boss. As he and Lamont exchanged handshakes, Garth had a feeling Jefferson was probably wondering why a boss would accompany his employee on a shopping trip.

"What brings you to Santa Cruz?" Garth asked Lamont.

"My wife and I came over on a cruise ship. We split up when I wanted to check out some sporting equipment, and she said she was looking for several new outfits. This was the first ladies' fashion store I came to and figured she'd be in here. While looking around for her, I ran into Regan. Small world."

Regan beamed. "Yes, it is, isn't it?"

Lamont then said, "I'd better check out the other shops for Monica. We'll need to return to the ship in a few hours. It was good seeing you again, Regan, and nice meeting you, Garth."

"Same here," Garth said.

When the man walked out of the store, Garth turned to Regan. "He seems like a nice guy."

"He is. Lamont and I dated for a semester while we attended UCLA."

Raw venom seeped into his gut. He'd gotten that same reaction when Charm had told him about Harold Anders's job offer. Garth had no clue why he would be feeling territorial either time. But then maybe the feeling wasn't territorial but protective. Yes, that had to be it.

"I bet you're getting bored."

Her words intruded into his thoughts. Did she think that was the reason he had come over here? "No, I'm not bored." He glanced down at the outfits slung over her arm. "I see you found several things."

"Yes. I feel like I hit the jackpot. I just have to pay for them and then I'll be ready to go."

He lifted a brow. "Aren't you going to try them on?"

"There's no need. I know my size."

He chuckled. "Charm claims she knows her size, too, but that never stopped her from trying on her clothes. Go ahead. I'll wait. Otherwise, I'm going to feel as if I rushed you."

"Please don't feel that way. I'm sure they'll fit me."

"Humor me anyway, or else I'll think Charm has deliberately taken advantage of my kindness all these years."

She threw her head back and laughed, having no idea

how beautiful her neck looked when she did so. "All right, if you're sure. It's your time."

"Yes," he agreed. "It's my time and I have plenty to spare. I'll grab a seat right here to wait."

He watched Regan disappear behind the door that led to the fitting room. While working, she wore her pilot uniform, and on occasion, when she doubled as his chauffeur, she wore a chauffeur uniform. Every so often he saw her dressed formally when she accompanied him to events. He rarely saw her in casual attire, so whenever he did, he couldn't help but appreciate the beautiful woman she was.

In addition to her good looks, Regan had a gorgeous figure, but she'd never been one to flaunt that fact. And he liked it whenever she wore her hair down, where it flowed around her shoulders, which was something she rarely did while working. Usually she wore a ponytail, or had it all stuffed beneath her pilot cap.

As he settled in the chair, he recalled how she'd looked at the Westmoreland Charity Ball, beautiful from head to toe. He released a deep breath, still not certain why that particular night in Denver had been a turning point for him. Not really a turning point but more of an eye-opener. Since then, he'd tried not to be aware of certain things about her, but he'd noticed them anyway. And putting distance between Regan and himself wasn't an option when he'd been flying around the country a lot lately.

He'd meant what he'd told Regan. Going shopping with her was a piece of cake compared to the times he'd gone with Charm. Early on, Bart had declared that one of the brothers would escort Charm whenever she went anywhere, including shopping. She hadn't liked that directive any more than they had.

Instead of taking out her irritation on Bart, she'd unloaded on her brothers and made their shopping trips with her a nightmare. At least for the others, she had. Garth had known how to handle Charm from the beginning, and when she saw that nothing she did rattled him, she soon began behaving. He could honestly say accompanying her on those shopping excursions had turned out to be rather enlightening. She'd told him more than he'd wanted to know about women's undergarments, and how to tell if a woman was wearing any. Charm said she preferred him taking her shopping because he never rushed her out of the stores like Cash, Sloan, Jess and Maverick did. And he never flirted with the sales clerks like Sloan and Maverick. She claimed that Maverick even disappeared a time or two, probably into the ladies' restroom, with a sales clerk. Garth had no reason to doubt her story.

"I'm ready, Garth."

He glanced up and met a smiling Regan. "That was quick."

She chuckled. "While modeling, I learned how to get in and out of my clothes rather quickly."

Why did the image of her doing that very thing suddenly flash in his mind? "I'd forgotten about that time you modeled." Franklin, fearful that his daughter was turning into a tomboy, had enrolled her into etiquette school at sixteen. One of her instructors had persuaded Franklin to let Regan participate in several teen modeling events.

"That was back in the day, but it was fun."

"Do you miss it?" he asked, getting to his feet.

The store clerk had placed all the items she'd purchased in a shopping bag emblazoned with the store's name and logo.

"I didn't do it long enough. Just two years."

He recalled that he and his siblings had attended several of her modeling events. She'd also appeared on the covers of a number of Alaskan teen fashion magazines. After glancing at his watch, he said, "It's a little past noon. I hope you're ready to grab something to eat."

"I am."

"I know how much you like tacos and I overheard someone mention a place not far from here that sells good ones."

They left the clothing store and headed to the taco shop. "Just so you know, Charm planned this entire trip for me and one of the things she included was a chef who will be at our disposal."

"Sounds nice."

"It is. I met him this morning. And breakfast was delicious."

As they strolled in silence, he was glad they were spending time together like Charm had suggested. The thought that Regan might accept Harold Anders's job offer was bothering him whether he wanted it to or not. The only possible problem he could see in them sharing space for two weeks was his inability to control his attraction to her.

That was basically his problem and not hers.

He credited himself as being a problem-solver and intended to do everything within his power to make sure his desire for her didn't become an issue he couldn't handle.

Regan watched Garth walk into the guest room of the château to place her luggage near the huge bed. Why did he always have to look sexy, no matter what he was wearing or what he was doing? Then there was his scent. Always fresh, robust and manly.

"Thanks for bringing that in, Garth."

"No problem. I hope you find everything satisfactory."

He had to be kidding. The room was gorgeous, and the view of the mountains outside one window and the sea out the other was spectacular. But then, she could say the same thing about the château itself. It sat high on a hill that overlooked the ocean as well as lush green valleys.

When they'd arrived, she'd been awestruck. The house

was a lot bigger than she'd thought, spread out in a way that there were views from every window.

"It's beautiful here, Garth. Thanks for inviting me to stay."

"What time do you want to eat dinner?"

Regan glanced up at him. She hadn't thought they would be sharing all their meals. She'd figured they each would be doing their own thing. "We ate a big lunch, so a late dinner will suit me fine." The tacos had been delicious, and she might have eaten one too many.

"Late is fine with me, too," Garth said. "I'll let you unpack. If you're not too tired in an hour or so, I'd like to give you a tour of the place."

"Okay."

He walked out, leaving her alone. Sighing deeply, she strolled to the window. How many times had she dreamed of this very scenario? To be alone with Garth on some remote island. In her dream it had been a lovers' tryst. One she had hoped for, longed for, for years.

A few minutes later she was unpacking, when her phone rang. She smiled when she saw it was Simone Brinkley, her best friend from college. "Simone, thanks for calling me back."

"No problem. Have you left Santa Cruz and headed my way?"

"There's been a change in plans. I won't be coming to LA just yet. Garth invited me to join him at the château for two weeks," Regan said, placing the phone on speaker so she could talk while putting her clothes away.

"Why would he do that? When we spoke yesterday you suspected he was meeting some woman for a romantic rendezvous."

"I still believe that was the plan, but for some reason, she didn't show up."

"The woman was a no-show and he invited you to stay with him instead?"

Regan began hanging her new outfits in the closet. "It's not like that, Simone. He's my boss."

"A boss you happen to be in love with. How can you do it, Regan?"

She opened one of the dresser drawers to place her lingerie inside. "How can I do what?"

"How can you love Garth the way you do and yet be okay that he only asked you to spend time with him because some woman didn't turn up?"

"Again, Simone, it's not that way. Garth has no idea how I feel about him, and I'm not taking any woman's place. At least not in the way you're insinuating. He doesn't see me that way. To him I'm his employee. He was merely kind enough to invite me to the château to enjoy myself. Not to enjoy him."

"But you love him."

Regan drew in a deep breath. "Yes, but my feelings for Garth are something I have to deal with. Eventually I'll fall out of love with him."

"So far you haven't, and it's been how many years now, Regan? When we were at UCLA, he was all you ever talked about, and whether you'll admit it or not, I know he's the reason you left LA to return to Fairbanks. Who in their right mind leaves sunny California to go back to icy Alaska?"

Simone was right: Garth was the reason she'd gone back. "It doesn't matter."

"It should matter." Simone paused and then said, "Umm…"

Regan frowned. "What is that 'umm' for?"

"I'm thinking."

Regan knew when it came to Simone, that could be dangerous. As much as she loved her best friend, she refused to let Simone pull her into any shenanigans, and with Simone there could be plenty. As the only child of a single mother, Simone had been raised to believe that she could get anything she wanted if she worked hard and went after it.

"Please don't think, Simone. I've got this."

"No, you don't have this. If you did, you would have Garth Outlaw right where you want him."

"Simone…"

"No, Regan, this might be your only opportunity to go after the one thing you want. The two of you being at the château together is perfect. If I were you, I would seduce the hell out of him. What do you have to lose?"

Regan rolled her eyes. "My job, for one. Are you trying to get me fired?"

"He won't fire you and you know it. You mean too much to him."

"I wish," Regan said, in a whisper.

"Then make it happen, Regan. All it will take is for you to give Garth a hint that you're interested. You're beautiful, smart and intelligent. Who wouldn't want to fall in love with you?"

Regan drew in a deep breath. "You're saying that because you're my best friend."

"No, I honestly believe in your abilities more than you do. You want Garth, and being there with him affords you the perfect opportunity to get him. If you don't go after what you want now, it might be lost to you forever."

Regan shook her head. "I feel sorry for the man you set your sights on. Once you decide he's yours, he won't stand a chance."

The sound of Simone's laughter came through the phone. "Not sure such a man is out there. But if there is, then damn right, I intend to go after him."

Four

Garth stood on the screened-in deck, thinking what a beautiful day it was for mid-October. The weather was perfect, unlike how he knew it would be back home in Fairbanks.

A few minutes ago he had spoken to Jess, who had called to let Garth know he'd returned to Washington. Jess had left Alaska right before what forecasters predicted was the start of the cold season, which was beginning a month earlier than normal.

Garth's gaze moved across the vast amount of land surrounding the château. The view was breathtaking. As far as he could see, there were lush green lands, mountains or ocean. A sense of peace settled over him. It had a lot to do with the view in front of him, and he knew, deep down, it had a lot to do with Regan being here with him.

She hadn't said much while they'd shared lunch, which he'd found odd, since they talked frequently during flights. But he realized they held different conversations then because of their roles. Now they were on equal footing.

He'd finally gotten her to open up by introducing topics

they were both familiar with. Like her father and his siblings. He'd enjoyed strolling down memory lane and they'd had quite a few laughs. They'd even talked about Bart and how he still refused to accept the Westmorelands as their kin. By the end of lunch, he'd begun feeling almost that same comfort level he was certain his siblings felt with her.

"I hope I didn't take too long to unpack, Garth."

He turned and immediately felt a sense of déjà vu. Seeing her now renewed the feelings he'd been overpowered by that night at the charity ball. Granted, she wasn't wearing a full-length gown today, but she'd changed out of her jeans and into a long, flowing skirt and billowy blouse. She looked downright sexy; her outfit was a total turn-on.

Instead of answering her question, he asked one of his own, stating the obvious. "You changed clothes?"

She smiled and he felt his gut clench. He knew he had to regain control of his senses or he would lose them totally. "Yes, I decided to wear as many of my new outfits as I could—the ones I bought today, as well as those I brought with me. You like this one?" she asked, twirling around.

He nodded. "Yes, you look nice."

Her smile seemed to brighten. "Thanks. Are you ready to give me a tour of the place?"

"Sure," he said, moving toward her. She had also taken a shower. He knew because her scent of jasmine was even more vibrant.

"We'll start at the front and work our way to the back," he said, leading her to the front door.

"All right."

From there he covered the massive living room and dining area, as well as a spacious eat-in kitchen. There were two sections to the house, east and west. He would be on the east wing and she would be on the west. In the middle was a colossal family room flanked by two Greek pillars.

A huge stone fireplace took up one wall. On the opposite wall were floor-to-ceiling windows that overlooked a mountainous waterway. There was also a screened-in patio with a pool and hot tub.

Garth noticed that what had excited her more than anything was the piano that sat in the middle of the living room. He recalled both she and Charm had taken lessons, but Regan had been the one who'd taken those classes seriously. He'd heard her play before and knew she was gifted. He wasn't surprised, since her mother had also been a gifted pianist. It then dawned on him how many things Regan was capable of doing well.

"Thanks again for inviting me to join you."

He smiled over at her. "No problem. It's important to me that you enjoy yourself."

She lifted a brow. "Oh, why?"

There was no way he could tell her what Charm had shared with him about that job offer from Harold Anders, so he said, "It can't be easy flying me all over the place. And this year has been an extremely busy one. I appreciate all you've done."

What he'd said was true. The company had brought on a number of new clients, which had required flying all over the country for negotiations. Once Bart retired, Garth had begun expanding globally. Sloan was put in charge of international sales and Maverick's job was overseeing the company's expansion into states like Texas, Florida and the Carolinas, for starters. Cash was Garth's right-hand man in the Alaska office, and Charm…well, they were still trying to figure out exactly what her duties were. For now, they involved anything that made her feel useful, and she seemed to be satisfied with that.

And because he didn't want Regan to assume her being here was nothing more than a job perk, he added, "Let me add that my appreciation for you goes beyond your duties to the company, Regan. I would not have issued this sort of invitation to any other employee. I consider our relationship special, mainly because of our family history and friendship. You are someone I trust explicitly."

"Thank you, Garth."

There was a quiet moment between them. Too quiet. He wasn't sure if she felt the sexual chemistry flowing between them, but he certainly did. He felt it to the point he took a step back so he could stay in control and not do anything he would later regret. He checked his watch. "Paulo will be here in a minute."

"Paulo?"

"Yes, he's the chef I told you about. He's on call for the entire two weeks. Because I enjoy cooking, I intend to whip up a few meals for us on my own."

"Like your pancakes?"

Garth chuckled. "Yes, like my pancakes."

During her teen years, when she would spend the weekend with Charm, he had cooked breakfast for everyone. Roberta, who'd been the Outlaws' cook for years, had made use of him in the kitchen when he'd been a kid and gotten underfoot. As a result, he'd discovered that cooking was something he liked, and he had a few signature dishes. After Roberta died, Bart had hired Maddie to take her place, but she wasn't Roberta in the kitchen. So on Maddie's off days Garth had enjoyed feeding his family.

After the tour of the outdoors, they returned to the kitchen to find Paulo had arrived. Introductions were made, and when Regan began speaking to the man in his native tongue, Garth recalled that like him, she was fluent in several languages.

Garth knew Paulo was in his fifties, married, the father of five kids and one grandchild. He had come highly recommended from Garth's cousin Jared Westmoreland. Jared, an attorney living in Atlanta, had brought his wife, Dana, to Santa Cruz last year for their wedding anniversary.

While Paulo was telling them what he would be preparing for dinner, Garth noticed Regan licking her lips. Need sprang to life in the pit of his stomach.

He needed to get a grip.

"I have several activities planned for the next two weeks, but don't let me tire you out. If at any time you prefer doing your own thing, just let me know."

"Okay, I will."

He glanced at a clock on the wall and saw they had a couple of hours before dinner. "I have an idea," he said.

"What?"

"I haven't heard you play piano in years. What do I have to do to get my own private recital?"

She smiled up at him in a way that warmed his insides. "Just ask. I would love to play something for you, Garth."

Regan ended up playing several pieces for him. Each time she finished one and glanced over at him, the look on his face made her insides tingle. It was obvious he liked listening to her play. And she liked looking at him.

Every so often she would find him staring at her. The first time, the sight of him had made her breath catch on a surge of yearning so abrupt it felt like pain. She had to force her fingers to keep moving.

The look had made her wonder if he was thinking of the woman who had not shown up here. How long had he known her? How had they met? She guessed the relationship was serious, since he'd insinuated he was thinking of settling down.

He stood and clapped when her final musical piece came to an end. "That was great, Regan."

"Thanks. That's how I wind down, by playing my piano." He knew about the Steinway Grand piano that she'd bought a couple of years ago.

"I wish Charm had kept up those lessons, but her heart wasn't in them."

She nodded. "No, it wasn't." There was no need to tell him why Charm's heart wasn't in it. At the time, Charm's heart had been into Dylan Emanuel. Dylan, then a seventeen-year-old from Memphis, had won a summer scholarship to attend the University of Alaska's Fairbanks Summer Music Academy. That was where Charm and Dylan had met. One of the instructors teaching Dylan that summer had also been Regan and Charm's piano teacher.

Garth had been away in the military at the time, and when Bart found out about the budding romance, he'd wasted no time putting an end to what he'd called utter teenage nonsense. He thought Charm was too young to consider herself in love with anyone, and that Dylan wouldn't ever amount to anything. Regan wondered if Bart thought that now, since Dylan, with several Grammys under his belt, was being lauded as one of the greatest jazz guitarists of all time.

Regan stood and glanced at her watch. "Goodness, I've been playing for over an hour."

"No problem. Paulo texted to let me know dinner was ready."

"Why didn't you say something? I would have stopped playing."

He smiled. "And that's why I didn't say anything. I didn't want you to stop. I loved hearing you play, and listening to music relaxes me."

She knew that. While in flight he would request all types of music, but he liked jazz and rhythm and blues the best. "I'll go wash up for dinner."

"Okay, and I'll do the same."

She headed toward the west wing, where her bedroom was located. As tempted as she was, she didn't look back over her shoulder. But why did she have a feeling he was still standing there looking at her?

When she reached her bedroom, she closed the door behind her and leaned against it. As she drew in a deep breath, a low moan escaped her lips. Garth Outlaw had no idea how sexy he looked sitting there with his head thrown back, his long legs stretched out in front of him, his eyes closed while listening to her play.

And then there had been those times when she'd glanced over at him to find him staring at her. Whenever their gazes met, she had fought hard to make her fingers not miss a note. Why had he stared at her that way? What had he been thinking? Maybe he was looking at her, but not thinking about her. Perhaps he'd been thinking of the woman who wasn't here. Longing for her. Wishing Regan was her.

Simone's insinuation that Garth had invited Regan here to take the woman's place came to mind and she pushed it away. She refused to even consider that as a possibility. But what if it was true? She shook her head, refusing to go there. Just like he trusted her, she trusted him.

But she recalled one of her ex-boyfriends once telling her that sex to some men was like an itch. For some, it didn't matter which woman did the scratching.

She was about to go to the bathroom to freshen up when she heard the sound of voices not far from her bedroom window. She moved toward it, staying back so she couldn't be seen. Garth was outside talking to Paulo, thanking him for preparing dinner and letting him know he would be doing all the cooking tomorrow.

Garth stood and watched Paulo get into his car and leave, but he didn't move to come back inside. Instead, he shoved his hands into the pockets of his jeans and stared out at the long driveway that bordered the beautiful grasslands. He appeared to be deep in thought, and she wondered if he was again thinking about her, the woman who hadn't shown up.

As she continued to watch him, she could no longer deny the intense desire she felt for him. Desire she had no right to feel, but felt anyway. It was the same with the love she'd harbored for years.

Her breath caught when suddenly he looked at her window. She was certain he couldn't see her, but had he detected her presence? The window was open, but she hadn't made a sound. She was sure of that. Yet he stared into the open window as if he was staring straight at her. Like he knew she was staring right back at him. She was conscious of everything about him. It felt like every part of her body was burning inside.

How was she supposed to share dinner with him and keep him from detecting her attraction to him? Granted, she'd done it for years, but this felt different. She was in his space and he was in hers in a way they'd never shared space before. There was no way she could sit across from him at dinner when the mere sight of him made her heart do handsprings in her chest.

She slowly backed away from the window. It was only then that she released a deep breath. A part of her wanted to go tell him she preferred staying at the hotel. But what would she say if he were to ask why?

Regan knew she had to make it through these two weeks without giving anything away. After that, it would be business as usual. He would be her boss and she would be his pilot, and nothing more.

Five

Garth knew the moment Regan had moved away from the window. He hadn't seen her, but he had known she was there. Her scent had given her away. He had looked toward the window, yet she hadn't said or done anything to give away her presence. Why? Why had she stayed hidden from him?

He remembered when she'd glanced up and caught him staring at her while she played the piano. Instead of looking away, she'd held his gaze while she continued playing. Intense heat had curled his insides as their gazes connected, held, locked. On top of that, he'd felt his body's most primal urges kick in, reminding him just how long he'd been without a woman. Too long.

He could blame his celibacy on his workload, but he knew it was more than that. Even the woman from the dating agency, although attractive in the photos and meeting all his specifications, wasn't the woman he dreamed about when he went to sleep at night. The woman he longed to make love to. The woman who'd become his fantasy girl.

That woman was Regan.

Just thinking about how much he desired her had a hard hum of lust rushing through his veins.

There was no way she hadn't felt something, as well. He'd known the exact moment her nipples had hardened into buds and pressed against her blouse. And the pulse in her throat had thumped erratically, a clear indication she wasn't immune to what was taking place between them.

And something *was* taking place, and not just on his end.

The question he needed to ask was whether or not this attraction between them was something he wanted to incite. If so, why? And if not, then why not? There was no way he would let her go work for another company without putting up a fight. She was a vital asset to his company—someone he depended on, someone he trusted. Then, on a more personal note, she was someone who stirred his insides and fired up his desire without even trying. No other woman had done that since Karen. And there wasn't a damn thing he could do about it.

Why was he even trying?

He knew one good reason without even thinking about it. *Franklin.*

Regan's father meant the world to him. Garth admired the man and highly respected him. In some ways, he had a closer relationship with Franklin than with his own father. Bart had been hard to deal with at times. He still was. But Franklin had always been Franklin. He'd been the one Garth had gone to for advice or when he needed an ear during those times he'd had to take on Bart.

Franklin had always been the voice of reason. The one who seemed to understand Bart to the point where he'd begged his sons to try to understand him, as well. Garth was certain Franklin was privy to secrets regarding Bart that Franklin wouldn't divulge. Like the reason Bart refused to acknowledge his relationship with the Westmorelands.

"I'm back."

He glanced up and released a deep moan, hoping Regan hadn't heard it. She was wearing the same outfit and her hairstyle was the same. So why had he gotten such a gut reaction upon seeing her again? That didn't make sense.

"I was hoping I had time to set the table before you returned," he said, trying to figure out why his attraction to her was more intense at this moment than ever before.

"Since I'm here, I can help you."

Her help was the last thing he wanted because that would put her too close for comfort. However, there was no way he could turn down her offer. "Thanks. I'd appreciate it."

"Do you think I can kidnap Paulo and get away with it?"

Garth grinned. "You want to kidnap Paulo?"

"Why not?" Regan asked, licking her lips.

Garth fought the heat curling in his gut every time Regan did that with her mouth. Watching her eat was arousing. She would do well to keep her tongue inside her mouth. Every time she licked her lips he was tempted to show her the proper way it was done. On further thought, it would be the improper way. Definitely indecent. Why did indecent appeal to him?

"For starters," he said, shifting slightly in his chair to relieve the tightness in his crotch, "there is the matter of a wife, five kids and a grandchild."

She lifted what he thought was a cute brow. "Do you think they could be bribed?"

He grinned again. "Possibly. But wouldn't it be less of a criminal offense and a hell of a lot cheaper if you ask him for the recipe?"

She pretended to give his suggestion serious thought. "Only problem is that I don't follow a recipe worth a damn, Garth. You of all people should know that."

Yes, he should. He recalled that time years ago when she'd been fourteen or fifteen and had gotten a recipe from him to prepare her father a batch of cookies. Franklin had nearly broken his tooth when he'd bitten into one. He'd told Garth—behind Regan's back of course—that he would use the things for target practice.

"That was years ago," he said. "I would hope you've gotten better."

She chuckled. "Nope. I hate to disappoint you."

"You could never disappoint me, Regan." Although she might not be the greatest cook, she definitely had other talents—like playing piano, speaking several languages, walking with perfect posture and flying a plane.

He pushed his plate aside, inwardly admitting his cousin Jared hadn't lied. Paulo was the best. Garth had eaten other veal dishes, but nothing like the one he'd eaten tonight. Paulo had roasted the veal with potatoes in some special sauce. The same sauce that had Regan licking her lips.

He had to stop himself from licking his own lips.

He glanced back at Regan. She was licking her lips again and looking blatantly sexy while doing it. She gazed over at him and smiled. "Now for the dessert."

The dessert Paulo had made looked delicious, but the man sitting across the table from her looked delectable. Regan leaned back in her chair and smiled. Sharing both lunch and dinner with Garth had brought back pleasant childhood memories, reminding her of how much they'd been a part of each other's lives.

She recalled Bart always being distant, at least until Charm arrived. And she knew he wasn't the easiest person to get along with. He and his sons had clashed a number of times. Regan had once asked her father how he could work for a man who at times seemed so detached. Her father had simply said he understood Bart. There were things that had happened in Bart's life that he was still trying to work through. Her father never said what those things were and he would not have said, even if she'd asked.

Regardless of Bart's moody ways, because of her friendship with the Outlaws, she'd had a fun childhood. But that didn't mean there hadn't been periods of loneliness as the brothers got older and before Charm arrived. Being an only child had been tough, especially during those times when her father traveled a lot. But whenever he came home, Franklin Fairchild made sure she'd known just how much she was loved and wanted.

"Which one of these you want to try first?"

A smile spread across her lips when Garth held up the platter of delicious-looking treats. "Um, I think I'll try that strawberry twist," she said, leaning up to get it off the platter.

When Garth's gaze dipped to her chest, she realized how much of her cleavage he was seeing. She quickly sat back down. "Ah, could you pass the tray to me?"

"Certainly." Instead of passing it, he stood and walked it over to her.

Regan's heart thudded while watching him. "Thanks."

"You're welcome. Anything else you want while I'm up?"

She nervously shook her head. "No. That's all."

She then studied him as he returned to his seat, appreciating every step. He had such a nice backside. Could she fault him for taking a peek down her blouse when she was definitely drooling over his rear end?

"I think an evening walk is in order."

She blinked. "Excuse me?"

He smiled. "After all we've eaten today, I think we need to walk off the calories."

Regan took a sip of her wine. "Taking a walk sounds like a good idea."

She bit into her pastry and glanced over to see his eyes were on her. Specifically, her mouth. "Is something wrong, Garth?"

"No. Is it good?"

She smiled as she licked a crumb that clung to her lower lip. "Very much so. You ought to try one."

"I might later."

Regan noticed he was still staring at her while she ate her pastry. What he was thinking? Could Simone have been right? Was he attracted to her, even a little? "Are you sure you want me to take a walk with you?"

His gaze held hers when he said, "I'm positive. Why wouldn't I?"

"Don't you remember what happened the last time we took a walk together?"

He didn't say anything for a moment and then a smile spread across his face. "Oh, yes. That was the time you were to keep me occupied while Charm tried sneaking that cat with all her kittens into the house. You pretended you needed to interview someone for one of your classes."

She grinned. "I *did* have to interview someone for one of my classes. I didn't lie about that."

"Whatever you say."

She tilted her head to look at him, unable to hide her smile. "Why do I get the feeling you don't believe me?"

He smiled at her. "Because I don't. So, eat all the sweets you want so we can take that walk."

Six

After Garth and Regan changed their shoes, they left the château. They'd seen a trail earlier and intended to find out where it led. It had been a gorgeous day that turned into a beautiful evening. Although the sun had gone down and the winds coming off the ocean were brisk, she was enjoying the mild temperature.

At first they walked side by side, not saying much. Then he started off the conversation as they continued walking down the path. "Are you missing Fairbanks?"

She glanced over at him. "Not really. The only thing I look forward to this time of year is the first snowfall and the northern lights. They're beautiful."

"Yes, they are," he agreed.

It felt odd taking the time to give a woman his undivided attention. Bottom line, he was enjoying Regan's company in spite of one unnerving problem: being around her was stirring his libido like crazy. Like now. And at dinner, when she'd caught him staring down her blouse.

Instead of talking about work, he discussed Maverick's latest escapades. She had known the family long enough to know that of all his brothers, Maverick always managed to live up to his name. He liked thinking outside the box. Maverick was the one Garth could count on to come up with innovative ideas.

Although she laughed, not surprisingly, in the end she came to Maverick's defense. Since he was closer to her in age than the other brothers, Regan and Maverick had spent more time together and had always gotten on well together.

They talked about worldwide events and music and the books she'd read. And he tried to keep his concentration on their discussion while studying the beauty of her eyes, the texture of her skin and the shape of her lips.

When he fell silent, she shifted the conversation again. "I like your cousins, the Westmorelands. I especially liked talking to Ian. It seems the two of you have a lot in common."

He knew what she was referring to. Although Ian owned a casino in Lake Tahoe, he was also big on astronomy like Garth. Ian had graduated from Yale University magna cum laude, with a degree in physics. After graduation he'd worked at NASA's Goddard Space Flight Center. Although he no longer worked there, he hadn't given up his love of astronomy.

Garth's own fascination with science had begun with the northern lights. He'd kept up the interest through high school, at the University of Alaska in Juneau and into the Marines. His degree was in Transportation and Logistics with a minor in Physics and Astronomy.

"Yes, Ian is a swell guy. It would have been nice to have known him years ago. Then I wouldn't have felt like the only geek in the family."

"You weren't a geek."

He shrugged. "For a while Bart thought so." And that was putting it mildly.

Bart had been disappointed to discover transportation wasn't foremost in his oldest son's mind when he'd left for college. Although Garth knew he would work for the company, he'd seen nothing wrong with getting a minor in a subject he loved.

He decided to ask Regan something he was more than mildly curious about. "Are you still seeing Craig Foster?"

She slowed her pace. "How did you know I was dating Craig?" she asked while pushing a lock of hair back from her face.

"Franklin mentioned him. Maverick and Sloan did, as well."

She nodded. "And I guess Dad also mentioned that he didn't like him."

"Yes, he did say something to that effect."

She shrugged. "There was nothing wrong with Craig other than that he was military. Dad never cared for me dating a military man for fear I would end up marrying one and moving away."

"Yes, there was always that possibility. I'm sure you would have moved to wherever your husband got stationed, right?"

"No. I would never have left Dad."

He wondered if that was her way of saying those military guys she'd dated were not serious involvements. "You would not have?"

"Nope. But then Dad left me."

Just like she'd come to Maverick's defense, he came to Franklin's. "The cold weather was getting to be too much for him, Regan. Surely you understood that."

"Yes, I understood it, Garth. But the decision to move to Florida happened so unexpectedly. I dropped by one day and he told me his mind was made up."

He smiled. "You know as well as I do that Franklin has

never been one to procrastinate about anything." Then, to get back to his earlier question, he asked, "So, what's the deal with you and Craig Foster?"

She sighed. "Craig and I aren't seeing each other anymore. It was a mutual decision to go our separate ways."

"I see." He couldn't help wondering why. She was right about Franklin not liking the guy. But not for the reason Regan assumed. Franklin was a good judge of character and sensed Foster was the overly jealous type. Garth hadn't met Foster, but Maverick and Sloan had. Not surprisingly, they hadn't liked him, either.

"So, what's the deal with you and the woman you were to meet here for two weeks?"

Garth figured she had every right to ask, since he had inquired into her business. "We've known each other for a couple of months and decided to get together here. Something came up at the last minute and she couldn't make it."

That wasn't totally true, but it hadn't been an outright lie, either. The dating service had provided him with details a couple of months ago and the mix-up in dates had been discovered at the last minute. He figured there was no need to tell Regan they'd met through a dating service.

"What are your plans for tomorrow?"

He glanced over at her and hoped his plans were her plans. He would make sure of it.

"We have a private tour of the island scheduled for tomorrow."

"A private tour?"

"Yes. The driver will pick us up and bring us back afterward. It's a four-hour tour with a number of interesting places for us to see."

They had come to the end of the walking path at a cliff overlooking the sea. "This place is beautiful," she said. "I bet it's beautiful at night, too."

He bet it was. He could just imagine how the stars would look over the ocean. "Ready to head back?"

A smile touched the corners of her lips and his breath suddenly caught on a surge of yearning.

"Yes, I'm ready to head back."

"What time do we leave for the tour tomorrow morning?" Regan asked when they returned to the château.

He glanced over at her as he closed the door behind them. "If we leave here by ten, we should be fine. And I plan to prepare breakfast before we leave."

"Pancakes?"

He chuckled. "Yes, pancakes. I suggest you get up by eight."

"Need help?"

A grin touched his lips. "You know better. Cooking is therapy for me. I like doing it myself."

She saw he was leaning against one of the gigantic pillars. It was one sexy pose, and for a minute she envisioned him as a Greek god. "I was just thinking how when we were kids, you liked cooking for us. We got to play cards or board games while we waited. You guys had a lot of them."

He chuckled. "And if I recall, Scrabble was your favorite."

She was surprised he remembered. "Yes, I loved Scrabble."

"You would challenge Sloan because the words he came up with were never real words."

"Yes, and he figured I was too dumb to figure it out," she said, laughing. "He was so arrogant."

Garth joined in her laughter. "Was? He still is."

Her shoulders shook again in laughter. "I have to admit, playing that game definitely enhanced my vocabulary."

"That was the plan."

Regan sighed deeply. "You were always the mature one.

Very responsible. Looking out for everyone. Taking care of us, with Walker's help of course."

He grinned. "Of course. I was the oldest and Walker was my sidekick. Someone had to keep you guys out of trouble."

"And then you and Walker left for college."

He nodded. "Yes, however, we didn't go far and came home practically every weekend."

But still, she thought, it hadn't been the same. Things had gotten interesting when Charm had arrived. By then, Garth and Walker had returned home for a year before going into the military. That was all the time needed for Garth to take a firm hand to Charm, then leaving it to his brothers to do the rest when it became apparent Bart wouldn't.

"I think I'll go take a shower now," Garth said.

"I'll take one, too, and get into bed early to make sure I'm up at eight."

"I'm sure all that shopping wore you out," Garth said, chuckling.

"For your information, it was the walk that did it. I'm not into a lot of physical activity."

"Well, that's going to change while you're here, because I *am* into physical activities. I suggest we take a walk every evening."

The expression on his face was serious. "I'll think about it," she said, grinning.

"Yes, you do that."

She would—and there were other things she would think about. Like should she consider Simone's advice. Simone hadn't been the only person who'd suggested Regan catch Garth's eye. Charm had suggested that same thing, but that had been years ago. Charm probably figured Regan had gotten over her crush on Garth by now. If Charm thought that, then she was partly right. It was no longer a crush.

Now it was a lot more than that.

"I'll see you in the morning, Regan."

"Okay, Garth. Good night."

She'd started moving toward her bedroom when he called out to her. "Regan?"

She stopped to turn around. He was still leaning against the pillar and looking so sexy that a deep hunger, one she'd never felt before, invaded her midsection. "Yes?"

"Pleasant dreams."

She swallowed and forced herself to speak. "Pleasant dreams to you, too."

She turned back around and stepped away, walking as quickly as her legs would carry her.

Garth stood there long after Regan closed her bedroom door. Was he wrong to fight this inner turmoil he felt whenever he was around her? Did it make sense to place distance between them? That would be hard to do since they were here together.

They'd again taken a stroll down memory lane, and the one thing he *could* accept was that Regan wasn't a kid anymore. She had stopped being a kid long ago. Now that he'd finally noticed, was it wrong to want to do something about it?

He rubbed his hand down his face. Had she felt the desire radiating within him? Had she detected his need, his passion, his wants? His attraction? It was an attraction he had controlled since last year.

How long could he continue to control it? Why was he even trying?

He pushed away from the pillar and moved toward his bedroom. He needed to take a shower and he intended for it to be a damn cold one.

Seven

The aroma of strawberry pancakes had Regan opening her eyes with a huge smile on her face. Shifting her body in bed, she glanced at the clock on the nightstand to make sure she hadn't overslept. In fact, she still had thirty minutes to spare.

She had gone to bed early last night, not because she was tired but because if she'd spent just one more minute in Garth's presence, she would have given away her true feelings for him. That was why she was glad he hadn't pressed her for more information regarding her breakup with Craig.

The last thing she wanted him to know was that the reason she and Craig broke up was that he'd accused her of having an affair with Garth. And all because one of his friends in Denver had texted Craig the link to an article about the Westmoreland Charity Ball. Just so happened the article included a photo of her and Garth dancing together. Craig believed she wasn't sleeping with him because she was sleeping with Garth. That was when she'd told him to leave and not show his face again. She was glad she hadn't heard from him since.

Refusing to think about Craig any longer, she got out of bed, showered and dressed. In no time at all, she was walking to the kitchen. The closer she got, the more she picked up the smell of coffee brewing and bacon frying.

"Good morning, Garth," she greeted, sliding onto a stool at the breakfast bar.

Garth turned around and smiled at her. This smile wasn't any different than the others he'd always given her, but for some reason this one made her feel special. He looked good dressed in a pair of khakis and a green polo shirt. She'd always thought the color green enhanced his features. And she might be mistaken, but his eyes appeared darker than usual.

"Good morning, Regan."

She smiled back and for just a heartbeat, their gazes held. He turned back to the stove, but she was certain she hadn't imagined it.

"I hope you slept well," he tossed over his shoulder.

"I did. Thanks."

She studied his body, and the woman in her appreciated how his slacks stretched across his well-rounded backside and tapered down a pair of muscular thighs. Why did it suddenly feel so hot? And why was her heart pounding? Clearing her throat, she asked, "Need help with anything?"

"You can set the table for me. I figure it would be nice to sit in the dining room and take advantage of the view."

"Yes, that would be nice," she agreed, sliding off the stool.

She leaned up to get a couple of plates out of the cabinet at the same time he turned to place a plate of bacon on the counter. They nearly collided.

"Oops. Sorry," he said.

"No problem." Moving out of his way, she got the plates. Yesterday, the kitchen had seemed huge. Why, with both her and Garth in it, was it as if it had shrunk? Going to the drawer for the silverware, she was tempted to glance over her shoulder at him, but she resisted.

"Glad you woke up on your own. I wondered if I would have to wake you."

Now she did turn to look at him. Was he serious or just joking? She could just imagine him coming into her bedroom to wake her. Then, no, she couldn't imagine it. She didn't *want* to imagine it. Doing so would play havoc on her hormones. From the mischievous look that appeared in his eyes, she figured he was just joking.

"You would not have had to wake me. I have a built-in alarm clock. Got it from Dad."

"Yesterday, I noticed something else you got from your dad."

"Oh, what?"

"Your ability to add stuff up in your head. You did it yesterday at the restaurant. It always amazed me how Franklin could do that. As a kid I struggled with math and he would give me pointers, or shortcuts as he would call them."

Yes, that was another gift she had inherited from her father. Because her mother had died when she was young, she didn't remember much about her. However, she knew how much she looked like her, because her father had kept pictures around the house.

"You okay over there?"

She closed the utensils drawer and glanced over at him. "Yes, I'm fine. I was just thinking of my mom."

"At least you have one to think about."

She met his gaze. There hadn't been any bitterness in his tone. The words had been spoken matter-of-factly. She'd been around the Outlaw brothers enough to know the subject of their mothers was a joke to them. Garth had written off his mother years ago when she had left him with Bart and then remarried. She'd had other children, but none of them had ever reached out to Garth. His mother hadn't, either.

"Do you ever hear from her, Garth?"

He would have every right to tell her it was none of her business, but he didn't. Instead, he said, "No. I understand her other son just finished law school and her daughter is in med school."

She wanted to ask where he'd obtained that information, but she didn't press her luck. Evidently, he read her mind.

"I looked her up once, right before I left for the military. I called to see if she would meet with me. At first, she said no, but then she agreed. I invited her to dinner, and she had pictures of her family. I asked if I could meet them, and she said she preferred I didn't. I was a part of her life she didn't want to remember. I suggested she let her son and daughter decide, and she said they had. They knew about me and didn't want to meet."

"You believe that?"

"No reason not to. Doesn't matter. I left satisfied that I had reached out to her. If she and her family didn't want me to be a part of their lives, then so be it."

She nodded. It was his decision to make. Moving out of the kitchen, she went into the dining room to set the table. He followed, carrying several platters.

"It's just the two of us. How do you think we'll eat all that food?" she asked him.

He shrugged. "It's not really a lot, and between the two of us none of it will go to waste, trust me."

"If you say so." She knew he was a hearty eater and figured the reason he kept in great shape was because he had a workout room in his basement and he stayed active.

Breakfast was enjoyable, and the pancakes were delicious. He told her of the places the private tour would take them and figured they should be back before two. What really sounded good was his offer to grill hamburgers for lunch.

"I talked to Maverick and Sloan last night," he said as they cleared the table. "I mentioned you were here with me and they threatened me bodily harm if I didn't make sure you had a good time."

After they'd loaded the dishes into the dishwasher, she glanced at her watch. "We've made good time. I'll be ready to leave once I change shoes."

"All right."

Regan walked off, and although she didn't look back, she again had a feeling Garth was watching her.

"Need help?" Garth asked, moving to assist Regan with her packages as they entered the château. It seemed every stop they made on the sightseeing tour, she had run into a shop to purchase souvenirs. She'd made a list that he knew included his brothers, Charm, her father and Bart, as well as some of her friends.

"Yes, thanks."

She passed one of the bigger bags to him. He got close enough to inhale her scent. He'd smelled jasmine on other women, but for some reason the scent was different on her.

"You're still grilling hamburgers?"

He glanced over at her. "Yes. You're hungry?"

She scrunched up her face. "I wasn't going to say anything, but with all that walking we did, breakfast has worn off."

"Then I'll get started right away. I've even thought about getting in the pool."

"Now that's something you wouldn't be doing this time of year in Alaska," she said.

"True," he said, placing the bag on the table. "You want to join me for a swim?"

Regan turned and lifted a brow. "You want me to go swimming with you?"

She seemed surprised that he'd asked. "Yes."

She smiled. "I'm glad one of the things I bought that day we went shopping was a swimsuit."

"That's good."

He had enjoyed her company again today. Her excitement had been contagious. Their tour guide had been thorough and full of historical facts, and Regan had asked a lot of questions.

Garth watched as she grabbed her bags and walked toward her bedroom. He rubbed his hands down his face. She was sexiness on legs. He'd never seen a walk so graceful be such a turn-on. Before closing her bedroom door, she glanced over her shoulder and saw him still standing there, staring.

A confused frown settled on her face. "Is anything wrong, Garth?"

For a quick second, he was tempted to give her a straight answer, to tell her that yes, something was wrong. He'd come here to meet a woman who was supposed to help him control his intense attraction to Regan. Because of a mix-up, the woman was a no-show, and now the very object of his desire was under the same roof, breathing the same air, sharing his space and blowing his mind every time she walked or talked.

Instead, he said, "No, nothing is wrong. I was just thinking about something."

"Oh. Okay." She closed the bedroom door.

It was only then that he turned to go to his own room.

Garth was already on the patio seasoning the burgers when Regan joined him. Although she wore a cover-up over her bathing suit, he could clearly see the outlines of a very shapely figure. He tried keeping his attention on the meat.

"You can go ahead and get in the pool if you want. I want to get the meat on the grill."

"Need help?"

He appreciated how she always offered. "No, I've got this. Thanks for asking."

Garth then turned his attention back to the grill. He heard her moving behind him, sliding off her sandals. Out of his peripheral vision, he saw her take off her cover-up. Every nerve in his body hummed with lust.

He was so consumed by his physical reaction that the loud sound of her splash made him jump. Deciding that he couldn't resist temptation any longer, he glanced at her in the pool and wasn't surprised that she was a good swimmer. Regan was good at so many things.

Garth turned his attention back to the grill. When he was satisfied it would be a while before the hamburgers needed him again, he left the patio and went into the kitchen to make a salad and fries. It was too early to start on the fries, but he could certainly get the salad into the refrigerator. He was almost done when he looked out the French door—at the exact moment Regan eased out of the water.

He nearly dropped the bowl while watching water pour off her skin. But what really held his attention was her bathing suit. It was a one piece, but for all he cared, it could have been a no-piece. It clung to her skin like a second layer. The shape and cut were perfect for every single contour of her body. He tore his gaze off her to quickly finish the salad, anxious to join her in the pool.

"I hope you're not through with your swim," he said, returning to the patio to find her stretched out on one of the loungers.

"No, I decided to take a break."

"I hope it's not a long one. I want to swim a few laps with you, after I take the meat off the grill."

Garth was a sharp businessman because he could read people. It bothered him that he saw apprehension in her expression now, which led him to say, "But only if you don't mind."

She met his gaze. "No, I don't mind."

It didn't take him long to finish the hamburgers and place them in the warmer. He walked toward where she lay on the lounger while flipping through a magazine. She had put her cover-up back on. Why? Was she nervous about him seeing her in a bathing suit that looked damn good on her?

Upon hearing his approach, she looked up. "Are you ready for me, Garth?"

Her words, innocently spoken, stirred something deep within him. It was a part of his body that just didn't want to behave around her. Regan was off-limits. When he returned to Alaska, he would call one of his female acquaintances to take care of his manly needs. But even as he had the thought, he said, "Yes, Regan, I am ready for you."

Eight

Regan watched Garth ease out of his jeans, and sensations she'd never felt before passed through her.

His swimming trunks looked good on him, fitting perfectly on his masculine thighs. Even in his business suits he could start her heart fluttering.

"I'll be back. I want to grab a couple more towels."

She watched him sprint off, feeling her heart against her ribs. Moving quickly toward the pool, she decided to be in the water when he returned. She was somewhat nervous at the thought of Garth seeing her in a bathing suit.

"You're in the water already."

Not only was she in the water, she was submerged in the deep end. Was that disappointment she heard in his voice? "Yes, I decided to go ahead and get in."

He jumped in, making a big splash. Her heart began beating fast as she watched him move agilely through the water, using a perfectly executed breaststroke.

"You want to do a few laps together?" he asked when they were less than a few feet apart.

"Sure."

"You have a nice bathing suit, by the way."

"Thanks. Ready for those laps?"

He nodded. "We are not competing, Regan. We're doing laps together. I felt I needed to say that just in case you're like Charm, who has a bunch of competitive genes in her body."

Regan tilted her head, chuckling. "I promise not to tell her you said that."

"Please don't. I have enough to deal with as it is, when it comes to Charm."

She could hear the brotherly fondness in his voice. Any other family that consisted of six siblings, all of whom had different mothers, would certainly be dysfunctional to the nth degree. But not the Outlaws.

"Ready to start?" Garth asked her.

"Yes, I'm ready."

Their bodies moved in sync as they glided through the water. The pool was large enough that they had their own space, yet their moves felt choreographed. As if on cue, when they reached the other side, they turned to go back to the other side of the pool.

They did a number of laps before she eased over to the side of the pool. She wanted to watch him work his body.

"You're leaving me?" he asked, treading water as he watched her.

"For the time being. I don't have as much stamina as you do."

When she was on the other side of the pool, he began swimming. His body maneuvered several different strokes masterfully, and he looked amazing while gliding through the water.

Regan lost track of time. Maverick was right about Garth having a lot of stamina. She couldn't help but be curious whether he took that same level of vigor to the bedroom.

She wasn't shocked to be wondering such a thing since she had long ago accepted Garth as a fantasy lover.

"Daydreaming?"

Regan sucked in a deep breath. She hadn't known he'd come to join her at the side of the pool. "Excuse me?"

A smile touched the corners of his lips. "I asked if you were daydreaming. You looked as if your thoughts were a million miles away."

Regan wondered what he would think if he knew her thoughts had been right here in the pool with him. "I was just deciding it's time to get something to eat."

He nodded. "Everything is ready but the French fries and that won't take but a few minutes in the air fryer."

"Okay." She just realized how close they were standing. She was tempted to reach out and rub her hands down his wet chest. But she wouldn't stop there. Then she would lean in and lick the side of his neck, and then…

"Did I tell you how nice you look in your bathing suit?"

"Yes, you did. Thanks."

"I got an idea of what we can do after we eat, if you aren't tired."

She licked her lips. "What?"

"Something we haven't done in a long time."

Her thoughts were on making love, but she figured that wasn't it, since they'd never done that before at all. "What?"

"Play Scrabble."

She couldn't help but smile. It had been years since she'd played. "Um, why do I get the feeling that I'm about to find out that Charm and Maverick aren't the only Outlaws with competitive genes?"

"What! You're challenging me again, Regan?" Garth said, grinning broadly.

"You bet I am. *Lionize* is not a word."

"Yes, it is." He didn't want to argue with her, but darn, she looked so cute when she was angry. Especially the way her lips formed into a pout. He took a sip of his wine, needing something to soothe the sensations rolling around too close to his groin.

"Then prove it."

"You do realize, Regan, that you can't afford to challenge me again, right?"

She lifted her chin. "Is that what you're counting on? That I'll let you get away with this one?"

"No.

"Then I'm challenging you, Garth. Prove it."

"Okay." He picked up his phone.

"No, this time, we are using mine," she said, standing to pull her cell phone out of the back pocket of the denim shorts she had changed into after their swim. He thought now what he always thought whenever he saw her legs. She had a gorgeous pair.

"Are you accusing me of cheating?" he asked, amused when he probably should feel offended.

"I'm not accusing you of anything. I'd just rather use my phone to look it up this time."

He shrugged. "Fine, go right ahead. And just so you know, you're cute when you're mad."

She frowned. "I'm not mad."

"If you aren't, then you could have fooled me. You know what I think?"

"No, what do you think?"

"I think you've been hanging around Maverick and Charm too long."

"Whatever," she said, rolling her eyes, as she pulled up the dictionary on her cell phone.

Garth watched her expression and knew the exact moment she saw challenging him had been a mistake. He couldn't resist adding salt to the wound by saying. "So, what does it say? What's the definition?"

"It doesn't matter," she said, placing her phone aside and picking up her wineglass.

"It matters to me. So, what does it say?"

Her annoyance was apparent when she picked up her phone and read aloud what it said. "To *lionize* is to treat someone as a celebrity." She looked back over at him. "Happy now?"

He leaned back in his chair and smiled over at her. Yes, he was happy. He had spent all day with her and tomorrow he would be doing the same—as well as the day after, and the day after that. He had twelve more days to be with her and he was looking forward to each of them. Around her, he felt relaxed. At least he did whenever he wasn't lusting after her.

"Yes, I'm happy, but I want you to be happy, too, Regan. So, I guess that means I'm going to have to start *lionizing* you."

A smile broke out on her pouty lips. Shaking her head, she said, "You just couldn't resist, could you?"

He chuckled, moving the board game aside to put it away. "Enough of Scrabble. The last thing I want is for you to walk around mad with me for the next two weeks."

"I couldn't ever get mad at you, Garth."

He glanced over at her. Instead of meeting his gaze, she was taking a sip of her wine while looking at the fireplace he'd lit earlier. Paulo had warned him that this time of year, Santa Cruz had warm days and cool nights. Since the château was right off the ocean, the evening temperature would drop rather quickly. They found his warning to be true. No sooner had they gotten out of the pool and eaten than the temperature fell. They were surprised, since it hadn't done so last night when they'd taken a walk.

"Besides," she said, finally looking at him. "I can't get mad at you since you're my boss and I need my job."

He took another sip of his wine. For some reason, it was important that while they were there together, their employer-employee relationship didn't exist. He wanted her to feel comfortable with him.

"That might be true, but while we're here together, we don't have a professional relationship. I invited you to stay here and to share my space not as my pilot, but as a friend. The person I cooked breakfast for this morning, went on a tour with today, went swimming with and beat at Scrabble, is someone I consider a friend."

A huge smile touched her lips. "There you go, rubbing salt into the wound again."

He laughed. "It's not intentional." He became silent for a moment and then said in a more somber tone, "But seriously, you understand what I'm saying, right? I don't want you to think I would invite other female employees to spend time with me this way. I feel comfortable with you and with being alone here with you. And I hope the same holds true for you."

She nodded, a serious expression appearing on her face, as well. "Yes, of course.

"Good. Do you have any questions or concerns you think we should address?"

She hesitated but then said, "Yes, there is one thing that's concerning for me."

"And what is it?"

Garth watched Regan nibble on her bottom lip. He'd known her long enough to know that whatever this concern was, she was nervous about bringing it up.

"You can talk to me about anything, Regan. That hasn't changed."

She met his gaze. "What about her? The woman you

were supposed to spend time with here, who didn't come? There are some women who wouldn't appreciate their man spending two weeks with another woman, no matter how innocent the relationship. What if she doesn't understand the kind of friendship we share and thinks us being here means more than it does? Will she understand our unique relationship?"

Their unique relationship…

He'd never thought of their relationship as such, but that was definitely one way to define it. For her to ask such a question showed the depth of her concern. And from her standpoint he understood why she would be concerned. But that was only because she didn't know the truth.

Although he wouldn't share any details about the dating service or his plans to settle down, he could certainly address her concerns. "Don't worry about her, Regan."

He could tell from the look on her face that those words hadn't waylaid her concerns. "Why not?"

He met her gaze and held it. "Because you don't have to. You're going to have to trust me on this."

Regan looked into his eyes, considering his words. Maybe the relationship with the woman who hadn't arrived wasn't as serious as she'd assumed. Even then, it wasn't like Garth to spend two weeks anywhere with a woman if it wasn't serious. Other men might do such a thing, but not Garth.

Knowing he was waiting for some kind of response, she said, "Then I guess that settles it, because I do trust you."

Looking at her watch, she decided it was time to retire for the night. "I need to call Simone to tell her about my change in plans." Simone already knew, but Garth didn't have to know that. At the moment Regan just needed to escape from his presence. There was only so much of him she could take. His entire aura was overpowering.

"Okay. Paulo will be back tomorrow. If you want breakfast, he will be here by nine. I plan to go sailing. You can join me if you like."

She would definitely like, but she didn't want to crowd him. They had spent today together, and it might be a good idea to have space for both of them tomorrow. "Thanks, but I brought a book to read. One written by your cousin Rock Mason. It's good." Rock Mason was the pen name of his cousin Stone Westmoreland.

"I heard his books are good. I haven't had time to read one. By the way, according to our agenda, we're to attend the opera tomorrow night. It's a dressy affair."

She'd forgotten all about that. When he'd shown her the itinerary a couple of days ago, she'd been excited at the idea of going. She'd brought a gown that would be perfect. At the time, she'd packed it just in case she and Simone decided to do something fancy while she was in Los Angeles.

"I'm good with dressy and would love to go. It doesn't start until eight, so I'll be well rested by then, but the question of the hour is whether or not you'll be rested, since you're going sailing tomorrow, Garth."

"I should be fine, so let's plan to go."

"Okay. Good night, Garth."

"Good night, Regan. Sleep well."

Later that night, when Regan slid between the sheets with her e-reader in her hand, she couldn't help but think about how much she had enjoyed today. She and Garth had done things together they hadn't done in years.

She could still hear music, which meant he hadn't gone to bed yet. Turning on her side, she opened the e-reader, while thinking about how he'd defined their relationship while they were here. They were not sharing space as employer and employee, but as friends.

Was there a reason he'd wanted to make that distinction?

She'd been serious when she brought up the issue of the woman who was to have met him here. Not all women, or men, would be so understanding. Regan couldn't claim that she would be. But she would let him handle his business.

Tomorrow they would have their space and maybe that was a good thing. Time would tell.

Garth stood and moved across the room to turn off the music. It was past midnight already. Shoving his hands into the pockets of his jeans, he threw his head back and inhaled deeply, drawing in Regan's lingering scent. She'd gone to bed hours ago, yet her scent was still here, and had stayed while the music played.

He had closed his eyes so his mind could absorb the music and his entire body could soak up her fragrance. He yearned for things he hadn't had in months and only wanted them with her.

That was the crux of his problem. He couldn't have them with her. This insane craving for her couldn't be normal, could it?

Why not? his mind countered. *She's beautiful and she's single. She told you she was not involved with that military guy any longer, so what's the problem? And tonight you defined your relationship as personal.*

He had enjoyed playing Scrabble with her and loved it whenever she had challenged him. Not because he'd known his word would stand, but because she was so intense about winning. It seemed his Regan had a few competitive genes, as well.

His Regan?

He frowned. She was not his, although tonight there had been a couple of times he'd thought of her as such.

Grabbing his wineglass, he stood and headed for the kitchen. Tomorrow they would do separate activities during the day. However, he had a feeling tomorrow night, attending the opera with her, would definitely be a test of his endurance.

Nine

Regan stood at the window and then looked down at her watch. It was almost six o'clock, and if she and Garth planned to attend the opera, they would need time to get dressed and leave at least by seven-thirty, since it began at eight.

"We're still going to the opera tonight, right?"

Regan jumped, startled. Turning, she saw Garth leaning against a pillar. She fought to keep her heart from racing. He was shirtless, with his jeans riding low on his hips. She'd seen him without a shirt before. Like yesterday, when they'd gone swimming, and at other times over the years. But that didn't mean a thing to her pulse rate.

"Where did you come from?" she asked him.

"My bedroom. I just woke up from my nap."

She could see that now. He still seemed drowsy around his eyes. The sleepy look was sexy on him. Way too sexy. "I didn't know you had returned from sailing."

"I came back three hours ago."

"Oh." That had to have been when she'd been in her bedroom talking on the phone to Simone...or rather listening to Simone, since her best friend had done all the talking.

Simone figured yesterday would have been a great day to seduce Garth. It had taken Regan a good half hour to re-iterate to Simone she intended to do no such thing.

"So, are we still going to the opera?" he asked her.

"Yes, I still want to go."

"Then we will."

"Paulo left food for you if you're hungry."

"I'm not. I still feel full from those sandwiches he fixed me for lunch."

"How was sailing?"

"Great. I loved being out on the water. I had my music with me. It doesn't get any better than that."

She nodded. "Well, I'm glad you're getting rest, Garth."

He smiled. "You and Charm both. She called earlier and threatened to disown me if she finds out I'm working on files while I'm here."

Regan lifted a brow. She'd heard the music playing last night from her bedroom. Jazz. What he usually listened to while working. "Are you working on files from here, Garth?"

"Nope. This has been a relaxing trip so far. Besides, I wouldn't undermine Cash like that."

No, he wouldn't. "I'm sure Cash is doing just fine running things."

"I'm sure of that, too. If something comes up that needs my attention, he knows how to reach me." Garth glanced at his watch. "I guess it's time for us to get dressed. You want to meet back in this same spot in about an hour?"

"That sounds good," she said.

"The opera lasts three hours, followed by a reception with dancing."

"I saw that. Do you think you'll want to stay up that late?"

He chuckled. "Need I remind you that you're the one

who goes to bed with the chickens. I should be the one asking you if you're okay with the late hour."

"I think dancing would be nice."

"So do I. Then let's do it," he said.

"Yes," she agreed. "Let's do it."

Regan looked radiant, Garth thought, watching her enter the room. She was so beautiful he was rendered speechless. He was grateful he had the pillar to lean on. Otherwise he would have gotten weak in the knees. With each graceful step she took, he was aware of her in every pore of his body. He could even feel blood rushing through his veins.

The gown she'd worn to the Westmoreland Charity Ball had knocked the breath out of his lungs. The one she had on tonight was having the same effect, tenfold. On top of that, the way it draped over her curves stirred sexual hunger to life in his midsection.

Even her hair was different. The curls were piled high, nearly forming a halo around her head. Regan was incredibly feminine from top to bottom, and the areas in between, he was certain. Her soft-as-sin curves were captivating his mind, making him appreciate being a man.

"I'm ready, Garth."

She might be ready, but he sure wasn't. Sharing space with her tonight would definitely be a distraction. A distraction he couldn't handle. "You look beautiful, Regan."

A smile spread across her face. "Just a little something I threw together."

If that was the case, and he figured it wasn't, she'd thrown it together rather nicely. "Well, no matter how you managed it, you look beautiful."

"Thanks, Garth."

Even her makeup looked good on her. She hadn't been

heavy-handed with it. It was light and blended perfectly with her skin tone.

And speaking of skin…

Was that a split up the side of that gown? One that went up past her knee and over her thigh whenever she walked? One that flashed skin? A lot of skin? When she came to a stop in front of him, he stared down at her generous cleavage that revealed even more skin.

He inhaled deeply, then wished he hadn't. Her scent was even more of an attention-grabber tonight. It was getting to him in ways a female perfume never had before. Tonight, he'd been bitten.

"Ready for an enjoyable night?" he asked her, leading her to the door.

"Yes. I'm more than ready."

Three hours later, Garth glanced over at Regan, who was sitting beside him in the huge opera theater. The theater lights were turned down, which afforded him an opportunity to study her. It was obvious from the look on her face and the focus of her gaze that she was enjoying the opera.

And he was enjoying her.

He shifted to sit more comfortably in his seat. If he continued to stare at her, she would eventually notice. Though maybe not, since her attention was clearly on the singer who was performing on stage. Pretty soon it would be time for intermission. No sooner did that thought pop into his mind than the lights came on.

He used that time to walk around and stretch his legs while Regan visited the ladies' room. Moments later, they met back up and he suggested they stop by the concession area for coffee.

Garth tried not to notice the men admiring Regan in that beautiful gown she was wearing. The same gown that draped across her curves, her breasts, and clinched at the

waist, showing a perfect hourglass figure. While he was in
one line getting their coffee, she was in another grabbing
snacks. He overheard the two men in line in front of him
remark to each other about what a gorgeous woman she was
and that they envied the lucky man she was with tonight.

They'd spoken not knowing Garth was fluent in Spanish and understood everything they said. He was tempted
to tell them he was the lucky man. However, he figured
they would find that out when they saw him and Regan
together later.

He glanced over to where Regan sat after she'd gotten
them a table. They had twenty minutes before the lights
would start blinking, letting everyone know intermission
was over and it was time to return to their seats.

He recalled the drive to the opera house. He'd ridden in
a car with Regan numerous times, but tonight had felt different. She had kept the conversation lively by telling him
she'd been asked to host a booth at a career fair at one of
the schools next year. She made sure to mention that she'd
only committed after checking his schedule to verify it was
a day he wouldn't need her. Since she was thinking about
his schedule that far in advance, he hoped that meant she
wasn't giving Harold Anders's job offer any serious consideration.

He joined her at the table with two cups of coffee. "Here
you are," he said, placing one in front of her.

"Thanks. Wasn't that singer superb?" she asked in an
excited voice.

There was no way he would admit he hadn't paid attention to the singer since his mind had been filled with
sexual thoughts of her. Sitting so close to her in the audito-
rium had played havoc on his libido. And when the lights
had come on for intermission, he'd glanced down to see

the split in her gown showing him a portion of her thigh. That hadn't helped matters.

"This coffee is good, Garth."

Her words intruded into his thoughts. Was it? He hadn't noticed even though he'd taken a couple of sips. He'd been looking at how perfectly her lips fit on the cup as she tried not to smear her ruby-red lipstick.

There wasn't much about Regan that didn't turn him on, leaving him longing. He'd known it, yet he had still invited her to join him at the château for two weeks. How crazy was that when his prime purpose for coming here had been to put an end to his intense attraction to Regan by meeting up with another woman? Things hadn't turned out that way, and now his attraction had become red-hot desire.

He was faced with two choices. He could either handle it or act on it.

He wasn't sure how he would handle it, but his mind immediately filled with ways to act on it. There was no need to blame not having sex for so long as the reason for his horny thoughts. Deep down he knew that was just an excuse. He could have had any woman he'd wanted, and he needed to stop claiming he'd been way too busy for one. A man made time for what he wanted, and the truth of the matter was—he hadn't wanted another woman.

Not even the one chosen for him by the dating service. He had thought perhaps seeing her in person might create a spark. But now, he had a gut feeling it would not have. He'd sought the woman out for the wrong reasons. He was glad she hadn't shown up.

The lights began blinking.

"I guess that means it's time to go back. But first I want to thank you for bringing me tonight, Garth. For sharing all the activities with me for the last two days. I know I wasn't the one who was supposed to enjoy these things with you, and I might be wrong for feeling this way, but I'm glad I got to do them, even if I was a spare."

A spare? Was that how she saw it? How could she not? At that moment he decided to give her something else to think about. Meeting her gaze, he said, "There is no other woman I'd rather be here with than you, Regan."

There.

At that precise moment, he had made a decision.

He wouldn't handle his intense attraction to her. He intended to act on it.

There was no reason for him to continue fighting his desire. Regan was a grown woman who could make up her own mind about whether she would want an affair with him or not.

She smiled. "That's a kind thing to say, Garth."

He had a feeling she didn't believe him. That meant he had eleven days to convince her he'd meant every word.

Ten

There is no other woman I'd rather be here with than you, Regan...

Garth's words were still warming Regan's heart when the opera ended, and they entered the room where the reception would be held. Had he really meant what he said or was he just being kind?

"This place looks nice," Garth said, and in a surprise move, he took her hand in his and led her through the throng of people toward an empty table.

The moment their hands touched, sensations spread up her spine. She inwardly told herself the only reason her hand was in his larger one was because the room was crowded, and he wanted to make sure they stayed together. But what about the other times he'd held her hand tonight?

Once seated, she glanced around. The table was perfect. It was close to the dance floor and not far from a buffet of hors d'oeuvres. A live band performed an array of music that ranged from classical, jazz, Latin and even R&B. Several couples were already out on the dance floor.

"I'll go get our drinks. What would you like?" Garth asked her.

"A glass of red wine will be fine."

"Okay, I'll be back in a minute.

She watched him leave while thinking how nice he looked in his tux. Of course, she'd seen him in a tux before, but still… It showed off his broad shoulders, muscled chest, firm thighs and muscular arms. He was a specimen of a man that any woman would appreciate. She hadn't missed the number of women checking him out tonight.

She switched her attention from Garth and his admirers to the architectural beauty of the room. Beams and columns framed high chandeliers. The outside of the building was built in the form of a massive wave. It was beautiful and could rival the opera house in Sydney, Australia.

"If you're alone, senorita, I would love to join you," a deep male voice said.

Regan glanced up to see a tall, handsome man standing by her table. She was about to tell him that no, she wasn't alone, when a familiar, authoritative male voice answered. "She isn't alone. She's with me."

"I'm sorry, senor," the man said apologetically and quickly walked off.

Regan looked up at Garth and understood why the man had left so quickly. A fierce frown covered Garth's face. He handed her a wineglass before sliding into the chair beside her.

"Sorry I took so long," he said.

"You weren't gone long, and thanks for bringing me the wine," she said, wondering why he'd acted so protective of her just now. She recalled him doing the same thing at the Westmoreland Charity Ball several months ago. The last thing she wanted was for him to start treating her like he was her protector.

She took a sip of her wine. "I could have handled him, you know."

He met her gaze. "Yes, I know. However, when you're with me you don't have to."

She didn't say anything, deciding not to make an issue of it. "So, what's on the agenda for tomorrow?" she asked, to change the subject.

"Hiking."

She blinked. "Hiking?"

"Yes. Of course, you don't have to go. You can sleep in if you like. But if you decide to join me, it's best if we get an early start to beat the sun."

Regan stared at him. They probably wouldn't get home before midnight tonight, and he wanted to get up early? She didn't have a problem being an early riser, but usually she would be in the bed early the night before, as well.

"Do you want to dance?"

Since she knew they would be hiking tomorrow, it would have been a good idea to suggest they return to the château. However, a part of her refused to give up a chance to dance with him. "Yes."

Garth stood and offered her his hand. Placing her wineglass down, she took his hand and he led her to the dance floor. She felt a tingling sensation just from touching him. She knew things were about to get hotter being in his arms.

He drew her to him, and she felt comfortable with her body meshed to his. When he began moving, she automatically followed. She loved remembering the last time they'd danced together. Now, tonight, she would have new memories.

He still held her hand in his, against his chest. Seemingly against his heart. "Did you enjoy the opera?"

She looked up at him when she wanted more than anything to place her face on his chest and draw in his scent. "Yes, what about you?"

"Yes, but I admit to watching you a lot."

Her eyes widened. She hadn't known. "Why?"

"Seeing the happiness on your face was priceless. I could tell you were really enjoying yourself."

A smile spread across her lips. "Yes, I was. But it doesn't sound as if you were if you were watching me."

"I enjoy watching you."

She swallowed deeply. "Why?"

"I just do."

A part of her wanted to ask him to be more specific, but she decided not to. The music would be coming to an end soon and she wanted to savor being in his arms while dancing. He then placed his hands around her waist. Was she imagining things or were his fingers at her waist nudging their bodies closer? Or was her body just naturally moving closer to his?

The music was a slow Spanish concerto. Garth was an excellent dancer and she followed his lead. He'd said he enjoyed looking at her. Was there more to it than that? Was she wrong to hope there was? Was she wasting her time even thinking such a thing?

At that moment she really didn't want to spend a lot of time thinking. Instead she wanted to bask in the feel of being in his arms.

So she rested her head on his chest.

Garth glanced down at Regan. He liked the feel of her head resting against his shoulder. He doubted she knew how many times tonight he'd thought about kissing her. He had admitted to not being able to keep his eyes off her and that would have been the perfect opportunity for him to tell her how much he desired her, ached for her.

But he hadn't.

However, he would—just not now, not here.

He was tired of resisting.

She lifted her head from his chest and her gaze locked with his. For the longest time, they stared at each other. Sexual hunger took over every part of his being. Surrendering to a primitive force he could no longer fight, he lowered his head to hers. Their mouths were a breath apart when he felt a tap on his shoulder. He swung his head around.

"May I cut in?"

Maybe Garth should have felt grateful that the man's untimely arrival had stopped him from kissing Regan in the middle of the dance floor, but he didn't. All he felt was a high degree of annoyance. "No, you can't."

Dismissing the man's presence, Garth turned to Regan. "I'm ready to leave."

She nodded. "So am I."

Twenty minutes later, Garth brought the car to a stop in front of the château. He noticed Regan hadn't said anything since leaving the opera house. Was she upset with him for behaving like a Neanderthal with that guy who'd wanted to dance with her? Acting territorial, as if he had every right to do so?

"Are you upset with me?" he asked. He wanted to know now, before they went inside.

She glanced over at him. "No, although I don't understand why you feel the need to act like my protector."

Was that what she thought? Even when he'd come within a moment of kissing her? "I wasn't acting like your protector, Regan."

"Then what?"

He broke eye contact to draw in a deep breath. She had to know, or at least suspect, he desired her. Was she waiting for him to spell things out? If so, then he would. "We'll talk about it when we get inside. Okay?"

She nodded. "Okay."

He got out of the car to open the passenger door for her. Then he took her hand in his, and they walked to the front entrance. He let them inside.

"I'd love a cup of coffee while we talk. What about you?" he asked her.

"Yes, I'd love a cup, too, but first I'd like to get out of this gown and shoes. Could you give me ten minutes?"

He nodded as a vision of her getting out of the gown and shoes filtered through his mind. "Yes, I could use ten minutes, as well."

Garth noted he was still holding her hand. Looking down at their joined hands, he lifted them to his lips. That wasn't enough. Releasing their hands, he placed his at her waist while staring down at her. He needed to do the one thing he'd almost done on that dance floor. The one thing he'd dreamed of doing to those lips for quite some time.

"Garth?"

He saw mixed emotions in her gaze and knew there was only one remedy. He lowered his head to hers.

She released a moan the moment their mouths connected. He heard it and the sound shook him to the core. When their tongues mingled, dueling like they couldn't get enough of each other, his control shattered.

Tightening his arms around her waist, he drew her closer as he deepened the kiss in a way that had him moaning right along with her. He was deliberately mating their mouths and he didn't want her to concentrate on anything other than the way his tongue was stroking hers. Fire stirred in his loins, arousing him in ways he hadn't experienced in years, if ever.

Knowing they couldn't stand here and kiss forever— although he wished like hell they could—he reluctantly brought the kiss to an end. He saw the desire in her gaze and was tempted to kiss her again. Instead he said, "We meet back here in ten minutes, right?" He dropped his hands from her waist and slowly backed up.

"Can we make it twenty?" she said softly, as she also began slowly backing away.

"Yes."

She turned and quickly walked to her bedroom and he walked toward his. Entering the bedroom, he eased the tuxedo jacket from his shoulders and then removed his tie. He wondered if Regan still thought he was acting like a protector. Would a protector kiss her the way he just had? He couldn't help wondering what she was thinking right about now.

Regan leaned against the bedroom door. Breathing in deeply to slow down the wild beating of her heart, struggling to come to terms with what had just happened.

Garth had kissed her. He had actually kissed her.

Nobody knew the number of times she had fantasized about him doing what he'd just done. Should she pinch herself to make sure she wasn't dreaming? Should she regret it, since technically he was her boss? Common sense told her that maybe she should do both of those things, but common sense was something she lacked right now.

She moved away from the door to the mirror on the wall to take a look at her reflection. Namely, her mouth. She smiled when she saw a pair of lips that had been thoroughly kissed by Garth Bartram Outlaw. A kiss that had shaken every nerve in her body. Even now, she felt her insides quivering.

Moving from the mirror, she slid out of her shoes and then danced around the room, on top of the world. What had Garth meant by the kiss? He had certainly put to rest her assumption that he'd been acting like her protector. As far as she was concerned, Garth was the epitome of every woman's fantasy. He'd certainly been hers. No matter how many guys she'd dated, they hadn't been Garth. No guy had held a light to him. None.

But what had that kiss meant? Was it just his testosterone acting up or could it mean more?

As she slid out of her gown, she hoped it was more. She traced her lips with her tongue. Yes, definitely she wanted more. But, she had to be realistic. She had to think about what *more* would entail. Yet, at the moment, she didn't want to think at all.

She glanced at her watch. She now had less than ten minutes to redress. What would they talk about? Would he tell her he'd decided after all this time that he loved her and—

Regan suddenly went still. She needed to calm down and stop acting like a sixteen-year-old who'd gotten kissed by the most popular boy in school. She had to stop thinking about things that might not happen…like another kiss, the feel of his hands all over her, him stripping off her clothes, taking her against that pillar he liked leaning against.

She needed to pull herself together, and no matter how difficult that might be, she would do it.

Precisely twenty minutes later, after changing into a pair of jeans and a shirt, Garth returned to the foyer just as Regan did. He nearly missed a step when he saw the outfit she'd changed into. It was a beautiful jumpsuit with an off-the-shoulder neckline that emphasized the curve of her neck.

His gaze traveled up to her face and zeroed in on her mouth, the lips he'd tasted earlier. She had applied more lipstick. He fought the urge to close the distance between them and kiss it off.

While getting undressed, several alarming thoughts had filled his mind. What if Regan wasn't ready for what he wanted? If he were to let his desires be known and they weren't reciprocated, it could push her toward ending her employment with the company. If he proposed an affair, things could get messy if it didn't work out. It would not only ruin his relationship with her, but also with Franklin. Could he risk all of that?

"There are a couple of Paulo's muffins left from this morning. I plan to grab one. Would you want one, as well?" she asked as they walked side by side to the kitchen. "I bet it would go well with the coffee."

He picked up on the slight nervousness in her voice. He didn't want her to feel uneasy around him. He would do and say whatever it took to remove any tension between them.

"I bet so, too, but I'll pass. I had enough sweets for the night. Go ahead and grab your muffin and I'll get the coffee started," he said in a lighthearted tone.

"Okay."

He moved to the counter where the coffeepot sat and couldn't resist glancing over at her as she moved toward the refrigerator. That outfit looked pretty damn nice on her. In fact, she looked good in anything she put on her body... even her pilot uniform. But what was on his mind now, more than anything, was her taste. No woman's mouth had a right to taste as delectable as hers had tasted.

Garth returned his attention to the coffeepot, wondering what he would say when they sat down to talk. He heard the movement behind him and fought the urge to look over his shoulder again. Was she thinking about the kiss as much as he was? Had she enjoyed it as much? Did she want to do it again? When the aroma of cinnamon floated across the kitchen to where he stood, he figured she was warming her muffin up in the microwave. A part of him wished she would come over and warm him up, too. In his present state, it wouldn't take much.

By the time he poured the coffee into cups and headed for the table, she was sitting there waiting. He forced a smile onto his features. Now he was the one feeling nervous. "I guess going hiking with me in the morning is off the table. It's after midnight," he said, placing the coffee cup in front of her, and then sitting down with his own.

She shrugged her shoulders—those beautiful shoulders left bare in the outfit she was wearing. "Who knows? I might surprise you." Then, taking a sip of her coffee, she said, "Mmm, you have the magic touch when it comes to making coffee, Garth."

He chuckled. She'd always told him that, which was why she left the making of the coffee on the plane to him. He would make a pot before the jet took off, and by the time it leveled off in the sky, he was ready for a cup. He would also take a cup to her in the cockpit.

He watched her take a bite out of the muffin. She looked over at him, catching him staring. She licked a few crumbs from around her lips. "You sure you don't want me to warm one up for you? It's delicious."

"Yes, I'd like one, but just a taste. May I have a bite of yours?"

He wasn't sure whether or not his question surprised her. Her expression was unreadable. She lifted the muffin to his mouth and he took his own bite, in the very spot where she'd taken hers. Then he licked the crumbs off his lips, knowing she was watching him.

"You might be right after all, Regan," he said. His gaze held hers, and he could see the pulse in her throat beating rapidly.

"Right about what?"

"Kidnapping Paulo."

A smile spread across her lips. "Think we can come up with a plan?" she asked, finishing off the muffin.

Watching her, knowing they'd shared that muffin, made intense desire heat his core. "With us together, Regan, anything is possible."

His words must have stirred something within her because he saw the pulse racing in her throat again. She took a sip of her coffee and then sat the cup down and looked at him. She licked her lips, which caused a hard jolt of need to pass through him. He picked up his cup to take a sip of his own coffee, wishing it was something stronger.

"You said we would talk, Garth."

Placing his cup down, he met her gaze. "What I have to say can be summed up in a few words, Regan."

She raised a brow. "And what words are those?"

"I want you."

Eleven

Sensuous shivers spread through Regan as she stared at Garth, speechless. First off, the kiss; then he'd shared that muffin with her. And now…

Granted, she'd known he was a straight shooter. However, she hadn't expected what he'd just said.

He wanted her?

"Yes, I want you," he said again, when she didn't respond. "I figured that kiss would have been a good indicator."

She drew in a deep breath. It had been, but still… "I worked for you for almost five years, and you never paid me any attention, Garth."

He leaned back in his chair as he picked up his coffee cup again to take a sip. "If you recall, Regan, after losing Karen, I wasn't paying any woman much attention. I barely dated."

As far as she was concerned, he barely dated now, and when he did, she figured it was to take care of his physical needs. "So why now and why me?"

"Why not you, Regan? You are a very beautiful woman."

She rolled her eyes. "I look the same as I've always looked, Garth."

"That might be the case, but I began truly noticing your looks a few months ago. I guess you can say my blinders were taken off."

She took a sip of her coffee and met his gaze over the cup. "And just when were these blinders removed?"

"The night of the Westmoreland Charity Ball."

She placed her cup down, remembering that night. He had surprised her by inviting her to go with him. She'd discovered later that Bailey, whom Regan had gotten to know after Bailey married Walker, had suggested that he bring Regan. She also recalled he'd been very attentive that night. Even his brothers had teased him about it.

"Do you remember that night?" he asked her.

She nodded. "Yes, I remember. I thought you were being overprotective."

"You assumed that tonight, as well. You were wrong both times, Regan. Both times I was being territorial. That night I felt something that I hadn't felt in ten years. Sexual attraction toward a woman, of a magnitude that it was hard for me think straight. It made me want to take you somewhere and seduce you."

She blinked, finding what he was saying hard to believe. "Seriously?"

A smile curved his lips. "Yes, seriously."

Regan took another sip of her coffee. Then with a boldness that surprised even her, she asked, "Why didn't you seduce me, Garth?"

She saw the flash of heat that appeared in his eyes. He quickly took another sip of his coffee. "There's no way I could have done that," he finally said.

She lifted a brow. "Why not?"

"The man who seduces you should be the man who plans to marry you. You would expect that."

He was right. Gone were the days when she was into

sex for the sake of sex. She was older, wiser and a lot more mature than she'd been in her early twenties. At twenty-eight, she wanted more from a relationship. For her, being intimate with a man meant marriage was in their future. That was one of the reasons she hadn't slept with Craig. In addition to him being the suspicious and jealous type, she hadn't loved him.

Was Garth letting her know any seduction on his part would be nothing more than casual sex? If that was true, had he planned to spend two weeks with a woman he wasn't serious about? Would his affair with that other woman have been nothing more than sex?

"Are you saying you're not interested in getting married ever, Garth?"

He shook his head. "No, that's not what I'm saying. In fact, I've been thinking about marriage a lot lately."

Hope sprang up inside of Regan. "You have?"

"Yes. In fact, that's the reason I came to Santa Cruz. I was to meet a woman I was contemplating marrying one day."

Regan's hope was replaced by disappointment and confusion. "Let me get this straight. The woman you were to meet here, the one who eventually was a no-show—you were thinking about marrying her?"

"Yes."

"But now you want me?"

"Yes."

She frowned. That didn't make sense. For him to think about marrying a woman meant that he and the woman were in love and sharing a serious relationship. If that was the case, then how could he tell Regan that he wanted *her*? Did he not think that was betraying the woman he planned to marry? Did he assume Regan would just step right in and take the woman's place in his bed? She expected better of him.

"Sorry to disappoint you, Garth," she said in a curt tone, standing to her feet. "There are some substitutions I will not do."

He reached out and took her hand. When she tried pulling it back, he tightened his grip. "I think you might have misunderstood me, Regan. Please sit back down so I can explain."

Regan wasn't sure what he could explain, but the feel of his hand touching hers caused all kinds of sensations to curl around in her stomach. She sat back down. Not because he'd requested it, but because she felt weak in the knees from his touch.

She lifted her chin. "You kissed me and said you wanted me. Yet, now you're telling me the woman you were to spend two weeks with here was someone you might marry. So, what did I misunderstand, Garth?"

Garth had made a mess of things, when all he'd been trying to do was have a totally honest discussion with Regan. But her assumption was pretty damn damaging. There was a lot she needed to understand.

"First of all, I don't expect you to take anybody's place in my bed, Regan. To be honest, the woman who was supposed to meet me here would have been taking *your* place. It was *you* who I originally wanted in my bed."

"What? You definitely need to explain that, Garth."

A part of Garth wished he hadn't been so blunt. But he had, and now he owed her an explanation. "My reaction to you that night in Denver, at the ball, bothered me. Like I said, it was the first time in nearly ten years I had felt such strong attraction to a woman. It also made me realize something else."

"What?"

"That you weren't Franklin's little girl anymore or Charm's teenage bestie. You had grown up to become a very beautiful woman."

She shrugged. "Not sure about the beautiful part, Garth, but I've been a woman for quite a while now."

"I honestly hadn't noticed you that way. But that night… your dress, the hair, the makeup, the total package…" He paused a moment. "Especially that dress. You were wearing the hell out of it."

"Thanks. I'll take that as a compliment, but it still doesn't explain things."

He nodded. "After we returned to Alaska we picked up our normal routine. I figured my attraction to you that night was one and done. But that wasn't the case. My desire for you grew stronger, taking over my mind and senses, interfering with the way I handled business matters. I knew I had to do something. That's when I came up with a plan."

"And what was this plan?"

"To turn my attention elsewhere. That meant meeting someone I could get serious about since I considered you off-limits."

She took a sip of her coffee before asking, "So how did you meet this 'someone else'?"

He shifted in his seat, deciding he might as well tell her everything. "Through a very private dating service. And for the record, we never officially met. Santa Cruz was to be our first meeting."

Garth and the woman hadn't met?

Regan was surprised. She had used an online dating service before, so she knew how it worked.

"So, if the two of you would have clicked, then you would have considered her wife material?" she asked, trying to understand. The Garth Outlaw she knew preferred handling his own personal affairs, and she would think that would include selecting the woman he might end up sharing his life with.

"Yes, and before you make more assumptions, I was pretty detailed in my specifications. They are thorough when vetting people and have an exclusive clientele. Their match for me rated highly and I thought she might be perfect."

Regan was trying hard to keep her composure when her heart was breaking. "Yet your perfect woman didn't show."

"No, but it wasn't her fault. It was a dating service error. Somehow there was a mix-up on dates."

"But you will reschedule?"

He shook his head. "No, I won't. Her not showing up was a good thing."

Regan glanced over at him. "Why?"

"Because I was only using her to help me get over my attraction to you. I see now that would not have been fair. And over these last few days, my desire for you has only increased. In fact, I can truthfully say that I desire you more than I've ever desired any woman before."

She fought back the hope that tried to return. She wondered if he realized the power of what he'd just said. What she still didn't understand, though, was why he'd felt he couldn't act on his attraction to Regan. Why had he gone to all the trouble of finding someone else?

"You were contemplating marrying her had the two of you hit it off?" she asked again.

"Yes. And there is one thing you need to know, Regan."

"What?" she asked past the lump suddenly forming in her throat.

He leaned forward in his chair and held her gaze. It was

as if what he was about to say was highly important. She had a feeling that, whatever it was, she was not going to like it.

"What is it, Garth?"

"Whereas I was willing to marry another woman, I am not willing to marry you."

Twelve

Regan snatched her hand from his as if she'd been physically slapped. She felt like she had been. Did he think she was not good enough for him?

As if he read her thoughts again, he said, "Let me explain—"

"You did already," she said, pushing her chair away from the table. "I got it. I'm good enough to sleep with but not good enough to marry. Can't have you marrying the hired help, right?"

"Damn it, Regan, that's not it and you know it. How can you say something like that?"

He honestly had the nerve to ask her that after what he'd said? "I say it because you're insinuating it."

"No, I'm not. I would marry you if I could, but I can't."

That didn't make sense. "And why not?"

He paused for a long moment. "My ability to love any woman ended the day Karen died. The woman I was to meet here knew that and was willing to accept a loveless marriage, but I don't expect you to accept one. I wouldn't want you to. You deserve better. You deserve to marry a man who will love you the way you should be loved. I wish I could be that man, but I can't. My heart will always belong to Karen."

He sighed deeply. "I'm being totally honest with you, Regan. I want you, but I can't love you, or any woman. All I have to offer is an affair that you won't forget or regret."

"For me that's not good enough, Garth." She then left the kitchen and headed toward her bedroom.

Regan forced herself to keep walking and not look back. She should be angry with him, but she was only angry with herself for loving him so much and believing that one day he would notice her existence and love her back.

But he couldn't love her.

She had heard something similar before…from her father. How many times had Franklin Fairchild told her that he still loved her mother and that no other woman would have his heart?

Regan would tell Garth the same thing she'd told her father more than once. He was a man with a lot of love to give and she knew the woman he'd lost would want him to move on with his life and love again.

Those words had fallen on deaf ears with her father, and she knew they would with Garth, as well.

Entering her bedroom, she closed the door behind her, tempted to throw herself against it and cry until she couldn't cry anymore. But she refused to do that, because something Garth said tonight stuck out in her mind…

"I desire you more than I've ever desired any woman before."

Did he truly mean that? And if he did mean it, did it mean he desired her more than he had Karen? She began pacing. When he and Karen had met and fallen in love, Garth had been about the same age Regan was now. From what Charm had told her, it was a whirlwind romance when the two had been stationed in Syria. Regan figured he had to have fallen deeply in love for him to still feel that way ten years later.

He'd said that if and when he did marry, it would not be for love. Some women would settle for that. Hell, a lot of them did.

Could Regan do the same?

She stopped pacing and sat on the edge of her bed. What about couples who didn't marry for love, but then the love came later? She knew of one such couple. Agatha Meadows was one of Regan's college friends. Agatha and Christopher had met on a cruise and were intensely attracted to each other. They'd engaged in a hot and heavy affair onboard the ship, and after the cruise, they'd gone their separate ways—without so much as an exchange of phone numbers to keep in touch.

Two months later, Agatha had discovered she was pregnant. Believing Christopher had a right to know he'd fathered a child, she'd hired a private investigator to find him so she could give him the news. Christopher, elated at the thought of being a father, had convinced Agatha to enter into a loveless marriage for the sake of their unborn child. That had been a hard decision for Agatha to make since she'd dreamed of marrying one day for love.

She'd told Regan she would settle on desire rather than love because there was no doubt in her mind that she and Chris desired each other. In fact, Agatha was convinced their desire for each other had been the catalyst to them falling in love. Now, after nearly seven years of marriage and two children, Agatha would be the first to tell you that their desire for each other had transformed into love. They'd been determined to make the marriage work and it had blossomed into something neither had expected.

Granted, the situation with Garth was different from

expecting a child together, but one aspect of their situation was similar. By his own admission he wanted her, and he had been willing to use another woman to get over his attraction to Regan. He'd even admitted that since being here with her, his desire for her had only increased. A part of her felt good knowing that, for the time being, she and she alone was the woman Garth wanted. The thought of that shouldn't make her heart swell, but it did. It gave her hope. Hope that what could start off as purely sexual could blossom into something more.

Regan began pacing again. Would any other woman fight for something more with Garth? Just like Garth thought Regan should marry for love, she thought he should marry for love, as well—even if that love was one-sided.

That was what he didn't know. She loved him.

Now she needed to somehow convince him that the woman he wanted could also become the wife he needed. The wife who could show him how to love again. He didn't need to marry someone from some dating agency, or any other woman for that matter. He needed to marry *her*. She knew him. Understood him. And more important, she loved him.

It was time she fought for the man she loved.

Now she needed to come up with a strategy to make things work in her favor. For the past five years she'd worked for Garth as his private pilot. Those times she doubled as his private chauffeur, she'd had a listening ear to how he transacted business while in the back seat of a limo. He was a brilliant strategist, so she'd learned from the best. Now she could put that knowledge into action.

She would use his desire to her advantage. She'd build on his desire and go from there. Regan was about to embark on one of the most important missions of her life. She had never seduced a man before, but she'd read enough romance novels to have an idea about how it was done.

What if she failed? What if he never loved her? Knowing Garth, he would still do all the things that would truly matter, for the woman he chose as his wife. He would respect her, be faithful to her, honor her and protect her. In his own way, he would even adore her, although he might not ever truly love her.

Regan decided then and there that even if Garth never fell in love with her, she had enough love for the both of them.

Garth paced his bedroom knowing he'd blown things with Regan. It wouldn't surprise him if she was in her bedroom packing. How could he have been so stupid to admit something like that to her in the name of being honest.

No matter how he'd tried explaining things to her, it had gone from bad to worse. He wouldn't be surprised if she took Harold Anders's job offer now. Hell, it would serve Garth right if she did.

He stopped pacing. He needed to talk to someone, confess to being stupid and have that person agree with him. Pulling his phone out of his back pocket, he called Walker.

"Hello?"

"You awake, Walker?"

"Awake? Man, it's daytime here."

Garth had forgotten about the time difference. "I forgot."

"Whatever. And since I know it's nighttime there, is there a reason you're calling me and not in bed with that woman? The one you met through the dating service?"

"She didn't show due to a mix-up in dates."

"Oh. So now you're alone and bored with nothing to do."

"I'm not exactly alone. Regan's here with me."

"Regan is always with you, Garth. She's your pilot."

Walker didn't get his meaning. "Regan was to leave after dropping me off and then come back for me in two weeks. I convinced her to stay."

"Oh."

He still wasn't sure Walker got it. "I want her, Walker. I want Regan."

His best friend laughed. Walker was honestly laughing.

"What the hell is so funny?" Garth asked.

"You. It took you long enough to figure that out, Garth. You don't think I haven't noticed that you want Regan? Hell, even Bailey noticed it. Why do you think she suggested you invite Regan to the Westmoreland Charity Ball?"

Garth rolled his eyes. "That's not possible. I only started wanting Regan at that ball."

"Wrong."

Garth frowned. "Wrong?"

"Yes, wrong. I began noticing how taken you were with Regan long before then. It might have been the night of that charity ball before you finally admitted it to yourself, but trust me. It's been long before that night. A year or so before. Maybe even longer."

Garth's frown deepened. Had it? As if Walker could read his mind, he said, "Trust me, Garth. I'm your best friend. I notice things, especially when they concern you."

"Then why the hell didn't you say something?"

Walker chuckled. "It wasn't my place. Besides, I was dealing with my own issues with Bailey. If you recall, I was fighting my own battles against falling in love. I didn't have the time or inclination to take on yours."

Garth leaned against the dresser in his room. "Love? Who said anything about love? I want Regan. I didn't say anything about loving her. You of all people know I could never love any woman but Karen."

Walker didn't say anything for a minute. "So, why are you calling?"

Garth rubbed his hands down his face. "I told you. I

want Regan. Desire got the best of me. With us under the same roof, I told her I wanted her."

"And?"

"And I also told her all I wanted was an affair and nothing more."

"Okay. That's fair. You told her what to expect and what not to expect, which is what all men should do with women. So, what's the problem? Regan is a grown woman. She either agrees to the affair or she doesn't."

"That's not all I told her."

"What else did you say?"

"I told her that the woman who didn't show up here, the one from the dating service, was someone I had contemplated marrying."

"And?"

"And that although I wanted Regan way more than I wanted that woman, I could not consider marrying her."

"You actually told Regan that?"

"Yes, but I tried to explain why. I don't want Regan to settle for a loveless marriage. She deserves more."

"I agree Regan deserves more, but I think you made a mistake in telling her that. Think about it, Garth. You're willing to marry a woman you're not even sure you'd want. Yet you know you want Regan, but aren't willing to marry her."

"I told you why."

"Yes, and if you'll recall, after Kalyn, I swore I would never fall in love again, either."

"Our situations are different, Walker."

"I've discovered a person's heart can expand to include others if they're willing to let them in."

Garth threw his head back and closed his eyes. Those would be emotions he never wanted to feel again. Emotions he doubted he *could* feel. "I can't."

"You can't, Garth? Or you won't? Think about it."

Thirteen

"Good morning, Garth."

The hot coffee nearly scalded Garth's tongue. Regan had entered the kitchen wearing a pair of skintight leggings and a long pullover top. Her hair was pinned up on her head with a few ringlets around her face. Why did she have to look so desirable this morning? So darn refreshed? On top of that, she smelled so darn good. She looked nothing like he felt, which was absolutely lousy.

After talking to Walker, he hadn't gotten much sleep. He felt even more like an ass for asking her to sleep with him when there would be no benefit for her other than the promise of great sex. Regardless of what Walker had insinuated, only one woman could or would ever have his heart.

"Good morning, Regan. I hope you slept well," he said, studying her and trying to decipher her mood.

"I slept great. I see Paulo's been here," she replied, checking out the platters of food Paulo had left warming on the stove.

He was about to answer when she moved to lift a lid and a shaft of sunlight came through the window blinds. The ray of light seemed to shine directly on her. She looked even more beautiful then. He couldn't help noticing the shape of her face from this angle, how refined it looked and what a graceful pair of shoulders she had. He had noticed those same shoulders last night and had wanted to place kisses all over them. He still did.

She'd obviously expected him to say something. But when he didn't, she glanced over at him and caught him staring, and he couldn't pretend he hadn't been.

Lifting a brow, she asked, "Is something wrong, Garth?"

He swallowed deeply. So much for trying to maintain his control with her today. "No, nothing is wrong." Then trying to regain his common sense, he added, "You might want to try the baked cinnamon apples. They're good."

"Um, I think I will."

He broke eye contact to resume eating, but he was aware of every move she made around the kitchen. She finally came to the table and sat down, taking the same chair she'd sat in last night.

"I guess you didn't go hiking after all," she said, after saying grace.

"No. I decided to put it off for another day." He was trying like hell to decipher her mood. He was convinced that when she'd left him in the kitchen last night, she'd been madder than hell. Now it was as if their conversation had never taken place. As if he hadn't proposed having an affair with her. Was she going to pretend it had never happened?

"About last night, Garth…"

Maybe she wasn't.

"Yes, what about it?"

"Your proposition. What time frame are you talking about for the affair, Garth?"

Did that mean she was considering it? A certain part of his anatomy wanted to leap for joy, but he refused to let it. "That will be up to you, Regan. Whatever you decide. However, if you decide to extend it beyond our time here, there's something you'll need to consider."

"What?"

"Are you willing for the affair to go public? You work for me and the last thing I want to do is to tarnish your good name. I couldn't do that to you."

"So, you would want us to sneak around?"

He could tell by her accusing tone that was honestly what she thought. "No. It wouldn't bother me if anyone knew we were seeing each other. I was merely thinking of your reputation, Regan. I don't want to hurt you in any way. I feel like a selfish ass even suggesting we have an affair, but…"

"But what, Garth?"

"I desire you more than I've ever desired any woman before. I should be able to walk away, but I can't. And that kiss we shared last night only made things worse."

"You said that last night and that's what I don't understand. You claim you desire me more than any woman before. Does that include Karen?"

He didn't say anything for a long while. She had every right to ask that. Hopefully, he would be able to explain and do a better job than he had last night. "Karen and I connected on a level beyond sexual chemistry. The desire was there, but not of this magnitude. When you're somewhere defending your country, desire and passion have to be placed on the back burner."

He paused. "There's nothing sexy about combat uniforms and fatigues. Karen and I managed a few stolen moments, but not many. We knew our situation was only temporary and there would be more time for the physical once our deployment ended and we returned to the States. That never happened, but there is no doubt in my mind that had Karen lived, and we had married, my desire for her would be a hell of a lot greater than what I feel for you, because she would have been my wife."

She didn't say anything, just continued to look at him. He couldn't help but wonder if his explanation had made things even worse.

"Thanks for explaining that, Garth. I fully understand now and I've made a decision."

He swallowed. "And what have you decided?"

"I will have an affair with you, Garth. However, it has to be short-term, only while we are here. Like you said, I have a reputation to protect."

He nodded. "Can I ask how you reached your decision?"

"Yes. You want me, and I want you, as well. More than I've ever wanted any man. I know what we're feeling is just a physical thing based on sexual need. Therefore, I need to get it on with you and move on."

Get it on with him and move on?

Move on to where? To whom? Did it matter as long as he spent time with her? If she could handle the type of relationship he'd proposed, shouldn't that be all that mattered?

"Are you sure about this, Regan?"

A smile touched her lips. "I'm sure. But I do need the name of that dating service you used."

He nearly choked on his coffee. "Why?"

"I'm thinking of giving them a try," she said, biting into one of the baked apples.

"Clearly, you're joking."

"Why would I be joking?"

"Because I told you about the women who apply to that agency."

She nodded. "Yes, women looking for a future with a man who would suit them and vice versa. I found the whole thing fascinating. I did online dating a few years ago and it was a total disaster. The guy wasn't at all what I thought he would be."

"Then why try it again?"

"Because according to you, this dating service is good at vetting people and they have an exclusive clientele. That's what I want. It sounds like their male clients would be of the caliber I'd like to meet."

He scoffed at that. "You need to meet someone who will fall in love with you, Regan."

"Is there a reason you think I won't? Do you think a man can't fall in love with me?"

"That's not what I'm saying," he said, trying not to grit his teeth.

"Then what are you saying, Garth?"

That was a good question. "Nothing."

She frowned at him. "No, I think you *were* trying to say something."

Garth broke eye contact with Regan. The last thing he wanted was to make her mad with him. He knew she dated, so why would it bother him how she went about obtaining those dates? She had every right to use that dating service if that was what she wanted to do.

"You know what I think, Garth?"

He looked back over at her. She was still frowning. "No, Regan, what do you think?"

"I think you assume I'm not good enough to go through that agency. That the women who do are polished, refined and sophisticated and you can't see me as any of those things. You can't see me as a wife to any of those men."

"That's not true."

"I think it is. Need I remind you that I went to an all-girls private school until I was sixteen, and that I can play the piano, speak six languages fluently, and I'm an ex-model, so I know a lot about fashion and poise. I can fly a plane, ride a motorcycle and shoot very well. I also like camping. I think I have a lot going for me and can hold my own."

He of all people didn't need to be told about her many skills and attributes. He knew them well. The one he didn't know about was her skill in the bedroom. That was the only one he was interested in right now.

"Of course, you can hold your own, Regan. All I'm saying is that most men who use that dating service might be looking for a wife, but they aren't looking for love. Are you willing to marry someone who doesn't love you?"

"I would think any man is capable of falling in love if the right woman came along, Garth. Except for you, and you've explained your reasons. Any man of wealth and influence has access to a variety of women if all they want to do is date or take care of their physical needs. A man using that caliber of dating service is looking for more and that's what I want, too. Just because you're not looking for love in a marriage doesn't mean every man who uses that dating service feels the same way."

She had a point there. Other men might not have an aversion to falling in love with the woman the dating service selected for them. There was no doubt in his mind that any man who chose Regan would be wowed by her. She was beautiful and accomplished. He could see any man falling in love with her.

"So when we return to Fairbanks, I'd like the information for the service so I can contact them before the holidays."

He pushed his plate aside, trying to hide his annoyance. "Why the rush?"

"No rush. I just figure that like most companies, they will have limited hours around the holidays. If I get my information in now, maybe by early spring I will have viable prospects. I will be twenty-nine by then. It would be nice to have someone special to celebrate my birthday with."

For some reason he felt a chill at the thought of her spending her birthday with anyone other than his family, like she had this year. Since Franklin had moved to Florida, Charm had known it would be Regan's first birthday without her father, so Charm had hosted a dinner party in Regan's honor at the Outlaw Estates. Even Bart had joined them.

"I'll make sure you get the information when we return to Alaska."

She smiled over at him. "Thank you, Garth."

Why did she have to sound so happy about it, and why did he feel like a selfish ass again? He wanted to have an affair with her with no promises of a future, but he was getting annoyed that she wanted to meet someone who could give her the love he couldn't.

He pushed the negatives to the back of his mind and decided to concentrate on the positives. Right now, the main positive was that she'd agreed to have an affair with him.

"What are your plans today?" he asked.

She shrugged. "It's too late to go hiking, so what do you suggest?"

He would suggest they head straight to the nearest bedroom, but as much as he desired her, he wanted her to decide when they would become intimate. "Whatever you want to do is fine with me. I told Paulo that he didn't have to return for the rest of the day. That means I'll be doing all the cooking today," he said.

"I'll help," she said as she stood to take their plates.

He watched as she walked over to the counter, loving the way her knit sweater fit over her leggings and across her backside. After placing the dishes in the sink, she turned and caught him staring again.

A smile touched the corners of her lips. "I just thought of something I'd like to do today."

"You did?" he asked in a voice that sounded almost too deep to be his own.

"Yes."

Their gazes held for a long moment. "What?" he finally asked.

"Come here and I'll tell you."

Garth heard a sexy catch in her voice, and it did something to him. Had him pushing his chair back to stand and cross the room to her. "Yes?"

"Move closer, Garth."

He could do that, and he did. A second later he was standing so close their bodies were touching. He could actually feel her nipples poking into his chest. "Yes?"

"Today I want to feel sexy, desired and wanted. Do you think you can handle that, Garth?"

Sexy, desired and wanted...

Images of how he could make her feel those very things spiked through his brain. "I know I can handle it, Regan."

She reached up and placed her arms around his neck. Tilting her head back, she looked up at him. "Then show me."

Fourteen

Garth drew her into his arms, lowered his head and kissed her. The moment their mouths touched, Regan knew she had made the right decision. This was what she wanted. Closing her eyes, she intended to get the full, unadulterated effect.

This was what she needed, and she hadn't known just how much until now. Seeing him walk toward her in those jeans and that T-shirt had made every hormone in her body burn. Seeing how the denim stretched across a pair of muscled thighs and how his broad chest and brawny shoulders were killing that T-shirt had made her heart flutter deep in her chest.

This kiss was different from the one they'd shared last night. It was passionate, but there was something else, too. It was seductive, fiery to the point where she moaned as their tongues mingled. Heat spread all through her body.

Garth's mouth was a perfect fit over hers. She'd noticed that last night and noticed it again today. His kiss drugged all her senses and made her want more, more and more. When he deepened the kiss, her moans deepened, as well.

He wanted her. She had the ability to taste the depth of

his desire in the onslaught of his greedy mouth. Was it intentional? Was he deliberately letting her know his desire for her hadn't changed? Was that why he was greedily lapping up her mouth, making her aware of his voraciousness? His insatiability?

She groaned in protest when he finally ended the kiss, but not before he used the tip of his tongue to lick her mouth from corner to corner. Opening her eyes, she gazed up into his dark brown ones while drawing in a deep breath. She loved him so much. He had no idea that she loved him. He thought all he wanted from her was sex, but she intended to make things so good between them that in the end he would think twice about letting her go build a future with another man. She was taking a gamble with her plan, but he was worth the risk.

"Are you sure about this, Regan?" he asked. "If you say yes, just know that before we return to Fairbanks, I intend to make love to you all over this house."

The thought had sizzling sensations spreading between her legs. If his words were meant to be a reality check for her, they had been. She was all too eager to mix her fantasies with his reality to see what they came up with. Her goal was to make him desire her more than he did now, more than he ever thought he could.

"I'm sure, but what about you, Garth? Are you sure, as well?"

"Sweetheart, I've never been so sure of anything before in my life."

He then swept her off her feet and into his arms and began moving. She knew he was taking her to a bedroom, and she didn't care which one. It didn't matter. Either would work.

Regan knew the moment he placed her on the bed that they were in the bedroom he'd slept in last night. His manly scent was all over the bedcovers. It aroused her. Made her feel as if her entire body was burning alive from the inside out.

"May I go on record to make something clear, Regan?" Garth asked, kicking off his shoes.

She swallowed. He was standing, all six feet and three inches of him, at the foot of the bed, staring at her with the same intensity that she felt. She wasn't sure what he had to say, but she definitely wanted to hear it.

"Yes," she said in an almost whisper.

"You don't need me to make you feel sexy, desired and wanted. You are those things already. What I intend to do is to make you feel needed," he said, stepping away from the bed to pull his T-shirt over his head and toss it on a nearby chair. "If only you knew the depth of my need for you."

She wondered if being needed also meant she was indispensable, essential, vital, crucial…all those things she wanted to become to him.

"Now I have you just where I want you, Regan. In my bed."

And whether he knew it or not, she had him just where she wanted him, too. Standing in front of her and stripping, for starters. As she watched, his hands went to the front of his jeans.

"And I have you doing what I've always fantasized about, Garth. Taking your clothes off in front of me so I can see you naked."

She could tell from the look on his face that her words surprised him. "You used to fantasize about me?"

"All the time. You always looked sexy in your business suits, but my imagination gets a little more risqué than that."

He shook his head. "I never knew."

"What? That I wanted you as much as you wanted me? I told you that in the kitchen earlier."

"I assumed that desire began since you've been here with me."

Boy, was he wrong. "No, it goes back further than that."

It was important that he knew everything. Not only that the desire was mutual but also that it hadn't just begun. If he understood that then it would be easier for her to build the kind of relationship they needed, regardless of whether he thought they needed it or not.

"I never knew," he said, looking a little confused. "You never said anything."

"I wasn't supposed to. You are my boss and I am a professional."

He nodded because she knew he couldn't refute that. "How long have you felt that way?"

There was no way she would tell him that she'd had a crush on him since she was sixteen, or that he was the reason she had returned to Fairbanks after her first year in college. She had heard he was back home from the military with a broken heart, and she'd been determined to fix it. Things didn't work out quite that way. He was deep in mourning for the woman he'd lost and had built a solid wall around himself, one that even his family hadn't been able to penetrate for a long while.

"The length of time doesn't matter, Garth. All you need to know is that the desire between us is mutual. Now are you going to finish undressing or what?"

He gave her that Garth Outlaw smile, and her gaze shifted lower, from his face to where his hand rested at his zipper. He was fully aroused. That much was obvious. Seeing him had the tips of her breasts responding.

Her heart raced in her chest and she couldn't recall another time when seeing a half-naked man had done that to her. But she knew it was more than seeing Garth without his shirt, because he'd been bare-chested around her before. It was Garth, period.

The man she had truly loved forever.

Her gaze was fixated on his zipper and it was quite obvious that he was aware it wasn't his zipper per se that held her interest. "Are you ready for me, Regan?"

She was ready for him, and ready to see him. "I am ready for you, Garth."

"Do you want to touch me now?" he invited, tapping his crotch.

She swallowed. That invitation was bold, and it made the tips of her fingers itch. She glanced up and met his gaze. "Copping a feel won't satisfy me. I'd rather touch you there when you're not wearing any clothes."

She saw the flare of heat in his eyes and smiled. Little did he know she intended to touch him—and taste him—all over. By the time they left for Fairbanks, she hoped he would have become so addicted to her touch that he would seek her out to continue what they'd started here.

"I'm not one to keep a lady waiting."

Her eyes were glued to his crotch when he began lowering his zipper. When he slid the jeans down muscled thighs and legs, her breath caught. The only thing left was his briefs and they were barely keeping him contained. She watched as he lowered them down his legs.

"Wow," she said, with both awe and feminine appreciation in her voice.

He smiled over at her. "Now are you ready to touch me?"

Garth knew that for as long as he lived, he would never forget the look on Regan's face the moment she saw him totally naked. She had no idea how much her expression boosted his ego. And he wasn't a man whose ego needed stroking. However, he was discovering that when it came to Regan, she got to him in a way that wasn't normal.

He'd been attracted to beautiful women before, but for some reason his attraction to her was different. For months, he'd tried to downplay it. Then he'd gone through a period of denial because there was no reason for him to all of a sudden become fixated on her. When ignoring it didn't work, he'd accepted his attraction to her was only physical. After sex, he thought, he would get back to normal. Once he'd gotten his fill of her—worked her out of his system while they spent time together here in Santa Cruz—then things between them would get back to normal when they returned to Fairbanks.

And for her to admit she'd wanted him long before now made desiring her even more acceptable to him. He didn't have to feel guilty about seducing her when she'd let it be known she wanted to be seduced. Just to think, they'd had the hots for each other, but had kept it secret. Imagine all the times he had wanted her and could have had her.

"Yes, I want to touch you, but shouldn't I take my clothes off, too?" she asked.

He nodded. "That might be a good idea because when you touch me, I'm going to want to touch you."

She grinned over at him. "Please do."

He'd been so used to the very professional, highly proficient Regan Fairchild that he'd have to adjust to the sexy woman reclining on that bed.

She eased up and pulled her top over her head and tossed it to join his T-shirt on the chair. Next came her black lace bra. She was taking her time unhooking it and he felt a stirring deep in the pit of his stomach as he watched her. Feeling a little impatient, he asked, "Need help?"

She shook her head. "No, I've got this."

When she removed her bra and tossed it aside to expose

a pair of gorgeous breasts with delicious-looking, darkened nipples, his tongue tightened in this mouth.

"Now for these," she said, working the leggings down her thighs. That left her clad in a pair of scanty, black lace panties.

"May I?" he asked.

She glanced over at him. "May you do what?"

"Take those off you?"

He watched how she drew in a deep breath as if his question had affected her. "If you want," she said. To him the sound of her voice was breathlessly husky.

"Yes, I want." Garth doubted she knew just how much he wanted.

He moved toward the bed and thought the same thing now that he'd thought when he'd seen her in her swimsuit. She had a gorgeous body. Seeing her small waist, flat tummy and a pair of long, beautiful legs made breathing difficult.

He felt heat in the tips of his fingers when he placed them beneath the waistband of her panties. He heard her sharp intake of breath when he touched her skin. When he slowly began easing the panties down her legs, anticipation took over his senses.

When he had uncovered her, Garth went completely still. He'd never seen anything so beautiful. Something passed through him, something akin to possession, which didn't make sense. They weren't in an exclusive relationship. All they would be sharing was an affair that would last only while they were here in Santa Cruz. Why did he need to remind himself of that?

"Garth?"

He shifted his gaze from her feminine mound to her face. "Who will do the touching first?"

He swallowed. The hell with touching, he wanted to

taste her, but she might not be ready for that yet, so he said. "Ladies first."

She evidently liked his answer. She crawled toward him and took him into her hands and cupped him. He knew he was a goner. "Not sure I'm going to last, Regan," he said, gritting his teeth to keep from groaning aloud when she worked her fingers on him.

Deciding he needed to touch her while she was touching him, he took her breasts in his hands, loving the way they felt. Then he leaned forward and sucked a hardened nipple between his lips.

"Garth!"

He released her breast as she released him. "I need you, Regan."

"And I need you. Now."

An aura of sexual chemistry surrounded them. He'd known for almost a year that he wanted her, but he hadn't expected to need her to this degree. Reaching over, he reached into the nightstand to retrieve a condom packet. He quickly ripped it open and sheathed himself, knowing she watched his every move.

Then, joining her on the bed, he straddled his body over hers. Her feminine scent fueled his desire. It had blood rushing fast and furious through his veins, causing a spike of heat to rush into his groin. Anticipation thickened the air and he bit back a guttural groan.

Leaning in, he captured her mouth with his, needing to taste her. When he couldn't wait any longer, he eased his engorged shaft inside of her, feeling how her body stretched for him. Glancing down, he saw the glassy look in her eyes, and when she whispered, "Deeper," he thrust hard, filling her totally and completely.

Garth gazed down at her and found her staring up at him. He loved the feel of being inside her, how her inner muscles clenched him. How her fingernails dug into his shoulders. He began moving, thrusting back and forth, and she extracted everything out of him.

Over and over he pounded into her, establishing a rhythm, a sensuous beat, that he could move to forever. He was taking her hard, fast and then harder and faster, not letting up. He needed this. He wanted her. He needed her.

The sound of her moaning and then purring and then moaning again pushed him over the edge. Throwing his head back, he continued to thrust hard, trying to go deeper with every stroke while loving the feel of her inner muscles clenching him even tighter.

Suddenly, he released a loud growl, one he was certain shook the rafters. But he couldn't stop. Wasn't sure if he would ever stop. His body bucked and she screamed out her pleasure. Every inch of him was filling her. Just the way he wanted. Just the way he'd dreamed. Never had he shared an orgasm with a woman who had rocked him all the way to the bone.

Her muscles continued to grip him, to pull everything out of him as he thrust hard, heading toward another climax right on the heels of the first. Then, when he knew he had nothing left to give, he collapsed on top of her before quickly shifting so his weight would not harm her.

"Regan."

"Garth."

Somehow, he found enough energy to kiss her again. What they'd shared wasn't ordinary. It was something he hadn't counted on. When had he ever desired a woman this much? Even now he felt himself getting aroused all over again.

Releasing her mouth, he eased out of bed to take care of the condom. "I'll be back in a minute and when I return…"

She glanced up at him with satisfied eyes. "Yes?"

"I intend to taste you all over."

Fifteen

Regan forced her eyes open and looked up at Garth. He had more energy than he knew what to do with. Well, that wasn't totally true since he did know what to do with it. He did her. Over and over again. Not once, or twice, not even three times. They had been going at it since breakfast, skipping lunch and napping in between. And when he'd told her he would taste her all over, he'd meant it. No man had ever done anything like that to her before. Making love to Garth had definitely been an adventure.

"No way we haven't worked up an appetite. It's time for me to get up and fix dinner since we skipped lunch," Garth said, easing his body off her and pulling her into his arms.

"Not sure I'll make dinner," she said. All she felt like doing was sleeping and burying her face in the bedcovers that smelled like him. The scent of a man. A robust man. A very sexual man. A man who had more stamina than the law allowed. But he'd also been tender and caring. He hadn't done anything without first making sure she was comfortable with it. Everything he'd done had filled her with pleasure, pleasure and more pleasure.

"You have to eat, Regan," he said, leaning down and placing a kiss on her lips.

She loved it whenever he kissed her, and he'd been kissing her a lot today. All over. "Why? So you can zap away all my strength and energy again?"

He grinned. "Did I do that?"

"Yes. And you don't have to look so pleased about it." And he was looking pleased. She'd seen Garth smile a lot of times, but this was a different kind of smile. One that showed an unusual side of him. A sensual side. A side that openly displayed emotions she hadn't seen him expose in a long time. Not since he'd returned from the military.

"Hard not to look pleased when I am. Not about zapping your energy or strength, but the fact that I'm here and you're here with me."

"News flash, Mr. Outlaw. I'm usually with you," she reminded him. Hopefully, to give him something to think about. "You've been doing a lot of traveling lately and I'm your transportation in the air and often on the ground."

"I like this way better. With you in bed with me."

She knew that for now, it was all sexual for him. She could deal with that as long as she believed there could be more down the road. "I guess I should get up and help you with dinner."

"You don't have to. I like taking care of you for a change. You're always taking care of me. Like you just said, whether it's in the air or on the ground, you're my girl."

She bit back the temptation of telling him that she wanted to be more than *his girl*. She wanted to be his wife, and she hoped one day he realized that she could be everything he needed. "Thanks. But staying in bed will make me lazy."

He smiled. "I doubt you know the meaning of the word, and if you do feel like slacking off, that's fine because you deserve it. Besides, you are on vacation."

"I've never helped you cook before," she said. "I want to do it."

"Suit yourself," he said, easing out of bed. Then as if he thought better of it, he leaned back on his haunches and threw the bed covers off her.

"Hey! What do you think you're doing?"

He grinned. "I just want to see you naked again," he said as his gaze roamed all over her. "You want to try out the hot tub after dinner?"

"Sure. Sounds like it will be fun."

"Trust me, sweetheart. I intend to make it fun."

"Grab that measuring cup over there for me please, Regan."

"Sure thing. But why don't you just estimate? That's the way Dad does it."

Garth was trying to keep his attention on what he was making and not on Regan, who was acting as his assistant. The distraction wouldn't be so bad if she wasn't wearing his T-shirt and nothing else. And he knew for a fact she was completely bare beneath it. No panties. No bra. Nothing but the most delectable and soft skin imaginable.

"Roberta was a stickler and felt everything had to be measured, and that's how she taught me. On the other hand, Franklin is such a whiz at everything he does. He could probably prepare a delicious five-course meal with his eyes closed."

Regan smiled. "Yes, Dad could probably do that. While growing up, whenever he left on a trip, he would prepare enough food for me to eat while he was gone." She chuckled. "He would even date the containers so I would know what to eat and when."

"Wasn't there someone staying with you while he was gone?"

"Yes, Ms. Petry. She was a good housekeeper, but couldn't cook worth a darn. I complained to Dad, but he thought I was being overly critical. At least he thought that until he ate some of the food himself. Since she was good at everything else, he didn't want to let her go. Besides, he liked knowing I was eating healthy."

Garth knew that Franklin had enlisted in the air force in his twenties, where he was a cook for a while. Four years later, when it was time to reenlist, he'd expressed his desire to become a pilot and was granted his request. What would Franklin think of the proposition Garth had made to his daughter? More than once Franklin had told him that Regan was no longer a child but an adult who was mature enough to make any decisions governing her life. Garth was glad Franklin felt that way, because her decision to have an affair with Garth had been hers to make.

He had a feeling his siblings wouldn't be as accepting of it if they knew. His brothers, on more their one occasion, had appointed themselves Regan's guard dogs. Especially Sloan and Maverick. For that reason, although they were aware Regan was here with him, he wanted to be sure they had no idea Garth and Regan had become lovers. It was a good thing their affair would end when they left here. Otherwise, there was no doubt in his mind his brothers would have a lot to say about something that was none of their business.

"Here you are."

He turned and accepted the measuring cup from Regan. The moment their hands touched, intense heat curled inside his gut. She'd been eager to help him with dinner, and he appreciated her enthusiasm. However, she had no idea what being around her in a T-shirt that barely covered her thighs was doing to him. Watching her swish around in the kitchen aroused him all over again. After finally leaving the bed, they had showered together, which had been something dreams were made of. If he wasn't careful, he could become addicted to all this passion, and this was just day one.

"Thanks."

"You're welcome.

Brownies were his specialty and one of the easiest things to bake—if he could just concentrate on making them. Instead, every time Regan moved, his gaze moved with her. He was trying really hard to retain his sanity, by telling himself he'd seen a pair of nice-looking thighs a lot of times. But his subconscious would counter: *never Regan's and never this much*. They just reminded him how it had felt being between those thighs.

"Will it be much longer?"

He glanced over at her. She stood close to him and he inhaled her scent. Shower-fresh, clean and jasmine. "Not too much longer. The baked chicken will be ready to come out of the oven about the same time I'll be ready to slide this batch of brownies in." He'd decided to bake brownies because he knew just how much Regan liked them. Now she would get a chance to try his.

A half hour later, he took off his apron. The baked chicken and rice pilaf were done, the broccoli and carrots were simmering and the brownies were in the oven. He glanced over at Regan. "Thanks. You were a big help."

She laughed. "I did my best. Are you sure I didn't get in the way?"

"No, you didn't get in the way." He glanced at his watch. "We have a little less than an hour before everything will be ready."

"Do you want to go for a walk?" she asked him.

He pulled her close and rubbed his hand down her arms.

He loved seeing her body's reaction to his touch. They didn't have time for a full-blown lovemaking session and he'd never been one for quickies. For him, lovemaking was something to be savored, appreciated and made to last as long as it could.

"We can take a walk after dinner. I prefer doing something else." He saw the way her eyes immediately darkened and knew what she assumed he was about to suggest. "Not that, either. I'm looking forward to tonight."

"Oh? Then what?"

Was that disappointment he heard in her voice? His hands slid from her arms to her waist. "You ever played a kissing game?"

She lifted a brow. "Kissing game? Can't say that I have. Have you?"

He shook his head, grinning. "No, but when I was in the Marines, it was a game the guys would talk about. Evidently, it's a popular game that the Lower 48 are used to playing, but me and Walker, the only ones from Alaska, had never heard of it."

"How is it played?"

"For starters, like this." Pulling her to him, he leaned down and captured her mouth in his. On her moan, his tongue slid inside her mouth. He loved the way her body automatically responded to him, whether to lovemaking or kisses.

He deepened the kiss, and she reciprocated. Their mouths mated greedily, voraciously. For a moment, he felt as if he could eat her alive. He had allowed his body to go without sex for a while. What would she think if she knew he hadn't made love to a woman since the Westmorelands' charity ball?

He released her mouth. She was panting, but then so was he. Every time he kissed her, desire twisted his guts. Maybe he should back out of this kissing game. He might not be able to stand the heat that would be generated.

Sweeping her off her feet and into his arms, he left the kitchen and walked to the living room. He eased down onto the sofa with her in his arms, his hand coming into contact with her bare bottom.

"So, what's this kissing game called, Garth?"

One of the things he liked about her was that she didn't have an aversion to trying something different. "Too Hot."

She nodded while adjusting her body to sit up in his lap. There was no way she wasn't aware of his aroused state. "How is it played?"

Just looking at her made him want to bury his face in the hollow of her throat to breathe in her scent. He was still that attracted to her. Making love hadn't even put a dent in his desire. She was still very much in his system, and he wasn't sure how he was going to get her out of there. But he had to do it by the time they left here. He had no choice.

"The object of the game is for a couple to kiss without stopping and without touching each other. If one of the players touches the other in any way, then he or she loses and the winner gets to do whatever he or she wants to the loser."

He saw the lifting of her brow and knew she had questions. "Yes?"

"What if I really need to breathe? I'm not good at holding my breath for a long period of time."

"All you have to do is break off the kiss, but you only get a couple of seconds to suck in air."

She frowned. "A couple of seconds?"

"Yes. I'm being generous."

"You really think so?" she asked him, looking none too sure of that.

He chuckled. "Okay, take no more than five seconds.

I am modifying the rules, but if you don't think you can stand the heat then stay out of the kitchen."

"Oh, I plan on getting you so hot, Garth, steam will be coming out of your ears. There's no way you won't lose."

Sliding her off his lap, he placed her on the sofa beside him and turned to face her. "Bring it on, Regan."

Kissing but no touching…

Regan was convinced whoever had thought of this kissing game needed to have their head examined, and she needed hers checked just for agreeing to play. But she would find any excuse to kiss Garth—the kicker would be not touching him. She liked rubbing her hands over his chest whenever his tongue was inside her mouth. Earlier, she'd even cupped him a few times and loved touching him there.

"Ready to start?" She looked at Garth, saw the dark heat in his eyes. He was so sure of his abilities that he'd basically already declared himself the winner. It was there in his gaze and the smile curving his lips. Well, she would have to show him.

More than anything, she had to stay in control of her senses. All five of them. Taste wasn't off the table because that was the main sense they would be using. Since touching was off the table, it would be the biggest temptation. Closing her eyes would take care of her sense of sight, but she wasn't sure about the hearing and smell. Just hearing him groan did things to her and he had a scent that turned her on.

"Regan?"

Drawing in a deep breath and forcing her hands to her side, she nodded. "Yes, let's do this."

Not waiting for him, she leaned in and went straight for his luscious mouth.

Sixteen

Mercy! Regan had charged into his mouth like her life depended on it. The action had surprised him so much that he had to remember where they were and what they were doing. On instinct he'd almost reached out to lock his arms around her, but then caught himself. Touching her was the one thing he couldn't do.

He had to calm his pounding heart and take charge of the situation. She'd gotten a head start and he'd been swept up in how she made him feel. Explosive sensations had settled right in his groin. Once he took control, he figured it would all be over. Already he was thinking about what he would have her do when she lost.

He returned her kiss with an urgency he felt in every part of his body. Deepening the kiss, he whipped his tongue from her grasp and became the aggressor. He knew he had succeeded when he felt her move under his mouth. He nearly lost it when he heard her moan. He balled his hands into fists at his side. Otherwise, he would be tempted to use those hands to stroke her all over, to slide them underneath that T-shirt and caress her breasts. Garth didn't want to stop there.

She suddenly snatched her mouth away to draw in a breath and then she was back at it, reclaiming his mouth as if determined to regain command. And for a moment she did. Regan had caught him off guard when she broke off the kiss. In those quick three seconds, he'd been focused on the sight of her wet lips, and now she'd gotten the upper hand. This was a full-contact, wet-tongued, bone-melting kind of kiss.

He was fighting like hell to get back his mastery but discovered it wasn't as easy as he'd thought it would be. She was kissing him in a way that spilled intense pleasure within his very soul. It was if this was a kiss of intent. One of possession.

Never had a woman kissed him like this before. A part of him suspected she'd never kissed a man like this before, either. She wasn't behaving like an experienced kisser, but like one who'd discovered something new that she liked. She was getting all she could out of it.

Damn. What had he created?

That question was lost on him when she used deep, hot glides of her tongue in his mouth, silently demanding that he return the favor, so he did. Then she sucked on it in a way that made his erection throb.

He knew what he wanted. Here and now. He wanted to take this kiss to a whole other level. He wanted more of her taste. He wanted all he could get. In every way that he could get it.

When she moved to take his mouth again, he tumbled her back on the sofa.

He could tell by her expression that she hadn't expected that maneuver. "You touched me, Garth."

That wasn't all he was about to do to her.

"I'm hot. I'll worry about all the steam coming out of my ears later, Regan."

Standing, he quickly pulled the shirt over his head and shoved the jeans down his legs. Regan was on her back with the T-shirt pulled up above her hips, her legs spread. He couldn't have dreamed a better pose.

"I want to kiss you there, Regan," he said, getting out of his briefs.

"That involves touching. Are you forfeiting the game?"

He grinned. She could honestly worry about the outcome of the game at a time like this? But then maybe he was the only one sexually riled to the point of losing control. Had he misinterpreted her arousing scent? Hell, he didn't think so.

"May I kiss you there?" he asked her, to make sure they were on the same page.

"You're forfeiting the game?"

Whatever it took. "Yes," he said, practically licking his lips.

"Then, yes. You may kiss me down there all you want."

Quickly dropping to his knees in front of her, he buried his head between her legs.

You may kiss me down there all you want…

"Ohhh," Regan moaned and wondered how she could have possibly told Garth something like that. Hadn't he proved that morning just what a naughty mouth he had? And just what wickedly sensuous things he was capable of doing with his tongue?

She couldn't believe all the attention he was giving to her. Right there. He was paying her back for all those things she'd done to his mouth while kissing him. Now he was doing them to her—there. He was making it nearly impossible to keep still. That was why her hips were moving and why he'd clamped down on them firmly with his hands to keep them steady. She was practically locked under his mouth.

Regan was dying of pleasure, she was sure of it. She bit down on her bottom lip to keep from screaming. Never had so many erotic points seized her senses all at once. She was tossed in a state of sexual frenzy, causing her to rock her body against his mouth.

He retaliated by sinking his tongue even deeper inside of her, pushing her over the edge. Unable to take this much pleasure any longer, she screamed his name when her body jerked into a shattering climax that seemed to go on forever.

The intensity of her orgasm brought tears to her eyes. She was still whimpering in pleasure when his body moved to straddle hers. Opening her eyes, she saw Garth, right there. Their gazes held and he kissed her tears away.

Such unexpected tenderness made her want to cry even more. Instead, she wrapped her arms around his neck and guided his mouth to hers. They kissed with a greed that renewed her desire for him, made her fall deeper in love with him.

He released her mouth and stared down at her. The desire in his eyes caused heat to reignite between her legs. As if he felt it, too, he entered her, fitting snugly in the vee of her thighs. He began moving, setting the rhythm while staring down at her. She was too transfixed to look away.

She watched as his brows drew together as if some thought had suddenly entered his mind. She knew what it was.

"I'm on the pill, Garth."

His brows relaxed. Leaning in, he kissed her. The moment his mouth touched hers, a climax rushed through her. It seemed hers triggered his own. Cupping a hand beneath her bottom, he tilted her hips then moaned inside her mouth when pleasure took him over.

No sooner had their bodies relaxed than the oven's buzzer went off. They had done all of that in fifty minutes? Amazing. When he eased off her, he pulled her up to a sitting position beside him. Instinctively, her body curled into him. At that moment she doubted if she'd ever felt more content.

Hours later, Garth entered his bedroom to change clothes. He would be rejoining Regan in fifteen minutes to enjoy the hot tub. Dinner had been awesome, if he did say so himself. Regan had said so, too. She'd gone on and on about how delicious it was. He'd been quick to remind her that they had prepared the meal together and that she'd been an excellent helper.

He hadn't been giving her any BS, because she had been a great assistant. He had enjoyed having her there with him, sharing his space. She was the first woman to ever do so. There was never a time that he and Karen had shared kitchen duties. Nor had they ever played any kissing games. And he'd never gotten the chance to perform oral sex on her. Hell, he wasn't sure if she would have liked it. He did recall that the few times they had made love, she'd gotten up immediately afterward, saying she wasn't the cuddling type. He'd gotten used to that.

Regan, however, was the cuddling type, and now he was getting used to how she liked things. Either way was fine with him, but he found Regan's way of wanting to be held afterward a lot more intimate.

He inhaled a deep breath as he began stripping off his clothes to change into his swimming shorts. He couldn't stop thinking of that kissing contest. Boy, had he enjoyed it, from start to finish. Of course, it hadn't finished the way it should have, but he had no complaints…other than one. Since he'd forfeited the game, that made her the winner. That meant she could do whatever she wanted with him. He couldn't help wondering what she had in mind.

Garth had finished changing when his cell phone went off. He recognized the caller as Maverick and was surprised his youngest brother had waited this long to call. Maverick had a tendency to make a pest of himself, but deep down Garth knew he wouldn't have it any other way. Maverick was Maverick.

He grabbed the phone off his bed. "What's going on with you, Maverick?"

"I should be asking that of you. Are you treating my girl right?"

His girl? "If you're referring to Regan, yes, I'm the perfect host."

"Good. She needs to enjoy herself. Working for you isn't easy, Garth. You're demanding. Too serious at times. Too driven. Hanging around you for any period of time can be stressful. You work too hard. Regan deserves time to enjoy herself. To chill. I just hope like hell that you're not boring her."

Garth smiled when he thought of what all he and Regan had done that day. He could safely say she wasn't at all bored. The sound of her screaming out her pleasure was still ringing in his ears.

"Look, Mav, I need to go take a shower," he lied.

"Okay, and tell Regan I said hello."

"I will. Talk to you later."

He clicked off the phone and quickly left the bedroom. He didn't want to keep Regan waiting.

Seventeen

The next morning, Regan slowly opened her eyes. The first thing she noted was that she was in bed alone. How had Garth left without waking her? When she had drifted off to sleep last night, he'd been holding her in his arms, with their limbs entwined. She must have been sleeping pretty hard not to have felt him disengaging their bodies.

She glanced at the clock on Garth's nightstand as the aroma of bacon flowed through her nostrils. It was breakfast time and Paulo was back. But she would have to say, Garth had done a great job at breakfast yesterday. In her book, Garth had done a great job in everything yesterday.

Dinner had been great and the brownies had been delicious. To top everything off, their lovemaking had been wonderful. Both before and after dinner. When she thought about what all they'd done in that hot tub, she couldn't help but blush. And then last night, right here in this bedroom. They'd taken another shower together—their second that day—and then he'd dried her off, swept her into his arms and carried her to his bed to make love to her again.

She'd made love more times in one day and night than

she'd done in the past three years. The mere thought had her pulse racing, mainly because it hadn't been with just anyone, but with the man she loved.

She eased up in bed, wondering where Garth had gone and why he hadn't awakened her before leaving. Did Paulo know they were sharing a bed? Did she care? No, she didn't, because she was an adult and free to do as she pleased. The same held true for Garth.

Even so, she had a feeling Garth wouldn't be mentioning their affair to anyone. At least that was the feeling she'd gotten when he mentioned last night in the hot tub that Maverick had called and sent his regards. There was no way Garth would have given Maverick a hint the two of them had something going on. If he had, Maverick would have called her, probably to try talking her out of it.

More than once, he had warned her about guys who meant her no good. She was the marrying kind and should never, ever settle for anything less. He would definitely see any affair with his oldest brother as settling. Especially if he discovered Garth had warned her he could never fall in love with her. Maverick, like everyone in their family, knew Garth was still in love with Karen. Maverick would never understand that although she knew it, too, she was hoping that Garth would see over the next two weeks that she was wife material as much as any other woman.

She wanted him to enjoy their time together so much he would be willing to take a chance on them as a couple. She knew it was a risk, but she didn't care. Some risks were worth taking.

"Whatever you're thinking about must be serious."

She glanced over to the doorway and smiled when she saw Garth leaning there. Why did have to look so jaw-droppingly gorgeous standing there shirtless, with his jeans riding low on his hips?

"Good morning. I was just thinking about Dad," she lied. There was no way she could tell Garth what she was really thinking about.

The smile disappeared from his face and he came into the room to stand beside the bed. "Why? Is something wrong with Franklin?"

She heard the panic in his voice and understood. He had a close relationship with her father, and she had been surprised he hadn't used that relationship as a reason for him not having an affair with her. She was glad that Garth had believed her father all those times he'd said he accepted Regan as the adult she was. Her father knew that if she made mistakes along the way, she would learn from them. Now she was beginning to wonder if loving Garth as much as she did would be a mistake she would eventually learn from. Her main question to herself was, if that was the case, would it be one she would recover from?

Franklin Fairchild believed that, like him, his daughter was a fighter. He had encountered the biggest fight of his life when he'd moved on with his daughter after unexpectedly losing the wife he adored. He had moved on without another woman to love.

Would Garth be like her father?

"Yes, Dad is fine. He should be returning from his cruise in a few days. He's had his cell phone off and I don't expect him to turn it back on until he reaches one of the islands that are part of the United States territories."

He nodded and she could see his features relax. "I'm glad he's enjoying his life."

"Yes, but I wish he could enjoy it more."

"How so?" He came to sit on the edge of the bed and—as if it were the most natural thing—he reached out and took her hand in his. An electric current pulsed where he touched.

"There were times when I would walk into a room and he would be just sitting there staring at Mom's picture. Those were the times when I knew his heart was in pain. He loved her so much that he refused to move on. Dad's a very handsome man, and a number of women made it known they would have loved for him to return their interest. But he didn't. He dated on occasion, but he pretty much decided that only one woman could have his heart."

Garth didn't say anything, and she knew why. He and her father shared the same views in that respect.

Maybe this would be a good time for them to talk about it again. A couple of days ago he'd told her he could never love another woman, but she wanted to believe his heart was big enough to share. Why, like her father, did he not believe that?

"I know where Franklin is coming from, Regan. It's not easy to fall in love a second time when your heart is still consumed with memories of the first. I recall the number of times Franklin would say you helped keep Geneva's memory alive because you looked so much like her. And you had her spirit and compassion. I agree. Geneva was a beautiful woman. I recall when she began working for the company and how smitten Franklin was of her. I was a kid and I walked in on them kissing once."

Her eyes widened. "You did?"

He chuckled. "Yes. However, before your mind gets overloaded with scandalous thoughts, they were married, but you hadn't been born yet. On that particular day, he'd flown my dad on a business trip somewhere in the Lower 48 and had been gone for at least two weeks. Roberta took all of us out to meet the plane when it returned. Geneva was there waiting, too."

He paused. "Your dad always looked dapper in his uniform, and being the professional that he was, he waited until he'd taken care of all the paperwork before he got off the plane. Your mom waited patiently. I remember having to go to the bathroom. I went down some hallway near one of the hangars and he and your mom were there. I guess you could say they were letting each other know how much they were missed."

"Ah, how romantic," she said, imagining the scene.

He looked over at her and smiled. "And if I do recall, nine months later you were born."

Regan threw her head back and laughed. She laughed a lot around him and she noticed he laughed a lot around her. She loved how he would share these fond memories with her.

Now she needed to ask him something that would place a damper on the mood, but she needed to know.

"Garth?"

"Yes, sweetheart?"

That was the second time he'd referred to her that way, and yes, she was keeping count. She doubted he was aware that whenever he used that term of endearment it made her heart swell. "Tell me about her."

He lifted a brow. "Who? Your mom?"

She shook her head. "No. About Karen."

For a long moment, he didn't say anything, and just stared at her. Then he slowly released her hand and stood. "Why do you want to know anything about Karen? I told you all you needed to know about her, which was that I love her and will always love her. What else is there for you to know?"

Regan nervously nibbled her bottom lip. She could give him a page of reasons, but none that she could tell him without putting him on the defense. Why was he hesitating? Her father would have seized on any opportunity to talk about her mother. A part of Regan didn't understand why Garth wouldn't do the same. Granted, any information about Karen wasn't her business, but a part of her wanted to know.

She shrugged her shoulders. "I just want to know about the woman who still has your heart. I think that's a special kind of love."

He didn't say anything for a minute and then he walked over to the dresser and leaned against it, as if he needed to put distance between them. Six feet of distance. He drew in a deep breath and said, "I don't think I will ever forget the first time I saw her. Walker and I went into a club on base and there she was, sitting at a table with friends, other female soldiers.

"I could tell she seemed nervous about being in the club. After I met her, I found out why. Her parents were very religious. Her father had been a minister. It was obvious she wasn't used to being in such a place. Guilt was written all over her face."

He rubbed his hand down his face and Regan knew reliving the memories was hard on him. "When we began dating, I would take her to nice places off base. The zoo, various museums and markets. Then we got our orders to leave and discovered we were headed for the same place in Syria. By then, we'd been dating exclusively for four months. I knew we were head over heels in love with each other. We talked about marriage. I'd even met her parents and her older brother when we had chance to go visit while on leave. Unfortunately, she never got to travel to Alaska to meet my family."

He paused a moment and she could see deep sadness in his eyes when he finally said, "I will never forget the day I got the word her chopper had gone down. We'd had a few stolen moments the night before. In less than a month, both our groups would be leaving Syria. I would be assigned to Camp Pendleton in California and she had orders for Virginia. She had less than a year left and I had a few months longer than that. She was to start planning our wedding."

"I'm sorry, Garth."

He drew in a deep breath. "So am I. For whatever reason you wanted to know about Karen, there you have it. Any other questions?"

"Yes, there is one. Do you stay in touch with her family?"

"Somewhat. Her parents are now deceased, and her older brother followed in his father's footsteps and is a minister in Kansas. I hear from him from time to time."

He didn't say anything for a minute. Then, he said, "I came to let you know breakfast was ready. That seems like ages ago. I'm sure Paulo has kept everything warming." His posture straightened and he moved away from the dresser.

"I'll be showered, dressed and ready to join you at breakfast in twenty minutes."

Garth nodded and was about to leave the room when she called out to him. "Garth?"

He turned around. "Yes?"

"Thanks for sharing that with me."

He nodded again and walked out.

Garth stood at the huge window in the dining room and looked out at the ocean. Today the gusts were high, and the waves were choppy. Regardless, the sea looked beautiful, and this spot was great to view it all. His waterfront home on the Chena River in Fairbanks, even with its rustic appeal, couldn't compare to this.

His lips curved into a smile. Nothing could compare to *Regan*. When he'd walked into the bedroom and seen her in his bed… With the sheet pulled up to cover her breasts and her hair all mussed around her shoulders, she'd looked like a goddess. A sexy, tumbled goddess.

Nothing could erase that image from his mind. Not even the question she'd asked about Karen. A part of him had initially felt Regan didn't have a right to ask anything. But then, when he'd begun talking about Karen, he'd realized he had needed to have that conversation. He wasn't sure why he felt that way, but he had.

Before walking out of the room, he'd come close to asking a question of his own. Was she honestly thinking about taking that job with Anders? Although Charm thought she wasn't, he wanted to hear it from Regan's own lips. However, to ask her about it would reveal where he'd heard it from and all fingers would point to Charm. He'd promised his sister he would keep the information to himself.

His mind filled with thoughts of yesterday. Especially their time in the hot tub. That had been the first time he'd ever made love to a woman in one. After getting out of it, they'd showered together, and ended up in bed making love the entire night. He could get used to this.

Suddenly, it flashed through his mind that no, he could not. Should not. In a few days they would be leaving, and when they did, their affair would end. She knew it and accepted it. No drama. That was the way he wanted it. Their affair had been a mutual, adult decision and was nobody's business. She would return to being his pilot and he her boss.

"Garth?"

He turned at the sound of her voice. If all these sexy outfits she'd been wearing every day were meant to grab his attention, they were working. Today she'd put on what looked to be an island dress that swished around her ankles and hung off her shoulders.

"Yes?"

"I'm ready for breakfast."

She seemed somewhat nervous. Did she assume he was upset because she'd asked him about Karen? If that was the case, he needed to arrest her fears. Crossing the room, he wrapped his arms around her as he looked down at her. "You look beautiful as ever, sweetheart. I love this outfit on you."

Her lips parted into a smile. "Thank you."

"I hope you know I'm wondering about my downfall—"

She lifted a brow. "Your downfall?"

"Yes. I forfeited yesterday's kissing game, so you're the declared winner. That means you get to do whatever you want to me. I hope you take pity on this poor soul."

Her smile widened. "Poor soul? I can't see you falling in that category. I've been thinking of just what I want to do to you, Garth. I've come up with plenty of ideas. Too bad I have to settle on just one."

He took a step closer to her. "Would you like to share that idea with me?"

She took a step back and grinned. "No, and our breakfast is getting cold."

She turned to walk away, and he reached out and pulled her into his arms, leaned in and kissed her. This was his first kiss from her today, but he was going to make sure it wasn't his last. Her taste did something to him each and every time.

When he finally released her mouth, he took her hand and together they headed toward the kitchen.

Eighteen

"Garth, could you come in here a minute, please?"

Regan knew what she intended to do to him would take more than a minute, but she couldn't think of a better way to end their two weeks in Santa Cruz. For as long as she lived, she would always remember the time they'd spent together here. They'd attended a couple more operas, shared dinner at several posh restaurants in town, gone to a movie and taken a drive along several of the scenic beaches. They'd eventually gone hiking in the tropical laurel forests and had spent an entire day kayaking and canoeing.

He'd even gone shopping with her again. They'd bought more souvenirs and she'd helped him find gifts for Walker and Bailey's twins. But no matter what they did during the day, they looked forward to each night when they returned to the château to make love until sleep claimed them. Often, they would awake in the middle of the night and make love again.

She also appreciated how they would spend time talking. Over breakfast Garth would tell her of plans he had to move the company forward, his concern for his father—

who still didn't accept that the Westmorelands were related to them—and how finding out about the Westmorelands had enriched his family's lives in many ways. Family meant even more to him now.

He told her about the renovations he intended to make to his home at the beginning of the year, which included adding a theater room. She loved his home and had visited him a number of times with Charm. She especially loved how she could see the Chena River from almost every room.

They'd talked about her father and how he was enjoying life in Florida and how she planned to spend Christmas with him this year. She told Garth about the trip she and Simone had planned to Ireland next year and the renovations she planned to do to her own home. Conversing with him was easy and she enjoyed it tremendously.

Tonight was their last night together. Tomorrow they would leave to return home. He probably assumed she'd forgotten about collecting her reward from the kissing game. If that was what he thought, then he was wrong, because tonight was the night.

A part of her wished they could extend their stay another week, month, year. She had enjoyed being here with him and hoped he had enjoyed being here with her. Her goal had been to make each day memorable for him. Ones he wouldn't forget. Ones he would want to continue, even when they returned to Fairbanks. She wasn't sure if she'd succeeded, but tonight would put the icing on the cake.

Glancing around the room, she saw everything was in place for Garth's hot oil massage. This wouldn't be the first time he'd been in her bedroom, since they'd made love in here for a change in scenery, but at the time the room hadn't looked like this. Tonight she had transformed the bedroom into a romantic sanctuary, complete with burning candles, dim lighting, the scent of lavender and relaxing music. She had set the mood for a night of intense intimacy.

She had taken her time in selecting the oil, glad Garth hadn't been with her at the time. She had talked him into going into a wine shop to select a bottle for their last night together. That was when she had doubled back to a shop that sold everything she needed for tonight. According to the salesclerk, who'd been very knowledgeable, the best scented oil would be lavender. It was relaxing, but also had an arousing effect on a person's mind. She even claimed it stimulated the brain like an aphrodisiac.

Regan looked down at herself. If her outfit didn't get his blood stirring, then nothing would. Garth had no idea what she'd set up for tonight, what her prize would be for winning the kissing contest. What she planned to do to him.

She intended to make it a night he would always remember.

Regan heard the knock on the bedroom door and moved in that direction. He had to be wondering what she'd been doing in here all this time. Maybe he assumed she was packing, since they would be leaving tomorrow.

When she opened the door, he stood there, looking sexier than any man had a right to look. She'd seen him in jeans so much over the past two weeks that it would be hard getting used to him wearing suits again.

"You need me for something?"

Boy, did she ever, she thought, roaming her gaze up and down his masculine form. They hadn't gone out today other than to take a walk around the shore after lunch. Then later, after dinner they had made love, showered and made love again. It was as if they'd wanted to get as much of each other as possible.

And she still wasn't ready to let go, which was why she'd decided to play her last card tonight.

"Yes, come in," she said, stepping aside.

He entered, stopped and did a full circle. Then he looked back at her. "What's going on?" he asked in a husky voice.

"Time for me to collect my kissing game winnings, Garth. I get to do whatever I want with you. And do you know what I plan to do?"

Regan watched his throat move in a deep swallow before he asked, "And just what do you plan to do?"

She moved close to him and rubbed his chest, wishing her fingers could touch his bare skin and not a shirt. "What I want to do to you, Garth Outlaw, is to touch you all over. Tonight, I will be giving you a hot oil massage."

A smile touched his lips. "Bring it on."

Regan returned his smile. "I'm glad you're a willing participant."

"Sweetheart, I don't know a man alive who wouldn't be."

She chuckled. "I need you to undress, Garth. Completely."

Regan stepped back to watch him unbutton his shirt and kick off his shoes. Blood rushed through her veins when her gaze drifted over his open shirt, bare chest and shoeless feet. Then he began shoving his pants and briefs down a pair of masculine legs.

When he was completely nude, she studied every inch of him. He had a body to die for, and she felt she was slowly drawing her last breath. It didn't go unnoticed that while she was ogling him, he was studying her just as intently. Probably wondering what, if anything, she had on under her robe. To appease his curiosity, she wiggled her shoulders to ease out of it and reveal a very sexy negligee.

"Damn, that's nice, Regan. Real nice."

"I'm glad you like it."

And it was so obvious he liked it. There were some things a man couldn't hide. A huge erection was one of them. Knowing she'd caused it was getting to her. "Now I need you to get in the bed and lie facedown, Garth."

She watched him walk over and stretch out on the bed, facedown. At that moment, an intense jolt of sexual need rocked her to the core. She had to get through this. She just had to. She would need the memories of being here with him, freely touching him, long after they'd returned home. She had to accept the reality that no matter what all she'd done here to make him want her, there was a chance he might never think she was wife material because he would never be able to love her. She forced that thought from her mind.

Once he had settled into position, he said, "I can't see you in that short thing you're wearing."

"You will soon enough, Garth."

She studied the contours of his back, which was military straight even while lying down. Coming to stand beside him, she poured heated oil into her hands and began to slowly massage the oil into his skin. There was something about the music playing, the scent of lavender flowing through the room, the low lighting and the gentle flames of the candles. She covered his back from top to bottom, gently rubbing her hands over his buttocks, down his inner and outer thighs, down his legs and all those areas in between.

"That feels so good, baby."

She smiled at that term of endearment. "Trust me, I'm probably getting more out of this than you."

"I doubt it."

What she'd said was true. The feel of her hands gliding across his skin pushed her to succumb to desire that felt like a living creature seeping into her pores, nervous system, the very essence of her mind. It caused an ache in the juncture of her thighs. Her nipples hardened and her heart skipped several beats.

"Now flip over on your back, Garth."

He complied and all she could do was stare at him, letting her gaze roam from the top of his head to the bottoms of his feet. He had beautiful feet for a man. But nothing was more impressive than the huge, engorged erection standing straight up for her. She licked her lips just looking at it.

"Don't do that, sweetheart."

She swallowed and moved her gaze from his midsection to his face. She saw longing so intense in his features that a ball of need burst to life inside her womanly core. Reaching again for the bottle of oil that had been kept in a warmer, she poured an ample amount in her hands.

She gently glided her hands all over his chest, working the oil into his skin, soothing any tense muscles she felt along his shoulders. Then she moved lower, tracing a path down his sculpted abdomen, loving the texture of his skin beneath her fingers.

And when her hands moved lower, their eyes met. She saw desire, more than she'd ever seen before, flare into his eyes. As she took him into her hand, his breathing became choppy.

Not removing her hands, she leaned in close to his mouth and whispered, "Breathe."

When he lifted his hand toward her, she said, "No touching. If you're good, I'll let you touch all you want later. I just want you to lie still and relax."

"You're killing me."

A smile touched her lips. "We are killing each other, and I promise to take us out of our pain real soon."

She moved lower, to his thighs, and began stroking featherlight touches down to his calves. From there she moved to his ankles and the soles of his feet.

After putting more oil in the palms of her hands, she

slowly retraced the path up to his shoulders. Once again, she paid a lot of attention to his midsection, letting him know how much she enjoyed touching him there. All kinds of sexual vibes poured off his body.

"Regan…"

She heard the burning sensuality in his voice and saw it in his eyes. The sound and sight made her tremble. "Yes?"

"I need you."

He'd just said he *needed* her, and not just that he *wanted* her. Regan tried not to let his words get to her, but the force of them came crashing down on her when she realized how much she had to gain—and how much she could lose. She refused to think of losing. She had to believe this night and all those other nights meant something to him.

"Regan."

When he said her name again, she leaned close to him and whispered, "You can touch me now."

As if those were the words he'd been waiting for, he quickly sat up and pulled her down on the bed with him. In seconds he had stripped her of her negligee and had her beneath him. He captured her mouth in his at the same time he entered her body in one hard thrust.

She let out a joyous scream and immediately climaxed. The intensity had hot blood rushing through her veins and sexual sensations flooding her stomach. When he threw his head back and let out a guttural moan while pounding hard into her, she screamed again. Another orgasm struck her, more powerful than the one before. He released her mouth and she looked up at him, saw deep-seated pleasure in his eyes. She would always remember putting it there. The questions she forced to the back of her mind were whether or not he would remember. Whether or not she'd done enough to engrave herself into his mind, if not his heart.

* * *

"I'm ready to leave, Garth."

Garth tossed aside the magazine he'd been reading and stood. When he glanced over at Regan, he went still. Gone was the sexy temptress who'd been rocking his world for the past two weeks. The woman who'd been his constant companion during the day and shared his bed every night. In her place was Regan, his pilot. Forever the professional. She'd dressed in her uniform to remind him of it. Even her hair was back to being hidden under her pilot's cap. Did she expect him to suddenly stop wanting her just because that uniform was a reminder that he was her boss? Was this her way of letting him know their Santa Cruz fling was officially over?

If that was the way she wanted things to end, then he would give her that wish.

But not until after he'd held her in his arms and tasted her lips one last time.

Crossing the room, he came to a stop in front of her. "I know what happens when we return to Fairbanks, Regan. But we aren't there yet."

He then pulled her into his arms and captured her mouth with his.

Nineteen

Regan dropped down on her sofa as she shifted her cell phone to the other ear. "I'm glad you enjoyed your cruise, Dad. It sounds like you had a great time."

"I did. What about you? That was nice of Garth to invite you to hang out with him in Santa Cruz. Did you enjoy yourself?"

"Yes, I enjoyed myself," she said, easing up from the sofa to cross the room and look out at the lake. Snow was falling. The usual for this time of year. In a week or so, they would be buried in it.

She drew in a deep breath, finding it hard to believe that she and Garth had returned to Fairbanks nearly two weeks ago. She wondered if he'd conveniently forgotten to give her the information about the dating agency that he'd promised her. She had reminded him before they'd left Santa Cruz and again when they'd landed in Fairbanks. He hadn't seemed to like the reminders, but she'd hoped they would light a fire under him.

They had parted at the airport like they usually did, with a "goodbye" and not an "I will see your later." She had checked her calendar, and the next scheduled flight, weather permitting, wasn't until December, when she would fly him to Denver to attend his cousins' charity ball.

Thanksgiving was in a couple of weeks and she'd thought about joining her father then, as well as for Christmas. There was no need to hang around here for the holidays. If Garth had any intention of suggesting they continue to see each other, he would have contacted her by now. Evidently, he had gotten back into his regular routine. For all she knew, he could have started dating again. The thought of that broke her heart, although she shouldn't let it. She had tried to make him see her importance, but obviously her risk hadn't paid off.

Suddenly, she realized she'd been distracted by thoughts of Garth and she'd missed what her father had been saying. She caught the tail end of it. "Excuse me, Dad, but what did you say?"

He gave a soft chuckle. "I said that I met someone. A real nice young lady."

That was what she'd thought he said. Quickly moving away from the window, she returned to the sofa and sat back down. "Young lady? How young, Dad?"

He chuckled again. "She's three years younger than I am, Regan."

Regan was glad to hear that. "You met her on the cruise?"

"No, I met her five months ago and invited her to join me on the cruise."

Regan didn't say anything because she was completely stunned. When she recovered, she said, "You've been seeing someone for five months and didn't tell me? I saw you this summer and you didn't say anything about it."

"I had to be sure, Regan."

She swallowed. "Be sure of what?"

"That Deena was someone I could fall in love with."

Regan swallowed again. "Is she? Have you?"

"Yes. I've fallen in love with her."

She didn't reply. Honestly, she should be happy for her father. She'd been trying to push him into serious relationships for years. She'd given up and thought he would never meet a woman he'd want to give his heart to again. "Tell me about her, Dad."

"Deena is a widow. Her husband died of cancer twelve years ago. She has two sons, both doctors, and a daughter who's a college professor. She's a retired nurse who moved to Florida from Wisconsin. Like me, she wanted to escape cold winters. She moved into the neighborhood around the same time I did, but we met at one of our homeowners' association meetings a year ago. We started out as friends, meeting for coffee and taking walks, and then it moved to something more serious."

Regan nibbled her bottom lip. "I see."

"Well, you don't sound happy for your old man."

"I am happy for you, Dad. Just surprised."

"I can't wait for you to meet her. I told her you were coming here for Christmas."

Regan was about to tell him she might be seeing him sooner than that, when his next words stopped her. "I'm meeting Deena's kids for Thanksgiving. We're flying to Wisconsin, where they live."

Regan didn't respond at first. Then, because she knew how she felt was important to her father, she said, "I am truly happy for you, Dad, and I can't wait to meet Deena when I come visit you for Christmas."

"Thanks, sweetheart. I need to go now. Deena and I have a date later. We're doing dinner and then a movie."

She nodded, hearing the excitement in his voice. "Enjoy yourselves."

"We will. You take care, sweetheart."

"I will, and you do the same, Dad."

After ending the call, Regan stood and walked back over to the window. At least her father had proved that one could love again—although it had taken him nearly twenty years to reach that conclusion. Better late than never. And he honestly sounded happy. She couldn't wait to meet Deena.

Should she take that as hope for herself? She would if Garth had given her any reason for hope when they'd parted at the airport. He hadn't. It was as if once he'd returned to his home turf, she was out of sight and out of mind. She had honestly thought he would have called her by now, if for nothing more than to see how she was doing.

She stood and was about to go into the kitchen when her phone rang. She quickly picked it up, hoping it was Garth, and then sighed in disappointment when she saw the caller was Charm. "Hey, Charm."

"Hello. I just got back from visiting Walker, Bailey and the twins in Kodiak. The babies are adorable."

"I bet they are, and I bet they are growing like weeds."

Charm chuckled. "Yes, they are. The reason I was calling was to see if you wanted to do dinner tonight at the Riverview? It seems like I haven't seen you in ages, and you need to tell me about Santa Cruz. I'm thinking of taking a trip there myself next summer."

Regan didn't have anything planned for later and getting out of the house to meet Charm was a good idea. "Yes, I'd love to have dinner with you."

Garth stood at the window in his office and looked out. It was hard to believe it had been fourteen days since he'd seen or talked to Regan, and a part of him missed her like crazy. For the past thirteen nights he'd gone to bed remembering how they would shower together, make love, share a bed, and how he would hold her in his arms while she slept and then wake up making love to her every morning.

Those had been the times when he had felt a degree of peace he hadn't felt in ten years. During those two weeks in Santa Cruz, he'd gotten used to being happy, satisfied, at ease with life and comfortable with having Regan around. He'd known her for years, all of her life, and she'd been his pilot for nearly five years, but he could honestly say that during those two weeks, he'd gotten to know her in ways he hadn't thought possible. Not all of it had been spent in the bedroom. However, he would be the first to admit the times in the bedroom had been special.

He'd even opened up and told her about Karen, not knowing how much he'd needed to talk about his past with someone other than Walker. Doing so had placed a lot of things in perspective.

Regan had captured his heart.

He had fallen in love with her.

Garth shook his head, not believing how things had turned out. Maybe he'd fallen in love with her last year when his blinders came off, but he'd been fighting it. He'd been convinced he would be dishonoring Karen's memory to give someone else his heart. It had taken ten years to discover he'd been wrong.

It had taken ten years to accept that losing the person he loved didn't mean losing their memory, as well. To love someone and then grieve for them—that was a transition in life that a number of people went through. Just because he felt emotions for another person didn't diminish what he'd once felt for the woman he'd loved and lost. It was about accepting that it was time to move on.

The relationship he'd shared with Karen had been unique, what he'd needed at the time. Now he was ten years older, and a different type of woman appealed to him. A woman like Regan. He admired everything about her. Her sexiness, her overall view on life and her ability to have fun and encourage him to have fun, as well.

Walker was right about a person's heart expanding to include others, if one was willing to let them in. Garth was willing to let Regan in. He *needed* her in.

It had taken fourteen long, tortuous days and nights to finally accept that. Now that he'd come to terms with the idea that Regan was the woman he loved, he knew it was time to act. There was a chance he would lose her if he didn't do something about it. Even now, she expected him to give her information on that dating service and he didn't intend to do that.

He would do whatever it took to make sure she loved him in return. He would court her properly. Take her to dinners, movies, concerts—prove there was more than sex between them. He'd once told her she deserved a man who would love her, and it was up to him to prove that *he* was that man.

He suddenly felt good. Totally rejuvenated. He would call her, something he'd wanted to do many times since returning, but he had fought against it. He would invite her to dinner tomorrow night. He would take her to some-place super nice.

Garth heard his stomach growl. He had skipped lunch due to a conference call and needed to have dinner. Grabbing his jacket off the coatrack, he was about to leave when his personal assistant beeped him.

"Yes, Helen?"

"Your sister is here to see you."

A smile curved his lips as he replaced his jacket back on the rack. "Please send her in."

A smiling Charm walked in. This was the first time he'd seen her since he'd returned. Cash had told him she'd gone to visit Walker and Bailey in Kodiak. "So, you finally remembered you have a job that you needed to come back to?" he asked, grinning. It was a joke with him and his brothers that Charm worked in spells. They just weren't sure when those spells would hit.

"Oh, stop trying to be a big bad CEO," she said, crossing the room to give him a huge hug. "I missed you."

"And I missed you, too. However, I do need to remind you that you're on the company's payroll and have an office here."

She waved a hand at him as she took the chair in front of his desk. "Whatever. How was Santa Cruz?"

"It was nice," he said, sitting down, as well.

"And did you show Regan how much she was appreciated?"

If only she knew how much, how often and to what extent he'd shown Regan, she wouldn't be asking.

"Yes, I did." Then he decided to quickly change the subject. "So, how's Walker, Bailey and the twins?"

"They are great, and it was fun hanging out with them. I kept Bailey company while Walker flew to Anchorage. I even got to feed the twins. Walker IV and Westlyn are so cute."

Charm looked at her watch and stood. "I need to get going. I'm meeting Regan for dinner."

Garth, who'd been fiddling with a file on his desk, jerked his head up. "You're having dinner with Regan?"

"Yes. I haven't seen her for a while and invited her to dinner. You want to join us? I'm sure she wouldn't mind."

More than anything, he wanted to see Regan again. He was about to tell Charm that yes, he would love to join them, when his personal assistant beeped him again. "Yes, Helen?"

"There's someone here to see you."

"Who?"

"A woman by the name of Josephine Harris."

Josephine Harris?

The woman from the dating service.

He immediately glanced over at Charm. "Did you not cancel my membership with that dating service?"

"I most certainly did," Charm said. "Her being here is breaking that company's policy and procedures. They are to handle any contact between the two of you. I wonder why she's here."

Garth reached for his jacket to put it on. "I don't know but I'm about to find out." He then said to Helen, "Please escort her in."

Josephine Harris was a beautiful woman. He'd known that since he'd seen photos of her. She was sharp, sleek and sophisticated, and looked good in the outfit she was wearing. The two-piece ensemble had the word *class* written all over it.

But she wasn't Regan.

As far as he as concerned, Regan had all those same qualities and more.

"Josephine, this is a surprise."

He then introduced her to Charm and noticed that the two women shook hands and said all the niceties, but he knew his sister well enough to know there was immediate dislike on her end.

He caught Charm's gaze. "Don't you have a dinner date?"

"Yes. I guess I'll be going. I'll talk to you tomorrow."

He nodded. "Okay and please tell Regan I said hello." There was no need to tell Charm to tell Regan he intended to call her later. For now, the less Charm knew the better.

"I'll tell her." She then turned to Josephine. "It was nice meeting you, Josephine."

"Same here, Charm."

The moment the door closed behind his sister, Garth returned his attention to Josephine. "Would you like to have a seat?"

"Yes, thanks." She sat down in the chair Charm had vacated and gracefully crossed her legs. Garth knew this was so he would notice. He had. Only thing, although they were a nice pair, he liked Regan's legs better.

"So, Josephine, why are you here?" he asked, taking a seat behind his desk. "Didn't the dating service notify you that I'm no longer a client with them?"

"Yes, I was advised of that. However, I figured the least we could do was officially meet. So here I am. I believe we would have enjoyed our two weeks together."

Garth had a feeling she might have, but he would not have. He was glad the woman he'd spent two weeks with had been Regan. "Would we have?"

"Yes, and I intend to prove it. I decided to come here to spend some time with you. I'll be here for a week."

She'd decided?

He needed to explain to Josephine Harris that any involvement they might have looked forward to at one time was no longer a possibility. Granted, he understood the mix-up hadn't been her fault, but now his heart was elsewhere. And for her to assume she could just show up here unannounced, with the expectation that he would make time for her…for a week…was ludicrous.

His brothers' offices were down the hall. They might pop into his at any time and the last thing he wanted to do was explain Josephine Harris to them. He was hungry and decided he would set her straight over dinner.

"How about having dinner with me?" he said.

Her lips curved into a huge smile. Too late he saw she'd taken his invitation as something positive. She would find out soon enough it wasn't.

"I'd love to dine with you, Garth. Then you can tell me if I'll be staying at the hotel for a week or at your place."

Garth stood and grabbed his jacket. Yes, he most certainly would be telling her that and a lot more.

Twenty

"I'm glad you enjoyed yourself in Santa Cruz, Regan."

Regan smiled over at Charm. Like Garth, Charm was known for her radiant smile. Unless she didn't like you, and then she had no problem making that fact known. "Thanks." And because Regan didn't want Charm to ask her any more questions, she decided to change the subject.

"When are you going on your holiday shopping trip?" It was a known fact that Charm traveled to LA around Thanksgiving every year just to do holiday shopping.

"Not sure. I just got back in town and Garth reminded me that I'm getting paid to do a job I'm rarely in the office doing. Like I don't know the only reason they gave me that cushy office and job title was to keep me out of their hair. He told me to tell you hello, by the way."

Regan's fork nearly slipped from her hand. "Did he?"

"Yes. I just left his office before coming here and mentioned I was having dinner with you. I invited him to join us, but that was before…"

Charm's voice trailed off and Regan glanced up from her meal to study her. Charm was staring at something across the room, and the smile that had been on her face earlier was gone. "Charm? What is it?"

"I don't believe it. Garth just walked in, and I can't believe he's actually having dinner with her."

Regan felt her heart drop. "Her who?"

"Josephine Harris. The woman who was supposed to join him in Santa Cruz."

Pain twisted in Regan's chest. "But I thought he'd decided not to reschedule a meeting with her," Regan said. At least that was what he'd told her.

"That's true. I canceled his membership with that dating service myself. But she showed up at his office today, right before I left to come here. He seemed annoyed that she'd showed up unexpectedly like that."

Regan took a sip of her wine. "Well, if they're here for dinner, that means he's no longer annoyed."

"Evidently not. They're being escorted to a table. They can't see us, but we have a good view of them. Look to your right."

Regan did and her heart felt crushed. "She's gorgeous."

Charm rolled her eyes. "Yes, if you like the phony type. I bet everything on her is fake. Her boobs, her hair, her nails. I'm even questioning that outfit. Not all women choose to show off their assets like that."

At any other time, Regan would have found what Charm said amusing, but not now. Not when pain had taken over her body. She'd honestly thought she had a chance with Garth, even after two weeks with no contact, but she was being proven wrong. All it took was seeing how the woman clung to Garth while being led to their table.

"Regan? Are you all right?"

She looked back at Charm and wondered why she'd asked. Had the tears she was trying so hard to fight been forming in her eyes anyway? "I'm fine, Charm."

Even when she spoke the words, she knew they were a lie, and she had a feeling Charm knew, as well.

Garth arrived at the office early the next morning because he and his brothers had a meeting scheduled at nine. Over dinner he'd finally gotten through to Josephine Harris. He was not interested in her. The woman had honestly thought a lot of herself. Had placed herself on a pedestal so high he'd gotten a crick in his neck looking up at her.

As soon as this morning's meeting was over, he would call Regan and invite her to dinner tonight. He would have contacted her last night, but it was late when he'd gotten in, and after dealing with Josephine, he hadn't been in the best of moods.

A short while later, he entered the conference room and found his brothers all there. As was Charm. He didn't recall inviting her to the meeting. And why did they all have serious looks on their faces?

"Good morning, everyone."

He was quick to note the greeting had not been returned. "Is there a problem?"

"We think so," Cash said, sliding an envelope to the middle of the table.

Garth lifted a brow. "What's this?"

"Why don't you read it and see?" Sloan said, and his voice had a sharp edge to it.

Garth wondered what the hell was going on. He picked up the envelope, opened it and read the document. He snatched his head up and saw four accusing pair of eyes staring him down.

"Regan is resigning."

"Apparently, and we want to know why," Sloan said in an irritated voice.

"What happened during those two weeks she stayed with you in Santa Cruz?" Maverick asked angrily.

Cash's gaze snapped around to Maverick. "Regan was with him the entire time?" he asked, making it obvious that this was the first he'd heard of it.

"Yes, she was with him the entire time," Charm said, in a disgusted voice. "I suggested he ask her to join him there as a way to show how much he appreciated her." She then turned her attention back to her oldest brother. "So, what happened in Santa Cruz, Garth?"

Garth narrowed his gaze at his four siblings. What they were asking was none of their damn business. But because he knew how much Regan meant to them, he would tell them what they wanted to know.

Placing his hands on the table and leaning on his arms, he faced them down. "Since the four of you want to know something that's really none of your business, I will tell you exactly what happened with me and Regan in Santa Cruz. I fell in love with her."

From the shocked look on his siblings' faces, his response hadn't been what they'd expected.

"You fell in love with Regan?" The question was asked from four sets of lips.

"Yes, I fell in love with her. I honestly believe I fell in love with her last year at the Westmoreland Charity Ball, but it took me this long to accept it."

"Hell, I suspected something was up," Cash said, a grin replacing his scowl. "You were acting so territorial that night and I figured it had to be for a reason."

"I suspected the same," Sloan said and Maverick nodded to agree.

"Not so fast," Charm said, tossing her hands in the air as

if she wasn't buying what he'd said as easily as her brothers. "If you love Regan, then explain last night."

Garth frowned. "Last night?"

"Yes, last night. Regan and I were having dinner at the Riverview when you and that Josephine Harris woman arrived."

Garth drew in a deep breath. "Damn." He recalled how Josephine had clung to him walking into the restaurant, wanting to make it seem like they were an item.

"Who is Josephine Harris?" Maverick wanted to know.

"The woman from the dating agency," Charm answered.

"What dating agency?" Sloan asked.

Garth ignored his question. Instead he kept his gaze trained on Charm. "I took Josephine Harris to dinner to tell her I didn't want to see her again."

"Well, it didn't look that way from where Regan and I sat. The woman was practically all over you. I would not have known that seeing you and the woman together bothered Regan if I didn't know her so well. And then when she called me this morning to say she was resigning and to make sure you got her note, that's when I put two and two together."

Garth straightened and shoved the envelope into the pocket of his jacket. "This meeting is canceled."

He then walked out briskly.

Regan stood back and studied the Christmas tree she'd just decorated. Granted, Thanksgiving was still two weeks away, but it didn't matter to her. She loved the holidays, Christmas especially. Besides, she needed to do something to keep her busy, to keep her from thinking about Garth. She checked her watch. He should have gotten her resignation letter by now.

She had cried herself to sleep last night, after calling herself all kinds of fool for thinking it would be easy to win him over. And what was even more pathetic was that she hadn't even gone after his heart. She'd figured desire would be the foundation and that one day he would eventually fall in love with her. She'd been willing to take that chance.

But things hadn't worked out that way, and it was time to move on to protect her heart. After all that time they'd spent together and what they'd shared—if Josephine Harris could easily walk in and erase it from his mind, then the woman was welcome to him.

He wouldn't need a pilot until the end of next month, which gave him plenty of time to look for her replacement. She would call Harold Anders later today and accept his job offer. Also, later today she would call her father and let him know of her decision to resign. For the first time in over forty years, a Fairchild would not be the corporate pilot for Outlaw Freight Lines. She would make both of those calls later. Right now, she wanted to stand here, sip her coffee and stare at her beautifully decorated Christmas tree.

Her doorbell sounded. She frowned, wondering who would be paying her a visit. She hoped it wasn't Charm. Last night she'd come close to spilling her guts.

Leaving the living room, she went to the door. "Who is it?"

"Garth."

Garth? What was he doing here?

If he thought he could talk her out of resigning, then he was wrong. But more than anything, she would not let him think the reason she was quitting had anything to do with him…even if it did. She had her pride.

She opened the door and pasted a cheery smile on her face. "Garth? What are you doing here?"

"May I come in?"

"Sure." She stepped aside to let him in.

He'd been to her house before, many times, when he'd

been kind enough to pick her up for the airport because of bad weather. This was the first time she'd noticed how his tall, muscular frame seemed to take up a large portion of her living room.

"That's a pretty Christmas tree."

She followed his gaze. "Thanks." She then looked back at him. "Why are you here, Garth?"

He pulled an envelope out of his coat pocket. "About this. We need to talk, Regan."

She lifted her chin. "Why? I resigned. There's nothing to talk about. I got a better job offer, and I'm taking it. End of story."

"I don't think that's the end of the story. We should talk."

Regan drew in a deep breath. She had given two weeks' notice, so technically he was still her boss for now. She would listen to what he had to say, and then she would ask him to leave. There was nothing he could say that would make her change her mind at this point.

"Fine. We'll talk. May I take your coat?" She watched him peel his coat off massive shoulders and a masculine body. A body she had tasted all over, straddled, laid hands on…

"Here you are."

She blinked, knowing he'd caught her staring. Fighting to regain control of her senses, she took the coat from him. "I'll be back after hanging it up."

When she returned, he was standing in front of the tree. As always, he looked good in his business suit, but she liked him in jeans, too. "So, let's talk, Garth."

He turned around and met her gaze, and she nearly got weak in the knees. He was staring at her the way he'd stared at her a number of times in Santa Cruz. There was so much desire in his dark eyes. She took a deep breath. She honestly didn't have time for any of his lusty dispatches. "Please say what you have to say, then leave, Garth."

He nodded. "I'm not accepting your resignation," he said, tossing the envelope on a nearby table.

She crossed her arms over her chest. "You don't have a choice. I've accepted another job that's paying me more."

"That's not the reason you're quitting and you know it. Charm said the two of you were at the Riverview for dinner yesterday."

"And what of it?"

"I think you got the wrong impression."

She rolled her eyes. "I have no idea what you're talking about. You're free to dine wherever you want and with whomever you want. My resignation has nothing to do with that."

"I don't believe you, Regan."

"You think a whole lot of yourself if you believe my wanting to advance my career has anything to do with you. I'd gotten that job offer weeks ago and was trying to decide whether I should take it or not. I've decided. Sorry my decision doesn't meet with your approval."

"Why are you doing this to us?"

"Us?" That one word made her snap. "There was never an us, Garth. I knew it and I accepted it, yet I'd come up with this brilliant idea, using all that strategy planning I've watched you use over the years. I figured if I could be the woman you wanted, then I could certainly become the wife you needed. Stupid me for thinking such a thing was possible. I was even willing to let love come later or not at all. But my plan backfired. After I gave you those two weeks, you weren't satisfied. I wish you the best with your perfect woman and I hope you wish me the same with my employer."

She hadn't meant to go off on him and say as much as she had. But it was too late to take any of it back.

"Now please leave, Garth, and take my resignation letter with you, because it's official."

Twenty-One

Instead of leaving like she requested, Garth moved away from the Christmas tree, took off his suit jacket and placed it across the back of her sofa. Then he rolled up his shirt-sleeves.

"And just what do you think you're doing?"

"I'm about to fight, Regan. Not with you but *for* you. While growing up, I resented Bart for not fighting for my mom when my parents split. He never fought for her. He just fought her for me. I don't plan to make that same mistake."

Garth paused and then said, "Yesterday morning, after thirteen sleepless nights of pure hell, I woke up ready to admit the truth. That you had somehow done something no woman was supposed to do after Karen. You had somehow wiggled your way into my heart."

She shook her head as if what he'd said was too far-fetched to believe. "No, I did not."

He held up his hand. "Hold up. You had your say and now it's time I had mine."

He was glad she tightened her lips so he could continue. "I had made up my mind to call you last night and ask if

I could take you out to dinner, so I could tell you everything. Especially what I felt in my heart. Then, unexpectedly, the woman who was supposed to meet me in Santa Cruz showed up, assuming we could hang out together for a week to make up for the time we didn't get in Spain."

He paused to draw in a deep breath. "The reason I took her to dinner was because I skipped lunch and was hungry. And I honestly didn't want to burst her bubble on an empty stomach, and I didn't want my brothers questioning me about the woman in my office. She broke the dating service's ironclad policy by even seeking me out. You of all people know what a stickler I am for people following the rules."

"But she's gorgeous."

"So are you. No comparison in my book," he said.

"She was all over you."

Garth heard the hurt in her voice. "But at any time did you see me all over her? I knew who I wanted, and nothing she said or did would have made me change my mind. I considered her of no significance."

He walked across the room to stand in front of Regan. "You're a different story. There were a number of things I had to overcome, and you helped me do that. I loved Karen and for years I refused to feel those same emotions for anyone else. However, you showed me that it was okay to be happy in a new relationship. And being happy didn't mean I was forgetting or replacing feelings I had for the person I lost. It meant I had discovered how to tuck those feelings into a special place in my heart and move on."

"What are you saying, Garth?"

He took a step closer to Regan. "What I'm trying to say is that I love you, Regan. I believe I fell in love with you at the Westmoreland Charity Ball. I told you why I even used that dating service in the first place. The more I saw you, the more I desired you. I figured that if I turned my attention to another woman, that would solve the problem because I honestly didn't think I could give you the love you deserve. Now I know I can."

A smile spread across his lips. "Whatever strategy you used on me worked. I love you and will continue to say it until you believe me, Regan. Yes, it took me fourteen days since we've been back to accept it. Go ahead and count it against me as being slow. But it has no bearing on the depth of my love for you. I love you, and I will spend the rest of my life showing you how much."

He saw the tears stream down her face and then she said, "And I love you, too. I've loved you forever."

Her words surprised him. She'd said she'd wanted him for a long time but had never said how long. "You have?"

She wiped away her tears. "Yes. The reason I returned to Fairbanks after just one year at the university in Los Angeles was not because of Dad. It was because of you."

He lifted a brow. "Me?"

"Yes. Even when I knew you were hurting after losing Karen, I still wanted to be there for you."

Her words touched him deeply. "I never knew. I love you so much." He reached out and pulled her into his arms, then lowered his mouth to hers.

Twenty-Two

"The decorating committee has outdone itself this year," Garth said, glancing around.

Regan thought the same thing. The ballroom of the Pavilion Hotel was absolutely gorgeous and set the stage for another Westmoreland Charity Ball. And because this was also New Year's Eve, everyone was in a festive mood and excited for the arrival of the new year.

She was one of those people.

So much had happened since that day in November when Garth had shown up at her home, refusing to accept her resignation and then proclaiming his love for her. Afterward, he'd called the office to inform Cash and the others he was taking the rest of the day off. He'd ended up taking the next three days off when he'd insisted they fly to Kodiak to visit Walker, Bailey and the twins.

Regan had spent Thanksgiving with the Outlaws and there was no doubt in anyone's mind, including Bart's, as to what type of relationship Regan and Garth shared. Then they'd spent Christmas with her father and met Deena. Regan liked her immediately and concluded the attractive woman was everything her father needed. He seemed truly happy.

"You're quiet."

She glanced up at Garth and smiled. He looked handsome in his tux. "I was just thinking about Dad and how happy he is."

"Yes, Franklin is happy and I'm happy for him. I hope you slept well last night."

Regan nearly choked on her punch and glanced up at him grinning. "Who slept?" she asked, knowing he'd kept her up most of the night making love.

Jason Westmoreland's wife, Bella, had renovated her ranch house into a bed-and-breakfast inn to be used by visiting relatives and business associates. Garth and all his siblings, as well as some of the visiting Westmorelands from Atlanta, Montana and Texas, were all staying at the inn.

Regan had met a lot of the Westmorelands at last year's charity ball. None of them seemed surprised to discover that she and Garth were now an item. Some of the ladies claimed they'd noted an attraction between them at the last ball.

A couple of hours later, Charm and Bailey came to grab Regan from Garth's side. "There's one of those photo booths downstairs. Let's take a picture together," Bailey said, grinning.

"Okay."

There was a line when they got there, and a number of the Westmoreland ladies were there to take pictures in the booth, as well. Someone suggested a group photo and several individual and duo shots. Regan figured a full hour had passed and was surprised Garth hadn't come looking for her. She glanced at her watch. Midnight would be in less than a half hour.

The first thing she noticed when she returned to the

ballroom was that it was completely dark. "I wonder what happened?" Regan whispered to Charm.

"I have no idea," was Charm's response.

Suddenly a bright light came on—a spotlight. And it was shining directly on her.

"What in the world?" she turned to ask Charm and Bailey, only to discover they were no longer by her side.

Then, unexpectedly, another group of lights came on. A portion of the dance floor was lit by candlelight in the shape of a huge heart. Regan was certain she had never seen anything so beautiful. Then, with the magic of a hologram, special effects and enhanced sound, a private jet landed in the center of the ballroom floor. Suddenly the cabin door of the jet in the hologram image appeared to open, and there stood Garth. He glanced over to where she was before walking toward her with a single red rose in his hand.

She couldn't stop the tears from falling when he stopped in front of her and presented her with the rose. Then, putting her arm in the crook of his, he walked her over to where the candlelit heart illuminated the dance floor.

Once they were there, a microphone was placed in Garth's hand. "I have a special dance for us, but first let me introduce the members of the band. We'll have Dillon and Micah Westmoreland with their guitars; Bane Westmoreland on keyboard; Riley Westmoreland on the piano; Canyon Westmoreland with his French horn; Jason Westmoreland and his saxophone; and Stern Westmoreland with his violin. The band will be conducted by the renowned Sampson Kilburn, who was once their music instructor. He credits their mother, Clarisse, an accomplished pianist in her own right, with making sure all seven of her sons had an ear for music."

The onlookers went wild when the seven Westmorelands took their place on stage with their instruments. With

Sampson conducting, the lights dimmed again. The music began playing and Garth drew her into his arms.

Regan was still speechless as she gazed up into Garth's smiling face. They were dancing inside the heart-shaped area. For the past two months Garth had done everything in his power to show her how much she was loved. At night they rarely stayed apart, and every day he showed her how vital he thought she was in his life.

When the music ended, she watched as he lowered himself to one knee and gazed up into her eyes. "Just so you know, I got your father's permission to do this," he said, taking a small box out of his jacket. "I love you, Regan. Will you marry me?"

More tears appeared in Regan's eyes. "Yes, Garth, I will marry you." She felt a ring slide onto her finger. Glancing down, she saw the huge, sparkling diamond. It was beautiful and so radiant it was blinding.

He got to his feet and pulled her into his arms for a passionate kiss as the Westmoreland band started performing again.

Epilogue

A beautiful day in June

"Garth, you may kiss your bride."

Garth had wondered if the minister would ever get to that part. He was ready. He smiled when he pulled Regan into his arms and lowered his mouth to hers. After Walker, who'd been his best man, nudged him in the side, Garth released her mouth. It was then that they turned to face all three hundred guests as the minister said, "I present to everyone Garth and Regan Outlaw."

Cheers went up and he figured it was a good time to kiss his wife again. Turning her to him, he took her into his arms again to do just that.

An hour or so later, after the photographer had taken a ton of pictures, he and Regan were making their way around the huge ballroom of the Pyramid Hotel in downtown Fairbanks. It was beautiful. After he'd told Regan how Riley's wife, Alpha, who was a party planner, and Dillon's movie star sister-law, Paige Novak, and several of her Hollywood friends had put together the theatrics for his proposal, Regan had been quick to hire Alpha as her wedding planner. Regan had chosen the storybook wedding theme and Alpha had delivered.

The Westmorelands were there in huge numbers, and when they saw Bart for the first time, the Denver group was shocked by how much he favored their fathers, Adam and Tomas. Of course, Bart was still in denial, although last night at the rehearsal dinner he'd tapped Riley on the shoulder, thinking he was Garth. Charm's mother, Claudia, the love of Bart's life, had arrived a few days ago for the wedding, and thankfully, Bart was on his best behavior.

"Hey, Garth, Regan."

They turned to face several of the Atlanta Westmorelands. "There is a bet going on as to which of you will be flying the jet to your honeymoon," Storm Westmoreland said.

Garth shook his head. The one thing he knew about his Westmoreland cousins was that they enjoyed betting and gambling as much as the Outlaws.

"Really?" he asked, ignoring Regan's chuckle.

"Yes, so who's it going to be?" Durango Westmoreland asked.

Garth shook his head. He and Regan would be leaving first thing in the morning for their honeymoon in the Netherlands. "I'll let my wife answer that."

All pair of eyes shifted to Regan, who said, "We both will."

"Okay, guys, pay up." Not surprisingly, it was Ian who won the money.

When they walked off, Garth glanced down at Regan and brought their joined hands to his lips. "Have I told you lately that I love you?"

"Only once since I became Mrs. Outlaw."

He threw his head back and laughed before leaning close and whispering in her ear. "I love you, Regan."

She beamed up at him with what he thought was the sexiest smile ever when she said, "I love you, too, and thanks for making me the wife you need."

* * * * *

TEMPTED BY THE BOSS

JULES BENNETT

I'm dedicating this book to all the women who decide to take a chance and go after what they want. Good for you!

One

"Not a damn thing seems to be working."

Kelly Prentiss stood opposite her boss's desk and listened to him rant once again. Same issues, different day, and burnout was threatening to become a real thing.

Trying to breathe new life into a multi-billion-dollar business after it had hit rock bottom was quite a task for anyone to take on. But Luke Holloway wasn't just anyone. He was the Vice President of New Product Development for Wingate Enterprises, he was her boss, and he'd starred in every single fantasy she'd had for the last several years.

The poor guy didn't even know how many hats he wore.

Thankfully it was Friday, but she knew Luke wouldn't be taking the weekend off...which meant she wouldn't be taking the weekend off, either.

"We need to think outside the box," she offered.

Those dark, brooding eyes landed on her and every nerve ending stood at attention. She thought after working for Luke for so long this sexual tension would cease at some point, but each day that passed she only felt that magnetic pull more and more.

How ridiculous was it to be infatuated with her boss? Could she be any more cliché? Added to that, the man was practically married to his job. He didn't make time to date anymore and, to her knowledge, he didn't even find her attractive. Never once had he flirted or even tried that fun banter men and women engaged in. All work, all the time; that was Luke.

He'd had a failed engagement three years ago and, since the downward spiral of Wingate, he'd poured every waking minute into finding the next big product, or miracle, to pull the company out of the ashes.

Luke either needed some grand new hotels, some phenomenal up-and-coming businesses…or, at this point, some fairy godmother to come save the day. Anything that would give the Wingates the boost they desperately needed to restore their reputation and breathe new life into the family-owned empire.

"You think I haven't been thinking outside the box?" he asked.

Kelly knew he'd been doing everything in his power to rescue the company, but she had to do something to get his attention. Desperate times called for desperate measures and all that. So she had a plan…an extremely *risky* plan. However, if Luke knew what she had in store for him, he'd fire her and never speak to her again.

And, if he realized this scheme was his brother's

idea, it might bring an abrupt end to their cozy family gatherings.

Good thing then that Luke didn't know anything about the detailed plans that had been building up behind the scenes between Kelly and Zeke Holloway.

"Listen," she began. "I've been doing some research on my own, and there's an investor that would like to meet with you. He has some great ideas and he's offering to help back the next project."

His brows rose as he listened, and Kelly knew she had him.

"He's ready to meet anytime you're available," she went on, not wanting to give him a chance to speak. "I can clear your schedule and contact your pilot. We could go as soon as tomorrow if that works for you."

Her heart beat so fast in her chest she could barely think straight. Kelly couldn't believe she was deceiving him. But the man didn't look out for himself, so *somebody* had to, right? And, considering she was the closest nonfamily person in his life, she took the liberty upon herself.

Actually, his brother Ezekiel was the one who proudly concocted this plan, but Luke's brother was the VP and had his own host of issues to deal with. Added to that, he had recently married the love of his life, Reagan.

Kelly was the one with Luke day in, day out. They spent hours upon hours together, and she knew how his mind worked, so she prayed she could pull this off. Zeke had told her point blank she was the only woman for the job.

Lying to Luke about an investor didn't feel right. But

she promised Zeke she'd whisk his brother away so he could relax and recharge, and considering he was putting up an insane amount of money for this plan, she couldn't back out now.

Silence filled his office and did nothing to calm her nerves. Kelly came to her feet and offered a wide smile, hoping she could at least fake some confidence.

"I think this is the exact thing you need to find your footing," she told him. "It wouldn't hurt to hear what this man has to say."

At least that first part of her statement was the honest truth. He needed a reset and, quite honestly, so did she. They'd both been working nonstop. She couldn't keep watching her boss beat himself up and she was running out of steam. At some point, someone had to take over and call the loss.

Taking a break didn't mean admitting defeat. It just meant their minds simply needed to be cleared of all the extraneous stuff that wasn't working and to allow for ideas of things that *would* work.

But, she had to be honest here, this trip was also about seeing if there was a spark. She never would have taken a chance on her own, but now that Zeke insisted on getting Luke out of the office and someplace relaxing, this was her only opportunity to take the biggest risk of her life.

"You trust me?" she added, knowing he did but needing to reel him in further to pull off her plan.

"With every secret I have," he told her.

The guilt hit her, but she had to shove it aside. Zeke had every good intention of making his brother take a forced vacation…but her carnal thoughts that were ac-

companying them weren't so innocent. Still, she had to
hold firm if she ever wanted to discover if this sexual
attraction was only one-sided.

Kelly figured one minor lie in the grand scheme of
things was nothing compared to what Luke had already
been through. He would forgive her—she hoped. If this
plan procured some new idea, then he might even give
her a raise.

Her breath caught in her throat.

And if the plan produced a successful seduction?
Well, she honestly didn't know what that would mean
once they returned to the office, but she couldn't think
about that right now. There was too much on her mind
to crowd any more worries in there.

"Ready for me to set this up?"

Luke blew out a sigh and held out his hands. "At
this point, I say we give it a try. What do you need me
to do?"

"Nothing." Kelly started toward the door. "Just leave
it all to me. What time should I have the private jet
ready for tomorrow?"

"Let's do noon," he told her. "I can't miss the nine
o'clock meeting with my brother. Ava wants to see us."

"Perfect," she said, her nerves now in full force. "I'll
make all the arrangements."

Ava was their aunt who had lost her husband, Trent,
to a stroke. It hadn't taken much time for Keith Cooper to swoop in on her during a moment of weakness.
While he might have been infatuated with her, Ava
hadn't returned his feelings. She'd only moved in with
him platonically when her estate had been foreclosed.
That had turned out to be a mess since, shortly after

she moved into her own place, Keith's nephew had revealed it was Keith who had embezzled money from Wingate Enterprises.

Among his many crimes against the family, Keith had used Ava to get closer to the Wingate money and pilfer funds, falsify records, arrange a fire, and frame them for drug trafficking over a period of time. And that's how the free fall had started and how Keith had wound up arrested and why Luke and Zeke ended up hating Keith for taking advantage of their aunt and nearly destroying the entire family.

Really, the whole sordid nightmare was a complete disaster. Kelly was glad to escape from all of that drama for a while, too.

She left the office and closed the door at her back. Leaning against it, she shut her eyes and pulled in a deep breath. She honestly hadn't been sure if he was going to say yes or not, but now that he had, there was no turning back.

So how was Luke going to react when he realized she'd double-crossed him and there was no investor? Not only that, but how would he respond when she finally made a move to seduce him?

The woman deserved a raise, or one hell of a hefty bonus for Christmas.

Kelly Prentiss had stood by his side through thick and thin. She'd been right there through his broken engagement, offering advice and never judging. There was something so comforting about having someone who would not only listen to him no matter what, but who he could also trust implicitly.

Then, with all of the destruction that had befallen the Wingates, she hadn't wavered one single time. She'd put in just as many hours as he had and she had also delivered her sound advice where needed. She was literally his right-hand woman, and he would be lost without her.

Luke had never met anyone more loyal, more hardworking or more dependable than Kelly.

And now she had a lead on a possible investment that could help not only Wingate Enterprises come back from the dead, but could also boost his reputation and get them on the fast track to regaining their billions.

Kelly was still keeping the meeting location a secret, but he counted on her to bring him only the prospects that would help the company. She understood time was of the essence and not to be wasted. Bottom line? If she was so excited about this potential investor and she wanted to keep everything under wraps, then he'd go along with her plan.

His work as of late had only taken him to the office and once to Dallas for the day. Getting out of Royal, Texas was going to be refreshing, and he almost didn't care where Kelly was taking him.

Luke relaxed against the soft leather sofa in his plane and glanced through his emails. He answered a few, but moved the others into their appropriate files to get to later. He'd barely slept last night…story of his life over these past few months.

The stress of carrying a company into a new territory and practically starting over was quite the load to bear. But Luke knew he could do it—he refused to admit defeat or ever give up and Kelly was just as much of a fighter.

He glanced across the aisle to where she sat with her laptop. Her tortoiseshell glasses outlined those remarkable green eyes, and her wavy hair had been pulled up on top of her head. With her legs crossed and her little pink toenails showing through her sandals, she looked like a mix of summer vacation and complete professional. He shouldn't find both attractive, but he couldn't deny Kelly was a beautiful woman.

No, *beautiful* seemed too tame a word to describe all of her complexities. *Striking* and *captivating* were much better descriptors.

An odd stirring shifted through him, and he chalked it up to lack of sleep and an overworked mind.

No funny business could ever happen between Kelly and him. Because no way in hell would he risk his one and only trusted right-hand woman just for a fling. And besides, he was in no position right now to even *think* of being with a woman. He couldn't even get his work under control, let alone have the time to feed into anything such as a relationship.

A relationship? That was so absurd. Clearly he was so stressed from lack of sleep, he was now delusional. Luke wasn't going to be that creeper boss. He respected the hell out of Kelly. Beauty was only part of what made her so special. She was extremely intelligent, with a sharp mind and quick wit. There was nobody else he'd ever want in the boardroom with him, fighting for his ideas and vision…just as soon as he had said ideas and visions.

Damn it, no wonder he was so confused about his unwanted attraction for his assistant. He'd never thought of her in a romantic manner, but now he couldn't help himself. Maybe it was the way she'd gotten a little demanding and a little controlling, taking over this whole plan...whatever the plan might be.

"Are you alright?"

Kelly's question caught him off guard, and he wondered how long he'd been staring at her. The last thing he needed was for her to think he wasn't stable or that he found this look of hers more than attractive.

Damn it, Luke. Get a grip. She's your employee and this isn't a pleasure trip. This is work and that's all there's time for.

"Fine," he quickly answered, then stifled a yawn. "Just anxious to get there."

He hadn't asked for many details, mainly because Kelly knew the ins and outs of Wingate Enterprises as much as he did. There was nothing about this situation he didn't trust her with.

"Tell me more about the investor," he said as he tipped his neck from side to side, trying to stay awake.

Her eyes widened a fraction before she glanced back down at her laptop. "Oh, let's wait to discuss work until we get there. I need to answer these emails. Sutton is looking for the projected numbers as we get ready to finish out the quarter, and it seems like you're tired."

Luke wasn't often dismissed by her, but they'd both been working so hard, he wasn't going to interrupt her now. Sutton Wingate was the company CFO, and Kelly might be Luke's assistant, but she did many things for many people within the family business, including Sutton's twin, Sebastian.

Kelly was an extremely busy woman and she'd put

all of this together for him. Luke couldn't help but feel hopeful based on her excitement over this trip.

Finding the next big investment or backer would be the break they so desperately needed once they came up with a plan to revamp their company. Naturally, there would have to be many steps taken. It wasn't just one miracle they were seeking, there were multiple, but they had to start somewhere to get that first leg up on rebuilding.

Luke settled back in and tried to refocus into work-mode. There was no reason he couldn't continue following his own leads on potential investors. He'd really love to acquire some other jets or bring something brand new to the market that Wingate could sink their teeth into and call their own. Getting in on the ground floor was always the best because, while there may be risk, the only way to go was up and, at this point, they had nothing else to lose.

Unfortunately, his eyes were burning from lack of sleep and he couldn't stop yawning. Any brilliant thoughts weren't going to come to him during this state of exhaustion.

"Why don't you lie down?" Kelly suggested. She removed her glasses and stared across the aisle. "I can move from the couch and take the captain chair. We still have a few hours before we land."

Luke shifted his laptop aside and came to his feet. "No need for you to move. I'll just stretch out right here."

He took a seat next to her and adjusted so his feet were propped up a little.

"I never knew this couch did that," she said with a laugh.

"That's because we're always working, but each seat has its own recliner." He settled in deeper and laced his hands over his abdomen. "I won't fall asleep. I rarely do these days."

"Don't worry if you do," she assured him, staring down at her screen. "I'll wake you when we're close."

He shut his eyes, focusing on the way Kelly pecked away at her keyboard and the hum of the engines. She said they had a few hours left, but he still couldn't guess where they were headed. Maybe the mountains for some resort idea or perhaps the coast to get some inspiration from a cozy town. Wherever they were headed, Kelly must truly believe this could help break ground on a new beginning...

"Luke."

He jerked awake, blinking against the brightness, and realized he had indeed fallen asleep.

Turning his attention toward Kelly, he adjusted his seat to sit straight up. "How long was I out?"

She shrugged as she put her laptop in the case. "About two hours."

Damn, that was a good nap and now he at least felt refreshed and revived.

Wait. Two hours? Where had they flown to? He'd been awake a while before he'd actually fallen asleep. Hadn't he?

No matter where they were, Luke couldn't wait to meet this potential investor. Every time he approached a prospect, Luke couldn't help but think this was the one that would save his ass.

Not that he was in jeopardy of losing his position within the company. He was too powerful and too wealthy to be pushed aside. But damn it, people were trusting him to bring the family business back in a major way. Luke didn't intend to fail and he didn't intend to do half the job, either. He would find the best investors and he would make Wingate Enterprises even more lucrative than ever.

Luke fastened his seat belt as the plane started the descent. "You must be like a security blanket or something, because I haven't slept more than two hours in a row for a while."

Kelly turned to face him with that stern look she always gave just before she lectured him. He'd gotten used to that look. It actually used to terrify him, but he knew his assistant only meant well. She watched out for everyone around her.

Which made him wonder who ever watched out for her?

"You can't save the company if you can't take care of yourself," she scolded. "Which brings me to the reason for this trip."

"What do you mean?" he asked.

Kelly bit down on her bottom lip for just a moment as she held his stare. Something was off. There was a niggle in his gut that seemed to be shooting off red flags, but he didn't know what he should be warned about.

"Kelly?"

"This is for your own good," she told him.

Dread replaced that niggle. "What have you done? Where are we?"

She tipped her chin and squared her shoulders. "We're in Oahu for five days of rest and relaxation."

"What the hell?"

"And there's no investor," she added. "Just you, me, and a private beach bungalow."

Two

Luke stepped off the plane and was greeted with a lei.

"Aloha, Mr. Holloway. Aloha, Ms. Prentiss. Welcome to Oahu."

Still confused as his anger continued to bubble up, Luke stepped aside as the young Hawaiian man, who was dressed in a crisp white suit, placed a lei on Kelly and then gestured toward the large silver SUV.

"Please, come this way," he offered. "We will get your luggage and take you to your resort so you can get started on your romantic getaway."

"I'm not going to any resort," Luke gritted out before turning to Kelly. "What the hell is going on?"

He overlooked the fact that the man seemed to think he and Kelly were a couple and had come here for some lover's retreat. But his mood soured even further when he noticed another man approaching the plane, presumably for their luggage.

Kelly's eyes darted from him to the driver as she offered a slight, nervous smile.

"Could you excuse us a moment?" she asked. "You can go ahead and gather our things."

Once the men were gone and working on the suitcases, Kelly focused back on Luke.

"You lied to me," he accused.

And that's what pissed him off the most. She'd never lied to him, but this was beyond lying. She'd been purposefully deceitful. How in the hell had she planned all of this without his knowledge? Using his own jet? His own pilot?

They'd flown all the way to Hawaii and he'd been utterly clueless and way too damn trusting. She had to have had help, and this reeked of Ezekiel. There was no way Kelly could've handled all of these details, let alone the financial aspect of this, without some major backer...

Like his meddling, yet well-meaning brother.

"This is for the best," she explained. "I've never lied to you before and I've never done anything like this. Don't you see that's how serious this whole thing is? You desperately need a break."

Luke heard her words, but that didn't calm his frustration and anger. What had gotten into his loyal, honest assistant? Or maybe he should be asking who?

"Did Ezekiel talk you into this?" he asked.

Kelly's eyes widened as her dark red strands blew across her cheek in the warm breeze. He could tell by her reaction that she didn't want to rat out Zeke, but Luke wasn't stupid.

"He told me to make sure you relaxed and ordered me to not let you steamroll me back to Royal before this vacation time was over," she explained. "So, you and I are both going to take a break and recharge. You've been working yourself to death and Zeke and I are not taking no for an answer. Now get in the car."

Luke blinked. He knew Kelly was a strong, determined woman—that's one of the reasons he valued her as an employee and his right-hand woman. But she'd never directed that attitude toward him. This side of her was new and he wasn't so sure he liked it.

Well, a commanding woman could be sexy in the right circumstances, but not when it was his assistant bossing him around like a toddler at the commands of his own brother. Luke would definitely be giving Zeke an ass-chewing about all of this.

"You can't make me stay."

Kelly took a step forward, coming toe to toe with him. Those green eyes seemed even darker now as she narrowed her gaze.

"You're right, I can't make you," she agreed. "But Zeke asked me to do this. He's gone to all of this trouble and your schedule is cleared for the next week. Please, do this for me. Take care of yourself so you can take care of Wingate."

The conviction in her tone had his anger subsiding somewhat. He still didn't like being tricked or hijacked or whatever the hell this was, but he also knew his brother wouldn't have enlisted the help of his assistant or gone to great lengths to get him away from the office if he wasn't worried.

Still, that attraction that had slapped him in the plane, coupled with sleeping so well next to her, would quite possibly lead to them crossing a line they could never return from.

"Can we get in the car?" she asked, her eyes pleading.

Luke glanced to see the driver had loaded their luggage and was waiting by the back door to allow them in. With a heavy sigh, he headed for the SUV. He assisted Kelly before climbing in after her.

Once the door was closed, he glanced over at her. She stared straight ahead, legs crossed, and those glasses back in place. This was his most valued assistant, but she'd been much more than that. She'd stuck by his side through hell in both his personal and professional life.

Never once in the five years that she'd worked for him had she ever asked a thing from him. She'd been so damn noble and now she was clearly worried about his mental state because of all the stress. Luke swallowed hard. She obviously believed following his brother's orders was the way to go, but Zeke wasn't aware of this stirring deep within Luke. Zeke wasn't the one turned on by his assistant's demands and her sexy little glasses.

But Kelly turned to face him, imploring him, clearly concerned for his well-being, and he would have to be an absolute jerk to ignore all of these efforts. A few days away from the office wasn't something he ever did, especially during such a critical time. However, his brother might have a point. If Luke could rest and possibly recharge his mind to start fresh, maybe that was the way to go.

Hell, he felt like he'd tried everything else at this point, maybe he should spend a few days in paradise with a gorgeous woman. Not that he could let anything happen between them. Because risking anything with this woman would be a recipe for disaster. She was too invaluable to him and the company.

And, while he did decide to stay, that didn't mean he was happy about being lied to.

"Who else knows you kidnapped me?"

Kelly laughed. "*Kidnapped?* Really, Luke, there's no need to be so dramatic."

"What else would you call it?"

"A much needed getaway."

He didn't know the last time he'd had a vacation, but that didn't mean he wanted one with his smoking hot assistant. Working with her in an office setting was one thing, but being in a romantic bungalow on an island resort was a whole different story.

"This might not be the best idea," he told her. "Us sharing a room."

She stared at him for a moment before turning and shifting to face him fully.

"Listen, we're obviously both adults and we're professionals. Besides, we have a house, it's not like a hotel room with one bed. Unless you're afraid you can't keep your hands off me," she joked with a wink.

Oh, hell. That wink and smirk shouldn't affect him, but he couldn't ignore that unwanted pull of attraction. How could this work? What the hell was his brother thinking?

"I'm just kidding," she told him. "Don't look so scared. But I do have to tell you about one rule Zeke was adamant about, and I have to agree with him."

He raised his brows. "Rule? You mean after all this craziness you two concocted, you only came up with one rule?"

"For now," she replied with a grin. "No electronics."

Luke waited for her to tell him she was teasing. When her smile vanished, he realized she was indeed serious.

"You cannot actually think that's going to fly with me." He laughed, then sobered. "How can I check in with work or my brother?"

The brother he wanted to berate for meddling in his life.

"I assure you, Zeke has everything under control back in the office and there's nothing for you to check in on. That's the whole point of relaxing."

"I won't be without my phone," he insisted.

Kelly tipped her head and smirked. "Oh, there will be no phone, no laptop, nothing. You will unwind, you hear me? We will get massages, food and drinks delivered to our private bungalow... And we will have our own beach and our own personal butler, as well. The point of this is to remove yourself from reality."

He stared, wondering just how far removed from his real life he had to be. "I'll give you the laptop, but not the phone."

Kelly laughed, and he found that anger bubbling up once again. He was not going to be bullied through this entire situation.

"I will be taking all of it, putting it in the safe, and

only I will know the code," she informed him. "This will be a complete reboot of your system. Got it? You will relax and you will have a good time. I'm here to make sure of it."

The thought of spending five days in a private beach house with his sexy assistant didn't sound like the smartest move he'd ever made. Not that he would ever make a move on Kelly. He valued her too much and would never disrespect her in such a way.

But, damn, being on the beach also meant he'd be seeing her in a swimsuit. If he thought she looked sexy on the plane with those little glasses and polished toes, how would he handle wet spandex wrapping her luscious body?

"Hell," he muttered. "I brought suits…not the swimming kind. I have nothing for a beach vacation."

She threw him a smile. "No worries. I've taken care of that part."

Something about that saucy grin terrified him and he had no idea what in the world he'd gotten himself into. He should've turned right around and gotten back on that plane. Kelly could have stayed and had all the vacation she wanted, he'd even give her paid time. Hell, he'd double it.

But somehow he'd ended up in the back of an SUV heading toward what some would say was a romantic, tropical getaway with his stunningly beautiful assistant.

Seriously. What could go wrong?

Kelly's heart beat faster as they were escorted to their bungalow. The walk through the opulent gardens and tall palm trees flanking the narrow path seemed even more exotic than she'd imagined.

Before Zeke booked this place online, he had shown it to her to make sure it was okay. Like she was going to turn down a free vacation with the one man she'd wanted for years? Any place would've been perfect, giving her the chance she'd been too afraid to take in Royal.

But now, well, they would be alone and there was nothing stopping her. Kelly had gotten online and called the resort, giving strict instructions for her and Luke to be left alone. She'd also gone ahead and set up times for food deliveries, massages, and two excursions to get Luke to lighten up even more. She'd promised Zeke she would do anything to make his brother decompress, and she wasn't going to let him leave this island until she saw an improvement.

As they got closer, the soft lull of the ocean waves lifted her spirits and calmed her nerves. The bright pink hibiscus trees lined the path of lush greenery. Then their home away from home came into view.

An absolutely adorable thatched roof covered the bungalow. The ocean was just on the other side, and she knew their private beach would have beautiful white sand. She couldn't wait to get inside.

"Would you like to explore on your own or do you need a tour?" their guide asked as he stood outside the door.

"We can take it from here," she told him, reaching in her purse for a tip.

"I will have your bags brought down at once," he said, taking the tip and nodding his thanks. "You just need to type the code and the door will unlock. It automatically locks for your safety. Please don't hesitate to call if you have any needs. Welcome to Malie Villa."

Tranquility Villa. So perfect. That name had pulled her in as soon as Zeke shared it with her and, once she'd seen the online photos, she'd been hooked. Never in her life would she have thought to come to a tropical paradise like this. It wasn't like she had a significant other to travel with...she also hadn't been looking. Luke occupied way too much of her headspace.

Kelly typed in the code and opened the door. "Welcome to your vacation," she said, gesturing for Luke to enter. "I'll even let you choose which room you want."

"Wonderful," he murmured as he stepped inside.

Kelly closed the door once she was in and her breath caught in her throat. The view was even more breathtaking than any photo she could ever see.

The entire back wall was comprised of folding glass doors that had been left open to allow the ocean breeze to filter through. There was a private infinity pool and an outdoor eating area. The open living room seemed cozy with all the white furniture with green accents. There was an eat-in kitchen to the right and bedrooms to the left. The entryway had a small Christmas tree all decorated with pineapples and flamingos.

"I'll admit, this place is gorgeous," Luke stated, turning to face her.

Kelly smiled. "Did you think your brother or I would choose somewhere subpar to make you miserable? You deserved the best."

"I didn't think you'd take me anywhere," he countered.

Kelly shrugged. "Well, now you know we'll do anything for you. Even if that means looking out for you when you don't look out for yourself."

He stared at her a minute and Kelly fully realized just how alone they were. They'd been alone at work, at lunch meetings, even in a plane when going to meet investors. But they had never been alone in such a capacity as this. There was something…very intimate about being in a romantic bungalow on an exotic beach with a man she'd been fantasizing about for years.

Could she actually pull this off?

If he was still peeved about being swept away on a forced holiday, she was going to have a difficult time taking a leap of faith with this man that she wanted as more than a boss. She would be sleeping only feet away from him. So close, yet so damn far…

Kelly could never, ever admit her feelings to Luke in a traditional setting. She valued him not only as her employer, but as a friend, and she wouldn't risk her position at Wingate.

When Zeke came to her with a proposition to get Luke out of the office under the ruse of taking him to see an investor, Kelly knew she couldn't let this golden opportunity pass her by. This was the only time they'd be together outside of the office for non-Wingate business. There would be no better option…and what better place than a romantic, tropical setting?

"Go pick your room," she told him. "I'll wait for the luggage."

He turned and went into one room, then the other. Kelly waited in the entryway, wishing they would hurry with the luggage so she could change and explore that beach. She couldn't wait to dip her toes into the sand

and water and start her vacation. Though she was a messed-up bundle of anxiety, she hoped she didn't lose her nerve after mentally preparing herself for weeks.

Luke came back out and sighed. Then he unbuttoned his sleeves and rolled them up onto his thick, muscular forearms.

If his bare arms were making her excited, she would be doomed when it came to seeing him in a bathing suit. She'd only seen Luke in dress clothes, or the occasional jeans and dress shirt, before.

"I'll give you the room with the view of the ocean," he informed her. "I'll take the room with the garden view."

Kelly jerked slightly. "You should take the room with the ocean view. The water is more relaxing and I'm so glad to be here, I'm certainly not complaining about a garden view."

"That one has a Jacuzzi tub," he said. "I wouldn't use anything like that."

She hadn't thought about the bathrooms. But she wasn't going to argue. She'd take whichever room he wanted her to.

There was a knock on the door, and Luke crossed to get the luggage. Once he had everything wheeled inside, along with a few extra items, and they were alone again, Kelly took her bag to her room.

"What's all this?" Luke came to stand in her doorway, holding up shopping bags from the resort.

Kelly sat her suitcase up on the stand in the corner. "That's the clothing I requested for you for the trip."

Luke shook his head and sighed. "Who paid for this? You or Zeke?"

She held up her hand. "Just stop worrying about everything. Zeke is the financial backer here, but I'm coordinating all the needs on this end. Your job for the next five days is just to enjoy the view, the food, the drinks, and not think about a thing."

His eyes held hers and Kelly held her breath, hoping he wouldn't argue. She just wanted to have a carefree, relaxing time with him. Selfishly, she wanted Luke to see her as more than an assistant, but she still had to work her way up to that.

Physical attraction had been present from day one. But there was more to Luke that attracted her. He was loyal, kind, powerful, and devoted to his career and his family. There was no way she could've ignored that extra tug toward him as time had gone on and this might be her only chance to make her move.

Time was not on her side right now. But she couldn't exactly attempt seduction on day one...could she?

"Fine," he told her. "I'm all yours for the next five days."

That's what both thrilled and terrified her.

Three

"What the hell did you ask them to send me?" Luke yelled through the closed bedroom door.

There was no way he was stepping foot out of here, not wearing this embarrassing excuse for a bathing suit.

Why was he being punished? Wasn't this supposed to be a relaxing trip? Nothing about this bag of clothes had him calming down. If Zeke was here, he'd likely be enjoying this misery a little too much.

Luke peeked at Kelly through the crack in the door. She stood on the other side wearing some floral cover-up and her long, red hair pulled up on top of her head. She had a beach towel tucked under one arm and her sunglasses perched in front of her bun. Now that was a beach look. What he had on was…hell, he didn't even know what to call this.

Why did Kelly look like she'd just stepped off a magazine shoot while he looked like he was ready to participate in some indecent bachelor auction? Because his goods were definitely on display.

"Just let me see," she told him, motioning for him to come out. "It can't be that bad. It's just a bathing suit. We're adults."

"Oh, this suit is *very* adult," he growled. "Did you tell them to find the smallest suit for me?"

Kelly's brows drew in. "Is the size too small? I didn't know how big your...how big... Uh, what size you'd need."

Her pink cheeks would be adorable in another capacity, but not when his nether regions were being squeezed to death.

"I don't think it's the size," he gritted through his teeth. "I think even two sizes up would be skimpy."

"Skimpy?" she asked, her eyes wide. "I certainly didn't ask for that. Can't you just put on another set of trunks? I asked for them to send three male bathing suits."

"Oh, they sent three," he countered. "They're all the same, but in different colors. Black, navy, and red."

And that wasn't all they'd sent. He'd opened the bags and gotten a sneak peek on the rest of his wardrobe for the week and he wasn't too keen on that either, but at least it would cover up his manly bits.

"Can I just see?" she asked. "I swear I won't take a picture and post it."

She snickered a little and he glared. "I have to say I'm not trusting you much right now. First you kidnapped me—"

"You really need to adjust your terminology," she corrected. "This is a much needed vacation."

"And then you have the resort deliver sacks full of tourist clothing with a bikini bottom only a woman should wear."

"If I'd told you what to pack, you would have known something was up," she explained. "Listen, you're just going to have to come out wearing that and I swear, I won't laugh."

"You already laughed and I'm not even out yet."

"It's out of my system. Promise."

As if to prove her point, Kelly shrugged, causing the cover-up to dip off one slender shoulder. He tried like hell not to look at the swell of her breast just above the bikini top, but he couldn't help himself.

This was *not* ok. None of it. He shouldn't be looking at his assistant's ample chest…and he sure as hell shouldn't be enjoying the way she looked. How the hell would he react when she took her cover-up off? One thing was for certain, she would definitely know if he liked it if he left these damn skimpy bottoms on.

Muttering under his breath, Luke closed the door and looked around the room for a towel. He grabbed one from his en suite and wrapped it around his waist before opening the door once more.

"Let's go," he told her, holding the knot at his side with a death grip. "You have to close your eyes as I'm getting in and out of the water."

Her eyes dipped to his chest, then lower, before she brought her focus back up to his eyes. Was that desire she saw looking back at him? No. No way. Kelly had been with him for five years and she'd never once acted like she was attracted to him.

He needed to ignore the fact she had more skin ex-

posed than he was used to and remember they were
adults and professionals. This was nothing more than
a relaxing vacation that she went to a good deal of trouble to make happen.

"No electronics?" he asked.

She held up her hand. "I promise, I put mine away
with yours. I won't post anything about your little boy
shorts."

Luke glowered at her. "You're enjoying this way too
much."

"Possibly, but it's only the first day," she told him.
"You'll learn to enjoy yourself, too. That's my goal."

"I'd rather your goal be to call the gift shop and ask
if they have real trunks for a man."

Kelly pursed her lips. "I suppose I can do that."

He waited while she stepped into the living room and
used the house phone to call the gift shop. A moment
later, she hung up and turned to face him.

"All done," she told him. "Someone is on their way
with more options."

"I'll pay for this pair," he told her.

"Zeke's card is on file. No need."

She shifted her towel to the other hand and headed
toward the opening to their own infinity pool.

"Just join me when you can."

Luke waited near the door, but couldn't take his eyes
off the view…and he didn't mean the ocean and tall
palm trees.

Kelly slowly pulled her cover-up over her curvy body
and tossed it onto a lounge chair. She adjusted her sunglasses over her eyes and dipped a toe into the water.

That bikini should be illegal.

The scraps of material and strings were just a simple black, but there was very little coverage. They made his bottoms look large.

Kelly stepped on into the pool and then dove under. She came up at the other end and rested her arms along the ledge as she stared out at the ocean.

Luke jerked when the doorbell rang. Clutching his towel in one hand, he opened the door with the other.

"Here you go, sir."

The worker handed over another resort bag and nodded his goodbye. Luke closed the door and slipped back into his room. The minute he pulled out the new suit, he groaned. He wasn't sure which one was worse, but this one did cover a little bit more.

Reluctantly, he changed and grabbed his towel. By the time he stepped outside, Kelly was lying on a chaise on her belly reading a book.

Those damn cheeky bottoms of hers were seriously taunting him. He should not be lusting after his assistant. He respected the hell out of her and his thoughts were taking a drastic turn from strictly professional to highly inappropriate.

Luke blew out a breath. He would just pretend they were in the office. That's all. Surely he could do that, right?

But in the office he wasn't looking at half her bare ass. He never would've made it through board meetings if that were the case.

"There has to be other trunk options than the two I've seen."

Kelly glanced over her shoulder and busted out laughing. "What? You don't like the big red lips on your...um...your..."

He resisted the urge to cover-up said lip section, but instead propped his hands on his hips. "Do I come across as the type of guy who would wear black spandex shorts with red lips on my junk?"

She rolled over onto her side, the sway of her breasts shifting with the movement, and Luke used a good bit of his willpower to keep his eyes on hers. Damn it, he needed a distraction.

"Do you have sunscreen?" he asked. "You don't want to burn."

"I sprayed myself, but I don't know how well I managed my back." She pointed to the table in the corner. "Grab that bottle and just give me a once-over, please."

Luke sprayed her back, even going on down over her cheeks that were only half covered. He sure as hell didn't want to have to rub aloe on her later if she got too much sun. He'd probably go up in flames if he had to touch her bare skin.

Once he was done—thankfully he didn't have to rub anything in—Luke went to the edge of the water.

"It feels really nice," she told him, turning back to her book. "We can go to the beach if you want. Or you can go alone. I don't want to smother you on your vacation."

For some reason, the moment she said smother, he got an instant image of her splayed over him. He was seriously going to have to create some distance between them or he would end up embarrassing himself.

"I think I'll go take a walk on the beach," he told her. "I need to clear my head. You just enjoy your book."

He headed down to the shore at a record pace and hoped like hell she hadn't noticed his blatant arousal.

There was no way in hell he was going to make it to the end of this trip without crossing the line with his assistant.

As if he didn't have enough to worry about with Wingate, now he wanted to strip that pathetic excuse for a bikini off Kelly and take both of their minds off their troubles.

Four

Kelly blew out a sigh when Luke left her alone. When he'd stepped outside, she nearly had a heart attack at how sexy he was. She'd known he was built, but she'd never seen him like *this*.

All that dark, taut skin with those black snug shorts—even the red lips right smack in the center didn't take away from his potent sex appeal. If anything, those shorts were damn hot on him, and she thought they were perfectly fitting for what she wanted to do.

The closer she got to trying to seduce him and make the biggest risk of her life, the more her nerves jumbled all together and her common sense told her not to take this chance.

But she had to. It was now or never. So no matter her fears, she had to push them aside and go after what she wanted.

As much as Kelly wanted to admire Luke even more, it was probably best that he went down to the beach alone right now. She hadn't missed the way his eyes had traveled over her body—the man really should wear some sunglasses to hide the fact he was giving her a visual lick.

She also didn't miss the obvious attraction he had to her. Those skimpy shorts hid nothing. Hmm…maybe getting him into bed wouldn't be as difficult as she thought.

Kelly smiled as she flipped the page in her book. Good to know this new bikini was working like a charm, just like she intended. Men were simply primal creatures…even men married to their jobs. They still had basic needs and still craved bare skin and a little temptation.

A fling wouldn't hurt, would it? They were adults and they could keep this separate from the office. She wasn't looking for a ring on her finger or any promise of commitment. The only relationship Luke wanted was his career…a situation she knew all too well because of her father. She'd seen the struggle her mother had gone through trying to get any attention from her husband. Kelly never wanted a life like that, and she knew she deserved better.

So, a little fun in the sun had to be the theme for this trip.

A bit later, the doorbell rang again. Luke was still not back, so she got up and went to answer.

"Aloha, ma'am." The concierge wheeled a cart of food and drinks inside. "Where shall I set up this dinner for you?"

Kelly glanced around and really wasn't sure. "How about you leave it here and we will take care of it?"

He nodded. "Please let us know if you require any further service this evening."

Kelly thanked him and showed him out. She went to the cart and lifted the domed lids. Surf and turf with grilled asparagus and a cauliflower rice. Wine, beers, and a particular bottle of bourbon that she'd requested.

There was also a white-and-gold card advertising their nightly resort entertainment. She was still tired from the trip and not really in the mood to be around a bunch of people, so she wasn't going to mention that to Luke.

Kelly figured the sun would start to set soon, so she carried the plates out to the patio area and set everything up. She poured herself a glass of wine and got Luke a beer, then put the alcohol in the fridge, save for the bourbon that she left on the counter.

Luke still wasn't back so Kelly went to her bedroom and changed into a pair of shorts and a tank. She took her hair down and brushed it, then put it back up into a top knot. The movement had her shoulders feeling tight, and she glanced in the mirror to see she'd gotten a little pink today. She'd have to be more liberal with the sunscreen tomorrow. Apparently she'd gotten so sidetracked with her Luke fantasies and then her book, she'd lost track of time and hadn't reapplied.

As Kelly stepped out of her room, Luke was coming up the steps by their pool. Water droplets ran over his broad chest and beaded all over his close-cropped hair and beard. He carried a towel and stopped by the pool to dry off. Since he hadn't spotted her yet, she felt a little voyeuristic standing here watching him rub his towel all over his very fine body.

Kelly cleared her throat and headed out to the patio.

"You're just in time," she told him. "I hope you're ready for dinner."

"I'll get changed and be right out."

He walked by her without glancing her way and Kelly ignored that twinge of disappointment. He seemed upset about something, but she had no clue what. He didn't have his cell to check emails or take calls, so what could have bothered him on a secluded beach?

Perhaps he was irritated at his attraction toward her. Luke wouldn't like that he was losing control over anything, especially his feelings. She'd never known him to mix business and pleasure. Even when he'd been engaged, he'd put his career first.

Kelly didn't want more than this right here. She wanted these few days alone with Luke to prove to him she was more than his assistant. Two adults in a romantic resort indulging in a heated fling that would stay just between them was all she was asking for. With the possibility of him finding her attractive, Kelly had a burst of hope that layered over all those nerves.

Kelly didn't mind one bit helping him take his mind off Wingate and everything they'd left back in Royal. She just hoped Luke was ready for all she had in mind.

By the time Luke came back out, he was still scowling, and she couldn't help but laugh when she saw his outfit.

"I swear, I didn't ask them to send all of these tacky things," she defended. "I just gave them your sizes and said I needed trunks, shorts, and shirts. I asked for a pair of sandals and sunglasses, too."

"Oh, I got everything you asked for. But this was the best outfit out of the eccentric variety."

Kelly couldn't help but laugh at the green-and-white plaid shorts and the white T-shirt that read EYE CANDY in bold, black letters.

"I seriously considered putting a suit on," he grumbled as he took a seat at the table. "And I mean the kind of suits I brought."

"Aw, now you're just being a grouch. It's Christmas time, and we're on a private beach. Perk up. I'm the only one who can see you, right?"

He met her gaze. "Believe it or not, I do demand respect."

"You think I don't respect you?" she asked, a little hurt he would even think that.

"It's impossible to respect anything I've got in there to wear." He leveled her gaze across the table. "The next time you kidnap someone to an unknown destination, maybe at least tell them what to pack or don't have their wardrobe left to the hands of a resort gift shop."

Kelly reached for her wine. "Oh, well. A minor hiccup. It's my first kidnapping."

He ate in silence for a minute, and she wondered if he was literally angry with her for being here and for the wardrobe. She wanted him to have a good time, and by the end of this trip she wanted him to see her in a manner outside of the office and in a more relaxed environment.

Was that too much to hope for?

"How was the beach?" she asked.

He drew his brows together as if trying to think of his day. "Peaceful," he told her. "Having a private beach is definitely a perk that almost makes up for my atrocious clothes. You'll have to go down there tomorrow. How was the book?"

"I'm almost done with it."

His eyes widened. "In one day?"

"Listen, when I get a break I take full advantage," she replied. "I love to read."

"How many books did you pack?"

"I brought seven." She held up her hands ticking off her fingers. "One for each of the five days and two just in case I finish early on the others."

He eased back in his seat and continued to stare at her. "You're really taking this relaxing period seriously."

"You will, too," she vowed. "I have a few surprises planned during our trip."

His eyes narrowed and his lips thinned. "I don't know that I'll survive anymore surprises from you."

She couldn't help but laugh. "I promise you will love them. I'm just trying to help you recharge, remember? You need a little fun in your life and to take time to forget about the office. Trust me, all of those issues will be there when we get back."

He continued to study her, then his eyes dipped to the scoop in her tank. Her heart clenched as the sexual awareness seemed to bounce between them.

"Your skin is pink." He motioned toward her chest. "You need to be careful and apply more sunscreen."

"I know. It's a little tender. I just got lost in the book and the time got away from me. I'll be fine."

Luke grabbed his small fork for the lobster tail. "I've

never read anything so entertaining that it caused me to lose total track of time."

"Well, you will have to read something other than spreadsheets then."

He shook his head and laughed. "You're awfully snarky. I bet you're feeling really sure of yourself now that you've succeeded in getting me here."

She clutched her wineglass to her chest. "I won't deny I feel pretty damn good. I was worried about lying to you, but I knew in the end it would be for your own good."

They finished their meal and then carried their dishes back to the cart. Luke pushed the cart out the door and left it for their private butler to get later.

"I did order your favorite bourbon," she told him as soon as he closed the door. "Would you like a glass?"

"I'm actually pretty tired. I might turn in early."

Another sliver of disappointment slid through her, but what did she expect? To ply him with bourbon and have her way with him? No, that certainly wasn't her style. She wanted him to come to her on his own. But she was also going to show him there was more to both of them than work.

Yes, she wanted him to reset his mind where Wingate was concerned, but she also wanted him to see what had been in front of him for the past five years.

Would he ever see her as more? And if so, would he ever admit to it…or would he be too afraid to take that type of a risk?

Kelly sighed. Well, no matter what might transpire between them, it wasn't going to happen on night one. It might not even happen on night five, but she had to try. She had to see if there was a spark between them and if he felt even an inkling of what she did.

When Luke went to his room, Kelly headed into hers to shower and put on her pajamas. Maybe she'd get started on another book. She figured she wouldn't get much sleep tonight…not with the man of her every fantasy sleeping only feet away.

Tomorrow, she would have to make a move. Time was running out.

Hell. He couldn't sleep. The image of Kelly in that damn bikini hovered in the forefront of his mind.

Maybe he should get that bourbon she'd gotten for him. Perhaps a little nightcap would help. It was nearly midnight and he hadn't heard her for some time. He'd listened to her showering earlier and he'd had to think of anything else other than her naked body so close.

There was no excuse for him lusting after her. He'd always found her attractive…any man with breath in his lungs would find Kelly Prentiss stunning. But he'd never looked at her in a sexual way—and now he couldn't see her as anything else.

Damn her for bringing him here and pulling these emotions out of him. Had that been her plan all along? To seduce him? Because she was doing a hell of a job.

He never mixed business with pleasure. He couldn't even hold an engagement together and keep his career. His job was his number one priority. Family loyalty meant everything to him, and in turn, that meant he had to give his all to Wingate.

Tossing his sheet aside, he swung his legs off the bed and headed for the door. Luke had on his own black boxer briefs which actually covered more than any suit he'd been given. He was at least comfortable, though back at home he slept nude. With a thin wall separating him from Kelly, he thought it best to at least have one more layer of protection.

Luke opened his bedroom door and headed toward the kitchen. The soft glow of light coming from around the corner made him pause. He took another step, then another, only to come up short and have his breath catch in his throat.

Well, damn it all. This is not what he needed in his line of sight.

He wasn't expecting to see Kelly standing there in some skimpy, silky blue romper with half her ass on display as she rubbed some aloe on her bare cheeks.

The way she was twisted around trying to hold up the hem of her practically sheer bottoms and rub lotion with her other hand all while trying to see behind her… which looked damn uncomfortable and near impossible.

An instant image of her in various other positions flooded his mind, and he cursed himself for even allowing that to happen.

Her eyes met his and she jerked her bottoms down as she straightened upright.

"Luke," she exclaimed. "What are you doing up? Did I wake you?"

Did she wake him? Hell yes she did. With the picture burned in his brain of her lying in that bikini, of her sashaying with those curvy hips, of her wet body from the pool…

There was no way he could sleep with all of those images rolling through his mind like some X-rated movie.

He remained still, the picture she'd made rubbing her backside now singed into his mind. "Couldn't sleep. I came to get some of that bourbon you mentioned."

And now he would need a double shot.

Luke motioned toward her. "You get burnt?"

Kelly sighed. "Yes. I put sunscreen on, but then I got so caught up in reading, I forgot to reapply. It's pretty painful on my…well, you saw."

He took a step forward, watching as her eyes widened. The unwanted lust and arousal slammed into him, but seeing a sexy woman in the middle of the night wearing nothing but silk would do that to any man… even if the woman was his assistant.

"Do you need help?" he asked. Why was his voice so husky? And why the hell had he offered his services? He couldn't assist Kelly…at least not in the way his body suddenly clamored to.

"Oh, um, no," she murmured. "I think I got it."

Silence settled heavy between them, and Luke wished he'd just stayed in his room. This trip was playing mind games with him, and he didn't even recognize his own thoughts. Up until now everything in his mind had centered on the company, but these last several hours had all revolved around torrid erotic fantasies involving his most trusted employee.

Was Zeke really trying to play matchmaker now that he'd found the love of his life? Was he wanting Luke out of the office to both take a break and have some fling? What was the goal, really?

Ezekiel had just married Reagan in some whirlwind Vegas wedding. The two were so in love, it was almost nauseating and definitely not something Luke believed would work for everyone.

Love sure as hell wasn't for Luke, and he didn't have time for any office romance, either.

"Do you want me to get you a drink?" she asked in that sweet tone of hers.

Luke jerked from his thoughts and shook his head. "I can get it. I'll probably go sit on the patio for a bit for some fresh air."

Kelly nodded. "Ok. Well, good night."

She stared another minute, her eyes landing on his bare chest, before she passed by him to go back to her room. It wasn't until that door closed with a soft click that he released the breath he'd been holding.

Damn it. He was going to have to pull himself together or he'd never make it out of this trip without surrendering to temptation.

Five

Kelly scooped up a seashell and rinsed it off as the tide rolled in. She ran her thumb over the smooth edges and slid it into the side pocket of her beach bag. As a child, she'd always loved looking for seashells when she'd gone on beach vacations with her parents.

That was something she and Luke had in common; they had both lost their parents when they'd been in college. Her parents had died within a couple years of each other, but Luke had lost his at the same time in a car accident.

Even though Luke was an adult, he and his brother, Ezekiel, were raised by their aunt and uncle, Trent and Ava Wingate. That's how Luke and Ezekiel had slid into the company.

Unfortunately, Trent passed away and a grieving

Ava had turned to Keith Cooper…who ended up being the downfall of Wingate, but that bombshell fact didn't come out until a very carefully placed wiretap.

The downward spiral of the company just seemed to steamroll with one unfortunate event after another between fake charges being brought against them, foreclosures of properties, and the embezzlement. Keith had been behind it all and would certainly pay for his crimes.

Sutton Wingate, the CFO, was doing all he could on his end to make the numbers work, but there just wasn't a way to bring this company back up from the ashes without some grand new project to give them that boost they needed.

That's why Ezekiel and Luke were feeling the pressure to make things right and eliminate the black cloud that had been looming over Wingate Enterprises.

The stress had just become too much and while Zeke had Reagan as an outlet, Luke only had his career. That's when Zeke had realized his brother needed to get away and clear his head.

Between all of the career ups and downs, Luke had been put through the ringer, but so had his personal life with the broken engagement a few years ago. Kelly had never been as happy as when his ex, Lily, had finally gotten out of his life. And as far as she was concerned, Lily had never been good enough for Luke. She'd been much too demanding, not understanding that Luke had an important role in Wingate and couldn't just take off on a whim. She never cared about Luke's feelings or his work, she had only cared about how big her ring was, or how fancy their wedding could be or having the grandest house in all of Royal, Texas.

And Kelly couldn't stand how Lily would look down on her when she came into the office. Like being an assistant was so far beneath a wanna-be trophy wife.

So when all was said and done, the broken engagement was for the best. Luke wasn't the marrying kind and clearly Lily didn't see that. Kelly knew exactly the type of man he was…and that's the sole reason a fling was her only option with the man she was so hopelessly infatuated with.

Moving on down the beach, she slid her toes along the wet sand where the tide kept coming in. She felt another larger shell and bent down to dig it out and rinse it off, too. Although she didn't know how long she'd walked, so far she'd found five shells that she wanted to take back to Texas. She wanted a reminder of her trip to this beautiful, exotic location.

And her trip with Luke.

That sounded ridiculous and naive, but she was the boss of her own little world and she didn't care.

She didn't see Luke this morning when she'd gotten up. Breakfast had been delivered at nine. She'd grabbed some fresh fruit and drank a mimosa before leaving and still hadn't heard a peep from his bedroom.

Maybe he was hiding or embarrassed after last night. Perhaps he was trying to figure out how to face her since he'd seen her bare ass?

All she knew was she hadn't missed the way he'd looked at her. The lighting might have been dim, but the raw passion in his eyes had been damn obvious.

He'd been turned on and those tight, black boxer

briefs did nothing to hide the fact he'd also been aroused.

Likely seeing any half-naked woman in the middle of the night would cause him to get turned on, but he'd never been turned on by her before…at least not that she knew.

Kelly turned and headed back toward the bungalow. She put on her yellow bikini and only threw on a white wrap around her waist. While she definitely needed less sun on her buns today, she still wanted to go back and get more sunscreen on her upper body.

She rinsed off her feet at the outside shower and left her bag and sandals on the chaise by the pool. The sun was already beating down and she couldn't wait to build on the tan she'd started.

Being stuck in an office for ten hours a day lately, she hadn't had much time for catching some rays. Not to mention December wasn't the best month to try to gain some color in Texas.

When she stepped into the bungalow, Luke stood at the breakfast cart picking at a piece of bacon. He glanced up and caught her eyes.

"Sleep well?" she asked, not really knowing how to break the ice. She also figured he hadn't slept too well if he'd needed the aid of some hard alcohol to assist him.

What was the protocol after your boss saw you rubbing your bare ass with aloe? Should she make a joke? Offer to rub *his* ass?

No, Kelly. Calm down. He was still her boss, he still deserved respect. She was just going to have to take this one minute at a time to see how he was going to handle everything.

The man had enough chaos in his life and here she was adding to his angst. She didn't want his worries to grow, she wanted to seduce him. She hadn't seduced a man before and she was starting to wonder if she was even able.

"After the bourbon and fresh air I slept fine," he muttered.

Okay. Well, clearly someone wasn't a morning person. He was always ready to go in the office in the mornings. How could he not be at such a dreamlike location? This place made her forget her worries...except for the fact she was sexually frustrated.

"I'm sorry about last night." Might as well bring out the proverbial elephant. "I found the aloe in the fridge so I just stood in here and applied it. Had I known you were awake, I never would've..."

He stared. Those dark eyes seemed to bore into her as if trying to uncover her deepest thoughts. He'd put on a pair of green shorts with a floral, very tacky button-up, but he'd left it completely open. How could the man make a tasteless tourist wardrobe look so darn sexy?

Maybe it was that bedroom glare, maybe it was the dark, black beard, maybe it was that exposed chest that made her want to run her hands over the taut muscles and chest hair... Or maybe it was the *entire* package that was still driving her out of her ever loving mind.

She'd asked for this. After all, she was the one who had brought him here under the guise of work. What did she expect? Of course his body would be on display. They were on a tropical island and the weather called for skin to be out...not covered up.

If only she had the green light to touch said skin she wouldn't be so cranky and frustrated.

Kelly cleared her throat. "Anyway, I'll be sure to stay in my room at night," she promised as she moved closer to grab a slice of pineapple. "The beach is beautiful. I found some really nice shells. I always collect some anytime I get to a beach. I keep a bowl of them on my desk at home to calm me when I'm feeling stressed."

He stared at her and she wondered why she'd started babbling and telling him random nonsense.

"Are there plans for the day?" he asked, clearly not impressed by her small talk.

She smiled. "Actually, yes. Later today we are getting a massage."

He stared at her once again. "A massage?"

"It's pretty much key to relaxing, Luke. I promise, you'll love it."

"Don't count on that," he told her. "I'd love to get my phone and check my work emails. That's what I'd love."

Kelly rolled her eyes and grabbed a strawberry. "Not going to happen. So, you want to swim or go to the beach or walk around the resort?"

"I don't even know what to do."

She couldn't help but laugh. "That's why I'm here," she informed him. "I'm going to teach you to relax."

"I'll relax when I think of a solution for Wingate."

Kelly actually felt sorry for him. He was wound so tight he couldn't think of anything else. She seriously had her work cut out for her.

"You know when you'll think of it?" she asked. "When you're not *trying* to think of it. I know that sounds strange, but it's the truth."

He reached for another piece of bacon and bit into it, then turned a mug over and poured coffee from the carafe. She waited while he sipped his java and continued to pick around at the breakfast.

"Why don't you get some trunks on and we can take a walk on the beach," she suggested.

"Didn't you just do that?"

"It's more fun with someone else."

"What do you do for fun back in Royal?" he asked curiously.

She'd worked for him for five years, and he knew most things about her, but she realized he never really asked about her personal likes or hobbies.

"Lately I've been too tired to do much else other than work, grocery shop, and do my laundry," she admitted. "I love to read and travel when I can. I've always been a beach girl at heart. Growing up we always vacationed at the shore. My parents chose a different beach locale each summer, so I guess that's where my love of travel also comes into play."

His brows drew in. "You haven't taken a vacation in the five years you've worked for me."

"No, I haven't," she agreed, pouring herself another mimosa. "When I first started working I wanted to be there to make a good impression and I couldn't afford to travel. Then everything went to hell. I couldn't leave when you needed me most. And now that we're trying to regain our footing and rebuild, I couldn't just take off."

"Yet you did," he reminded her.

She leveled his stare. "Because you're working yourself to death, which wasn't helping anyone. You'd gotten cranky with the staff."

"You mean with you," he corrected.

Kelly took a drink and shrugged. "I can handle your growling, but when I see that it's not just a bad day here and there and you're starting to form a long-term pattern, I need to intervene. I care for you, Luke."

There. She'd put that nugget of information out in the open and he could take the statement the way he wanted.

A corner of his mouth kicked up in amusement. "Are you my self-appointed keeper?"

She crossed her arms, still holding onto her mimosa. "I'm your assistant. I wear many hats under that title."

"Did you and my brother have a long talk about me?" he asked.

"We did. He's just as concerned as I am."

Luke sighed and raked a hand over his beard, the bristling against his palm had all of her nerve endings standing on edge. She could practically feel that coarse hair along her bare skin as he pleasured her.

"Then why didn't he say anything?"

Luke's demanding question brought her back from her fantasy. "Did you want Zeke to take you on a getaway?"

His eyes slowly ran over her body, giving her even more ammunition for her arousal. How could the man be so potent when he wasn't even touching her?

"We both can't be away from the company," he stated, his eyes darting back to hers. "Ava is just getting back into the swing of things and we need to support her all we can."

Kelly was proud of the fierce woman Ava Wingate had proven to be. After Keith had been pilfering money over time and destroying everything they had, she had decided to jump back into Wingate and make the company stronger than ever.

She was still fragile from all the heartache, but she'd always been a strong role model for Luke and Zeke.

"Then don't you think you should just listen to me?" Kelly asked. "Ava needs you at the top of your game, and one week will not make or break the company. With her and Zeke there, everything will run just fine. After all your family has gone through, I think you can take this time to regroup."

Luke came around to the other side of the breakfast cart to stand next to her. He continued to stare at her like he could read her thoughts…which was terrifying if he knew what she'd been thinking about him.

"Fine," he stated. "For the next five days, I'm yours. Do what you want."

Kelly nearly stripped his clothes off, but regained her common sense before embarrassing herself. The next five days would surely prove to be extremely memorable…and maybe just a little thrilling.

Six

"Are we having fun yet?"

Kelly laughed and he hadn't realized how sexy that soft chuckle of hers could be. Maybe it was because he was lying within inches of her on their private patio or perhaps it was due to the fact that his eyes were closed and his other senses were heightened. Or maybe it was because she kept wearing the skimpiest damn bikinis he'd ever seen.

"I'm having a blast," she answered.

"I'm not doing anything but sitting still," he grumbled.

"That's the point."

That made no sense to him. He needed his phone, he needed to be setting up meetings of potential investors, he needed… Hell, he needed to be doing something. He'd never just sat still before. What did that accomplish?

And not only was he sitting still without his work, he had to be subjected to this unwanted jolt of desire every single time he was around Kelly.

Which was all the damn time.

"Is Ezekiel meeting with—"

"No work talk," she demanded.

Luke sat up and swung his legs over the side of the chaise so he could face Kelly. She continued to lie there with her eyes closed, driving him crazy with those little yellow strings tied at her hip bones, and he knew good and well she heard him sit up. The woman might be the death of him.

If he didn't know better, he'd think she was doing this on purpose.

"How come you aren't this annoying in the office?"

Now she did turn to face him, pulling an arm over her forehead to shield the sun as she flashed him a smile.

"Because you're in charge in the office," she told him. "I'm in charge here. If you're getting restless, we can take a walk around the resort or down on the beach."

"I need to do something other than sit here."

She abruptly came to her feet and motioned for him to get up, too. "Go throw on something else and we'll take a walk. The resort is beautiful. We can go have a drink or something."

That sounded somewhat better. At least she'd be wearing more clothes, which would certainly help his mental state...and his growing attraction. He absolutely could not see Kelly as more than a friend or assistant. He refused.

Which is why he was going to push away all of those mental pictures of her in those damn bikinis and remember he was her boss. He could not cross that invisible line because there would be no coming back.

Kelly would much rather spend her time relaxing on the beach and catching some rays, but if Luke wanted to walk around, she'd go with him.

They made their way along the paved paths through the lush gardens and past other bungalows. The few couples they saw were walking arm in arm or holding hands. Kelly bit the inside of her cheek to keep from laughing. Probably not many boss/assistants on romantic getaways.

"Do you want to look in the gift shop?" she asked. "Maybe you'll find some other things to wear that aren't so bad."

Luke glanced her way and nodded. "Couldn't hurt."

"I mean, you do look like a tourist, so that's what you are. But if the plaid, floral, and tacky tees aren't doing it for you, then I guess we can shop."

"You are seriously getting your kicks out of this," he chuckled. "I'm sure you can't wait to get back to tell my brother."

Kelly laughed. "Oh, he'll definitely be informed of how well we spent his dollars."

They passed a couple of restaurants, one Mexican and one Italian. There was a buffet on the other side of the resort and a few other themed restaurants. Kelly loved that they could order from any of the places, or a combination of them, for any meal. So far, everything they'd eaten had been amazing.

They passed workers who merely smiled, nodded, and murmured a polite Aloha. Everything was so laid back and easy going here.

Luke reached the gift shop door and reached to open it, gesturing for Kelly to enter first. Even though he was a tad disgruntled, that Southern charm was always present.

"Aloha," the pretty female worker greeted. "What can I help you find?"

"We're just looking," Kelly told her with a smile.

"Let me know if you need any help."

Luke went immediately to the men's section and began perusing the swim trunks. Nearly everything was small, skimpy, and extremely garish. Kelly picked up a pair of boxers that claimed they glowed in the dark with little lips all over the material.

Kelly held them up and smiled, shaking the hanger. "How about a pair of boxers to match your trunks?"

He glared at her over the rack. "I've got my own, thanks."

She shrugged and hung them back up. "You can look here. I'm going to check out my section."

"See if you can find a suit that covers more," he muttered.

Kelly jerked. "Excuse me?"

His eyes met hers. "A one piece or something."

Irritation quickly slid into anger. "So you want me to get a different suit?"

"That would be nice."

She offered a sweet smile. "Sure thing. Anything to make you relaxed."

Turning toward the bathing suits, Kelly started

searching for the perfect one. She found something in white that she believed would work just right. She also selected a cute little backless sundress in a pale pink and a pair of colorful sea glass earrings.

Kelly went to the register and had everything charged to her card because she wasn't putting it on the room for Zeke to pay for. She grabbed her shopping bag and turned to see Luke empty-handed.

"Nothing capture your attention?" she asked.

He shook his head. "I'll make do with what I have."

Kelly shouldered the shopping tote and headed toward the door. "Well, I have a new suit so what do you say we grab some drinks from the bar and head back to the room? We can get changed and go down to the beach for a few hours."

"I could use a drink," he agreed.

As soon as they stepped outside, they headed to the bar closest to their hut and grabbed a few tropical cocktails. Kelly couldn't stand the silence or the questions nearly exploding in her mind.

"What was your issue with my suit?" she asked as they walked side by side.

"What suit?" he grumbled. "You've been wearing scraps."

Kelly bit the inside of her cheek. She wasn't sure if she should be pissed or amused. Either way, he noticed her and he was irritable. That was a great sign that her plan might be working.

"I'm getting sun and I'm on vacation," she reminded him. "Everyone has a home wardrobe and a vacation wardrobe."

"Not me."

She rolled her eyes as she sipped from her hot pink straw. "I'm not surprised," she retorted. "You don't go anywhere to need a vacation wardrobe."

They reached the door and he punched in their code. Luke held the door open for her and she brushed by him as she entered. She hadn't done it on purpose, but there wasn't much room. A small thrill shot through her. She didn't miss his swift intake of breath or the way that hard, muscular body felt against her own. Granted the moment only took a second, but it was enough to have her wondering if he was finally seeing her in a different way.

"I'll get changed," she told him as she headed toward her room. "Meet you out on the patio in five minutes."

"I've never known a woman who can get ready that fast."

Kelly tossed a glance over her shoulder. "It's the beach, Luke. There's not much to do. Besides, you've never been with a woman like me."

Seven

Luke stepped from his room just as Kelly did. He shouldn't have said a damn word about that bathing suit. Because he couldn't run the risk of her realizing that she was getting to him.

In any event, he hoped like hell she got something that covered her butt cheeks and her boobs. Maybe she found one of those surfer-style suits with the higher neck and sleeves. That would certainly help.

Or maybe it wouldn't. Kelly Prentiss was a hell of a beautiful woman. Even in the office, she was a head-turner. When they'd go out for meetings in restaurants or to meet potential investors, she definitely got the attention of men.

"Ready to go?" she asked, holding onto her straw bag.

At least she had on a cover-up that he couldn't see

through. She'd tied the wrap around her waist and pulled her hair up on top of her head. Just a few pieces fell down along her neck, caressing her creamy skin.

He seriously had to think of anything else so he didn't give away exactly what he was thinking. These damn lip bottoms didn't hide a thing.

"Let's go."

"I also have the butler bringing more drinks," she said as she headed toward the patio. "I told him we'd be on the beach so he is bringing them down there along with some snacks."

She thought of everything. If he wasn't so turned on by her, and angry with himself for allowing those unbidden emotions to slip in, he'd be impressed with how she continued to stand by him.

He couldn't deny that he would've been lost these past five years without her. From having his back in board meetings to rallying around him emotionally during the crisis, Kelly was one of the strongest, most loyal women he knew. She was absolutely invaluable to him in all aspects of his life.

He followed her down to the beach and to the cabana they had. Kelly sat her bag down and reached for the tie of her wrap. Luke adjusted his sunglasses and slipped off his flip-flops, turning them over so the sun didn't make them too hot.

When he glanced back up, he nearly choked.

"What are you doing?"

Kelly glanced to him, her hand in her straw bag. "Getting sunscreen," she said as she pulled out the green can.

"What the hell is that suit?" he demanded.

She glanced down, then back up. "You told me to get a new one. You like?"

She did a slow turn. The top barely covered her nipples and the back… Luke swallowed…was a damn thong.

"No, I don't like," he growled. "You're my assistant."

Kelly laughed as she sprayed her arms. "Does my status change with each suit?"

Luke rubbed his jaw. "You can't… I can't—"

She stopped spraying and stared at him.

"This isn't right," he bit out.

"What?"

He motioned with his arms, pointing toward her very tempting display. "All of this. You, me…all of your bare skin. You're my assistant."

Her lips quirked in a grin. "You keep saying that, Luke. I'm well aware of my job title, but right now neither of us are working. I assure you, if I was another woman on vacation with you, this bathing suit wouldn't be a problem."

She went back to spraying herself, totally ignoring him. Luke clenched his jaw. *Nobody* ignored him. And when the hell did she get so mouthy? Was she trying to drive him out of his mind?

Luke moved around the cabana, his eyes locked on her gorgeous body. He stopped inches from her and she instantly stopped spraying to stare up at him.

"Need some spray?" she asked, holding up the bottle.

"I need you to stop this," he commanded. "What are you doing to me?"

"Forced vacation, remember?"

He jerked his sunglasses off and tossed them to the

cabana bed before doing the same with hers. He wanted total honestly and he needed to see her eyes to try to get a read on exactly how she was feeling.

"You bought this suit to be spiteful."

"So what if I did?"

Those green eyes seemed to be even brighter out in the sun. They held him captive in a way he'd never noticed before.

"You didn't like the other one," she went on. "You told me to get something different."

"I told you to get a one-piece."

She cocked her head and tipped her chin in a defiant manner. "You don't get to give the orders here," she reminded him, pointing a finger into his chest. "If you don't like what I'm wearing, then stop looking at me."

Something in him snapped. Luke grabbed her finger and pulled her hand aside so he could step right up and into her face. He held onto her hand as his mouth came within a breath of hers.

"You think you're in charge?" he growled. "You think I can just stop looking at you? Wrong on both counts."

Luke leaned in, gazing into her eyes for a moment, silently making sure she was definitely on board. The intense desire staring back at him gave him no reason to stop.

He claimed her lips, ready to put them to better use than sassing him.

Never in his life had he wanted to kiss anyone more. He'd never been more sexually frustrated in such a short time and he'd never in his wildest dreams thought he would want his assistant in such a carnal manner.

Damn this woman could kiss. Her nearly bare body pressed against his as she met his passion with a heated desire all her own. He still held onto one of her hands, but her free hand came up to the back of his neck, as if holding him in place…

Had she been keeping this inner vixen bottled up? Did she have feelings for him or was she just taking advantage because he'd gotten in her face?

He didn't give a damn right now. There was a need, an ache that he needed to feed. Something burning inside of him that he'd suppressed for far too long.

Kelly's hips ground against his, and there was absolutely no denying exactly how aroused he was. No matter how irritated he tried to be, she knew the truth now.

"Excuse me, Miss Prentiss."

They jerked apart, his hand still holding hers as he turned to look over her shoulder. The butler stood there with a large tray full of snacks and drinks.

"I'm sorry to interrupt," he went on. "I just didn't know where you wanted these?"

Kelly stepped back from Luke and eased around him. "Thank you so much," she said sweetly. "Just set everything here."

She pointed to the table next to the cabana and pulled money from her bag for a tip.

Once the butler left them alone, Kelly turned back to face him. Her lips were swollen and damp, and he had to clench his fists at his sides to keep from closing the gap between them and finishing what he'd started.

"Are we going to talk about that or do you just want a drink?" she asked.

Was she seriously just going to move on to the refreshments? Like what just happened hadn't taken them across some invisible line they could never come back from?

"How long have you wanted to kiss me?" he asked bluntly.

"You kissed me first," she retorted. "So I guess I should be asking you that same question."

Fair enough.

"For about a day now."

She crossed her arms and shifted her hips as those breathtaking green eyes continued to hold him in place. "Well, I've been coveting your kiss a little longer. You didn't disappoint."

Kelly didn't say another word as she reached for one of the tall piña coladas with a bright pink flower on the side of the rim. She eased the flower out of her way before taking one long drink.

"This is amazing," she said, going in for another sip. "You ready for one?"

"How long?" he asked again, his patience at an all-time low.

Holding onto her glass, she glanced over her shoulder. "Years."

Luke remained still, absolutely stunned at her admission. How had he not known? How had he missed the signs? She'd never said one word or even flirted.

"That's a long time to keep your emotions to yourself," he told her.

"You were engaged and my boss, so that's not exactly a time to reveal my inner desires."

Desires. That word slipping through her lips had his body aching even more. He'd always known she was beyond brilliant, independent, strong-willed…but sexy hadn't entered his mind. And now that's the only word he could use to describe her.

"You didn't think I deserved to know before now?" he demanded, taking another step toward her.

"And when would that conversation have taken place, Luke? During a meeting where we were all stressed trying to bring the company from the ashes? Or maybe when your engagement fell apart? Tell me when exactly I should have opened up my most vulnerable thoughts to you."

When she sounded like that, so exposed and bold, he felt like a complete jerk.

Luke pulled in a deep breath and propped his hands on his hips to keep from touching her again.

"Would you have ever said anything?" he asked softly.

She dropped her arms at her sides. "I was letting my swimsuits speak for me."

He said nothing. What was there to say? He was sinking here and there was absolutely no lifeline anywhere in sight.

"Listen," she started. "We kissed. We don't have to do anything else. My attraction to you doesn't have to change anything, either. It's not like you're the only guy I find sexy."

Luke moved before he even thought about his actions. His feet slid through the sand as he shifted to stand directly in front of her.

"Do you kiss those other guys like that?" he demanded.

She tipped that chin again and he was finding he

wanted to nip at that as well. There had been way too damn much brought to his attention in the past day and he still wasn't sure how he felt about that... But he knew he needed to fix this ache, this gnawing need he had.

"I don't believe that's any of your business," she answered pertly.

"You just threw other men in my face," he countered. "You made it my business."

Her lips quirked in a grin and her eyes sparkled with mischief. "So what are you going to do with all of this information?"

Was she challenging him? Luke didn't know if he was amused, turned on, or peeved. Likely a healthy dose of all three.

"Figure out where the hell my mind is at."

He left her standing there as he went straight to the ocean, welcoming the cool water in a vain attempt to calm his raging hormones.

What the hell was he going to do? she'd asked. He had no idea, but he was stuck alone with her for four more days, and he had a feeling that kiss was a stepping stone to something much more.

Eight

As much as Kelly had wanted to follow Luke into the ocean, she'd decided they needed space. She lay on the cabana with her drink, and his since he ran away, and picked up her book.

Since the white material draped all across the top of the cabana, she didn't need sunscreen after all. She lay on her stomach reading, popping the fresh fruit and enjoying their piña coladas.

And thinking about that kiss.

Mercy, her boss could make a woman's toes curl. Her suit nearly melted off and that had nothing to do with the heat. The way he'd grabbed her, commanded her without a word, and then claimed her... Kelly's wildest fantasies hadn't even been that good

What would happen if they did more than kiss? If

her entire body had responded to just his lips, would she be able to even handle more?

Oh hell yes she could. She'd been dreaming of that moment for quite some time. As much as she found Luke attractive and sexy and intelligent—and pretty much the perfect man in every way—she also knew a workaholic like him would never share his life with a woman… Not when he had such a demanding career. Kelly had known that in advance, which is why she always told herself if she ever got the chance with him, they could only be physical. Nothing more.

She flipped the page in her book and took another sip of her drink. The sand shifted and water droplets splattered onto her legs.

Glancing over her shoulder, she saw Luke raking a hand over his hair, clearly the source of the droplets. She thought she'd only give him a glance, but a body like that really deserved so much more.

All of that dark skin with water clinging to those impossibly broad shoulders and then losing the fight as the moisture slid down over his muscular torso and right toward those lips on the front of his tight trunks.

At this point she really had no idea who was seducing whom, but she wondered if the battle of control would continue to volley back and forth.

"How was the water?" she asked.

"Refreshing." He glanced down toward the drinks. "Did you take mine, too?"

She rolled back to her stomach and put her mouth on the straw in lieu of an answer. Kelly flipped a page in her book, though she wasn't even focused on the actual words. She needed something to do with her shaky hands.

"I'll go get us more drinks," he told her.

"No need." She still kept her attention on her book as if everything in their little world hadn't exploded an hour ago. "I already asked for another round. The butler came by a minute ago."

"Will I be able to have my own drink this time?"

Kelly closed her book, grabbed the piña colada from the holder on the bed, and turned to sit up and face Luke. She smiled, though nerves danced in her belly at so many unknowns that would be facing them in the next few days.

"I ordered doubles, so you will get your own."

"How much do you plan on drinking?" he asked.

She shrugged. "Considering I'm on vacation, who knows. I do love a good fruity cocktail, though. I might have some wine with dinner. But don't worry, I'm also getting plenty of water."

Swinging her legs over the side of the bed, she came to her feet and held onto her almost-empty drink. "Were you concerned for me, Luke?"

"I just don't want you getting dehydrated."

She laughed. "Whatever you say. Lunch is also being delivered in about an hour, so if you want to swim or just relax here go ahead. I plan on heading to the ocean to cool off."

As she spoke, his eyes would dip to her body, then back up to her face. The man was fighting with his willpower, and she couldn't wait for him to cave and just take what he wanted. There was no way, from that red-hot kiss, that he didn't want her.

Honestly, she wasn't looking for some ring on her finger or happily-ever-after. Oh, she was attracted to his intelligence, his determination, his compassion for those he cared for.

But the man fueled literally every one of her fantasies. Dates she'd gone on over the years just didn't compare to Luke...not that she'd ever tell him that. His ego was growing by the minute and didn't need more help.

As she started by him, he reached for her arm and stopped her.

"You've intrigued me," he murmured. "I don't know what the hell to do about this. I'm still processing everything."

He eased her around so she faced him fully. She stumbled in the sand and threw her hands up. They landed on his chest, and he steadied her with both hands on his upper arms. She had no choice but to stare up at him as he loomed over her with that hard, wet body pressed to hers.

"The ball might have been in your court all this time," he murmured. "But now that I know the truth, I'm in control."

The way he delivered that delicious threat had her body heating up in anticipation and arousal.

"Sounds like fun," she replied with a smile. "Can't wait to see what you come up with."

Kelly pulled from his grasp and made her way to the ocean, knowing full well Luke's gaze was firmly planted on her ass.

"I think we need to focus on investors for our overseas resorts."

Kelly glanced across the patio table as Luke cut into his baked fish and attempted to discuss business. Seriously? Her body had been about to go up in flames all day and he was trying to talk shop?

"Save it for the boardroom." She stabbed one of her fresh pieces of pineapple and popped it in her mouth. "No work while we're on vacation."

His eyes met hers across the small round table. "That's the only way of life I know."

Kelly dropped her fork and curled her hand around her glass of sweet tea. "Luke, you honestly need a hobby or something to take your mind off work."

"Your kiss took my mind off work," he tossed back. "That damn strappy suit took my mind off work."

"Glad I could help," she joked with a smile. "Let me know anytime you want to be distracted again."

Luke sighed and eased back in his seat. He still hadn't put a shirt on, but she'd thrown on her wrap cover-up. Still, sitting here having a meal while barely dressed was a level of intimacy she'd never shared with him before.

"You think this is a good idea?" he asked gruffly.

"Whether it's a good idea or not is irrelevant," she countered. "That doesn't change the sexual tension between us."

"There shouldn't be any," he snarled.

Kelly couldn't tell if he was angry with himself for being turned on or if he was upset that he hadn't noticed before.

"I know you've had me in this nice little assistant box for a long time, but it's okay to move those boxes around."

He continued to stare at her, those dark, penetrating eyes seeming to go almost black. Oh, he was aroused and not happy about it. That delighted her more than she thought possible because that smoldering passion was no doubt going to explode, and she planned on being right here to enjoy it.

"I don't like change," he told her. "I don't have time for it. I have a company to save and a family that is counting on me."

Kelly laughed. "No wonder you're cranky. You don't make time for fun because it's not work."

"I have fun," he defended.

"Doing what?"

He shrugged. "I do things."

Kelly crossed her arms and pursed her lips. "Buying new cars or upgrading your jet doesn't count."

"Funny," he mocked. "For your information, I enjoy working out and running marathons."

That was news to her. Well, not the working out part. A man didn't get a sculpted body like that without putting in the time and effort. But she truly had no idea about the marathons.

"I've worked for you for five years and I'm just now learning about these marathons?"

Luke shrugged. "Should I come to work and display my medals in my office?"

No, he would never do something like that. When Luke Holloway was at work, his mind was solely on the job. But he'd never been one to brag which made him all the more attractive.

"So how many marathons have you done?" she asked.

"A few."

Kelly snorted. "Oh, please. What's the number? You

have your spreadsheets memorized, so you know how many marathons you've run."

"Forty-seven."

Her eyes went wide at that number. She was expecting him to say like five or even ten. But forty-seven? Good heavens.

"That's quite remarkable," she told him. "I assure you, if I ran forty-seven marathons, I'd sure as hell be hanging up those medals. The only thing I run for is the coffee pot first thing in the morning."

Luke eased back up and went back to his lunch. "Running is therapeutic for me."

"I'm ashamed to admit, I don't work out." She took another sip of her tea and grabbed her fork. "I try to offset that by eating somewhat healthy."

"Your body is just fine."

She glanced across the table to see his eyes firmly on hers. There went those butterflies once again. How could she have schoolgirl giddiness and very adult fantasies all rolled together?

Anticipation. That was the only explanation. She had no clue what was going to happen here and that level of the unknown might be just as thrilling as anything else.

"Speaking of bodies, our massages are scheduled soon." Kelly sat her cloth napkin on the table and eased her chair back as she came to her feet. "I'm going to go rinse off in the shower to make sure all the sand and sunscreen are off."

He sat back in his seat, looking all relaxed and sexy. "I don't really need—"

Kelly held up her hands. "Stop right there. You are

getting a massage. You will love it and you will thank me afterward. End of discussion."

His lips quirked. "Yes, ma'am."

Oh, she could get used to those words coming out of his mouth. She nodded her silent thanks and turned to head to the shower. Although she could have invited him to join her, she rather liked this sexual tension and naughty flirting. She also wanted him to make the next move. Kelly had laid out her feelings. Luke knew full well where she stood, so the ball was in his court.

But, that didn't mean he held all the power here.

Kelly made her way into her bathroom and stripped down as she stepped into the large open shower with the rain head. She fully intended to hold tight on the reins of control during this trip. However, she couldn't let her heart get involved, not with knowing Luke was cut from the same cloth as her father. Both workaholics with no time for anything else.

When Kelly entered into a serious relationship, she wouldn't settle for less than being first in her partner's life.

But, she wasn't going to turn down a fling with the one man she'd been fantasizing about for years. This was the chance she'd been waiting on.

Nine

Luke didn't do massages. He didn't do facials or ped-
icures, or any other spa, self-care nonsense. How did
people make time for this? His mode of relaxing was
running, and that was when his work schedule allowed.

He felt like he was on display here. Nobody had
warned him he'd be bare-ass naked with only a thin
towel covering his backside.

Kelly lay on the table next to him on the beach.
Which, thankfully, provided a delicious distraction from
his cringe-worthy state of undress. And he grudgingly
conceded that the sound of the ocean waves in the background did have some of the tension leaving his body…
or at least some of his work tension.

The sexual frustration was practically exploding all
around him because, every now and then, Kelly would
let out the softest moan and his entire body would

tighten with a need he shouldn't have for his assistant. He had to think of something else, *anything* else, before he embarrassed himself when he turned over to lay on his back. That towel wasn't going to be able to conceal anything.

Kelly might have told him not to discuss work, but that wouldn't stop him from thinking about it and all the ways he could potentially jumpstart Wingate.

That would definitely keep his hormones in check because there was nothing about this situation that was enticing. He carried the weight around everywhere, desperately seeking the answers to bring the company into the next phase of their future projections.

He sighed. Their loyal employees were counting on him; his brothers and aunt were, too. Granted, his family was also involved and everyone was working like never before to make this black cloud disappear. But with Luke being VP of New Product Development, he shouldered the majority of the responsibility.

Ava had taken him in when his parents had died and there was a large part of him that felt obligated to take this burden from her. She'd been through so much and she deserved to be cared for, to be protected from all of this.

The masseuse dug into that crook between his neck and his shoulder, and Luke nearly moaned himself. As much as he'd been against getting a massage, those hands were magical.

An instant image of Kelly running her hands all over his body instantly popped into his mind. He wouldn't mind giving her a rubdown as well.

Damn it. He was supposed to be concentrating on

anything other than Kelly and that body she kept displaying.

She was more than just sexy curves, though. That did not even *begin* to scratch the surface of what this woman was made of. He'd always known how intelligent and astute she was, and to that end, he never went into a meeting without her. Heck, his assistant was like the second half of his brain. If there was something he didn't think of, he knew she would. Many times she was already ahead of him and he'd never had to ask her to do anything twice.

But it wasn't until yesterday that he discovered just how persistent, demanding, and strong-willed she could be. All of that combined was too damn sexy and he was having a difficult time resisting her.

He *should* be resisting her. She worked for him, after all, and he had to keep reminding himself that if they entered into a fling and it ended badly, then what would happen? He couldn't risk losing her as an assistant or a friend. She'd been there for him through so much and there weren't many people he trusted. He had to keep everyone in those labeled boxes like she'd mentioned. Moving anything around would completely throw off his entire life.

"You can roll to your back now," the masseuse whispered into his ear.

She lifted the towel slightly as he turned to his back. Next to him, he caught sight of Kelly rolling over as well. That glimpse of side breast was seriously not helping him keep his hormones in check.

And this massage was doing the opposite of relaxing him. If anything, he was more revved up than ever.

He wanted her in the worst possible way but, for all the reasons he'd just listed to himself, having sex with Kelly Prentiss was a horrible idea.

Maybe he should think about Christmas instead. Less than a month away and he still needed to get Kelly something. He was so bad at this. For the past five years, he'd given her a hefty bonus. Even when the company was plummeting, he'd given her money from his personal account. She was too invaluable to not show his appreciation.

Yet now…now everything had changed and he was absolutely clueless.

Luke focused on breathing slowly, trying to get his mind to calm down from going a hundred different directions. However, trying not to think about Kelly next to him wearing nothing but these damn towels? Well, that proved nearly impossible.

But, regardless, he *had* to stay strong because too much was at stake. They still had four days here, and somehow, someway, he was going to have to muster some serious willpower to resist her seductive charms.

The massage was absolutely fabulous. Kelly finally felt relaxed and ready to tackle anything.

The masseuses left them alone on the beach to dress in private. She smiled, knowing the ladies had just assumed she and Luke were a couple. There was really no need to explain otherwise.

Kelly swung her legs over the side of the cabana and reached for her cover-up. She slid the simple black sheath over her head and came to her feet.

When she glanced back, Luke was laying on his side

staring up at her. Between that little towel covering his most essential parts and his skin glistening from the oils used during the massage, Kelly had to pull in a deep breath to calm herself. Gah! Even having normal thoughts around him was starting to become difficult.

"What do you have planned now?" he asked.

That low, husky voice reminded her of her fantasies. She knew full well what that voice would sound like in the dark as his body slid over hers beneath the sheets.

"Is there something you want to do?" she asked.

That naughty grin had her smiling right back at him.

"I know, that was a loaded question," she said before he could comment. "Dinner won't be for several hours still. We can always rent a car and drive around the island, or we could hang here and continue relaxing without thinking of work."

Luke's eyes raked over her, something he kept doing lately, and she didn't miss that hunger staring back at her. Was he about to suggest they go back to the room? Or maybe he'd tell her to lay back down with him, as they had their own private beach and she'd paid for total privacy.

She wanted him now more than ever. And the best part was that she knew the feeling was mutual. He'd been eyeing her for days and there was no longer a doubt in her mind that he craved her with just as much fervor as she craved him.

Even so, she assumed Luke was still battling between his professional and personal life—not wanting to mix the two considering their positions. She hoped like hell this was the one time he'd put his work mode on hold to go after what he wanted… She was banking on that.

"Exploring the island might be the best," he told her gruffly. "Staying here alone isn't the smartest idea."

Oh, she thought it was a *fabulous* idea, but she was also up for a little exploration.

"I'll go get ready and meet you in about thirty minutes," she said. "I know just where we should go."

He continued to hold her gaze. "You're not taking me to a nude beach, are you?"

"Now why would I do that when we could get nude on our own private beach?" she volleyed back with a smile. "It's a surprise, so go get ready."

"I'm starting to become afraid of your surprises."

Kelly laughed. "I just like to keep you on your toes."

Turning away before he could comment, she headed up the beach toward their bungalow. She'd done enough research online and made some calls in advance to learn the areas to explore that would be private and dodge all the tourist hot spots. After all, she still wanted this time for Luke to be relaxing, and she really didn't want to be around a bunch of people.

Kelly quickly showered and pulled her hair into a top knot. She threw on her black bikini, a pair of cut-off jean shorts, and a white tank. Then she slid on her canvas shoes, tossed some necessities into her beach bag, and checked her cell to make sure the car was ready and out front.

Zeke had left instructions with the owner to ensure the staff knew Kelly was in charge and anything she wanted would be at her disposal. She appreciated that, she truly did, but she couldn't imagine what all of this was costing him.

She'd come to realize that it paid to have money and people on standby.

There was nothing she wouldn't do for Luke and lying to get him here was something she would never regret…no matter how things turned out. Yes, she wanted him to cleanse his mind and get a fresh start back at work, but she wanted him to see her as more than his assistant and sometimes buddy. She wanted him to see her the way she'd seen him all these years.

With each passing moment, that was becoming a very real reality. Something was developing between them and she wasn't sure if this was just a physical bond or whether there was more. The anticipation was part of the thrill and she couldn't wait to see what today brought them.

But…the more she learned about Luke on a personal level, the more she wondered how difficult it would be to keep her heart out of the equation.

Kelly stepped out of her bedroom to find him waiting in the living area. He glanced up from his spot on the couch and came to his feet. She couldn't help but laugh.

"Another new outfit," she stated with a nod. "I hope you're going to sport some of this snazzy wardrobe back at the office."

He glanced down to the T-shirt that read "Don't Worry—Beach Happy" and the bright pink shorts.

"These clothes will never make it back to Texas," he growled.

"Aw, now you know that shirt would be a big hit at the next board meeting," she told him. "Why be so predictable with a suit and tie?"

He glared at her. "Because I'm the VP and nothing about this is professional."

"But it's fun. Remember that word?"

Luke blew out a sigh and started toward the door. "You keep reminding me."

Kelly shoved her cell into the bag on her shoulder and stepped out of the bungalow. The warm afternoon sun fell on her face and she was so excited to spend the day frolicking with Luke without a care in the world. Her greatest fantasy was coming to life and, for now, she was going to enjoy the moment and not worry about what would happen once they left this paradise.

As they made their way to the front of the resort, a bellman greeted them and opened the doors to the white Jeep that awaited them.

"How the hell did you get a vehicle this fast?" Luke muttered as they got closer.

"Stick with me and you'll have all the fun things in life." She sent him a wink. "Just kidding. Zeke left his card and said I was to use it as I saw fit."

Kelly circled the hood and jumped into the driver's seat, thanking the resort employee for his help. When Luke settled in beside her, he turned to her.

"Where are you taking me?" he asked.

She put the Jeep in gear, so glad they had given her one with the top off, and adjusted her sunglasses.

"You trust me?" she asked.

Luke merely chuckled as she tore off out of the resort, heading for their day of fun.

There was still that guilt that seemed to have settled in deep. The guilt for being away from the office, the guilt for enjoying the hell out of this flirtation with Kelly, and the guilt that he still hadn't found a way to save Wingate.

Luke glanced from the picturesque blue water to the woman in the driver's seat. That glorious red hair blew all around her shoulders and face. She drove with a smile as she tapped her fingers on the steering wheel as if she had a steady beat in her head. He'd never seen her so calm, so free and spirited.

Something shifted inside of him. Something he couldn't quite put his finger on. All he knew was there was so much more to Kelly than he'd ever realized. She was more playful, more alive, and vibrant...and a hell of a lot sexier than he'd ever imagined.

She hadn't a care in the world right now. In the office, she was always on top of everything, her mind often worked like his and they were always in sync. Now though, she had clearly pushed Wingate aside and was solely in the present. Part of him envied her that she could compartmentalize her life in such a way.

Kelly loved Wingate just as much as he did, so it wasn't that she didn't take her job seriously. Her title might be assistant, but she really was so much more. She busted her ass to make him look good in front of potential investors. Her spreadsheets and slideshows were spot on for each board meeting and he was always proud to give her the due credit she deserved.

In the distance behind Kelly, the mountains peaked. There was something extremely calming about Oahu. He'd never been before and any time he traveled, he never did so for pleasure, or even with a female companion.

Everything about this trip was foreign to him. How could he ignore these strong, albeit brand new, emotions he was having for Kelly? Was it smart to even think about acting on them? They were just so damn potent, but he had to wonder if that was because they were alone on a tropical island that just screamed romance and sex.

Romance and *sex* were definitely two words he had never associated with her, but they were all he could think about now.

What started out as a crazy plan from his brother had quickly morphed into an incredible adventure. How could he not enjoy himself here with Kelly? Maybe if he made more time for decompressing, he'd be at the top of his game.

Kelly tried tucking her hair behind her ears, but the wind continued to whip it about. He had a sudden image of that hair sliding over his body as her mouth explored him and his tacky shorts just got a bit tighter.

Kelly pulled onto a narrow road leading away from the ocean. He wanted to ask again where they were going, but he knew she wouldn't tell him. She was having way too much fun with all of these surprises and, other than the terrible wardrobe, he was having a pretty good time. That massage had been amazing and the food had been incredible.

When she pulled the Jeep over on the side of the road and killed the engine, he glanced around to the base of the mountains and the rocky area surrounding them.

"We're here?" he asked.

Kelly climbed out of the vehicle and grabbed her bag from the back. "We are. Let's go."

He didn't know where they were heading, but he obliged and followed her. He wasn't one to typically take orders, but again, he couldn't deny this was part of the appeal of Kelly and this impromptu trip.

The rushing water seemed to echo off the rocks. He heard before he saw, but as soon as they walked a little farther and rounded the bend, Kelly stopped and gasped.

"It's even more breathtaking than they said," she murmured.

Luke came up beside her and stared at the rushing waterfall as it flowed into the crisp blue water below. It seemed so far away, yet still close enough to touch.

"I was given a tip about this place," she told him, her eyes still locked onto nature's beauty. "It's a waterfall only the locals know about and it's usually pretty private."

She started toward the path that would take them down to the base and Luke set out behind her. Beyond the beauty of this place that amazed him, he was also stunned at all the trouble she'd gone to now that they were here. Zeke might have footed the bill, something Luke would discuss when he got back, but Kelly had planned all the fun. This was only their first full day in Oahu and he had no idea what else she had in store.

Once they reached the bottom, Kelly sat her bag on the ground and toed off her shoes. When she slid that tank overhead, leaving her in only short denim shorts and a triangle bikini top, Luke had to fight back the urge to grab her and see if those kisses from earlier were still just as hot and arousing as he remembered.

"Want to get in?" she asked, that voice and smile so damn tempting.

"You didn't tell me to wear a suit."

Her eyes widened. "I didn't? Oops."

She unbuttoned her shorts, and he watched as they slid down her tanned legs and she kicked them aside. She stood there in her black bikini that looked like the other one that drove him insane. So much skin practically begging for him to explore with his hands and his mouth.

"Maybe you could jump in with your boxer briefs," she suggested. "They'd be no different than the trunks you have."

He took a step toward her, then another, until they were toe to toe. She tipped her head up to keep him in her sights.

"I'm not wearing any underwear," he told her.

Her face tinged a pretty little pink and, for the first time since he'd known her, she'd gone speechless.

"Well, then…" she stammered. "You can just, uh, I guess you can go skinny dipping. Nobody is here."

Luke took a step back and reached for the button on his shorts. Her eyes locked right onto his hands and that hunger and desire he saw had lust pumping through him. He couldn't exactly act on his attraction here in the open. Granted they were secluded, but anyone could come down at any time.

Luke decided since she'd teased the hell out of him, he'd turn the tables. He released the button and reached behind his back to grab a fistful of his T-shirt. He tossed it to the ground and couldn't help but swell with pride as her bright eyes traveled all over his bare torso.

He shouldn't be relishing in having his assistant look at him like he was everything she'd been starving for, but he couldn't deny that he wanted those eyes on him. He wanted her hands and her mouth on him, too. Damn it all…he wanted her and everything about that was completely wrong.

What would his family say if he came back from this and there was a shift in the dynamics between Kelly and him? Because if they ended up having sex, nothing would ever be the same back at Wingate. Hell, he'd already done everything in his mind so how could anything ever go back to the way it was before?

When he unzipped his shorts and started easing them down, Kelly pulled in an audible breath as her eyes widened.

"You big liar," she swatted at his chest. "You wore underwear."

"Oh, did I?" he asked. "Oops."

She continued to grin as he tossed her joke back in her face, but she still had that passion heavy in her eyes.

"Race you," she called a second before she took off toward the water.

Luke had barely gotten out of his shorts before he was issued the challenge and took off after her. She beat him by a step and he was surprised how warm the water was as it lapped up around them.

Kelly continued to laugh as she dipped her body

down and came back up. He'd never been so jealous of water droplets in all of his life. They ran over her bare shoulders, they ran between her breasts, they ran down her abdomen. Everywhere he saw a trail of water, he wanted to lick it.

"This feels amazing," she exclaimed. "I'm so glad I found out about this."

She had to nearly shout because the waterfall echoed. He'd traveled all over the globe for business, but he'd never seen a more beautiful sight than Kelly with all that wet, bare skin with the most spectacular waterfall in the background.

The water came to his waist, but he made his way deeper to where she stood. As he approached her, her breathing seemed to come out in pants and those green eyes mesmerized him in a way he'd never been before.

This was Kelly. His Kelly. The woman who spent more time with him than any other woman ever. Even when he'd been engaged, Luke still spent the bulk of his days at the office—something his ex never could understand.

Luke didn't reach for Kelly, but the way the force of the water kept rushing against them, there was no way to prevent their bodies from rocking against each other.

"You seem relaxed." She reached up and smoothed her fingertip down the space between his brows. "No worry lines. That's a first for you."

That simple touch snapped the very last bit of will-power he had. Luke took her hand and flattened her palm against his chest as he rested his free hand against the curve of her hip. He gripped her, pulling her pelvis closer to his.

The tips of her fingers dug into his chest and she tipped her head just enough for him to lean down and feather his lips across hers.

With their bare torsos suctioned together by the water, their hips held together from his grip, Luke wanted more.

He opened his mouth and covered hers, taking what he wanted and damning the consequences. She opened for him just like before only this time he knew what to expect. He knew how hard this punch of desire would hit him and how he might never recover from such an impact.

Kelly slid her hand up to his shoulder and around the back of his head. She gripped his hair and gave a slight tug, only adding to his arousal. He never knew how much an assertive woman would turn him on, but she'd shown that her ability to take control in any situation was damn attractive.

Luke reached around, grabbing her entire backside and lifting her body against his. Kelly wrapped her legs around him, grinding her hips, silently begging for more.

They were out in the open. At any given moment, another couple, a family, hell an entire tour group could start coming down, and he didn't care. He wanted Kelly with a fierceness he didn't even recognize within himself.

"Luke."

Even over the roar of the waterfall he heard her panting his name. Considering he wasn't used to her in this capacity, the newness of everything had him desperate for more, had him wondering how soon they could get back to their private bungalow where he could show her exactly what he wanted to do to her.

"Not here," he murmured against her lips. "I want you, Kelly. Just…not here."

She eased back, those bright eyes sparking with desire. "You can't tell me that and then put the brakes on. I've wanted you too long, Luke."

She was right. He couldn't imagine the need she'd had for so long. He'd only just come into these overwhelming emotions and she deserved to at least have the edge taken off. Luke wasn't so sure he could wait either, but he would for her. He wanted her in bed and in private, where he could show her exactly how much he hungered for her.

With one arm banded around her waist, Luke used his free hand to slide between their bodies. He grazed his fingertip along the elastic at the curve on the inside of her hip, causing those hips to jerk again.

She settled into his touch, wrapping her arms around his neck and resting her forehead against his. When he eased his finger beneath the edge of her bottoms, Kelly let out a cry and nothing could stop him from pleasuring her now. He wanted to take all of her passion, he wanted to *own* it.

Luke eased his finger into her, gritting his teeth as his own arousal continued to spike. This was all for Kelly, though. Later, he vowed, later they would take their time and explore each other.

Suddenly all those reasons this was a bad idea completely vanished from his mind. Nothing mattered except Kelly and giving her everything she wanted, everything she'd been waiting for.

He continued to pleasure her, sliding his thumb over her core to add even more to her experience. He wanted this to be perfect for her, he wanted to be remembered and branded in her mind forever.

How the hell had he come to this? Kelly was too damn powerful with this invisible hold she had over him. Damn it, he wanted her more than his next breath, and he wished like hell they would have stayed back at their beach house.

Her body jerked faster as he continued to touch her in just the right spot. Getting to know her body in such an intimate way wasn't something he ever expected... and now he didn't know how he could do without.

Kelly continued to cling to him as the wave of pleasure overcame her. Luke continued to work his hand against her, drawing out every bit of ecstasy. There was so much more he wanted to show her, to *give* her, but this would have to do for now.

When her body calmed, Kelly eased back and stared into his eyes.

"Luke, I—"

He quickly cut her words off with a kiss, then pulled back.

"No words," he rasped. "Whatever is happening here, we just need to let it happen."

He never thought those words would come out of his mouth, but this woman had changed so much within him in such a short time.

Kelly pulled in a shaky breath and shook her head.

She unhooked her legs from his waist and smoothed her hair from her face.

"Fine," she breathed. "But just know when we get back to the bungalow, I plan on returning the favor."

And with that wicked promise she dove under the water and took off swimming toward the waterfall.

Eleven

Kelly's body tingled the entire rest of the day. Once they left the waterfall, she ended up driving them around the island, hitting some local shops to buy trinkets she didn't need. She'd never expected to have had such a memorable day.

From the waterfall in Luke's arms to traveling around an exotic location with a man she was falling for, she couldn't imagine what else was in store for them the rest of their days here.

Kelly sighed. She didn't *want* to be falling for him—she had initially thought she could keep her heart out of this equation. But apparently some things were beyond her control. Even so, there were still too many parallels between Luke and her father. Kelly had seen the way her mother had suffered, vying for the attention of the man she loved. Kelly always vowed she would never let herself get into such a position.

She had to keep reminding herself that she couldn't hinge a life after this with Luke. He would go back to his job and she would go back to being his assistant. There would be no happily-ever-after or ring on her finger. And she was okay with that. This was her greatest fantasy and she would ignore the reality that awaited them when they returned to Texas.

Once they were back at the resort and headed toward their bungalow, the anticipation continued to build even higher, faster. Kelly wanted him out of those silly clothes and she wanted to explore every delicious inch of his body.

Luke stepped up to their door and punched in the code. As soon as they stepped inside, she noticed their dinner had been delivered and was set up out on the patio. The cart with everything extra sat in their dining area. There were rose petals leading from the front door, down in the sunken living area, and on out to the patio, circling the table.

She certainly hadn't told the resort that this was a romantic getaway. She knew Zeke had tipped heavily in advance for extra privacy, to keep the drinks and snacks always stocked, and only notify her if they needed anything. She didn't want Luke interrupted by anything or to be distracted by any outside issues…hence the electronics ban.

"I didn't realize we were gone so long," she told him.

Kelly went to take her shopping bags to her room. When she came back out, Luke still remained by the front door, but his eyes were solely on her. And there it was. She had hoped that hunger in his eyes back at the waterfall wasn't just because he'd pleasured her and that he fully intended to fulfill his promise that they would pick up where they'd left off once they returned.

And apparently that wish was not for naught.

"Do you want to go eat?" she asked.

Luke stripped that shirt off once again. She would never tire of seeing that magnificent physique on display. There was so much to take in, so much to admire and appreciate. Starting with that dark chest hair splattered over his smooth, satiny skin and trailing down to his ripped abs. And *hot damn*! Where had that dragon tattoo, which covered his entire back with a portion coming around his side, come from?

She'd never seen his ink before, and he'd never talked about it. Now she was even more curious about the man she'd been intrigued with for years.

"Dinner can wait."

Luke stalked toward her like a panther to his prey and Kelly took a step back. The closer he got, the more she eased back, excited for the thrill of the chase. She'd never guess he would be this commanding, this *primal*. The way he looked at her with a need so intense, she couldn't wait to fulfill his every fantasy.

Fantasy…that was the word she had to keep focusing on because that would certainly keep her heart protected. Nothing about this was real and nothing would be long-term.

When her back hit the wall next to her bedroom door, Luke came right up against her, resting one hand on the side of her head and then caging her in with the other hand.

That bare, muscular chest kept rubbing against her tank, and she wished he'd strip her out of her clothes. She wanted to feel him against her like she had at the waterfall. There was nothing stopping them now, no chance of being interrupted or seen.

Luke's dark eyes remained locked onto hers as he eased one hand between them. He never looked away from her as he jerked the snap on her shorts. Kelly reached down and shifted her hips from side to side as she wiggled out of them. When the shorts fell to her ankles, she kicked them aside.

Smiling with pure male satisfaction, Luke gripped the hem of her tank and jerked it up and over her head, leaving her in only her bikini and him in his black boxer briefs.

Exchanging a few heated kisses in the waterfall was one thing, but what was about to happen now was entirely different. He'd never seen her completely naked and vice versa. She wanted those briefs gone. She wanted to fulfill her promise of returning the sexual favor.

Kelly had waited so long for this and, as much as she wanted to hurry and get to the good stuff, she also wanted to take her time and relish every single moment and every single touch.

She arched to reach behind her back to undo the strings of her bikini top, but Luke beat her to it. He had those knots ripped away in record time. The garment fell between them, leaving her entire chest exposed. Then he did the same to the strings along her hips.

Suddenly, she stood before him completely naked and more turned on than she could ever remember. Luke took one step back, his eyes raking over her from head to toe. He made no apologies or excuses; in fact, he said nothing as he took in all of her in her most vulnerable state.

And Kelly didn't mind one bit. She wanted him to look. She wasn't shy of her body and, from the hunger in his eyes, Luke most definitely liked what he saw.

"Take them off," she ordered, nodding to his briefs.

With a crooked, naughty grin, he continued to stare back at her as he hooked his thumbs in his waistband and shoved the briefs to the floor. He kicked them aside and merely stood there with his hands on his hips.

If she looked as chiseled and perfect as Luke, she'd go around parading her body, too. Suddenly, she didn't feel so confident about her own.

Kelly started to cross her arms, but Luke stepped forward and gripped her wrists. He held her arms out wide and left plenty of room between them so he could see her entire body.

"Never hide from me," he commanded. "Nothing this beautiful should ever be hidden. You deserve to be explored, to be treasured."

Kelly swallowed, unsure of what happened to make him switch from putting a stop to this, to suddenly wanting everything she was willing to give.

"I didn't expect you to be so..." She knew she sounded ridiculous and likely her cheeks were flushed. "Perfect and well-toned."

"While I appreciate that, I want you to know that this body of yours has driven me out of my mind," he admitted. "Someone who wears a thong in front of her boss shouldn't be embarrassed to be naked."

She smiled and shook her head. "It's not that I'm embarrassed, per se, but I guess I just want to be everything you want…if that makes sense."

He pulled her hands to his chest and stepped against her, trapping their joined hands.

"You are everything I want right now."

Right now. Another reminder of how temporary all of this was.

"I guess I'm nervous," she admitted. "I've wanted you for so long, I just—"

Luke cut her off with his mouth on hers. Kelly opened for him, glad he'd taken control because she didn't want to think, she only wanted to *feel* and to return this passion he offered.

He lifted her against him, as he'd done at the waterfall, and she locked her ankles behind his back as he carried her into his bedroom.

Suddenly she was being tipped backward, and she landed on his soft bed. Luke went down with her, his weight pressing into hers on the mattress. His arousal settled perfectly between her thighs and she had to muster all of her willpower to not cry out.

The waterfall climax had taken some of the edge off, but she wanted so much more. She wanted to explore him and take their time. She wanted to know what made Luke come undone…and she wanted to see him lose control because of her touch.

"Do you have protection?" she whispered against his lips.

Luke eased back and shook his head. "I wasn't planning on this when we left."

"I have condoms," she admitted. "I *was* planning on this."

His eyes seemed to grow darker. "Where are they?"

"My room. In the drawer of the nightstand."

Then he was up and off of her. Kelly glanced out the patio door to the ocean and drank in the backdrop of the orange sunset. This was really going to happen, and she couldn't wait.

Her focus shifted back to the bedroom door when Luke stepped in fully naked and wearing the protection. The way he crossed the room to climb back up onto the bed had her sitting up on her elbows and pulling her knees up, ready for him to settle back where he'd just been.

"You look so damn sexy," he said as he loomed above her.

His hand went between her legs and Kelly bit her lip as intense pleasure pulsated within her. Then that touch vanished a second before he gripped the sensitive spot behind her knees and jerked her legs back even farther.

She kept her gaze locked onto his as Luke joined their bodies. There was no way to keep from crying out and arching against the glorious sensation.

With her legs dangling over his arms, Kelly reached out to grip his biceps. The muscles strained beneath her touch as Luke continued to work his hips against hers.

She couldn't control her moans and sighs, not when this felt so good and even more intense than she'd ever fantasized about.

Luke gripped her backside, lifting her farther into him as he increased the pace. This new position completely undid Kelly as her climax overcame her. She dug her fingers into his arms and called his name, begging him not to stop, begging him for more.

She knew he followed her in his own release with the way he'd stilled and held her so tight, like he never wanted to let her go.

Luke stayed with her until his body stopped trembling and then he slowly released her legs and came down to lie half on her, half on the bed. With one long leg and one strong arm draped across her, she'd never felt more protected or cherished. Yes, this was just sex, but to her this moment was so much more....

Kelly kept her eyes closed as if she could remain in this euphoria forever. Opening her eyes would bring back the reality that they weren't on this romantic getaway as a real couple. Rather, they were here because she'd tricked him.

She wasn't contrite, though. Luke needed the break and she'd wanted to see if they could be more. She couldn't be sorry for going after what she wanted.

His warm breath fell on her shoulder, sending even more tingles through her body. The low hum of the large fan suspended from the peaked ceiling relaxed her and settled her nerves. While she'd always wanted this to happen, she was never sure it actually would, and she certainly hadn't planned for how to react after.

"Should we go eat now?" he murmured against her shoulder.

Kelly was relieved he was the one to break the silence. She trailed her fingers up and down his arm across her chest.

"I'm in no hurry to get out of this bed," she answered honestly.

Luke came up on his elbow and glanced down at her. Those dark, heavy-lidded eyes had gone all soft and sexy. She wondered what he was thinking, but she wasn't going to be that woman who wanted to have postcoital chat sessions. She didn't need reassurance that he enjoyed himself or that he wasn't having regrets. She knew Luke enough to know that he wasn't ready to run out the door.

"How about I bring dinner in here?" he suggested.

Having dinner in bed with Luke sounded like a dream, but she couldn't let herself get too wrapped up in this fantasy world. Because as much as she wanted this to be reality, Kelly also had to use her head here.

"Let's eat outside," she told him. "It's so beautiful here, I want to take advantage of it before we go back to Royal."

His lips quirked into a grin. "And here I thought you just wanted to take advantage of me."

Kelly couldn't help but laugh. "I think it's you who took advantage of me, remember? You stripped me as soon as we got inside."

"*You* seduced me with this trip."

She reached up and ran her fingertip along his stubbled jawline. "You've been seducing me for years," she murmured.

Luke's face sobered as he leaned in closer. "How did I miss this?" he whispered against her lips. "How did I not see you?"

He folded her into his embrace, holding her on top of him as he rolled to his back. Kelly straddled his lap and braced her hands on his chest.

"I take it dinner can wait?" she asked with a grin.

He reached up with one hand, gripping the back of her neck and pulling her down for a kiss.

Dinner would most definitely have to wait.

Twelve

"So how did you guys choose this place?" Luke asked.

Kelly sat in the cabana, staring out at the darkened ocean and the starry sky. The calm, warm breeze washed over her, and everything in her world seemed so right, so perfect.

For now, while they were in this island paradise, she was going to just live in the moment and not worry about Wingate or her job or what would happen once they returned. Nothing mattered but Luke.

Their time was running out, though, and she knew there would be no romantic evenings after this trip. Her boss would go back to diving headfirst into work and ignoring the rest of the world. She had to brace herself for that because this wasn't a trip designed to make him fall in love…this only started out as a means of relaxation and seduction. And while she'd taken the risk and it had paid off, there was no way she would risk her heart; that was a sure bet to lose.

Kelly glanced over her shoulder to where Luke lay reclined beside her. He wore nothing but a pair of black boxer briefs and she had on a wrap cover-up with nothing beneath. They'd eaten dinner on the patio and had come down to the cabana once the sun had already set. They had complete and utter privacy.

"Zeke found the resort and showed me one day. Once I saw the place, I was in love and started planning," she told him. "He knew you needed a break and he needed me to accompany you pretending the trip was about business. I knew this was my only chance to show you how I felt. I couldn't do it in Royal or near the office."

Luke slid his fingertips over her arm and braced his other arm behind his head. She would never tire of seeing him like this. So relaxed, so…unencumbered. The man was sexy as hell in a suit, but seeing him on a tropical island all wet and bare-chested, highlighted by the sun, did something else entirely to her.

The physical attraction had always been there, but as she'd gotten to know him, she'd appreciated his loyalty to his family. Not to mention the fact that when things got tough, he still stuck around. She'd dated a few men who fled when things got complicated instead of trying to work things out.

Stability hadn't been too strong in her personal life over the past several years. Her career was all she could cling to and Luke had always had her back. But she knew he couldn't be there on a long-term-relationship level. Luke wasn't made up like that and ultimately that's what she would need.

"This place is perfect," he agreed softly. "So...you ready to tell me why you never revealed how you feel?"

"We've already been over this," she reminded him. "The timing was never right and I couldn't take that chance."

"I never took you for someone to back down from what you wanted."

Kelly smiled and turned back to the breathtaking ocean view. She pulled her knees up in front of her and wrapped her arms around her legs.

"I did go after what I wanted," she said. "I just took my time. Patience is everything."

Luke sat up next to her, the cabana shifting with his weight. The man wasn't just formidable in the board-room, he emanated power everywhere. All big and dominating and absolutely perfect. She couldn't find a single flaw with Luke Holloway.

"You dated while you've been employed with me," he murmured. "There have been flowers on your desk from time to time."

Kelly nodded. "That's true. I even dated a guy for several months about a year ago, but I was never really into them. I wanted to be. I wanted to get you out of my mind because I kept telling myself this was wrong. I mean, how cliché can I be to want to have sex with my boss? That's not professional and how would the rest of the employees react if we were...you know."

Luke's chuckle vibrated against her. "You think I'd send out an office email and inform everyone we had sex?"

"No," she laughed. "But the dynamics between us have changed and someone might pick up on that when we get back. I worry how that will look for me."

Luke reached over and slid a finger beneath her chin, turning her head to face him.

"Nobody will know a thing," he assured her gruffly. "We went away on a business trip and that's all."

Kelly really didn't know how she'd go back to work and see him in that capacity after being so intimate with him here. She knew how he tasted, how he touched and liked to be touched, what it took to make him come completely undone…

"It sounds easy enough," she agreed. "But I'm not sure I won't be able to stop—"

"From jumping me on the boardroom table?"

"No, silly!" Kelly laughed again and swatted his chest. "I was going to say I won't be able to stop from staring at you and I hope nobody picks up on that."

"Maybe I'll be the one caught staring at you," he tossed back with a grin. "Did you ever think of that?"

Kelly swallowed and shook her head. "I never thought this would actually happen. I wanted it to, but I wasn't sure you'd ever see me as more than just your assistant."

He gripped her chin between his thumb and finger again. "First of all, you have always been more than *just* an assistant. I wouldn't get anything done without you. You deserve more credit than what you give yourself."

His words warmed her deep into her heart. She knew he valued and appreciated her. Luke had always been the best boss and treated her with such respect. Even if she wasn't halfway in love with the man, she would love him simply for the way he treasured her.

"Second," he went on. "Since my engagement ended, I don't do much with dating or even looking to add someone into my life. I'm devoted to Wingate and determined to grow our product line."

"Your ex wasn't right for you."

Kelly hadn't meant to let that out, but now that she'd expressed her true feelings, she didn't care that he knew.

"Did our engagement affect how you felt?" he asked.

Kelly didn't want him to think she was looking to slip into that role of trophy fiancée. "Despite wanting you, I wasn't looking for more. I just didn't think she fit into your world. She seemed to… I don't know. Needy."

"She was," he agreed. "I'm glad I realized it before we married. I wasn't in love with her and she wanted a social status that she thought I could give her. It seemed like a good fit at first, but I seriously dodged a bullet with that one."

Marrying someone like Luke Holloway would certainly give someone a bump in their standings. It would get someone invited to the poshest parties, an automatic in with the elite Texas Cattleman's Club and money would never be an issue. Luke would give his woman everything she could ever want, and he would totally treat her like a queen.

Kelly never wanted a man to take care of her, she was more than capable of taking care of herself. She wasn't looking to marry Luke, she'd just wanted him in her bed. She wanted him to make her feel alive, to fulfill these fantasies she'd had for years.

But now that she knew they would make one hell

of a team in the boardroom *and* the bedroom—it still didn't change anything. Because when it came down to it, they wanted different things out of life.

"She didn't find the work hours too appealing," Luke went on. "She wanted the prestige and the money, but without the work."

"Well, that's impossible, especially during crisis mode."

Luke snaked an arm around her waist and hauled her back down onto the bed. "I don't want to talk about my ex anymore," he told her brusquely.

That was something Kelly could definitely get on board with. She'd rather talk work than the woman who used to wear Luke's ring.

"I didn't even know I needed this," he stated after a minute of silence. "You were right."

Kelly snuggled deeper into his side, tucking her head just beneath his chin. "I'm always right."

His laugh vibrated against her cheek.

"What?" she asked. "I am. Where would you be without me? You've admitted you couldn't live without me in the office and now I'm right about you needing this break."

"I would have never left for anything other than meeting with an investor or finding a way to fix Wingate."

He didn't have to admit that, she knew, and that's why she had to essentially lie to him to get him on that plane. When Zeke approached her, he'd told her there would be no way his brother would meet with anyone without her by his side. He trusted her with every aspect of his business.

"I should feel guilty for deceiving you," she finally said. "But I honestly don't."

"You could have seduced me in Royal."

"As I told you before, the timing was never right." Kelly eased back and rested on her elbow to stare down at him. "And that's not the sole reason I brought you here. I really was worried about you and so was your brother."

"He's just as much of a workaholic."

"That's true," she agreed. "It's in your blood, but he does know when to take a day off here and there to give himself some space. Everyone needs to recharge at some point in time. And besides, he has Reagan."

He tucked her hair behind her ear and trailed his fingers down her cheek. Her body had never really calmed since the waterfall and now each touch and each smoldering gaze from Luke only revved her up all over again.

"How many more days do we have?" he asked.

"Three." Not long enough. "I have a fun day planned tomorrow, but if you want to stay here and be lazy and naked, I can cancel."

Luke smiled. "You've gone through so much to get everything organized and planned."

"Think of it as part of your Christmas present," she told him. "Though I didn't actually pay for anything here."

Now he did laugh. That low, rumbling laugh that she rarely heard since he was so consumed with work. She wanted more of that in her life…she wanted more of that for him.

Ugh. This couldn't be happening. She could not fall

for her boss. There was no room in his life for her and
she would not fall down that same loveless hole her
mother did.

"I better step up my game for you," he joked. "I
haven't even started shopping, but I typically get you
the same thing each year."

"I'm not worried about my Christmas present, Luke."

There was nothing else she wanted from him than
what he'd already given her. This whole trip was much
more than she'd ever hoped for.

"Why don't you just promise to take more time for
yourself after you get back?" she asked. "That would
be a great present, because then this wouldn't have all
been for nothing."

He eased her back and came to hover over her. The
way he always maneuvered her to where he wanted her
was just another layer of sexy she hadn't anticipated.

"You can ask me for anything," he told her. "Consider it yours."

Could they try to keep a physical relationship once
they returned? Was that even possible? Because at this
point, she wasn't sure she could just turn off that switch
and act like nothing had happened between them…

But was continuing their sexual liaison something
Luke wanted? Was he even thinking that far ahead?
She wanted to give him some time to get used to this.
She'd had years to accommodate to her feelings, but
everything was still so new to him.

"No Christmas present necessary," she reiterated.
"There's nothing I need." *But then again…*

Kelly eased her knees up beside his hips to allow
him to settle in between her legs. Then she laced her

fingers behind his neck. "Or maybe we could come up with something you could give me."

Nodding approvingly, Luke slid his hand up the hem of her cover-up and found her more than ready. She cried out and pushed into his touch.

"I'm sure I can do something for you," he promised.

Making love by the ocean in the dark of the night was a moment she would never forget. Kelly hoped this was just the beginning of their intimate relationship and that her boss would want to keep things going once they returned home.

Thirteen

"I didn't take you for someone afraid of heights."

Luke held onto the edge of the deck and stared across the vast expanse of trees and lines. Nothing like looking like a complete wimp in front of the woman who went to so much trouble to prepare these plans.

"I'm not afraid of heights," he scoffed, trying not to lose his breakfast. "I'm just…getting acclimated, that's all."

"Sir, you do not have to go," the worker assured him. "We have people all the time that back out. It's different once you get up here and see."

"I'm not backing out," he stated.

Damn it, he *wouldn't*. He ran a multi-billion-dollar company and he'd never shied away from a challenge in his life. There was nothing he'd ever turned away from when he wanted it. And he damn well wanted to impress Kelly right now.

"Do you want me to go first?" she asked, placing a gentle hand on his arm.

He glanced to her, finding her absolutely adorable in her protective gear, with worry glimmering in her eyes. She'd do anything for him. She'd proven that over and over again. Now he needed to man up and show her that he wasn't someone who couldn't have a good time.

Unfortunately, his idea of a good time was hitting the weight room or going for long-distance runs. Nice things on solid ground. That was more his style.

Flying never bothered him, but this…this was a whole different level of crazy. Now there was just a thin cable holding him up and he wasn't necessarily a small guy.

"I'll go first," he gritted out, ignoring the churning in his gut. "Let's do it."

He listened once again as the worker went over the basic rules and what to do at the other end. Finally, he stepped to the edge, pushed aside the fear that nearly took him out at the knees and just stepped off.

The second he dropped and started gliding, he squeezed his eyes shut. But then something changed within him. His trepidation gave way to exhilaration and the smooth ride seemed almost *liberating*. Luke opened his eyes to see the treetops below and the bright beautiful ocean in the distance. Before he knew it, he was landing on the other deck and another worker was patting his back on a job well done.

Luke turned in time to see Kelly's big, wide smile as she rushed toward him from the cable. She was absolutely breathtaking like this. And apparently had needed this adrenaline rush just as much as he did.

Something shifted inside him once again. There was something about her that propelled him to take risks, that had him wanting to know even more about what made her smile like she hadn't a care in the world.

"You did it!" she exclaimed. "Did you like it?"

Luke nodded as he was assisted in removing his helmet. "I did. It was pretty awesome."

"I really am sorry I terrified you."

Luke didn't want pity, good grief that was like just adding salt into the wound. He might as well turn in his man card.

"Honestly, I didn't know heights bothered me that much until now," he admitted.

"Do you want to go again?" she asked.

There was a sparkle in her eyes that he couldn't resist. This woman was a risk-taker, which was a hell of a turn-on. He wanted to see that smile more. He wanted her to be happy. And most importantly, he wanted to be the man to ensure that joy never faltered.

This side of Kelly was not one he typically saw in the office and he realized he wanted to keep uncovering those layers to find out her true essence.

He dropped a kiss to her lips. "Let's go."

After several hours of zip-lining and hiking through trails along the mountainside, they headed back to the resort in their Jeep. Kelly loved the freedom of driving with the top down along the ocean road and having Luke by her side made the experience even more special.

"How about a walk along the beach?" she suggested once they were back inside their bungalow.

"Sounds good to me."

She slid her arms around his waist and stared up at him. "I really am sorry you were scared earlier. I just assumed—"

"That I was brave?" he laughed. "Don't tell anyone I nearly passed out looking at treetops."

"Your secret is safe with me," she assured him. "We're all afraid of something."

His brows drew in as he tipped his head, studying her. "You've found my kryptonite. What's yours?"

Kelly's heart clenched. What she *truly* wanted, more than anything was a family of her own one day. And a solid, loving relationship with a man who would put her first. But that man could not be Luke, no matter how much she might want him to be. There was no use in getting her hopes up or even letting her mind go in that direction. She'd been with him for five years and it wasn't like one week of great sex would reprogram this incurable workaholic.

"I think a girl needs to keep some secrets." She smiled and kissed his bearded chin. "Let's get our suits on and go to the beach. Maybe wear that suit you had from the first day."

"That tight thing? It will cut off circulation to the most important parts."

Kelly slid her hand between them and cupped those said parts. "Well, we certainly can't have that. I have plans for us later."

He instantly jerked against her palm. "Later?"

She couldn't help but smile as she eased her hand inside the waistband of his shorts for full-on contact.

"Now is fine, too."

Luke groaned and dropped his head back. This is what she wanted. She wanted him to come undone for her, knowing she'd caused him to release such passion. For now, he was hers, and she planned on taking full advantage...*literally.*

She eased his shorts down to his ankles and dropped to her knees.

"Kelly—"

"Let me," she whispered.

His hand went into her hair as she started to pleasure him. She had never done this to any other man and she only wanted this level of intimacy with Luke.

As she continued to stroke him, his hands tightened, pulling her hair just a bit and she knew he was getting closer to the edge. She increased her speed, hoping she was doing this right. But clearly he was enjoying himself and that's all she really wanted.

When the climax overtook him, he grunted her name over and over and the moment turned her on more than she ever dreamed possible. Who knew pleasuring someone else in such a way would be so arousing?

Kelly waited until he was finished before coming back to her feet and adjusting his shorts back into place. She stared up at him, and he smiled back at her.

"I still owed you a favor," she reminded him. "It's not the waterfall, but I couldn't wait."

He framed her face in his big, strong hands and pulled her within a breath of his face.

"You're going to be the death of me," he murmured. "What am I going to do with you?"

Was it too soon to ask about continuing this physical relationship once they returned? He was still adjusting to this fantasy life they were living. And she knew everything might be entirely different once they were back in Royal.

Would he still be married to his work or would he find a way to make room in his life for her?

She was reminded yet again of growing up with a father who was a workaholic. Kelly and her mother always came in behind board meetings or work trips. Her father loved them in his own way, but he just prioritized his life in the wrong order.

Luke had done that with his fiancée, but they weren't compatible so...what all did that mean? Would he consider putting her first in any manner?

Wanting anything more than a fling was so naive, but there was that sliver inside of her that wondered if anything more would be possible. Kelly shouldn't allow her thoughts to stray, yet there they were. She was human and had waited so long for Luke to see her as more and now...hell. She was in trouble. She knew it, but how did anyone just turn off feelings?

"Hey."

Luke's intense stare and calming word pulled her away from her thoughts.

"Sorry," she told him. "I was daydreaming."

He slid his thumb across her lower lip. "I'd love to hear about your dreams."

Kelly hadn't expected that. She hadn't expected him to want to learn more about her as a person, so maybe he *was* interested in exploring more. With every fiber of her being, she wanted someone to share her hopes and dreams with, someone to confide in, someone she could discuss her day with.

She couldn't help but smile at the idea of going to work together and coming home and unwinding with a drink cozied up on the couch.

Damn it! Why was she going there again? She couldn't want more with him, she absolutely could not. An intimate relationship was pushing it once they returned. Asking or wanting more was just waiting for a crushed heart.

"Let's go take that walk on the beach," she told him. "Then maybe we can have a relaxing swim in our pool later after dinner."

"During the sunset," he added. "I never thought I'd appreciate a sunset until I spent this time here with you."

He had so much going on with his family and with Wingate Enterprises. What would happen if they got back home and he left all these feelings behind? Would he just go back to business as usual? Would they keep their affair a secret?

There were so many questions swirling around in her mind. Kelly wished she had all the answers, but all she could do was continue to guard her heart and show Luke she wasn't ready for this to end.

"I think we're late for dinner again."

Luke wrapped his arms around Kelly as they sat in the sand. She'd nestled between his legs and leaned back against his chest as they watched the sunset over the ocean. He didn't recall ever feeling this calm or stress-free before. And, while he wasn't sure if this was because of the tranquil atmosphere or Kelly or the amazing sex, part of him never wanted this to end.

The other part knew he had to get back to Royal and

help his family pull Wingate back from the brink. There were so many people counting on this company to keep them employed and that was aside from his own family. He wanted to make something grand happen so he could ensure Ava kept her beloved company and didn't have to sell off anything else just to live. She didn't deserve that and Luke was damn well going to be the one to save Wingate.

Yet for the past couple of days, he'd forgotten all about his phone and work emails. He'd forgotten the burden that would be waiting for him upon his return.

All he'd wanted to do was lose himself in Kelly and this place. She'd whisked him off like some dream, knowing exactly what he'd needed to pull him out of the work cycle he'd been drowning in.

He hadn't seen it for himself—or maybe he hadn't wanted to. But Kelly had. She'd been in tune with him from day one. No matter what he'd needed, she'd been there by his side. How had he missed the fact she had personal feelings for him?

Because he'd been utterly consumed with saving the world, at least that's what it felt like most days, and he'd had complete tunnel vision.

That's what had ended his engagement, though he wasn't sorry that had happened. The feelings he had for Kelly over these past few days far surpassed anything he'd ever felt before.

And that scared the hell out of him.

"You're thinking," she murmured, wrapping her arms around his over her chest. "I can practically hear you."

"Just thinking of work," he admitted.

Kelly tipped her head back and stared up at him. "That's not allowed."

He kissed her forehead. "I know, but I'm just wondering how you could be so aware of what I needed and I couldn't see that you had feelings for me."

"Who said I had feelings? Maybe I just wanted to jump your bones."

Luke laughed. "Because I'm wide awake now and I can see it. You wouldn't have gone to all this trouble for seclusion and you sure as hell wouldn't have been intimate with me if you didn't harbor strong feelings."

She rested her head back against his shoulder and crossed her ankles out in front of her.

"No, I wouldn't have," she admitted. "But I also know this intimacy is all we can have. I won't play second fiddle to anything, not even a career. I just wanted you to see me as more and I wanted to take this chance to make that happen."

Oh, he saw her. He had no idea what to do now with all these emotions raging inside of him. Hearing her say she wouldn't come second to anything made sense, but there was a ping of disappointment that she agreed they couldn't be more. Clearly that's what he had thought, but having the words out in the open seemed so final.

But what about a physical relationship? Who said they had to stop once they returned to Royal?

Only time would tell, and their days here were quickly coming to an end. They would both have to decide what would happen once they returned home and Luke had to find out if there was room in his life for anything other than Wingate.

Fourteen

Kelly let herself back in the bungalow after going to the gift shop once more. She'd seen a new sundress she wanted in the window the other day, but had gotten sidetracked by Luke and hadn't gotten around to buying it. So she'd left him out on the patio drinking by the pool after their lunch and finally purchased it. She couldn't believe they were leaving tomorrow morning. A part of her wanted to stay here forever, but they had to get back and start work again.

Not to mention the Christmas parties coming up, and then rolling into the new year, which would mean more meetings regarding the best ways to increase sales and generate new ideas for the company.

Kelly snuck into her room where she still kept her clothes, but she'd been spending her nights in Luke's bed. She slid into the new strapless white dress that hugged her curves and had a wide slit going from her ankle to mid-thigh.

She made her way to the patio and stepped outside. Luke stood facing the ocean with his back to her, clearly still wet from his time in the pool.

"You like?" she asked, holding her arms out to the side.

He turned around and his mouth dropped. "That's damn sexy."

As much as his compliment warmed her, she couldn't help but notice what he was holding. Kelly's arms dropped to her sides as she took a step toward him.

"How did you get your phone?"

He had the widest smile on his face. "I saw you punch in the code once and I'm glad I did because I just had the best idea and I couldn't wait to text Zeke about it."

"What was that?"

As much as she didn't want work life to interfere with what they had here, they *were* leaving tomorrow. She just wished she could've kept him from this for one more day. She wasn't ready for that other life to creep in on their alone time.

"Why don't we package our resorts to couples?" he suggested. "Instead of trying to appeal to families or corporate events, I think we should look into romantic getaways. Honeymoons, anniversaries, just-because trips. We need to market those to make guests feel like you and I do. Like work doesn't exist or matter and they can escape from their problems."

But work *did* exist and he was proving that. She

wanted to take that phone away…she wanted to focus back on them. But Luke had been away from work for four days now and, clearly, he couldn't take it anymore.

"That's great," she told him, forcing a smile. "I'm glad you came up with a solution that will work."

"Do you really think it will?" he asked.

That was one other thing about him. He always valued her opinion and seriously wanted her input on each phase of anything he worked on at Wingate.

"If we can get guests to feel like us, then I think our hotels will skyrocket with bookings. You would have to think of not only the rooms and how that is laid out, but also the staff. You would need the couples to feel like they are one-on-one with a particular staff member. For instance, they need to be on a first name basis and know they can call upon one of our employees for anything at any time."

Her mind started working even though that was the last thing she wanted. But she couldn't help herself. Maybe a little of Luke rubbed off on her.

"Privacy will be the key to any couples' retreat," she added. "You want them to feel like they are living in a dream."

Luke stepped forward, set his phone on the patio table and slid his hands around her hips. He glided those talented fingers up into the dip in her waist and higher until he reached the top of her dress where it stopped just at the swell of her breasts.

"Is that what you feel like?" he asked huskily. "Like you're living in a dream?"

Kelly pulled in a deep breath as arousal coursed

through her. The man had barely touched her, and she was ready to go up in flames. Would he always affect her this way? Would she always want him with such a fierceness that she couldn't even describe?

"I *am* living a dream," she admitted, closing her eyes to his touch.

Luke peeled the dress down over her chest, leaving her bare to the warm, evening breeze.

"You're so damn sexy, Kel."

He'd never called her by a nickname before and, now that he had, she couldn't help but wonder if they'd reached a deeper level of intimacy.

His thumbs raked over her nipples and she wished he'd tear this dress off of her...who cared that she'd just bought it. Having Luke lose his control and have his way with her would be worth it.

His cell vibrated on the table and she nearly cursed.

"Leave it," she begged.

He hesitated for a split second and she thought for sure he was going to reach for it, but he ended up lifting her into his arms and walking inside.

"I have more important things to tend to," he told her. "Work can wait."

Her heart leapt with joy. She'd never seen him put work on hold for anything and now he was putting it on hold for her...for them. Maybe Luke had changed over the course of this trip.

He carried her into his room and sat her down at the foot of the bed. She'd gotten wet from his trunks and bare skin, but she didn't care. A man who looked like Luke should never be clothed. Kelly could stare at him all day long and never tire of it.

Her hand went to his side, where she saw the tail of the dragon tattoo.

"What's this about?" she asked.

"Strength. After my parents died and Ava took Zeke and me in, I vowed to remain strong no matter what. I vowed that I would take care of my family, my friends and never let anyone fall."

Which was why he was so damn protective of Wingate. She understood his burning need to save the company, but he couldn't keep carrying the weight of the world on his shoulders.

"I never thought a tattoo could be such a turn-on," she murmured, tracing her finger along the point of the tail and back up the other side.

His body trembled beneath her touch and he kept those dark eyes locked onto her.

"What am I going to do with you?"

She smiled. "You keep asking that. When are you going to figure it out for yourself?"

In lieu of an answer, Luke dipped his head and captured one breast. Kelly's head dropped back as she closed her eyes and slid her hands through his hair to hold on.

The way this man could drive her wild with the simplest of touches was amazing. She whispered his name, begging him for more. And that's when his hand found that slit in her dress that stopped just shy of being indecent.

She'd put nothing on beneath when she tried the dress on, always eager to give him easy access.

"I take it you like my new dress," she murmured.

His hand found her core, and Kelly stepped wide to allow his touch to work over her.

"I'd love you out of it even more," he muttered against her skin.

She gripped the material below her breasts and shoved the stretchy dress down her body. Luke only released her for a moment to get the garment out of the way before he was back on her.

"I need you now," he told her, lifting her to toss her onto the bed.

Kelly laughed once again, because the man went from erotic to playful so fast, she couldn't keep up. Always keeping her on her toes and wanting more.

He climbed onto the bed and rested a hand on each side of her head.

"I want you," he repeated. "Without a barrier."

His words sunk in and that's when she knew he cared for her more than she thought. He wouldn't want to be this intimate if this was just a casual fling.

Kelly eased her legs apart to accommodate his large frame. "I'm clean and protected without anything."

That jaw muscle clenched as his nostrils flared. He was hanging on by a thread. She could read him so easily now.

With this knowledge, Kelly locked her ankles behind his back and urged him closer to where she so desperately wanted him to be.

Once he sank into her, she couldn't help but cry out. Every time they were together she wanted more. She wanted to consume him and never stop loving him, both physically and mentally.

She did love Luke. There was no denying the facts and, quite possibly, she'd loved him for a long time.

But now she could admit it to herself and not be

worried or afraid. Because she had a feeling he might be falling, too.

"You're so damn perfect."

Those whispered words falling from his lips only heightened her arousal. He was everything to her and she wished she could tell him she loved him.

But she had to wait. There was no way she could pour her heart out to him this soon. He might not believe her and she didn't want to scare him off or confuse him. There was too much going on in his life with his family and the company. Adding to his stress would get them nowhere.

His body rocked harder, faster, his lips seemed to travel everywhere. He covered her face, her neck, back down to her chest, where she instinctively arched to his mouth. Her legs tightened even more around his waist and, with all of the pleasure points being hit at the same time, Kelly lost control and fell over the edge.

Luke followed her, ravaging her mouth as he went, and Kelly kissed him back, hoping her passion and love would come through without saying a word. She needed him to know just how special he was to her and just how much she wanted to be with him.

As they lay in his bed in the silence of the aftermath, Kelly wondered how long she could hold out before confessing that she'd fallen in love with her boss.

Fifteen

The flight back proved to be business as usual. Kelly tried not to take offense. They were, after all, away from the resort and the fantasy they'd been living for five days.

Luke sat across from her on his phone sending emails, then talking, then sending more emails. She had her laptop, but it remained closed at her side. The only reason she'd brought it to begin with was to keep up the ruse that they were meeting with an investor.

She wasn't in the mood now, though she knew there would be plenty of emails and work she could get done. Nothing needed her attention until Monday. She planned on taking tomorrow off and trying to transition from exotic island to Royal, Texas.

"This is going to be amazing," Luke exclaimed, setting his phone at his side. "I need you to take some notes."

Kelly pulled up her phone and sighed. Yup, they were definitely back to business as usual.

"We're going to throw a lavish party," he started. "We're going to have it at the Clubhouse and this needs to be bigger and better than anything we've ever done."

"How soon do you want this?" she asked.

"Next weekend."

Kelly stared across the aisle at him. "Luke, you can't possibly plan something of this magnitude in such a short time."

"Oh, I'm not planning it," he corrected. "We are."

She laughed. "You're insane."

"No, I'm optimistic," he told her. "Listen, we need to do this. My mind is back working overtime and you were so right when you said I needed this break. I know exactly how to fix Wingate and we are going to unveil our plan to our family and friends and look to the future with hope. It's Christmas, Kelly. There's so much to celebrate right now."

Having a festive, holiday party and the big reveal of his idea seemed fun and exciting in theory, but how in the hell would they pull this off?

"Do you even know if the Clubhouse is available that day?" she asked.

Luke merely raised a brow and she realized her question was ridiculous. If Luke Holloway wanted something, he was going to get it.

"Ok, so the venue is done." She made a note in her phone. "What about food or music or decorations?"

"I'm putting you on decorations," he stated. "You've used that one place before."

He snapped his fingers as if trying to recall, but

Kelly chimed in with the local company and typed in its name.

"Music and food can be done easily," he told her. "The club has people on file and we will use their services."

Kelly made some quick notes to follow up with all of these people tomorrow...clearly she'd be working Sunday instead of waiting until Monday.

"You've thought of everything," she told him with a smile. "What about banners or pamphlets for guests to see what you're envisioning?"

"Yes, that's where I really need you." He stood up from his seat and crossed the narrow space to sit next to her on the sofa. "We need to pull up all of our resorts and do mock-ups of exactly what we plan on adding to each place. We have to list the new amenities specifically designed for the couples."

He started naming off several things and she was typing as fast as she could. Maybe she should have brought up her laptop.

By the time they touched down in Royal, Luke was ready to go. He'd already made several calls and had set up meetings...for tonight...as in Saturday night.

Kelly wasn't surprised, but she was still disappointed. Although she should have realized that, the second he was back, the old Luke would take over and hit the ground running.

Perhaps that's part of the reason she loved him. The man was diligent, determined, and let nothing stand in the way of his success. He didn't work for the money; he worked to make things right, to help his family get back their tarnished reputation and regain footing with their company.

As they made their way toward their vehicles, Luke put Kelly's suitcase in her trunk. He had his own suitcase and she honestly didn't know if he'd packed any of his tacky resort wear or if he just had his suits inside. He'd worn a pair of navy dress pants and a dark gray dress shirt for the ride home. But she knew exactly what was beneath all of that. There were no fancy clothes that could erase her memory of every mouthwatering muscle he had, because she'd explored each and every one.

"I'm heading to Zeke's to discuss the plans," he told her, shoving his hands in the pockets of his dress pants. "If we can get this in motion quickly, then we could use all of these pre-bookings at the resorts to really pull the company back up."

"That's a solid plan," she agreed. "Just don't rush too much or everything could backfire and then we'd be worse off than we are now."

He shook his head and sighed. "I doubt things could get worse, but I refuse to let that happen."

Kelly felt his angst, knew the turmoil and the worry that flooded him. She'd seen it firsthand over the past several months. His family had been through hell at the hands of someone they trusted and Luke bore all of the weight of the company upon his shoulders. He didn't want to burden others; he wanted to be the one who came up with some magical resolution.

She also knew how much he loved Ava and appreciated all she had done for him after his parents passed. And Kelly understood that, deep down, his gratitude was the driving force behind him wanting to be the white knight who swooped in and saved the day for the woman who basically raised him.

"Come back to my house," he told her.

Kelly was surprised those words came out of his mouth. She hadn't been sure exactly where they'd land once they returned, but she had planned on letting him set the tone and the pace.

"Aren't you going to see your brother?"

Luke nodded and took a step toward her. He reached for her, curling his hands around her shoulders and pulling her close.

"I am, but I want you at my house when I get back." He dropped a kiss to her lips, then eased back. "I want you by my side through this."

As his assistant or his mistress…or something more? She wanted to ask, but the pain laced with worry in his eyes had her simply nodding in agreement.

"I'll be there."

"You know the code to let yourself in, right?"

Being his assistant for five years had given her access to nearly everything in his life. She'd never been to his house for more than quick drop-offs or pick-ups for various work things, but she wasn't about to turn down his invitation. This might be their chance to see if they could be more.

"Good luck with Zeke." She stepped back and opened the driver's door. "I'm going to pick up some things at my place and then I'll be at yours."

Luke smiled. "I like the sound of that."

Then he turned and went to his vehicle and Kelly was

left wondering exactly what he was thinking as far as they were concerned.

All she knew was Luke had recharged and seemed more hopeful than she'd seen him in a long time. Maybe he needed her emotional support, maybe he wanted more. No matter what, she still had to guard her heart. Even though she'd fallen for him, she still realized Luke wasn't going to put aside his work to make her first in his life. No matter how much she wanted a family and a husband, Luke could not fill that role. All she could do was enjoy their time together until it came to an inevitable end.

"It's genius."

Luke released a sigh of relief and sank back into the leather sofa in his brother's living room. Zeke sat across from him on the other sofa with his wife, Reagan, by his side.

His brother and sister-in-law had found love in the most unconventional of ways. A fake relationship for a front fell apart, but the two had married in Vegas anyway...and then fell in love. A little backward, but everything worked out in the end for Zeke and Reagan. Luke couldn't imagine them apart. They were so perfect for each other and complemented one another in every way.

Reagan slid her hand over Zeke's thigh and offered a sweet smile. "Luke, you have been so stressed lately. It's nice to see you relaxed. Wherever you went on a trip sure did wonders for your smile."

Luke wasn't about to admit anything or why he was smiling so much. Kelly had pulled something from him he hadn't even known was so hidden and buried. After

months of working so damn hard, staying up count-
less nights, worrying if he'd ever come up with the answer, Luke finally had a solution, and he only had her
to thank.

"Kelly played a huge part in coming up with this
plan," he admitted. "She's brilliant."

"You're a lucky man to have such an amazing right-
hand-woman," Reagan stated.

Assistant seemed so odd a term now. A week ago
Kelly was his assistant and now, well, she was his assistant, lover, and he wasn't sure what else to label her, because he was still trying to figure all of this out himself.

Between Wingate and his unexpected feelings for
Kelly, Luke really had no idea which way to direct his
attention right now. There was so much going on at
once, tearing him from one side of his heart to the other.

He cared for Kelly, there was no denying that. Making any type of label beyond that was naive and foolish.
Just because his brother had found the love of his life
didn't mean that was in the cards for Luke. He had much
too much on his plate right now to feed a relationship.
Look at that past engagement? That had been a disaster.

"Kelly *is* amazing," he agreed. "She's working right
now on getting the arrangements all set up for the party
at the Clubhouse this Saturday."

"So I take it you're not angry with me for deceiving
you with this getaway?" Zeke asked.

Angry? How could he be angry? That had been one
of the best weeks of his life. But he didn't like that
Zeke paid for everything and he would be rectifying
that soon. He just didn't want to get into a financial ar-
gument right now.

"You look like a different guy," his brother added. "You don't have those frown lines and you don't look so pissed off at the world. Maybe we should incorporate forced vacations quarterly to keep everyone at the top of their game."

Another trip with Kelly? He sure as hell wouldn't turn that down.

"I hate admitting you were right," Luke stated. "But we need to push forward and focus on this party this weekend."

Zeke chuckled. "You don't waste any time, brother."

"We don't have the time to waste. We need these pre-sales. That money will help launch us into the next phase."

"This is big," Zeke agreed, sliding his hand over Reagan's. "I knew you'd stop at nothing to come up with some miracle way to preserve the company."

Pride swelled within him. Luke hoped like hell this plan worked and would help protect the jobs of their two hundred workers. This next plan wasn't just about saving his own ass, but looking out for those who would have to seek employment elsewhere if something happened to Wingate.

"It's not going to solve everything," Luke replied. "But, it's a solid start that will have our shareholders and investors believing in us again. This will definitely boost everyone's moral."

"I think it sounds wonderful." Reagan beamed as she patted Zeke's leg. "You and Kelly have really outdone yourselves with this plan."

Luke knew his brilliant assistant was the backbone of his operation. He literally couldn't do his job to the best of his ability with anyone else by his side. Never in his life had he thought he'd find someone so compatible in the boardroom and the bedroom.

So what the hell did that all mean?

"Beyond the amenities—" Luke went on, forcing himself to stay focused on work "—we should add in upgraded packages for when someone really wants to impress or go all out. We can offer up private jet transportation and a car once they reach their destination. Our guests shouldn't have to worry about one thing once they book with Wingate."

Reagan's smile widened. "This will be a total sellout," she announced.

"I couldn't do any of this without Kelly."

Zeke tipped his head and drew his brows in. "Did something happen on this trip?"

"Yeah, we came up with a genius plan."

"Beyond that," his brother clarified. "Is there something more going on?"

Luke had no idea how Zeke had honed in on that, other than the fact they were brothers and shared a very close bond.

"Zeke, she's my assistant."

His brother continued to study him with that dark gaze that resembled his own.

"Nice dodge of the question," he said. "Something did happen. I can tell. You know, it's ok to admit anything. I know you feel the weight of the company on your shoulders, but you're not alone in this. Kelly is a great woman and she'd be good for you."

There was absolutely no way in hell Luke would

ever admit anything to his brother…not this early in their relationship.

Wait. *Relationship?*

Yeah, he supposed it could have that label, but just because they were physical and he'd asked her to stay at his house didn't mean he was ready by any means to settle down.

Luke shrugged. "All that happened was Kelly finally got me to see that I needed to recharge because I was being too hard on myself and that wasn't doing anyone any good. The getaway really helped me see things so much clearer."

All of that was the truth, Luke just opted to omit the R-rated version of the trip. Everything going on between Kelly and him had to remain confidential. Letting anyone else inside their personal bubble wasn't an option… not even his brother.

"I'm not so sure that's all there is to tell," Zeke added.

Reagan smacked his leg. "Would you leave the guy alone? He's come up with a brilliant plan to save Wingate and make the company profitable again. If something is going on in his personal life with his assistant, that's his business."

Luke could jump across the coffee table between them and kiss his sister-in-law. She had a way of keeping Ezekiel in line. Zeke never backed down to anyone, but he would do literally anything his wife told him to do and he'd do it with a smile on his face.

Luke wasn't about to say anything more. He didn't want to lie to his brother and he sure as hell didn't want to discuss Kelly.

A part of him was thrilled knowing she'd be back at

his home waiting for him. He wondered if she was currently exploring his house, his bedroom. Maybe she'd be waiting in the bed or the hot tub on his balcony off his master suite.

Luke came to his feet, more than ready to get home and start working on this party in a relaxed atmosphere with Kelly.

His brother and Reagan also stood and started toward the foyer.

"I'll go ahead and send some texts out about the party," Reagan told him. "I'll be sure to really talk it up as one not to be missed. Christmas is a magical time and I really think the timing couldn't be better for you guys to unveil this endeavor."

"I hope so," Luke replied. "I'll have some banners printed up with marketing and copy you on the email with the design."

"Sounds good," Zeke said with a nod of approval. "I'll start getting the word out to the TCC members, as well."

By the time Luke left and was headed home, he finally felt a sense of accomplishment. He hadn't had this feeling in so long and he absolutely owed everything to Kelly. Before their trip to Hawaii, he'd worked for hours on end, never finding anything resembling a solution that would help Wingate get that extra leg up they needed. But now everything was falling into place.

Luke stifled a yawn as he maneuvered the roads that took him home. It had been a hell of a week in the very best way and he couldn't wait to lie in his own bed tonight. Yet, much as he wanted her right beside him, a part of him wondered if asking Kelly to stay had been a mistake. He sure as hell didn't want to give her the wrong impression or to make her believe they could be more. Luke's hands clenched around the steering wheel as more self-doubts began to creep in. He knew Kelly well enough to know she would get attached and he didn't want to be the one to break her heart.

Sixteen

"Something smells good."

Kelly turned toward the wide, arched opening of Luke's kitchen and smiled as he stepped through.

"I made dinner," she stated, spreading her hands open to the display on the island. "I hope you don't mind. I rummaged through your cabinets to find something. I figured you'd be hungry when you got home."

Nerves swirled her belly as he came on into the kitchen and stood on the other side of the island. Being in his house was so much different than the neutral ground they were in in Oahu. She'd felt so strange walking through his house when she'd first gotten here. For one thing, the place was enormous. She'd peeked in each of the six bedrooms and deduced his was the one done in all navy and rich woods and the entire room had his masculine essence.

Everything in this place reminded her of him. The classy decor, the strong beams accenting the ceiling, the commanding two-story stone fireplace in the living room. It was all quintessential Luke and she loved getting another insight to his personal life.

Zeke and Luke had been living together, but Zeke had moved in with Reagan once they married. Kelly could easily see two bachelors living here in this vast domain.

She'd spotted a photo of Luke's parents on his dresser, and a piece of her heart tumbled for him. She knew that ache of not having parents in your life. At least he had his brother and aunt. He had some family left and she was glad he still had a strong bond with those in his life.

Kelly longed for such a bond but, more than that, she longed for a life partner. She longed for a family of her own and a man who loved her. She saw how her mother had missed out on so much and Kelly knew she would never live that way.

"I didn't mean to be gone so long," he told her. "Zeke and I got to talking, and I just wanted to make sure I filled him in on every detail."

"What did he think?" she asked. "Was Reagan there, too?"

Luke nodded. "They both thought it was brilliant. Reagan is sending out some texts and phone calls to some of her friends and Zeke is talking to the members of the club."

"It's going to be a busy week getting everything ready," she told him. "I hope I can pull all of this off to your satisfaction."

Luke circled the island and came to stand directly in front of her. Taking her hands, he looked directly into her eyes.

"You will pull it off," he assured her. "There's not a doubt in my mind that this will be the greatest party and re-launch ever. You're a mastermind when it comes to organizing and bossing people around."

Kelly couldn't help but laugh and shake her head. "I'm not bossy."

"You did a hell of a job bossing me in Oahu," he reminded her, then placed a quick, sweet kiss on the tip of her nose. "I need to grab a shower before I eat. I'm still straight off the plane and I want to change."

"No problem. I'll just fix up a plate and get us some wine."

He stared at her for a moment and she thought he was going to say something, but he ended up just releasing her hands.

"Give me ten minutes," he told her before he left the room and headed toward the stairs.

Kelly hoped he didn't mind coming home to her in the kitchen like she belonged here. She'd gotten fidgety waiting on him and then her stomach had started growling. Next thing she'd known she was boiling pasta and making marinara sauce.

Searching through the cabinets once again, she found plates and utensils. It took a bit to find the wine opener, but then she realized he had an electric one on the counter above the wine fridge.

When he still hadn't come down, she wondered if he'd gotten busy with emails or phone calls. She waited nearly twenty minutes before heading upstairs to check on him.

The minute she rounded the corner of his bedroom, she stopped short. There he was wearing only a towel around his waist, face down on his bed…fast asleep.

A twinge of disappointment coursed through her. So much for a romantic evening and picking up where they'd left off at the resort.

Kelly snuck away and went back downstairs. After eating a quick dinner, she cleaned up the kitchen and put the leftovers away. She'd already showered and changed at her place before she came here and now she needed to unwind. Her mind was racing and her thoughts too revved up to go to sleep.

With her laptop and phone, she decided to go to the back enclosed patio that overlooked the pond. The cozy oversize chaise in the corner called her name the moment she'd seen it earlier.

She settled in and started working on emails, spreadsheets, decor ideas, and everything that would be involved in throwing a last minute, lavish party. Her work was definitely cut out for her, but she'd never failed Luke before, and she certainly didn't intend to start now. Their professional relationship was stronger than ever, but she had no clue about their romantic future. She had a sinking feeling someone was going to get hurt…and that someone would likely be her.

"As you can see here, there would be specialty suites in an entirely different area of our resorts."

Luke pointed to the mock-up slide he'd put up on the screen in the boardroom. Kelly sat at the opposite end of the table and tried to gauge the faces of everyone in attendance.

Ava seemed completely enthralled at the ideas Luke presented. She'd eased forward in her seat, with her brows raised, and it was clear her nephew had her undivided attention.

Zeke seemed relaxed, as usual, as he sat back in his leather chair. The other board members were all staring up at the screen and, every now and then, Luke would glance her way and the butterflies would start fluttering all over again.

She'd spent the past two nights at his house, but this morning he'd been up and gone before she even woke. Since Saturday night, they had shared a bed, but nothing more than a few sultry kisses had been exchanged. He was all in work-mode and ready to get this morning meeting to the members of the board.

He'd been so restless last night. At one point she'd just rested her hand on his back and he'd calmed down. She knew he was nervous, but she also knew this whole plan was so splendid, there would be no way it would fail.

She didn't want to bring up the proverbial elephant: their relationship. Once this party was over and they were riding the high of moving forward, she would talk to him. He deserved to know how she felt and give him the chance to tell her how he felt.

They were so connected on the island, and they weren't necessarily disconnected here, but they also weren't as open and talkative. Right now it was just all work. She wanted more…she shouldn't, but she did.

"We can still appeal to the corporate travelers," Luke

went on, pulling her focus back to the meeting. "But that will no longer be our target audience. We will transform seventy percent of all resort rooms to accommodate couples for special, tranquil retreats. And we will offer a diverse range of packages for people on a budget all the way up to people who don't care how much they have to spend for their significant other."

Luke pivoted from the screen and tapped on his laptop, then turned back to the new slide.

"This would be the projected budget," he added. "And if you look on the next slide, you will see the projections of income if we have eighty percent booked by spring."

Kelly watched him in action, never more proud of the position he was in and the stand he was taking to protect his family, his company and the employees who depended on Wingate.

"This is a risk," Ava finally said when Luke was finished.

Luke nodded in agreement, his eyes meeting Kelly's briefly. She gave him a reassuring nod and he focused his attention back to his aunt.

"There's going to be a risk in any decision we make moving forward," he agreed. "This is the best-case scenario. Honeymooners, couples celebrating anniversaries, someone trying to get back in a partner's good graces, or a suitor pulling out all the stops to win someone's love…these are all everyday people who need a nice, reputable resort. Wingate can and will provide those services and be the greatest name when people go to book their getaways."

"Reagan's ready to book the first platinum package,"

Zeke chimed in. "I reminded her we already have a private jet at our disposal."

Ava tapped her short nails on the glossy table and Kelly couldn't stop staring, waiting for her final reaction. Although she knew the family matriarch wouldn't have the ultimate say on the matter, especially since the party and roll-out were already in place. This board meeting was more of a formality and a heads-up so everyone would be on the same page and able to answer any questions at the event.

"I trust you on this," Ava told Luke and Zeke. "I know you boys wouldn't steer this company in the wrong direction. You clearly believe this is the way to go and I am behind you a hundred percent."

Luke smiled, and Kelly could see the relief cross his face. He wanted Ava's approval. They'd been through so much together since his parents' passing. Not only had they been through heartache personally, they had also endured it professionally.

And with Keith being exposed as the criminal bastard he was, that had been another hard blow to all of them. He'd been a trusted figure in their lives. Now he was behind bars awaiting a trial. Kelly didn't even know how difficult that day would be when several of them had to testify...namely Ava and Luke.

"We have marketing working on the designs and various information for the guests this weekend," Luke went on. "Kelly has already contacted their caterer and set up the music. She's got the decor sorted out, as well."

"We'll be working around the Christmas decor the Clubhouse already has in place, but it will have a flare for romantic getaways, as well," she told everyone.

Luke caught her eye again, and she smiled. Then he went on to discuss the party in more detail and the way the evening would play out and the roles each of them would have.

Kelly continued to add to her notes. Luke had already gone over everything with her before they came in, but as he spoke, more ideas popped into her head and she wanted to type them in before she forgot. They needed to send out a company-wide memo in addition to an invitation to the party with a message to bring as many guests as possible. This needed to be a grand event to celebrate Wingate's big comeback.

As the meeting came to an end and everyone filed out the door, Kelly saw Zeke go to the head of the conference table and mutter something to his brother. Luke glanced up to her and she stilled.

"Could you excuse us?" Luke asked.

Kelly nodded and gathered her laptop and left the room, pulling the door closed behind her. She didn't know what the brothers needed to discuss, but she had a sinking feeling this wasn't about work and had everything to do with her.

"What the hell are you doing?" Zeke demanded.

Luke stared at his brother. "About what?"

"Don't act like you don't know what I'm talking about."

Rubbing his coarse beard, Luke shook his head. "I don't know. I thought the meeting went really well."

Zeke stepped closer. "You mean while you were shooting smiles and heart eyes at your assistant at the other end of the table? I asked what happened in Oahu and you denied everything."

Luke pulled in a deep breath. Had other people noticed? Had Ava or the few other members around the table? Hopefully they'd been too focused on the presentation to catch anything he had been unaware he was giving off.

"Do you want to tell me what's going on with Kelly?" Zeke asked. "And don't tell me she's just your assistant. I know that trip changed both of you."

"Fine. She's more. Is that what you want to hear?"

Zeke stared for another minute before taking a step back and cursing beneath his breath.

"What in the world are you thinking?" he demanded. "We're in crisis-mode. That wasn't my intention when I sent you on that trip."

"What I do in my spare time is none of your damn business." Luke willed himself to have patience here, because his brother didn't know the details. "Kelly and I have nothing to do with you."

Zeke nodded. "When it starts interfering with meetings, it sure as hell does."

His brother continued to glower at him, obviously waiting on more of an explanation.

"Kelly and I got closer on the trip," Luke added. "Details aren't necessary, but that's how we came up with this idea for Wingate."

Silence surrounded them and Luke hated that he felt like he had to justify his actions when none of this was Zeke's concern.

"Nobody is aware and I want things to stay that way,"

Luke explained. "Kelly wasn't just a fling and she's not fodder for office gossip."

Zeke's brows drew in as he jerked slightly in obvious surprise. "You care for her."

This was sure as hell not a conversation Luke had time for, nor did he want to get into with his brother at the office. There were too many other things to be doing, and Luke hadn't even sorted out his emotions yet. If he had serious feelings, then Kelly was the first person who needed to know.

"Your silence speaks for itself," Zeke stated.

"My silence is because I'm ignoring you. Nothing is said to Kelly or anyone else."

Zeke's face split into a wide grin. "Hey, if you want to keep your love life a secret, that's fine. But it will come out sooner or later."

Luke absolutely refused to answer. He could only handle so much at one time and he was juggling too many balls. If he dropped any, there would be another crisis.

He couldn't let Wingate down and he couldn't let Kelly down, either. He cared too much for the both of them and that scared the hell out of him.

Seventeen

Kelly hung her dress back in the walk-in closet and zipped the garment bag before closing the closet doors. She couldn't believe she had time to find a dress and one that fit perfectly without alterations.

She wanted to look her best for the party and for Luke. Every detail had been worked out and the buzz around Royal was spreading like wildfire, with everyone wondering what the announcement could be from Wingate.

Luke had worked late every night this week, falling into bed almost immediately after he'd gotten in. They'd barely talked, except at work, while finishing up the final touches of the party. But he had so much more to do, because the resorts were all being informed of the upgrades and the changes. He'd been busy, in contact with all of those managers and having conference calls.

He'd stolen a few kisses and ass-grabs here and there, but nothing more. The real world really did hit them hard now that they were back, but there was so much to be done to move into this next phase.

She still felt a little strange being at his house, but since he'd asked her to stay, he'd never mentioned her leaving and she'd fallen into a pattern.

She'd been here nearly a week and they hadn't made love one time. Had she just become an afterthought for him? Had their getaway been just a fling? Why had he asked her to stay to begin with if he didn't want to keep up what they'd had?

Once the party was over tomorrow, she would talk to him about where they stood. She understood his work was important to him, but now that her heart was involved, she didn't want to come second place if he was having feelings for her.

But she had to finesse this carefully. Because on one hand, she didn't want to come across as his needy ex. Kelly truly valued his commitment to his job. But on the other hand, if they were going to try at any type of relationship, she needed to know she was an important part of his life as more than his assistant.

A gnawing pit in her stomach opened up at the realization that maybe Luke didn't want more. She knew he'd always been career-oriented. That part of his life was actually appealing to her, but he'd never claimed to want a serious relationship. He'd never claimed to want a family or a wife.

Kelly cursed herself for being naive, for letting their trip clog her mind with romantic notions about the two of them that might never be fulfilled. She had to talk to him, openly and honestly, and she had to stop trying to dance around the subject.

Luke needed to know she'd fallen in love with him. He deserved to have all of the information so then he could decide where he stood and what he wanted from this relationship.

She didn't expect him home until late tonight, either. She knew he was at the office with Zeke working on the steps to take to make this transition with the resorts as flawless as possible.

Kelly had spent the evening at the TCC clubhouse decorating and making sure everything was absolutely perfect. She planned on being there tomorrow afternoon, as well. Reagan had offered to meet her and work on the final touches and helping the caterers get everything set out exactly where she wanted the dishes to go for easy flow.

Kelly couldn't help but have that rush of excitement over this party. She felt sexy in her dress and she couldn't wait to show Luke. Maybe tomorrow, after she told him she loved him, they could reconnect and pick up from where they'd left off in Hawaii.

She had hope. The way he looked at her, and the way he appreciated her, gave her that spark of encouragement. She wasn't one to be clingy or beg, though. If Luke didn't have the same feelings or want to work on something more solid than a work relationship or a quick fling, then she would have to move on. Just because she felt so strongly, didn't mean that he did. Her feelings had nurtured and grown over the years and Luke had just seen her as little more than his right-hand-woman less than two weeks ago.

Kelly tried to put her nerves to rest and decided to give herself a home manicure and pedi. She wanted to look her best for the re-launch party, and she just needed a little self-care time.

Tomorrow was going to be memorable in both her personal and professional life. She only hoped everything went the way she'd hoped and planned…otherwise, her heart was going to be shattered. If he didn't want more, they would have to part ways in all aspects and that meant she'd have to find a new employer. She had no Plan B, but while she was confident she could recover from her job, she wasn't so sure she'd bounce back from losing Luke.

"Wow. You look hot."

Kelly laughed and did a slow turn in her emerald green strapless ball gown. Reagan let out a slow whistle and a clap.

"There won't be a single man here with his eyes in his head," Reagan laughed. "And maybe some women, too. Damn, that dress is *amazing*."

Kelly loved it from the moment she'd seen it online. She'd paid for overnight shipping and prayed it would fit. The deep V in the front was nearly indecent, but the flare of the skirt gave it a softer touch. It was the best of both worlds, being classy and sultry at the same time. And the emerald green both set off her red hair and celebrated Christmas. She loved this dress so much, she might never take it off. Cleaning house and doing laundry was about to get a face-lift from her usual sweats and tees.

"I'm not looking for the guests to check out this

dress," Kelly stated. "I'd rather they look ahead to book a suite."

Reagan slid her hands in the pockets of her full red shirt and smiled. "Honey, they will flock to those rooms and be sure to tell all their friends they were the first to book at the newest, poshest resorts. And then those friends will get jealous and the trickle down effect will begin."

Kelly sighed. "I hope you're right. I'm so nervous."

"No need to be nervous." Reagan leaned in so the workers setting up the tables wouldn't overhear. "Unless you're nervous how a certain someone is going to react when he sees you in that dress."

Kelly's unease grew even more and she wondered how much Reagan knew.

"Don't worry," the other woman stated with a soft smile. "I don't officially know anything, but I saw the way Luke talked about you the other day, and I see it in your eyes now."

How had Luke talked about her, and what was she giving away right now? Did others know? Was there gossip flooding the office that she didn't know about?

"I can't do this right now," Kelly murmured.

Reagan reached for her hand and gave a gentle squeeze. "I'm so sorry. I didn't mean to freak you out. Listen, believe me when I say I know how it feels to keep a secret about someone you love."

Kelly closed her eyes. "I'm still processing all of this."

"Does he know you love him?"

Kelly shook her head and focused back on her friend. "Please don't say a word to Ezekiel," she begged.

"Of course not." Reagan reached now for both her hands and laughed. "Sometimes girls just need to have their own pact of secrecy."

Relief filled Kelly. She didn't have many girlfriends and due to her long work hours she didn't get out much to socialize. Reagan being close to Zeke just put her in close proximity to Kelly and she found the woman to be absolutely a joy and a treasure. Zeke had really lucked out.

"Thank you," Kelly said, returning the smile. "I'm sorry, I didn't tell you how amazing you look tonight."

"Red is Zeke's favorite color," she stated with a naughty grin. "Sometimes we just have to remind our men what they're dealing with."

Our men. Kelly wasn't sure how true that statement was, but she did like the sound of it. It reminded her of the conversation she wanted to have with Luke later. But, for now, nothing else mattered but this party and the success of Wingate's relaunch. They needed this big push to get off on the right foot for the first of the year.

Over the next hour, Kelly and Reagan worked on making sure the centerpieces were perfect, leaving pamphlets at each place setting. They also displayed information about the new amenities/travel packages in oversize frames and set it out on the informational table where two employees from Wingate would be stationed all night to answer questions and start the booking process.

She couldn't wait for Luke, Ava, and Zeke to see what all had been done to get this new plan off the ground. The idea had come on so quick, Kelly only hoped they weren't missing anything.

"Is there anything else that we need to do before the guests arrive?"

Kelly turned to Reagan and shook her head. "I think we did it. I seriously appreciate all your help."

Reagan moved toward the bar and motioned for the bartender to come over. "I'd say we deserve a celebratory glass of wine before everyone gets here."

"I like how you think," Kelly laughed. "But I might need the bottle to get through this night."

"We've got the time." Reagan smiled and lifted her glass in a mock cheer. "This is going to be a night to remember."

Kelly took a sip of her pinot and welcomed the tart taste. This would indeed be a night to remember.

Eighteen

Luke stepped into the Texas Cattleman's Club lodge and was blown away by the space and everything Kelly had accomplished in such a short time.

He tried to take in everything all at once as he adjusted his Stetson. There were easels propped up all around the ballroom with large, colorful posters exhibiting the new suites designed for romance, the prospected spa rooms, and the showcase also unveiled how the changes would look in the various locations by spring/summer.

His savvy assistant had managed to display everything in rich colors of gold and white, matching the Christmas decor the lodge already had in place.

There were twinkling lights draped like a canopy of stars from the peaked, wood ceilings. Tall Christmas trees adorned with gold accents and glittering ornaments flanked the entrance to the ballroom. And the tables had centerpieces that looked like something straight from the pages of a magazine.

This level of grandeur surpassed his every expectation, and he vowed to give Kelly a raise. Without her, the idea wouldn't have been born and this party would not have met the high standard people had come to expect from the Wingates.

The caterers were setting up the tiered stands with food at each end of the ballroom. The music had started over in the corner and there was a space for dancing. The lodge doors in the back were open to let the crisp air in and allow members to mill about inside and out. Even though it was December, this was still Texas and the evenings weren't too chilly.

Luke scanned the room once again, looking for Kelly. He hadn't seen her before she'd left. He'd gotten up and gone for a run, then he'd gone to see Ava, and by the time he got home, she'd been gone. He knew she and Reagan were working here for the past couple of hours, so he hadn't wanted to bother her. The party was due to start in thirty minutes and he wanted to steal her away for a moment before they were flooded with nearly all of Royal.

He saw a flash of red, but that was Reagan on the other side of the room. His sister-in-law was definitely a knockout, but Luke only had eyes for one woman.

Luke crossed the wood floor. "Reagan," he called as he approached her. He grabbed her hands and kissed her cheek. "You look beautiful as always."

"You don't look so bad yourself," she murmured, offering her signature smile. "If you're looking for Kelly, she's in the back office. She was touching up her hair."

The back office sounded perfect for that alone time he wanted to have with her. Even five minutes of complete privacy would be great. He'd been so busy this week and, when he'd gotten home, he'd always had every intention of stripping her and making love.

Love? That wasn't the term he should be using… not quite yet. But he did feel much more for her now than when they were in Oahu. Her loyalty, her compassion, her drive all matched his, and the more time he spent with her, even though they were back in reality, the more he realized he liked having her in his home. Knowing she was there waiting for him had him more eager to be home than he ever had been. Unfortunately, the timing of this project didn't allow him all that he craved.

The back office door was cracked and he eased it open, glanced in, and nearly gasped at the beauty before him.

She stood at the decorative old floor mirror propped against the wall in the corner. Her hands were in her hair. which was draped over one shoulder. She wore a shade of green that did amazing things to her skin, her hair, and her eyes.

Kelly caught his gaze in the reflection and her hands instantly stilled. She spun around and that's when he caught the full view of this dress that would surely bring him to his knees.

Man, he missed their intimacy and he missed when they could just be together without all of these outside complications.

"Kel." He closed the door at his back, unable to take his eyes off of her. "You look… Damn, you look sexy and gorgeous and I don't even know what all else."

She laughed and started toward him. With that full skirt, she seemed to be floating like an angel, but that deep V in the front proved she had a little side of vixen thrown into the mix.

"I was hoping you'd love this," she told him. She reached for his black tie and straightened it, then flattened her hands on his chest. "You look incredible, too."

He could barely speak. Kelly had always been a stunning woman and now that he'd had her in his bed, he knew she was absolutely, utterly perfect.

"Speechless?" she asked, tapping his lips. "That's fine. I plan on doing a good bit of talking later."

Luke swallowed. "I wasn't thinking about talking at all once I got you home," he assured her, reaching for that dip in her waist just above the skirt. "I owe you so much more after falling asleep on you all week."

Kelly smiled, her red lips practically begging him to mess them up. "I know you've been working hard. It's ok. But we do need to talk."

There was no man alive who wanted to hear those words come out of the mouth of a woman. They never led to anything good.

"That sounds serious," he told her.

She framed his face with her hands and stared back at him with those expressive green eyes. "Nothing to worry about," she promised. "I just have some things I want to tell you."

Luke cringed. "You're pregnant."

"No," she laughed. "Though I do want kids someday. Nice to know where you stand on the topic."

He shook his head as all the thoughts of what she'd want to discuss kept swirling around. "Sorry. I didn't mean to seem paranoid, but well, that would be terrifying right now."

Luke slid his hands along her hips and tugged her closer until her body aligned with his. He captured her lips, needing to feel her, to taste her. He couldn't wait to get her home and peel her out of this dress.

He eased back and stared down into those expressive eyes so full of passion, then she smiled.

"I like my lipstick on you." She slid her thumb over his lips to clean the mess. "Later, you can mess up the rest of it."

Oh, he loved the sound of that, but he still was itching to know what she wanted to talk to him about. Unfortunately, that would have to wait, because guests were going to be arriving soon and he needed to be out front and center the entire night.

"You did an amazing job out there," he said, taking her hand and leading her toward the door. "In case I haven't said it this week, thank you. It's not much, but I really wouldn't have been able to do this without you."

She tipped her head and the rest of her red curls fell down over her shoulder. "I'm glad I could be the one to help you. This is going to be an extraordinary ride and I want to be on this journey."

Which is exactly where he wanted her.

Later, he would tell her he wanted more. He still wasn't sure exactly what that looked like, but he wanted her to move in with him so they could see where things went.

Luke led Kelly back out to the ballroom, but made sure he wasn't holding her hand or even touching her. He wanted to stop hiding this and just be himself in public with her. He wanted to wrap his arm around her waist and not give a damn what people thought.

Yes, she was his assistant, but there was much more to their relationship. If people wanted to gossip about that, then that was their problem. All he cared about was getting more from Kelly, more from what they had started and seeing where they could go.

Kelly couldn't believe the turnout. She couldn't stop smiling and, every time she glanced around the crowded ballroom, she only saw people having a great time. She had answered questions about the new turn in the Wingate resorts and had even directed many people to the informational area in the back.

Luke and Zeke were milling about and she'd seen them pass by every now and then as they also were busy talking with guests.

The party was most definitely a success.

"I'd say everyone is having a good time."

Kelly turned to see Sutton Wingate, the CFO, nursing a drink and glancing around the room as he came to stand beside her.

"They are," she agreed. "I think this new phase of Wingate is really going to be something huge."

"Luke is taking a chance, but I agree there has to be a big risk for a big payoff."

Sutton's fiancée Lauren came from the bar with a glass of wine in hand and a smile on her face. She looked absolutely stunning in her floor-length gold dress.

"Kelly, you look gorgeous," Lauren stated. "I love that green on you."

"Thanks. I love that gold, too."

Sutton slid an arm around Lauren and a sliver of jealousy slid through Kelly. She wanted to know where she and Luke stood and if they were working toward something. And most of all, she wanted to come out in the open. Stolen kisses and staying at his house, but driving separately to work, wasn't any type of relationship she wanted to have.

"I'm about ready to book one of these getaways myself," Lauren said. "I love my life here, but being pampered with Sutton for a week doesn't sound bad at all."

Kelly gestured toward the back wall. "You can sign up right back there," she joked.

"What's everyone congregating over here for?" Sebastian asked. "Are we having a staff meeting?"

Sutton shook his head at his twin. "Just chatting. The party is already a success. I'm anxious to see the numbers shoot up over the next few weeks with these pre-bookings."

"Always a numbers man," Sebastian joked. "Just relax for the night and let the plan do its work. Everyone is loving the idea of a couple's getaway."

"That's because everyone is getting married or engaged lately," Lauren chimed in with a smile.

Sebastian shook his head. "Not everybody. Right, Kelly?"

She couldn't help but smile at the CEO, who obviously wanted nothing to do with commitment, but he didn't know that's exactly what she wanted from Luke.

"Marriage isn't for everybody," she stated with a

shrug. "If you all will excuse me, I need to refill my glass and chat with some guests."

Kelly eased away from the group and nodded her greeting to people she passed by as she moved her way through the crowd. The ballroom was absolutely packed. She was almost positive all of Royal had turned out to see what exactly Wingate was planning next.

She noticed living here that people with money wanted to spend it. They not only strove to have the newest and the nicest things, but they also wanted bragging rights and first dibs on social media status. Fine by her, because that would only give a burst of sales that would create a snowball effect that would generate more money than Wingate had seen since their funds had been pilfered by a trusted source.

Kelly turned and bumped into Gracie Diaz.

"Oh, Gracie," Kelly exclaimed. "I'm so sorry."

Gracie had her hand up to prevent more of a collision and held tightly to a glass of water in her other hand. She looked a little pale, but still gorgeous as always with her long, dark hair and striking brown eyes.

"Are you alright?" Kelly asked.

"Yes, yes. I'm fine." She attempted a smile, but Kelly didn't think Gracie was quite feeling it. "I was just feeling a little tired. I was going to go find a quiet place to sit."

Concerned, Kelly reached for her friend. Gracie scored a winning lottery ticket that had completely changed her life. She was now a multimillionaire and searching for something else to do with her life.

"I was in the back room earlier getting ready," Kelly stated. "I know it's empty if you'd like to go back and close the door. Can I get you something? Do you need to eat or can I get you more water?"

Gracie shook her head. "I just need to sit. I'll be fine, really. Go back to the party."

Kelly hesitated, but the young woman moved away and headed toward the hallway. Kelly wondered what was wrong, but she didn't want to pry. Everyone around here had something they wanted to keep to themselves and Kelly was no different.

Her eyes scanned the room and locked on Luke. He stared across with a hunger in his eyes she'd hadn't seen since Oahu, and her entire body tingled. There might as well be nobody else in the room with the way he was gazing at her.

Beyond the hunger, she saw a desire and a promise staring back. Tonight. She couldn't wait until they were done here and back at Luke's house where they could be alone and she could finally tell him she loved him.

Nineteen

"Your forgiveness means everything," Ava stated as they hovered in the corner of the ballroom at the party.

Luke glanced to Zeke. They'd all had a difficult time after Keith's actions had come to the surface for all to see. Ava obviously didn't know he had been stealing from the Wingates, but Luke and Zeke didn't want a repeat of the past. It was imperative that Sutton keep a tight rein on the numbers of the company and make sure nothing like that ever happened again.

Every division of the company had been impacted and hit hard. So many families had been affected by Keith's embezzlement scheme. The reputation of the company had been tarnished as well and every piece of the company struggled to find footing once again. It was going to happen, but they all knew this would take time and take several steps. Unfortunately, there wasn't just one blanket fix for all.

Justice was served though and Keith would be spending the next fifteen years behind bars where he couldn't hurt anyone again.

"We're only looking forward now," Luke told her. "This next phase is a whole new chapter for everyone."

"I know this isn't the time, but I was talking with Sutton and he believes we will need to sell Wingate estate to have the liquid cash for the hotel expansion."

Ava pulled in a deep breath and nodded. "I figured there would have to be an extreme decision, but the company has to come first."

Luke hated the idea of selling the estate, but Ava was right. The company had to come first. There were so many people depending on them to turn this disaster around, not to mention they had to rebuild their reputation. None of them were quitters and even though selling the estate would be emotional, they would all do what was necessary to start the upward climb.

"I love you both. Thanks for staying by me." Ava smiled and hugged each of her nephews. "I better get back to the party. Great job, by the way. I'm going to see Kelly to tell her what an amazing job she did with the decor."

Once Ava was gone, Luke sipped his bourbon and eyed the full room. He and his brother stood back in the hallway around the corner from the offices. Ava had wanted to talk to them away from the crowd and the noise.

Luke started to shift from leaning against the wall when Zeke stepped to block him.

"One minute."

Luke stared back at his brother. "What?"

"I know I was giving you a hard time about Kelly—"

"We're not doing this again, are we?" Luke asked curtly.

"I just want to make sure you don't hurt her or screw this up," Zeke stated. "The last thing we need is another shake-up on any level at the office. Kelly is the foundation in your department. If things went wrong with you two and she left…"

Luke had already thought of that. He didn't want to lose Kelly in any capacity—personal or professional. He wanted her in all aspects of his life, but that confession would have to wait until they were alone tonight.

And he sure as hell wasn't about to tell his brother how he truly felt for Kelly. That was something she deserved to hear first. He might not be ready to profess his love, but he did want to see where this would go and he fully believed he was falling for her.

"She's not going to leave," Luke stated firmly. "What Kelly and I have going on isn't a big deal or anything for you to worry about. She's been my assistant and she'll always be my assistant."

In the office and in his personal life. He wanted her with him. Damn it, he couldn't wait to get home and tell her.

Home. He liked thinking that she would be home with him. He wondered if she would even be interested in this giant step. After all, they'd only just started seeing each other in an intimate way two weeks ago.

Was this too soon? How the hell would he know if he was making a mistake or not?

Luke didn't know and that risk was both thrilling and terrifying. All he knew for sure was that this was nothing like when he'd been engaged before.

"I'll drop the subject," Zeke told him. "You know I just worry about the company and you and Kelly. She's like a sister to me."

"I get it," Luke said and blew out a sigh. "We better get back out there. I need to make a formal announcement. Care to join me on the stage?"

Zeke nodded. "Sure, but feel free to do the talking."

Luke shook his head and headed down the hall and made his way through the crowd. With his brother at his back, Luke took the three steps to the stage at the end of the ballroom and stepped up to the podium. There were several more easels and large posters propped on the stage showcasing the various resorts from Wingate. Luke was damn proud to be part of this company.

He tapped the mic to make sure it was on and then tapped a little louder to get the attention of the crowd. The roar of the guests started to calm down and Luke cleared his throat.

"First of all, I want to thank you all for coming out tonight to the relaunch of Wingate Enterprises."

A round of applause went up and Luke waited until the noise died down again.

"As you all have seen and heard, we are taking Wingate in a new direction," he announced. "We have a wide variety of packages for romantic getaways and those can be pre-booked starting right now. Every budget was taken into consideration and we have something for everyone."

Luke glanced around the room at all of the familiar faces and couldn't help but smile and be filled with hope at all of the people who had come out to support the company.

"I can't take all of the credit for this brilliant plan," he added. "My assistant Kelly Prentiss has truly been the brains behind the operation. If I could get Kelly to come up here."

He tried to scan the crowd for where she'd be coming from, but he didn't see anyone. Luke glanced to his side where his brother stood, but Zeke just shrugged.

Luke waited another minute, but Kelly never showed. Where could she be? She hadn't mentioned needing to leave.

"Well, I'm sure Kelly is here somewhere," he added with a chuckle. "I know she would appreciate you stopping her and thanking her for putting this amazing party together and helping with this next journey for Wingate Enterprises. Thank you all again for coming and, please, continue to enjoy the open bar and the rest of the evening."

Luke stepped from the podium and off the stage.

"I'm going to look for Kelly," he told his brother. "That's not like her to leave or just be gone. Maybe she's in the back office or the restroom."

Luke checked everywhere and couldn't find her. He pulled his cell from his pocket, but there were no texts or calls from her. He sent her a quick text asking where she was and if everything was okay. He waited a few minutes, but there was no reply.

Now he was starting to worry. As he asked around

about anyone seeing her, everyone said they'd just seen her moments ago, so he had to believe she wasn't far.

A loud shout caught his attention, but it was just the Wingate twins laughing and they were being hoisted into the air by some rowdy guests. Clearly people had taken advantage of that open bar.

Luke watched as the rambunctious celebration continued on outside and he saw it coming before it happened. Sutton and Sebastian were launched into the swimming pool by a group of cheering guys.

Was this the equivalent of dumping the ice bucket on the coach at the end of a big win?

Luke had bigger issues to deal with however, and he sure as hell didn't want to be part of that pool club. It might be fairly nice for December, but that didn't mean the pool water was warm.

When he turned back toward the ballroom, he spotted Gracie.

"Hey, Gracie." He stopped in front of her and noted how she looked like she wasn't feeling well. "Have you seen Kelly anywhere?"

"I just spoke to her," Gracie said. "Maybe thirty minutes or an hour ago. Is something wrong?"

He shook his head. "I just can't find her, that's all."

Something caught Gracie's eye over Luke's shoulder and she gasped. Luke turned and saw the Wingate twins dripping by the pool and Sebastian had stripped out of his jacket and shirt. A long scar ran down his back.

When Luke turned back to Gracie, she appeared even paler than before and looked on the verge of passing out.

"Are you alright?" he asked, reaching for her.

"I-I have to go."

She fled the ballroom, and Luke had no idea what had spooked her, but she was gone.

His cell vibrated in his pocket and he pulled it out to see a text from Kelly. Relief spread through him, quickly followed by confusion.

I overheard something you probably didn't intend for me to hear. You need to check your email.

His email? Had something important come through while they'd been at the party and she was working on it now? That would be just like her to take the stress off him and try to get everything taken care of while he was at the party. He smiled as he tapped the email icon. She was too damn good for him.

The confusion grew and along with it came astonishment.

Kelly's resignation letter? The date at the top was today, and she stated the notification was effective immediately. She indicated a difference of goals and her life going in a different direction now.

What the hell?

Luke read it again, still unsure about what was going on. What different direction? Wasn't this the same woman who wanted to talk to him for hours on end when they got home? The same woman who'd worn a dress she thought he would love?

The same damn woman who'd deceived him and swept him away for a romantic getaway for five days?

Anger slid right on in with all of his other jumbled emotions. Luke sent a text to his brother and Ava that he had to leave and he would get with them later. He assured them nothing was wrong just because he didn't want them to worry, but everything seemed to be wrong right now.

He had no idea where Kelly was or what she was thinking. Her email had been so vague, other than the part where she quit on him without notice or logical reasons.

Luke tried calling her over and over and no answer. She was ignoring him, and he wanted to know why. Whatever she had overheard had made her jump to conclusions and he needed to fix whatever the hell was going on.

He went to his house, hoping to catch her if she went there to retrieve her things. Who knows how long she'd been gone from the party before he realized it?

The moment he pulled into his drive, he saw her car and a heady sense of relief spread through him. At least he knew where she was, now he needed to know what the hell had happened this evening.

He barely had the engine off before he was out of the car and rushing up the stairs to the front door. He couldn't let her leave without finding out where her head was and who had hurt her.

And then he was going to have to tell her how he truly felt.

Twenty

Kelly heard the front door open and close, and she cursed herself for coming back here to retrieve her things. She should've just gone home and worried about her clothes and toiletries later.

A lump rose in her throat as the events of the night assailed her once again She had been a fool to believe they could have been more. For five years she'd slowly fallen for Luke, calling herself naive every step of the way for allowing thoughts of a relationship with her boss to creep in. She was not only foolish and naive, she was stupid and gullible.

And now she had to move on.

"What are you doing?"

Kelly cringed as she tossed her leggings into the suitcase on the bed. She pulled in a deep breath, willed

herself not to cry until she was home alone and turned
to face Luke.

"I'm packing," she replied simply. "Did you get my
email?"

"Of course I got your email, that's why I'm here."
He took a step farther into the room, then another, but
he didn't come too close. "What happened at the party
to make you want to resign? Did someone say something to you? Why wouldn't you bring the issue to me
instead of just disappearing?"

Kelly laughed bitterly. "The issue *is* you," she
stressed. "I'm just your assistant, Luke. That's all I'll
ever be and what we shared wasn't a big deal, right?"

Her heart started beating even faster when he took
another step toward her. "What are you talking about?"

Swallowing her emotions, Kelly crossed her arms
over her chest. "I heard you in the hallway talking to
your brother. I was coming out of the office from checking on Gracie because she didn't feel well, but I heard
you tell him that I was your assistant, that's what I'd
always be and he didn't need to worry about what we
had going on because it wasn't a big deal."

When he started to take a step forward, she held up
her hand. "No," she commanded. "Don't touch me and
don't come near me. I shouldn't have let myself get so
caught up in my own thoughts and fantasies."

"Kelly—"

"Stop."

She shook her head and went back to the closet to
get a few more things. She really wished she would've
taken this dress off when she'd gotten back, but she'd
been in a hurry to grab her things and leave.

"I just want to get out while I can and save my-self any further embarrassment," she went on, grab-bing clothes and giving them a toss into the suitcase. "I'm not upset with you, I'm angry at myself. You never promised me anything and you never acted like you wanted more than what we had. I should've made my feelings known so everything was out there between us, but I thought—"

"Kelly," he bellowed to get her attention.

She jerked back and cringed. He was smiling at her. *Smiling.* How dare he smile when she was clearly torn in two and she just wanted to get out of here with some sort of dignity intact.

"What you overheard was just for my brother's sake," he stated. "Zeke kept grilling me on what was going on and I kept telling him it was nothing and you were just my assistant. I didn't want to tell him that I was developing feelings for you, because I wanted to tell you first."

Kelly stilled, her heart in her throat as she tried to process his words. "What?"

Luke slowly closed the gap between them as he con-tinued to hold her gaze and widen that smile.

"I want you to continue staying with me," he told her. "I want more with you, because I'm falling for you."

"Wait…what?"

Luke reached for her and slid his strong hands over her shoulders. "I told Zeke you would always be my assistant because I do always want you by my side. I want to see where this takes us. We're so damn com-patible everywhere, did you think I'd honestly want to let you go?"

Kelly pulled in a shaky breath and willed herself not to cry. He wanted her to stay? She was so confused and clearly had almost let miscommunication and eavesdropping ruin her life and her career.

"You're falling for me?" she asked.

"I didn't realize how much so until I saw your email," he admitted. "I knew I wanted you to keep living here and I knew I wanted to try for more… But that ache in my heart and in the pit of my stomach had never been so strong than at the thought of losing you. I'm pretty sure I ran at least one red light to get here."

Kelly closed her eyes and dropped her head between his arms. "I'm so foolish. I just heard that and assumed you were once again putting work ahead of everything else and I couldn't live like that. My mother did and it destroyed her marriage to my dad. I don't want to be miserable like she was."

Luke gently lifted her head and started leaning in. "You'll never be miserable as long as I'm around," he vowed. "And I'm about to mess up that lipstick you re-applied earlier."

Anticipation quickly replaced sadness and frustration. She tipped her face up to welcome his kiss, and joy flowed through her as his lips hungrily claimed hers. His hands slid down her bare arms and went to her waist as he tugged her closer. Her breasts flattened against his chest and she was so glad he'd come after her. She was so glad he explained what she'd heard. She'd just been so afraid of getting her hopes up that when she overheard him and Zeke talking…

Kelly pushed away those negative thoughts and concentrated on the man who was kissing her, the man who wanted to be with her in his home to see exactly where this relationship could go.

"Did I mention how much I love this dress?" he asked as he eased back.

Kelly nodded. "I believe you mentioned it, but I'm ready to get out of it."

She turned her back to him and glanced over her shoulder. "Care to help me out of this?"

Luke let out a guttural growl as his hands went to the zipper. The dress parted and his warm breath grazed her back, instantly giving her goose bumps.

The garment fell away from her chest and then he was shoving the full skirt on down until it pooled in a thick puddle of material around her ankles.

Luke cursed beneath his breath, and Kelly turned back around and stepped out of the dress, wearing nothing but her heels and her earrings.

"Have you been like this all night?" he demanded, his voice thick with arousal.

Kelly merely smiled.

"You are trying to kill me."

"I was hoping we'd come back here and you'd strip that off me," she told him. "I figured wasting time with anything beneath was just silly."

He reached for her again, his hands suddenly all over her bare skin.

"I do love how you think," he murmured. "Just make sure you wear the proper clothes to board meetings or I'm not responsible for my actions."

Kelly reached for his suit jacket and slid it off his arms, but before she could get to his buttons, Luke was lifting her in his arms and capturing her lips once again.

He shifted a few steps and her back was against the wall. Then he held her in place with her legs locked around his waist as he fiddled with his pants.

Kelly couldn't help but laugh. "In a hurry?"

His dark eyes locked with hers. "You have no idea."

In the next breath, he joined their bodies and Kelly laced her fingers around his neck and pulled his lips to hers. She wanted all of him right now. She wanted to consume him, she wanted him to feel her love, to know that this was real and she wasn't going anywhere.

He'd come for her. That thought completely overwhelmed her. She'd tried to make an escape and he'd been right after her. The man always went after what he wanted, and now that was *her*.

Kelly had never been so happy or felt so treasured.

Luke reached between them and cupped her breasts as he worked his hips.

"Not fair," she panted.

He nipped at her earlobe. "What?"

"You have too many clothes on."

"Later," he promised. "We'll go slow later."

She liked the sound of that.

Between the ministrations to her chest and the way he worked those talented hips, Kelly was already on the verge. It had been a hell of a night, and she was just too revved up.

She let go and cried out his name as he plastered one hand on the wall next to her head and increased his pace moments before he lost himself in his own climax.

Kelly focused on her breathing, on keeping her shaky legs from falling. She wanted to stay right here, wrapped in Luke's love. She knew he loved her. He'd admitted he was falling for her and all she wanted was to start this new chapter with him.

"Kelly," he murmured against her ear. "Never leave me again. I couldn't stand it."

She smiled and took his face in her hands to ease him back. She wanted to look him in the eye when she told him how she felt.

"I love you, Luke. I'm never going anywhere."

"Good because I need you in every part of my life and I want to be able to tell you every day that I love you, too."

Kelly couldn't suppress her smile or her tears. "This is going to be the best Christmas ever."

He sealed their promise with a kiss and Kelly knew this was only the beginning of their lifelong journey.

* * * * *

COMING SOON!

We really hope you enjoyed reading this book.
If you're looking for more romance, be sure to
head to the shops when new books are
available on

Thursday 10th December

To see which titles are coming soon, please visit

millsandboon.co.uk/nextmonth

LET'S TALK
Romance

For exclusive extracts, competitions and special offers, find us online:

 facebook.com/millsandboon

 @MillsandBoon

 @MillsandBoonUK

Get in touch on 01413 063232

For all the latest titles coming soon, visit
millsandboon.co.uk/nextmonth

MILLS & BOON
A ROMANCE FOR EVERY READER

FREE delivery direct to your door

EXCLUSIVE offers every month

SAVE up to 25% on pre-paid subscriptions

SUBSCRIBE AND SAVE

millsandboon.co.uk/Subscribe

MILLS & BOON

THE HEART OF ROMANCE

A ROMANCE FOR EVERY KIND OF READER

MODERN

Prepare to be swept off your feet by sophisticated, sexy and seductive heroes, in some of the world's most glamourous and romantic locations, where power and passion collide.
8 stories per month.

HISTORICAL

Escape with historical heroes from time gone by. Whether your passion is for wicked Regency Rakes, muscled Vikings or rugged Highlanders, awaken the romance of the past.
6 stories per month.

MEDICAL

Set your pulse racing with dedicated, delectable doctors in the high-pressure world of medicine, where emotions run high and passion, comfort and love are the best medicine.
6 stories per month.

True Love

Celebrate true love with tender stories of heartfelt romance, the rush of falling in love to the joy a new baby can bring, and focus on the emotional heart of a relationship.
8 stories per month.

Desire

Indulge in secrets and scandal, intense drama and plenty of hot action with powerful and passionate heroes who have it all: wealth, status, good looks…everything but the right woman.
6 stories per month.

HEROES

Experience all the excitement of a gripping thriller, with an intense romance at its heart. Resourceful, true-to-life women and strong, fearless men face danger and desire - a killer combination!
8 stories per month.

DARE

Sensual love stories featuring smart, sassy heroines you'd want as a best friend, and compelling intense heroes who are worthy of them.
4 stories per month.

To see which titles are coming soon, please visit

millsandboon.co.uk/nextmonth

JOIN US ON SOCIAL MEDIA!

Stay up to date with our latest releases, author news and gossip, special offers and discounts, and all the behind-the-scenes action from Mills & Boon...

 millsandboon

 millsandboonuk

 millsandboon

might just be true love...

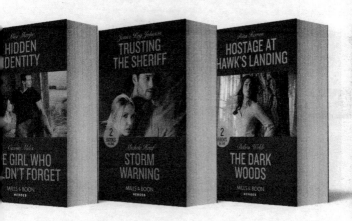

MILLS & BOON
True Love
Romance from the Heart

Celebrate true love with tender stories of
heartfelt romance, from the rush of falling
in love to the joy a new baby can bring,
and a focus on the emotional
heart of a relationship.